Raelia

The Medoran Chronicles: Book Two

Lynette Noni

 dyslexic books

Copyright Page from the Original Book

PanteraPress
great storytelling

First published in 2016 by Pantera Press Pty Limited
www.PanteraPress.com

A Cataloguing-in-Publication entry for this book is available from the National Library of Australia.

Cover and Internal Design: Xou Creative www.xou.com.au
Author Photo: Lauren Ami Photographs
Typesetting: Kirby Jones
Printed in Australia: McPherson's Printing Group

TABLE OF CONTENTS

From nurturing the **NEXT** GENERATION of best-loved **authors** ➤➤ TO CHAMPIONING LITERACY AND THE joys OF **READING** we're all about great storytelling!

 SCAN HERE for more on our GOOD BOOKS DOING GOOD THINGS programs.

And drop in to our website: PanteraPress.com for news about Lynette Noni and our other talented authors, as well as sample chapters, author interviews and much, much more.

To those with the courage to take a step forward.
Choose your path.

One

"Introducing their Royal Majesties, King Aurileous and Queen Osmada Cavelle."

Alex watched from the corner of the palace's grand ballroom, catching her first glimpse of D.C.'s parents as they descended the gold-lined staircase.

King Aurileous was tall and intimidating, but even from where Alex stood she could tell he had a kind face with prominent laughter lines. His eyes were warm as he scanned the sea of cheering people and his smile made her feel relaxed despite the overwhelming atmosphere.

Queen Osmada seemed, in a word, lovely. She was beautiful, with her dark auburn hair, and her smile was even more calming than the king's.

Alex's attention was diverted when her best friend appeared at the top of the staircase and the room fell silent as everyone gazed upon their princess.

"Presenting Her Royal Highness, Princess Delucia Cavelle."

The cheers were deafening as D.C. walked gracefully down the staircase to stand beside her parents, her lavender-coloured gown sparkling silver wherever the light touched it.

Both the king and queen reached across to kiss D.C. on the cheek before her father stepped forward to address the crowd.

"Beloved friends, we thank you for joining us in celebration of our daughter's seventeenth birthday. This is a momentous day for her and we are thrilled to share it with you," King Aurileous said. "Now please, eat, drink, dance, and be merry as we revel in this special occasion."

As if the end of his speech was an invisible cue, the orchestra hidden in the balcony above the ballroom immediately began playing an upbeat melody. The guests proceeded to move about and make pleasant conversation, while Alex stood awkwardly on her own as she waited for D.C. to make her way through the crowd.

Glancing around, Alex marvelled at her surroundings. She wondered if she should pinch herself to see if she truly was standing in the royal palace of Medora's capital city, Tryllin, when just a few short weeks ago she'd had no idea how to sort out her mess of a life. That was because, as far as her parents had known, Alex had spent most of the previous school year at the International Exchange Academy just outside Portland, Oregon. In reality, she'd actually been stranded for eight months in the fantasy world of Medora, attending Akarnae Academy—a school for teenagers with extraordinary gifts.

Alex was *supposed* to have spent her summer coming up with an excuse to leave Earth—or 'Freya' as it was known to the Medorans—so she could return to Akarnae when it reopened in the fall. But when she'd arrived back home for the holidays, her parents had been waiting for her, along with a dizzying assortment of federal agents.

Apparently the International Exchange Academy had finished classes a week earlier than Akarnae, and her parents had returned from their Siberian sabbatical in time to greet her. When Alex hadn't shown up, they'd contacted the school and discovered that she'd never enrolled as a student there. This news had sent them straight past panic mode and directly into full on hysteria. Their daughter had been missing for the better part of a year and they'd had no idea. Cue the plethora of police, private investigators and federal agents all on the hunt for their lost teenager.

With Alex's imagination frozen and her flippant story about having joined the circus for a few months falling on deaf ears, she'd been forced to tell her parents the truth and hope they wouldn't have her committed. It had been touch-and-go for a few minutes, so Alex had decided to prove to them that she wasn't stark raving mad. After willing a doorway to open in the middle of their living room, she'd dragged her stupefied mother and father through to Medora.

With them wide-eyed and slack-jawed, Alex had guided them straight to Darrius Marselle's office—her headmaster and friend—knowing he'd be able to 'speak parent' better than she could. And he had indeed come through for her, offering a detailed rundown of Alex's months spent at the academy in a way that her parents had been able to not just understand, but also see the changes in their daughter for themselves. In the few short months Alex had spent at Akarnae, her dedication to classes had made her both mentally and physically stronger, and she'd found good friends who made her happier than she'd ever been before.

Be that as it may, they'd still gone ballistic when Darrius had mentioned Alex's misadventures with the banished Meyarin prince, Aven Dalmarta.

Alex wasn't sure what had concerned them most: the fact that an immortal being was determined to use her influence over a sentient library to open a magical doorway to a missing city—and said like that, Alex couldn't blame them for worrying—or the fact that if his plans succeeded, he intended to carry out a mass extermination plot against the humans of Medora.

At that point in the conversation, Alex found herself wishing Darrius had gone for a 'less is more' approach. In fact, she'd gone back to wondering if her parents would find a way to lock her up—this time for her own protection.

To calm her parents it had taken several cups of something Alex could tell by the smell alone wasn't just tea. When they had relaxed somewhat and Darrius had answered most of their questions—thankfully leaving out the part where Alex had been stabbed and nearly died—they followed Alex home in stunned silence.

Thinking she was doomed to be superglued to their protective sides forevermore, it came as a great surprise when, a few days later, her mother and father informed her that she could go back to the academy for her next year of schooling. Apparently once the shock had worn off—and they'd likely repressed everything regarding Aven—her parents had realised just how valuable the last eight months at Akarnae had been for Alex.

Intrepid explorers themselves, it would have been hypocritical of them to keep their own daughter from her chance at a real life fantasy adventure—or so they'd told her.

Whatever their reasoning, Alex had been too thrilled to question their decision. Until they'd informed her that they would also be joining her in Medora for the year.

Her parents.

In *Medora*.

Apparently her mother and father had become so intrigued by the possibility of the unknown that they'd decided their next great archaeological adventure was to be of the otherworldly kind. As such, they'd spent the entire summer packing their earthly belongings into storage in preparation for spending some quality time in Alex's new world.

Alex, however, had spent that time freaking out about how to keep them safe from Aven since, if he found out about them, she was certain he would use them as leverage against her.

In the end they'd come to a compromise, one that Alex had cunningly offered to them on her seventeenth birthday, using that fact to help guilt trip them into accepting.

Having thought about it endlessly, she had decided that the best place for her parents was *inside* the Library itself. While Aven now had access to the unending corridors of doorways, the chances of him locating them in there were slim to none even if he somehow learned of their existence in Medora. As far as Alex could tell, it was the most secure place available to them.

Birthday-blackmail or not, it had taken some work for Alex to convince her parents to agree to remain locked away when they were so curious about the rest of Medora. But Alex explained that if Aven ended up getting his hands on them, and thus Alex in turn, their otherworldly adventures would come to a swift conclusion—as would the lives of all the humans populating Medora.

Doom and gloom aside, Alex's parents had accepted the truth of her words and reluctantly agreed to her terms. That reluctance had quickly turned to delight, however, when, with Darrius's help, Alex had managed to find them a place to stay in the Library that came with an ancient ecosystem as their scientific playground.

Having relocated from Freya just this morning, Alex had left her parents more excited than she'd ever seen them, even after she'd hesitantly informed them that she'd have to limit her visits to keep from drawing attention to their unorthodox location. But distracted by the wonder of the impossible discoveries awaiting them, they hadn't minded in the slightest. Instead, they'd kissed her absentmindedly on the forehead, wished her good luck for the year and encouraged her to enjoy her 'adventures'. Alex, for her part, had just rolled her eyes, hugged them, and promised to keep in touch as best she could.

Knowing that her parents were safely tucked away deep in the Library was all Alex had needed to switch her focus onto what came next: returning to the academy—and reuniting with her friends.

She had missed Jordan, Bear and D.C. fiercely over the holidays and couldn't wait to be back with them again once Akarnae reopened. They'd kept in regular contact via their ComTCD holographic communications devices, but she hadn't been able to leave the academy grounds to see them in person. They had, however, been able to meet up without her. It was easy enough for the boys, since Jordan always spent his summers with Bear's family, but Alex had no idea how D.C. had managed to sneak out of the palace, especially given that the boys were unaware of her royal status. As much as Alex kept telling her friend to let the others in on the secret, she knew D.C. was afraid that Jordan and Bear would treat her differently once they learned she was the princess. Alex knew them better than that, but she had yet to convince D.C.

Honestly, between organising a new life for her parents and arranging their long-term, secretive stay in Medora, Alex hadn't had much of a chance to try and break down D.C.'s arguments. But that was also because what little spare time she'd had over the holidays had been allocated for her to get beaten up, over and over again.

It was sad, but true. For three days each week Alex had endured hours of training with her Combat instructor, Karter, developing her previously non-existent fighting skills. In Karter's defence, Alex could admit that he'd done wonders with her in the nine short weeks they'd trained together. Their final session had been just yesterday, and while Karter hadn't shown any last lesson leniency with his fighting—not that she'd expected him to—at the end of their time he'd gruffly conceded that she'd learned enough to join the rest of her classmates in the coming school year. Despite her anxiety, she was actually looking forward to seeing how well she handled the class. And her classmates.

She would know soon enough, since all Akarnae students were due to arrive back at the academy tomorrow, with classes beginning first thing the following morning. All Alex had left to do was make it through tonight—D.C.'s birthday party at the royal palace.

Unfortunately, it seemed like every single invitee wanted to pay their respects to the ruling family, and D.C. was stuck playing the good little hostess until she could escape to Alex's side, as they'd arranged earlier that evening while getting ready in D.C.'s bedroom.

At least I'm dressed for the part, Alex thought while she waited. The dress she wore was almost as beautiful as the gown Bear's mother had designed for her as a Kaldoras present the previous year. Unlike that one, which had been a stunning sky-blue colour, the dress D.C. had given her was emerald green and cut on the bias to drape over one shoulder, leaving the other bare. It was made of the highest quality material, flowing softly over her body to compliment her figure. Her dark hair had been piled on top of her head with a few wispy tendrils left out to frame her face, and her smoky makeup accentuated her brown eyes. All in all, her regal look gave her the confidence she needed to wait, and keep waiting, on her own.

With nothing but the company of her thoughts, Alex mulled over everything that had happened that day, from saying goodbye to her parents—and Freya—to activating her personalised Bubbledoor invitation that was pre-programmed to whisk her directly to the palace where D.C. had been waiting with open arms and excited squeals. The last few hours had been filled with Alex's awed delight at wandering the majestic hallways, along with pampering fit for a princess in preparation for the night's event. But now, especially given her exhausting weeks filled with packing and Combat training, all Alex wanted to do was walk back up the shiny gold stairs and curl up on the couch in D.C.'s room—a room she was sure measured about the size of a small city.

That, however, wasn't an option for her just yet.

After what felt like hours, D.C. finally managed to escape the hordes of people demanding her attention to arrive at Alex's side.

"I'm so sorry!" D.C. said, her vivid blue-green eyes filled with apology. "I didn't think it would be so difficult to get away."

"That's okay," Alex said. "I've just been hanging with my new friend here." She slung an arm around the statue of a dragon-like creature beside her and added, "His name is Spitfire and he likes long walks on the beach at sunset. I think we're a match made in heaven, don't you?"

D.C. shook her head. "You must have been bored out of your mind!"

"Seriously, it's fine," Alex laughingly reassured her while untangling herself from the dragon. "I actually kind of enjoyed watching how everyone reacted to seeing you and your parents. They really do adore you, you know."

D.C. smiled wistfully. "It's my parents everyone loves. No one has seen me up close for years. This is the first birthday in a long time that I've celebrated with an actual party."

Alex had heard the warm reaction to D.C.'s arrival and she wholeheartedly disagreed that the crowd's adoration was solely for the king and queen. But she let it go and instead asked, "How are you able to be here so publically now?" She gestured at the room full of guests. "Won't people realise who you are after this? What if there are other students from the academy here?"

D.C. waved away her concerns. "Don't worry, Alex. The guest list is highly exclusive. There might be some people from Akarnae here if they're relatives of the royal council or on-duty Wardens, but they're all people I've grown up around. They know how important it is for me to remain anonymous."

Accepting her explanation, Alex took a moment to scan the room. Her gaze snagged on a familiar face and she had to do a double-take to make sure she wasn't seeing things.

"Is that...?" Alex's eyes narrowed and she hissed, "I can't believe it, that's Marcus Sparker! What is *he* doing here?"

D.C. followed Alex's line of sight. "The Sparkers are an important family," she said in a hushed voice. "There was no way for us to get out of inviting them without causing more problems than it was worth."

"You're not worried that Jordan might have decided to come along with his parents?" Alex asked, sounding a little more aggressive than she'd intended. She *really* didn't like the idea that the man who had once held her semi-captive for information was in the same room as her again.

"Jordan's never come to a palace event before, so I doubt he'd suddenly decide to now. Plus, he's staying with Bear, remember?" D.C. answered. "Relax, Alex. Marcus and Natasha won't dare try anything here."

"If you say so," Alex murmured, choosing to trust her friend. But despite her acceptance, she still felt antsy. Seeking a distraction, her eyes fell on the bar and she said, "I think I'll go grab a drink. Do you want anything?"

"Some of that fruit punch would be great, thanks."

Alex left D.C. and headed towards the beverage table. She would have made it there much faster if she'd crossed the centre of the ballroom, but she didn't want to risk running into Marcus, so she took the longer route and hugged the walls. The closer she moved to the beverages, the louder the music became, since the refreshments were located directly beneath the orchestra. When she finally reached the table, she felt overwhelmed by the vast array of coloured liquids to choose from.

"What are you after?" asked a male voice in her ear. It was only his proximity that allowed her to hear his question over the music.

"The fruit punch," Alex said loudly as she continued to search the kaleidoscopic contents of the table. A hand reached out from behind her and pointed towards the bubbly pink liquid served in dainty crystal glasses. Alex retrieved two of them and turned to thank the person she presumed was a waiter.

"Thank—Kaiden?" Alex stared up at his familiar face in surprise.

"Alex," Kaiden responded, with a hint of a smile.

"What are you doing here?" Alex gasped, glancing nervously to where D.C. was waiting. Was Kaiden one of the people who had grown up around D.C., or was he a threat to her friend's secret identity?

"It's the refreshments table," Kaiden said pointedly, reaching around her and grabbing a glass filled with a glowing green liquid.

"Not what are you doing here, what are you doing here?" Alex asked, flustered.

He raised one dark eyebrow and she struggled to fight off a blush. If it was possible, he was even more attractive than the last time she'd seen him in her Combat class. And considering he was wearing a tuxedo and not covered in sweat and grime, it was definitely possible.

"By 'here', I presume you mean the palace ballroom?" Kaiden clarified.

She shook off her dazzled feeling and pursed her lips. "Obviously."

"It's the princess's birthday," he stated. "There's a party going on, in case you haven't noticed. And I never turn down an invite to a good party."

Alex couldn't quite interpret the depth behind his humour-filled expression, but before she could ask anything else, they were joined by another familiar face.

"Alex! Fancy seeing you here!"

"Hey, Declan," she greeted the massive hulk of a boy. His tux was practically bursting at the seams and he didn't appear at all comfortable—unlike Kaiden, who looked as if he was born to wear formal attire. "How was your summer?"

"You didn't ask how my summer was," Kaiden said, looking even more amused for some reason.

Alex felt her left eye twitch and was glad when Declan started speaking so she didn't have to respond to Kaiden's remark.

"Yeah, all right. Not too exciting, but good. You?"

"Same here," she said, not wanting to go into detail. While they were definitely the nicest of her Combat classmates, the first time she'd met Declan he'd ended up sending her to the Medical Ward, unconscious. As for Kaiden, well, she wasn't sure what to make of him. Needless to say, neither of them were what she would call close friends.

But speaking of close friends...

"Oh, no," she said, looking across the room. "I'm so sorry, but I have to go."

Alex set both drinks back on the table and lifted her floor-length dress high enough to move quickly without tripping. She didn't care about avoiding Marcus Sparker this time as she hurried across the middle of the ballroom, weaving between dancing couples and political dignitaries. Her focus was solely on the two people who had arrived at the entrance to the room and were now heading towards the corner where D.C. was speaking to a small group of people. Alex knew she had to warn the princess, but she was too far away to capture her attention.

The king and queen came into Alex's peripheral vision as they waltzed along to the music and she groaned inwardly when she recognised the opportunity they presented. With a mortified breath and a silent apology, Alex picked up her pace...

...And launched herself at the dancing couple.

The three of them tumbled to the floor in a pile of limbs and formal attire. Alex could hear people shrieking around them, and before she could so much as blink, she was forcibly hauled off the royal couple with her arms wrenched behind her back.

With no chance for her to explain, two guards promptly dragged her from the room. She felt like her face was on fire as the entire ballroom of people watched the guards manhandle her, but she managed to lift her head and meet D.C.'s stricken gaze. When her friend stepped forward to intervene, Alex shook her head and subtly gestured in the direction of the two boys who were now gaping in shock along with everyone else.

Alex offered Jordan and Bear a weak smile as she was escorted past them. She turned back to D.C., relieved when her noticeably pale roommate nodded to say she understood why Alex had acted as she had.

'I'll fix this,' D.C. mouthed.

Alex smiled ruefully, fully aware that they would have a difficult time coming up with an acceptable excuse for her attack on the ruling monarchs of Medora.

The two guards frogmarched Alex out of the ballroom and through the resplendent corridors, before hustling her down a dark, winding staircase that led underneath the palace. Once they were on level ground again, they strode past more guards wearing armour and through what could only be described as an ancient stone dungeon.

Fortunately, it was empty of prisoners—as far as Alex could tell.

They stopped in front of a grimy cell and she was shoved none too gently into it. One of the guards immediately pressed on a touch-screen TCD terminal attached to the wall and a semi-transparent barrier appeared, zinging with what appeared to be live electricity. It didn't take a genius to work out that the barrier could do some serious damage, but Alex still had to struggle against the temptation to touch the almost hypnotic entryway.

When the guards took up sentry positions opposite her, Alex began pacing back and forth in the small space, preparing herself for whatever would come next. It wasn't long before she heard the sound of approaching footsteps and a young woman stepped into view. She had dark hair and striking features, and wore a black uniform with a gold emblem stitched above her heart—two swords crossed together behind a crown.

"I'm Warden Jeera," the woman said without preamble, her title telling Alex that she, like Bear's dad, was one of Medora's peacekeepers and responsible for the safety of the kingdom. "And you just tried to carry out an assassination attempt on the king and queen."

Alex sucked in a startled breath, realising that her current circumstances were perhaps more dire than she'd presumed. "I didn't—"

"What's your name?" Jeera interrupted.

Swallowing thickly, she answered, "Alex." But at seeing the Warden's *I-hope-you-can-do-better-than-that* expression, she cleared her throat and quickly added, "My full name is Alexandra Jennings, if that helps. I'm Princess Delucia's best friend."

The Warden raised a sceptical eyebrow. "I've never seen you at the palace before. That doesn't sound like best friend behaviour to me."

"We only met last year," Alex defended. "We go to Akarnae together—we're roommates, actually. You can check if you want."

"You're a student at Akarnae?" Jeera asked, her head tilted thoughtfully.

"Yes," Alex said. "I'm about to start as a fourth year. Provided that you let me out of this cell sometime before tomorrow."

Jeera's face transformed as if she'd come to a sudden understanding. Her harsh demeanour changed into something that looked very much like amusement. "Epsilon Combat, right?"

Alex felt confusion wash over her. How could Jeera possibly know that?

Before she could ask—or confirm her answer—Jeera waved her hand and said, "Never mind. But answer me this: if you claim to be the princess's best friend, why did you just attack her parents?"

Alex shook her head in denial. "I didn't attack them." When Jeera's brow rose again, she amended, "I can see how it might have looked that way. But I promise there's a perfectly good explanation."

Even though Jeera opened her mouth, it wasn't her words that responded to Alex's statement.

"This I'd like to hear," came a dry male voice. "Especially given that you accosted me and my wife in the middle of our waltz."

Two

Alex's eyes widened when the king stepped into view outside her cell, but she quickly came to her senses and dropped into a curtsey. "Your Majesty."

"Alexandra Jennings," King Aurileous returned. "I've heard a great deal about you, and none of it leads me to believe you have any kind of ill intent towards my family. So, tell me, what brought on that display upstairs?"

"I'm not sure what to tell you," Alex answered honestly, looking from him to the now very clearly entertained Jeera and back again. "You see—"

"Alex, where are you? We've come to bust you out of here!"

She groaned at the sound of Jordan's whispered voice echoing along the stone corridor. Only he and Bear would think they could break her out of a palace dungeon. Actually, considering both of their gifts, they probably *could* get her out, but that would just cause her more trouble when she was inevitably caught again.

She looked at the king and he gave her a 'go ahead' gesture.

"I'm over here," Alex called weakly, hoping they'd have the presence of mind to get out of there while they still could. But no such luck, since a few seconds later, both Jordan and Bear sprinted around the corner and came to a wide-eyed halt.

Jordan rallied himself first and said, "Uh, hello, Your Majesty." He bowed regally, with Bear following his lead. "We didn't expect to see you down here."

"I'm sure you didn't," the king said with a touch of amusement. "Nor did I expect to see anyone but my guards and their prisoner. For future reference, no one has ever broken out of my dungeons before. Or been broken out."

Jordan sent him a cocky grin. "With all due respect, Your Majesty, there's a first time for everything."

Alex couldn't believe he'd actually said that—and to the king of all people—but she was more shocked when the monarch smiled.

"Indeed there is," King Aurileous acknowledged. "But not in this case, I'm afraid. Unfortunately—"

"You have to let Alex go! She was only trying to help me!"

When D.C. came running around the corner mid-yell, Alex felt the need to bang her head against the cell barrier, regardless of the live electricity. *So much for trying to* keep her identity a secret, she thought. What a wasted effort.

"Dix? Is that you?" Bear asked, squinting into the shadows where D.C. had skidded to a stop at the sight of him and Jordan.

"Sweetheart, what are you doing down here?" the king asked.

"I ... Uh ... That is..."

For the first time since Alex had known her, D.C. appeared lost for words.

Jordan, however, looked like he wasn't sure whether or not to laugh. "Did the king just call you 'sweetheart'?"

There was a loaded silence where everyone appeared to be waiting for someone else to jump in and explain what was going on.

In a quiet voice, Alex said, "Dix, you're going to have to tell them now."

Bear glanced between them. "Tell us what?"

D.C. looked like she was frozen to the spot.

"Dix!" Alex called, trying to snap her friend out of her shock.

D.C. flinched and locked eyes with Alex, begging for help.

"Tell them," Alex encouraged softly, and D.C.'s shoulders sagged.

"Could you please give us a moment?" she asked her father, her eyes flicking to include Jeera in her request.

"You want me to leave you alone in a dungeon with the girl who just threw herself at your mother and me, and who is now under suspicion as an assassin to the throne?" The king sounded both sceptical and incredulous. "Not to mention her trespassing friends, who are here to to stage a prison break."

Put like that, Alex realised the situation wasn't all that wonderful for any of them.

"I guess not," D.C. murmured her acceptance. She stepped closer and turned to face Jordan and Bear. In a wavering voice, she said, "I wanted to tell you sooner, but I wasn't sure how."

"Tell us what?" Jordan asked, repeating Bear's question.

"I'm the—" D.C. began, but she coughed mid-sentence, as if the words were stuck in her throat. She moved her eyes to Alex again who nodded reassuringly, prompting D.C. to take a wobbly breath, stand up a little straighter, and say, "I'm the princess. Of Medora. And, um, it's my birthday party that we're celebrating tonight. Surprise?"

Jordan and Bear stared at her in silence, their expressions not giving any indication as to what they were thinking.

Alex could practically feel D.C.'s tension until, finally, both boys looked at each other and shrugged.

"It makes sense, if you think about it," Jordan said contemplatively. "You always were a prissy little—"

When the king cleared his throat loudly, Jordan's gaze flicked up to the monarch's stern face, and he finished lamely, "—uh, princess."

D.C. released a breathy laugh filled with relief. "You're not angry that I didn't tell you?"

"We didn't know you properly until recently," Bear pointed out. "What right do we have to be angry?"

D.C. beamed at them both and rushed forward to wrap her arms around them.

"Can someone kindly explain the apparent importance of this moment and why we're all down here in the dungeon to witness it? I presume the events are linked?" King Aurileous asked.

"Yes, Father," D.C. said, stepping away from the boys. "You see, these are my friends, Jordan Sparker and Barnold Ronnigan."

The boys waved cheerily to the king as she said their names.

"For a while now I've been putting off telling them who I am," she said. "I wasn't expecting to see them here tonight, and I'm guessing Alex was just as surprised."

D.C. looked at her for clarification, so Alex picked up the story from her side.

"When I saw Jordan and Bear enter the ballroom, I knew I had to get Dix's attention so she could escape before they recognised her," Alex said. "Launching myself at you and the queen seemed like a pretty good distraction."

Jeera let out a quiet snort and Alex looked at the king sheepishly. "I'm so incredibly sorry, Your Majesty. If I'd been able to think of an alternative, please believe that I would have taken it."

There was silence while everyone mulled over her explanation.

"Oh, and I'm not an assassin, by the way," Alex quickly added. "Promise."

Someone around the corner laughed quietly and she wondered who else was listening to their conversation.

After a moment the king nodded to Jeera to open the cell. When the barrier was down, the Warden gave a quick nod of deference to him, sent a mysterious yet entertained smile in Alex's direction, and walked away, leaving their small group alone but for the company of the dungeon guards.

The king stepped into the cell to join Alex. "Loyalty can be the strongest motivation for courage, Alexandra." He held her gaze with the same uniquely coloured eyes that D.C. had inherited. "What you did was very courageous, if somewhat dramatic, and I thank you for being loyal enough to my daughter that you would risk your own well-being. Twice, now, if we consider what happened with Aven a few months back."

"At least this time she didn't end up with a knife through her lungs," D.C. said. "That's progress."

"No, but the penalty for an assassination attempt is execution," the king said, causing Alex's breath to hitch. "Alexandra had no guarantee that any of us would have come to stop that from happening."

Alex hadn't considered the idea that someone wouldn't have come to help her out. And considering the consequences, she was glad the thought hadn't crossed her mind. Execution? Seriously? Yeesh.

"Thank you, Your Majesty," Alex said, uncertain how else to respond after receiving a compliment from the king. "I, uh, promise not to do it again. Or, worst case, I'll try to let you finish your dance first if there is a next time."

King Aurileous laughed, causing his entire face to light up. "I'm sure my wife would appreciate that, Alexandra."

"Alex," she insisted.

He smiled at her warmly. "Alex, it is. And now it's time for us to get out of here and enjoy the rest of the party."

"You can't be serious?" Alex said, forgetting that she was speaking to the ruler of Medora. "I can't show my face up there again!"

"Nonsense," the king said. "No one will recognise you."

Alex doubted that, but she obediently followed as he led them out of the dungeon and through the maze-like corridors back to the ballroom.

"Perhaps I was mistaken," the king murmured, when the room full of people went silent upon their entry. Even the orchestra stopped playing mid song.

"You think?" Alex muttered sarcastically, attempting to hide behind her friends. It was no use though, as it was clear that everyone recognised who she was.

The king apparently realised that as well, and raised his voice to address the crowd. "My friends, I hope you enjoyed our earlier re-enactment of *The Inebriated Guest*. Rest assured that it was a theatrical act for your entertainment, and not, as some of you might have presumed, an assassination attempt. In fact, I would like to present the leading actress, Alexandra Jennings."

Alex's jaw dropped at the king's declaration that she'd been acting like a drunken fool on purpose. She was even more surprised when the audience started applauding her performance, hesitantly at first, and then more boisterously.

D.C. pushed Alex forward to stand beside the king who whispered for her to take a bow. She'd never felt more uncomfortable in her life, but she did as she was told, and the people cheered louder as she curtsied.

"Now that the entertainment is over for the night, please continue to enjoy the celebrations," said the king, and the guests slowly turned their attention away.

"That worked rather well, if I do say so myself." King Aurileous sounded pleased. "Now, off you four go, and do try to stay out of trouble."

The king walked away and Alex hoped he was off to explain to his wife the truth of what had happened.

"So Alex, how does it feel, being known as 'The Inebriated Guest'?" Jordan asked, smirking.

Alex sent him a dry look. "Better than it felt being known as the assassin. I'm making my way up in the world."

"What are you two even doing here?" D.C. interjected, and Alex was grateful for the change in topic.

"Don't ask," Jordan grumbled.

"Gee, thanks," D.C. said, fluttering her eyelashes. "I'm glad you're so excited about celebrating my birthday with me."

"Oh, that's right." Jordan winced apologetically. "Sorry, it's going to take some getting used to." When D.C. nodded her understanding, he said, "My parents contacted me at Bear's house and ordered me to come, saying it was about time I met the princess since it's her—your—first public appearance in years. I, in turn, pulled the 'bring a friend' card and dragged Bear along with me."

"I didn't mind coming," Bear said. "I've never been inside the palace before. But Dad freaked out this afternoon when I told him where we were going. It was really strange. And it meant we got here late because he wouldn't let us leave until we listened to a lecture about palace etiquette and not embarrassing 'the family name'. He's never cared about that stuff before. Like I said, really strange."

D.C. burst out laughing.

"What's funny?" Bear asked.

"Your dad's a Warden here," D.C. explained after her amusement settled. "He's known about me for years, but when he learned we'd become friends, I made him promise to keep it secret until I found a way to tell you myself."

"He was probably concerned we'd all run into each other tonight," Alex guessed, smiling at the thought of poor William having to keep D.C.'s identity to himself. "I bet you were late because he was stalling, keeping you away as long as possible so you would miss Dix's big entrance at the beginning of the party."

"Why were you so worried about our reactions?" Jordan asked D.C., looking genuinely perplexed.

"I just didn't want you to be all weirded out or act differently around me," D.C. said, blatantly ignoring Alex's 'I told you so' expression.

"Are you kidding? You already behaved like a princess before, now I can legitimately call you that!" Jordan said, grinning.

D.C.'s face fell. "You can't tell anyone. Please, Jordan. There's a reason people don't know who I am. I just want to be 'D.C.', not 'Princess Delucia', especially at the academy."

"Hey, relax," Jordan said, pulling her in for a side-hug. "Your secret's safe with us."

Bear nodded his agreement and D.C.'s expression lightened.

"So, this is a birthday, right?" Jordan said. "Does that mean there's cake?"

"It sure does," D.C. answered. "And lots of it."

Jordan bowed with a flourish and held out a hand. "Then lead the way, Your Highness."

"I'll go get those drinks from earlier," Alex offered. "Second time lucky."

"Do you want company?" Bear asked.

Knowing he was more interested in the cake option, she let him off the hook. "I'm good, thanks. I'll meet up with you all in a minute."

Alex headed across the middle of the ballroom, lost in her thoughts about the past half hour and oblivious to her surroundings. She was startled when a hand grabbed her arm roughly and pulled her into an uncomfortably tight embrace.

"What a fortunate surprise."

Her heart leapt into her throat momentarily before her panic quickly turned into annoyance.

"I can't say the same for you, Marcus," Alex said, trying to wriggle free from his grasp.

"Be still, Alexandra. You don't want to cause another scene, do you?" Marcus hissed into her ear. "Why don't you dance with me instead?"

Without waiting for a response, he tightened his grip and forced Alex into a stiff waltz.

"You're a stubborn little thing, aren't you?" he said, keeping a fake smile plastered to his face even when she deliberately stomped her spiky heel on his foot for the third step in a row.

"The word 'stubborn' has such negative connotations," Alex said. "I like to think of myself as determined."

"You're certainly determined to make my life more difficult than it needs to be, I'll give you that," Marcus said. "We never did get to finish our New Year's Eve discussion, you know. And your mind remains silent to me. I don't like unsolved mysteries."

She tried to shrug, but he was holding her too tight. "I don't like to wear running shoes without socks, but you know what they say. When life gives you lemons..."

Marcus clenched his jaw and his eyes narrowed. "You don't seem to understand the predicament you're in. I have questions that only you can provide the answers to—and you *will* answer them, Alexandra, one way or another. Unfortunately, I have no easy way to spirit you out of here, not after your humiliating display earlier. Every single guard in this place has their eyes locked on you as if they're waiting for a repeat of your imbecilic behaviour."

"Imbecilic, huh?" Alex said. "Ouch, Marcus. That hurts."

"You need to stop testing my patience," he said through gritted teeth.

She returned his glare. "And *you* need to let me go before I deliver that encore performance you're so worried about."

"You can make a scene all you want—as soon as we're gone from here."

Alex felt her stomach dip unpleasantly at his implication.

"In case you hadn't noticed, we're in the middle of the royal palace," she said with much more confidence than she felt. "I'm not leaving, and you can't make me."

Marcus looked at her with a knowing glint in his eyes. "I believe you'll find I can, in fact, make you."

He released one of her hands and reached into his jacket, but Alex didn't have a chance to be concerned about what he was reaching for because Kaiden chose that moment to tap on Marcus's shoulder, diverting his attention.

"May I cut in?"

Marcus seemed just as surprised by the interruption as Alex was, and he loosened his hold on her enough that she was able to yank herself away from him.

"Absolutely," she said, facing her would-be saviour. Thankful for the perfect timing of Kaiden's intervention, Alex had to resist the urge to throw her arms around him in a grateful embrace.

"I apologise for the interruption, Mr. Sparker, but your dance partner is just too lovely for you to keep to yourself," Kaiden said charmingly to the older man.

"She's all yours," Marcus returned politely, as if he hadn't just been threatening her. He walked away from them with only a hint of a 'we're not finished' glance towards Alex.

Exhaling with relief, she looked back at Kaiden. "Thank you. Really, *really*, thank you."

"Do you want to tell me what that was all about?" he asked as he drew her close and led her into a smooth waltz.

"Not particularly," Alex said, easily following his confident lead. "But needless to say, we don't get along."

"I could tell." Kaiden nodded towards the pink marks blossoming on her upper arms from Marcus's rough grip. "Marcus Sparker isn't someone you want to have as an enemy."

Alex sent him a bland look. "I promise to keep that in mind next time he invites me over for tea."

"I'm serious, Alex. He's dangerous."

She stared into his troubled blue eyes before she broke the contact and focused on his shoulder instead.

"I know," she said quietly.

They moved in silence for a few moments before Alex decided to speak again. "You're really good at this. Dancing, I mean."

"We've danced before," he replied, and when she looked up, his eyes were no longer troubled—in fact, they were sparkling with amusement. It was a startling change from the serious expression they'd held just moments ago.

All the same, Alex frowned slightly, having no memory of ever dancing with him—and that was something she would definitely remember. But then she understood what he meant and replied, "Sword fighting hardly counts as dancing, Kaiden."

"I disagree." He spun her away from his body in a complicated three-step manoeuvre before guiding her back to him, keeping perfect time with the music. "It's all in the movement."

"Now you're just showing off," she said, now smiling herself. She was impressed he'd managed to not only surprise her with the move, but also guide her in and out of it without her having to do anything but follow along. She hadn't even stumbled—which was quite the miracle considering the heels she was wearing.

"Maybe," he admitted, with humour in his voice. "But it's not every day I get to dance with 'The Inebriated Guest'."

Alex groaned and leaned forward to hide her face in the crook of his neck as he laughed at her.

"It's not funny," she muttered.

"I disagree again," Kaiden said, and she moved her head back so she was looking at him once more. "Both the act and the explanation were the textbook definition of 'funny'."

She scrunched her face up. "Good to know I'm still a verifiable source of entertainment."

"I heard a rumour that you'll actually be participating in Combat this year," Kaiden said. "If that's true, I'm sure the entertainment will continue."

"Thanks for the vote of confidence," she said. "I can't tell you how much I appreciate your support."

"I'm here for you," he said mock-seriously.

"Hey, Alex, what happened to our drinks?" D.C.'s voice interrupted their conversation.

Alex hadn't realised that the orchestra had stopped for a brief intermission, so wrapped up was she in Kaiden's easy banter—and his arms. But her friends had found her and they looked between the two of them with unbridled curiosity. She hastily let go of him.

"Guys, this is Kaiden James," she introduced. "He's in my Combat class at Akarnae."

"We know who he is," D.C. said, amused. "We've been at the academy together for years."

"Oh. Right," Alex said, wincing inwardly. Of course they all knew each other.

"Thanks again for helping us out earlier," Jordan said to Kaiden.

Seeing Alex's questioning look, Bear explained, "Kaiden and Declan showed us the way down to the dungeons and then kept watch to make sure no other guards turned up. We didn't know the king and that Warden were already there."

"So that's why you were waiting around the corner when I ran past?" D.C. said to Kaiden, who shrugged noncommittally in response.

"Hey, guys. What am I missing out on?" Declan asked as he joined their group.

"Nothing important," said Alex. She wasn't sure how she felt knowing the two Combat boys had heard her interaction with the king down in the dungeons, so instead of dwelling on that thought, she motioned to them and D.C. and asked, "Have you all grown up together?"

"For the most part, yeah," Declan said. "Both my family and Kaiden's are closely associated with the royal family in one way or another, so we've all known each other since we were kids."

Alex wondered why the two boys hadn't befriended D.C. at the academy, but then she remembered that her roommate hadn't wanted to be known as the princess, and these two probably treated her like one, even if it wasn't deliberate. Plus, they were both a year ahead of Alex and her friends, and unless she was mistaken, D.C. didn't share any of their potential-based classes.

"What do your families do?" Alex asked, curious.

Before they had a chance to respond, the king called for everyone's attention.

"We would once again like to thank you for coming to share in the birthday celebrations, but the night is getting away from us and we ask that you begin to say your farewells so our daughter can get some sleep before dawn. Not to mention, her parents as well."

There were a number of chuckles and the king offered a general "goodnight" and left the ballroom with his wife.

"Ever the concerned parent," D.C. said, her face showing how much she loved her family. "I'd better go make my rounds, but I'll see you guys tomorrow at the academy. Alex, I'll meet you upstairs in a little while."

"Sure thing," Alex said.

Everyone else disbursed soon after that. Kaiden and Declan took off after a quick farewell, leaving Alex with Jordan and Bear.

"Are you both truly okay with Dix being the princess?" she asked.

"I had a feeling it might have been her, even before we were friends," Jordan said. "You don't grow up in my family and not have some kind of intuition about certain people."

"Well, I had no idea, but like we said down in the dungeon, it makes sense," Bear said. "And it's not like she's a different person. As long as she doesn't want us to bow when she walks into the room, then I'm cool with it."

"You guys are so great," Alex said, pulling them in for a spontaneous hug.

Jordan patted her on the back. "We sure are."

"Time for us to get out of here," Bear said, drawing away. "I told Dad we'd be back by midnight and we're cutting it close."

"We'll see you back at the academy tomorrow," Jordan promised, and the two of them took off into the departing crowd.

Alex looked around and noticed that D.C. was surrounded by admirers, so she quickly ascended the staircase and headed up to the royal suite. She'd had such a crazy day and couldn't wait to put her feet up and rest—and *finally* get her hands on a drink.

When she entered D.C.'s room, Alex had to pause for another moment just to appreciate her surroundings. She'd spent hours with her friend that afternoon but she still couldn't get over how royal the bedroom was. Like the rest of the palace, it was richly decorated in hues of gold, with lighter and darker shades complementing each other, and white, pearlescent undertones.

Everything from the carpet to the walls, the bed and the curtains, was a mixture of gold and white. The effect was stunning. However the best part, in Alex's opinion, wasn't the décor, but rather the view.

Although she was practically dying of thirst and ready to drop on her feet, Alex didn't hesitate to walk across the room and open the glass door that led out to a turret-style balcony. Earlier that evening she'd watched the sun setting across the shining city of Tryllin, the dying light reflecting off the ocean and bouncing along the windows of the city below. At night it was no less breathtaking, the moon bathing the view with an iridescent glow. The sight was enough to send a wave of relaxation over Alex, helping her shake off the stress of the evening.

With a contented sigh, Alex wandered away from the balcony, heading back into D.C.'s suite for a much needed glass of water before she curled up on the lounge to wait for her friend. She must have been more tired than she'd thought, because she was woken later by D.C. poking her in the shoulder. After a sufficient amount of grumbling, Alex had just enough energy to stumble into bed and fall straight back to sleep.

Three

"What do you say we get out of here for a while?"

Alex looked at D.C.'s excited face and replied, "I thought we weren't allowed to leave?"

It was midmorning and they'd been roaming the halls for a few hours, with D.C. giving Alex the official tour. The palace was incredible—and huge—but what both of them wanted most was to get outside. Unfortunately, during breakfast the king had ordered that they remain inside for the day because there was some kind of parade in the city and he was concerned for their safety. The queen, in turn, had sent them both an apologetic look, but she too had agreed with her husband.

Alex had been so awed by the fact that she was sharing a meal with the ruling monarchs of Medora—and the knowledge that they'd both very graciously forgiven her stunt last night—that she'd simply nodded her agreement and ignored D.C.'s huff of annoyance.

"You can't seriously want to be stuck in here until we have to leave for Akarnae? You haven't seen any of the city yet!" D.C. said, bringing Alex back to the present.

It was true that Alex desperately wanted to explore at least a small part of Tryllin before they left. Especially after having seen the stunning view from D.C.'s balcony.

"Besides, I sneak away all the time," D.C. continued, reminding Alex of how often she'd visited Bear and Jordan in Woodhaven over the holidays. "Trust me, I'm a pro."

True enough, D.C. did manage to get them out of the palace without being seen, but that was more thanks to the contraband Bubbler vials she'd somehow pilfered rather than any real skill on her part. It helped that both she and Alex had donned disguises in the form of cape-like cloaks made out of a shimmery charcoal-coloured material with hoods that cast shadows over their faces, making them indistinguishable even with light streaming straight into their eyes. D.C. claimed the cloaks were made of Shadow Essence, a special kind of energy used by Shadow Walkers—a race of grey-skinned beings who walked around on swirling clouds of shadows. Caspar Lennox, the professor who taught Alex's Studies of Society and Culture—or SOSAC—class at Akarnae, was so far the only Shadow Walker she had encountered. It took her a while to move past her inclination to compare him to a vampire, but once she did, she'd ended up becoming rather intrigued by him and his perpetual cloud of wispy darkness.

According to D.C., Shadow Walkers were well known in Medora for being mysterious but also doing exactly what their name implied—walking through shadows to transport themselves to new places. Hearing that, Alex had asked D.C. how it was possible, and her friend's answer had caused her head to spin.

"You know how the sun gives off energy?" D.C. had said. "Well, long ago there was a race of beings who discovered that darkness also has its own unique energy. They found a way to trap the energy of shadows and refine it to a point where they could use it. They became known as Shadow Walkers, because the first thing they learned was how to use the energy to walk through shadows."

When Alex had pressed for more details, D.C. had shrugged and said, "I've never Walked before, so I can't tell you much about how it works. But from what Bear told me, the ring you were given from Blake last Kaldoras has enough Shadow for three Walks, so you can see for yourself what it's like if you figure out how to access the Shadow Essence inside."

Even now, wandering around outside under the heat of the sun, Alex glanced down at the ring on her finger, repeating the conversation in her head. It looked the same as it had the day Bear's brother had surprised her with the gift. The band was black and the onyx-like centre stone of the ring coiled with darkness. Knowing it was infused with Shadow Essence made Alex realise it was more mysterious than she'd originally thought—but she still had no idea what it could actually do.

"What do you want to see?" D.C. asked, reclaiming Alex's attention from her ring as they walked casually along Tryllin's harbour.

Alex was entranced by all the sights, sounds and smells surrounding them. Apparently Sunday was the local fish market day, or so she guessed from the not-so-pleasant aroma that came in wafts strong enough for her to wrinkle her nose and hold her breath.

"It's your city," Alex responded. "Surprise me. But, uh, let's maybe go somewhere away from the fish."

Alex was certain her friend was grinning beneath her Shadow-infused hood, but D.C. didn't comment as she led them away from the harbour and up one of the well-travelled, cobblestone roads. It made Alex wonder about something.

"Why do you have roads if you don't have cars?" Then, not sure if D.C. knew what a car was, Alex added, "Or, um, transport vehicles?"

With a shrug, D.C. said, "Back in the days before Technos invented Bubblers, we used horses and carriages to move people and things around. The roads were necessary then, but that was long before I was born. These days the roads are mostly used as large pathways for walking traffic."

Alex nodded in understanding as the two of them continued up the cobbled street until they reached the outskirts of the city.

"This road will take us into the centre of the city and then right back to the palace," D.C. said. "It's my favourite street in all of Tryllin. There's so much to look at, with so many people bustling around."

True enough, the moment they turned around a bend in the road, Alex discovered exactly what she meant. It was as if they'd walked into a whole new world. The noises, the colours—it was overwhelming. There were people everywhere: children running and screaming, adults calling out to one another, street vendors bartering prices with customers. Alex had never experienced anything like it before. The entire street was a trade market. Even the buildings that lined the sides of the roads had salespeople calling out to promote their wares.

There were people everywhere.

"Come on, I need to eat," D.C. said, dragging Alex forward.

They stopped walking after a few minutes and D.C. stepped up to one of the shopfronts on the side of the road and entered the doorway into the building.

Inside, Alex was hit by an aroma so incredible that her mouth instantly began to water.

"This is the best shop in the whole city," D.C. said with a contented sigh.

Alex looked around the comfortable room with its cosy couches and coffee tables. She followed D.C. to a glass-fronted bench and her eyes widened at the cakes and slices on display behind the barrier.

"It's a bakery?" Alex asked.

"Mmm-hmm, and it's amazing," D.C. said.

Alex had visited plenty of bakeries and patisseries, but she decided to humour her friend and see what all the fuss was about. And it turned out that D.C. was right; Mrs. Gribble's Cupcakes and Nibbles provided them with delicacies that, in Alex's honest opinion, defined 'ambrosia'. Food of the gods, indeed.

After half an hour of scrumptiously decadent binging, Alex's moans of pleasure turned into groans of discomfort.

"I'm never eating again," she said, pressing her hands to her aching stomach and following D.C. back outside. "But that was incredible."

D.C. nodded emphatically and asked, "What now?"

"I'm the tourist. You're the guide," Alex reminded her as they set off again. The streets remained crowded with people but they seemed less congested than earlier.

"Yeah, but is there anything in particular you want to do before we leave?"

Alex thought about for a moment then said, "I'd like to see the parade your dad mentioned."

"Sure, we can do that, so long as we keep out of sight. My parents will be able to recognise the cloaks, even if they can't identify us through them," D.C. said. "If we keep following this road, it'll take us right to where we need to go."

They picked up the pace and continued onwards, with Alex marvelling anew over the energy and vibrancy of the street vendors and their customers, but her focus shifted when the throngs of people became thicker the closer into the city they travelled. The congestion deepened until Alex and D.C. were forced to walk in single file as they pushed their way through the crowd.

"If we get lost, meet back at Mrs. Gribble's, okay?" D.C. called over her shoulder. "Just follow the street back."

"Sure thing," Alex called back.

There were so many people that Alex began to feel claustrophobic. But she continued to follow D.C. and soon enough the noise of the crowd was drowned out by a loud voice speaking through some kind of amplifier.

"...is such an honour, and we hope you enjoy the rest of the festivities."

Alex and D.C. finally pushed through to a clearer spot that gave them a view up to a platform in the distance where the king and queen stood addressing the crowd.

The sound of cheering and applause drowned out all else and Alex realised they must have just heard the end of the king's speech. People began to surge towards the stage and Alex was hard-pressed to keep her feet on the ground in the mass of bodies.

"Bad timing, hey?" she called to D.C. over the noise.

D.C. didn't respond and Alex turned around to get her attention, only to discover that D.C. was nowhere in sight.

"Dix?" Alex called out. But the cheering crowd was too loud for her voice to carry very far.

Despite the clearer area, there were way too many people nearby and D.C. could have easily been swept up in the crowd.

"Dix!" Alex called again, and she started moving forward with the people in the hope of finding her friend. She continued with the flow of bodies for a few minutes before realising that finding D.C. in such a large crowd was on par with finding a needle in a haystack. She knew her best course of action was to head back to Mrs. Gribble's like they'd agreed and wait for D.C. there. Her friend might already be waiting for her, if she'd taken the wiser option and left straight away.

Alex managed to forge a path through the crowd until she was snugly against the wall of a building. The traffic was still flowing heavily, but the wall next to her made it easier to move than when she'd been in the middle of the mass. She fought to walk against the tide of bodies and slowly managed to break through the crowd.

"Excuse me, pardon me, sorry, excuse me..."

The apologies poured from her mouth as she pushed against the stream of people. They grumbled and glared, but she didn't care since she was focused on reaching her destination.

Finally the crowd started to thin out and her excuses were needed less and less. A few minutes later she could see the doorway to Mrs. Gribble's store about fifty yards away on the other side of the street, and she was relieved to see D.C. standing out the front.

"Di—"

A hand reached out from the doorway she was walking past and covered her mouth, muffling her call. Too shocked to react fast enough, Alex was yanked roughly into the building, the door slamming shut behind her.

"I told you we'd meet again, Alexandra."

Alex's blood froze at the sound of Aven's smooth voice whispering into her ear.

"Mmmfffnn!"

She struggled against his hold but was powerless against his Meyarin strength.

"Uh-uh-ah, we can't have you calling out to your friend," he said calmly as he tightened his grip on her. "You wouldn't want anything to happen to her, would you?"

Alex didn't know why Aven was warning her now, when only a few months ago he'd intended to kill D.C. himself—or use Alex to do it. But despite her lack of understanding, she wasn't willing to risk her friend's life, so she stopped struggling. Her efforts weren't getting her anywhere, anyway.

"That's a good girl," he said mockingly. "I'm going to let you go now, and you're not going to scream, understand? If you scream, the princess will die before the breath has even left your mouth."

Alex swallowed and nodded against his hand. The moment he released his hold on her, she jumped away and turned to face him, vaguely noting that they were in some kind of unused storage room.

"It's good to see you, Alexandra," he said, moving to lean casually against the wall of the empty room. "You're looking well."

Alex didn't let her guard down. Regardless of his relaxed demeanour, they weren't exactly old friends. Aven's calm façade worried her, especially since the last time they'd seen each other hadn't ended well for either of them. He'd been forced to flee, and she'd nearly died.

"What are you doing here, Aven?"

His golden eyes lit with amusement. "You're not happy to see me?"

She wasn't willing to play his game, whatever it was. Instead, she stood with her arms ready by her sides, waiting to see what he would do next.

Aven realised she wasn't going to answer him, so he continued, "Imagine my surprise when I learned that Marselle had finally allowed you to leave the safety of his precious academy, knowing that you could so easily fall into my hands."

"The security at the palace more than covered the risk," Alex defended. "I was perfectly safe there."

Aven's mouth curled into a slow grin and Alex hated that, despite his inherent evilness, he was still devastatingly attractive. Apparently it was a trait that all Meyarins shared, but since he was the only one of his race she'd ever met, she had no one else to compare him with.

"The security you speak of wouldn't have stopped me," Aven said. "Those pitiful palace guards and their ridiculous Warden superiors would have merely been an annoyance and waste of my time. But I knew all I had to do was wait for you to come to me."

"In case it escaped your notice, I'm not in this room by choice," Alex told him. "You're awfully confident for someone who happened to stumble upon me by chance."

"Chance had nothing to do with it. Only a fool would believe you wouldn't leave the palace to explore on your own. I just had to wait for the perfect opportunity to get you alone. Granted, your Warden friend is more talented than I gave her credit for, and she has admittedly made this day more tedious for me than I would have liked. But no matter, you're here now."

Alex didn't know what he was talking about. "What Warden friend?"

"The one who has been following you and the princess all day," Aven informed her with a smirk on his face.

Alex was shocked. If what he'd said was true, then she and D.C. were going to be in so much trouble when they got back to the palace.

...If they got back at all.

"Wait," she said, thinking fast. "How can a Warden have known who we were? And for that matter, how did you recognise us? You shouldn't be able to identify me through this cloak."

She fingered the material that covered her head and Aven barked out an incredulous laugh.

"I'm Meyarin, Alexandra," he said, as if that was an answer in itself. Maybe it was. "A touch of Shadow Essence isn't enough to fool me. But I can't speak for your Warden. And I don't care to."

Alex frowned and hoped D.C. was all right. But it was also a relief knowing that there was someone out there watching over them, despite the problems the Warden might cause for them later.

"Do you plan on telling me why we're here, or are we just going to exchange small talk all afternoon?" Alex asked. She wanted to get out of there—preferably in one piece—and to do that, she needed to know what Aven was after.

"You still have no patience, I see," Aven said.

She shrugged unrepentantly. "Patience is overrated."

Aven raised his left hand and looked at his scarred palm thoughtfully. "Perhaps it is a virtue you lack, but you certainly do make up for it with your strength of will."

Alex had to resist a shiver of apprehension when she felt her own palm tingle along the line of her identical scar. She would never forget the terror of being subjected to Aven's commands and stripped of her freedom. If she'd been born with any gift other than her willpower, she would have been Claimed as his slave for the rest of her life.

"You haven't answered my question," she said, forcing the fear from her mind. "Why did you pull me in here?"

In the blink of an eye, Aven pushed off the wall and stepped directly in front of her, trapping her in his gaze. His casual attitude was gone and the dangerous look on his face caused Alex to inhale sharply.

"Why do you think you're here?" Aven asked, his voice soft but with a harsh edge.

Alex refused to step back despite the fact that he was well and truly invading her personal space.

"If I knew the answer, I wouldn't have asked," she stated. "It's not like I can help you get into the Library and to Meya from here. We're nowhere near the academy."

Aven laughed derisively. "If I wanted to get into the Library today, I would have waited until you were back at Akarnae. No, that isn't why I sought you out."

He leaned closer and she struggled to hold her position. He looked even more amused, as if he knew exactly how uncomfortable he was making her feel.

"What I want is for you to know that at any time, in any moment, I can and will appear," he whispered into her ear. "I want you to live with the knowledge that I'm watching you and waiting for the perfect moment to strike. I want you to know that when that time comes, my plans will succeed. And I want you to know that you will be the reason for my success."

Alex shuddered, but before she could reply, the door burst open and Aven pulled away. She whirled around to see D.C. and another cloaked figure standing in the doorway.

"Alex!" D.C. cried, running towards her.

Alex spun back to face Aven, but it was too late. He was already gone.

Four

"I don't want to hear your excuses," King Aurileous said, pacing around his private meeting room. "I explicitly told you not to leave the palace today. You disobeyed my direct order, and because of that, you could've been hurt—or worse."

"Father, please—"

"No, Delucia," the king interrupted. "You need to understand how serious this is. If Warden Jeera hadn't followed you into the city, who knows what might have happened!"

D.C. dropped her head, remaining quiet.

The king hadn't taken the news of their visit into the city very well at all. Nor had he reacted calmly to the news of Aven's threat. But something had to be done to tame his wrath before he decided to lock them both in the dungeons and throw away the key.

"It was my fault, Your Majesty, not Dix's," Alex said, attempting to defend her friend. "She knew how much I wanted to see Tryllin. We didn't mean to cause any problems."

King Aurileous stopped pacing and turned to face both girls.

"Your loyalty is once again commendable, Alex," he said. "But my daughter should have known better—especially with the Meyarin on the loose."

"I'm sorry, Father," D.C. said quietly, looking at the floor.

The king sighed and opened his arms. "Come here, sweetheart."

D.C. hesitated a moment, but then stepped forward into her father's embrace.

"He almost took you from me once, my darling girl. I can't bear the thought of it happening again," he whispered.

Although the words weren't meant for her, Alex had to swallow back tears at the raw emotion in his voice. Before she could decide if she should give them a moment alone, they ended their hug with watery smiles.

"We're due to leave for the academy soon," D.C. told her father, "but will you keep us updated about Aven?"

"My best Wardens are searching for him now," the king said, looking at Alex thoughtfully. "I can't believe he approached you in the middle of the day like that. And then just let you go. It's ... concerning. But I promise to let you both know if we find him or learn anything more."

Alex thanked him, relieved that he seemed to have calmed down.

He kept his eyes steady on her and asked, "You'll look after my baby girl this year, won't you, Alex?"

She blinked with surprise. "Um, sure. I mean, yes, Your Majesty. As much as I can, anyway. When I'm with her—which is most of the time." She snapped her mouth shut in an effort to keep the words from continuing to spill out, but it was too late, and both the king and D.C. were already laughing.

"I can't tell you how safe I feel," D.C. said, still sniggering.

Alex decided to keep her mouth closed, but that just caused the king and his daughter to laugh even more.

"At least she's enthusiastic," King Aurileous said.

"That she is," D.C. agreed, smiling fondly at Alex.

"Don't we have to go?" Alex asked, trying to cover her embarrassment.

"Yeah," D.C. said. "We don't want to be late."

"Make sure you say goodbye to your mother before you take off," the king said, hugging his daughter again. "She misses you when you're gone."

"Of course," D.C. promised.

King Aurileous smiled at her one last time and turned to Alex. "You take care,

Alex. I have a feeling we'll need you more than we yet know."

She looked at him wonderingly, trying to fathom the meaning behind his ominous words. But then he winked at her, easing her concern. She couldn't tell if his comment was serious or a joke, but she was certain he didn't mean to cause her any anxiety.

"Thank you, Your Majesty," she said with a slight bow.

D.C. led the way out of the room and Alex followed her through the corridors and up the numerous staircases until they reached the princess's room.

After some quick packing, D.C. grabbed her small bag of belongings and said, "Okay, I'm ready. Let's go find Mother and get out of here."

Locating the queen in the palace's butterfly garden—and yes, to Alex's shock, it was an actual garden full of live, fluttering butterflies—D.C.'s goodbye with her mother was short but heartfelt. Queen Osmada even wrapped Alex in a motherly hug, saying that she looked forward to getting to know her daughter's best friend better in the future.

After their fleeting farewell, D.C. handed Alex a Bubbler vial and, with an excited gleam in her eyes, offered, "After you."

Alex grinned and threw the glass to the ground, sending butterflies scattering when the Bubbledoor rose up in front of them. As she stepped into the colourful mass, she thought of exactly where she wanted to arrive, and within a matter of moments she was out the other side and staring up at the academy's Tower building.

D.C. stepped through after her and they both grinned at each other, pleased to be back at Akarnae.

After stashing D.C.'s belongings with Alex's in the dorm room they'd shared the previous year, they headed directly over to the food court.

Alex was relieved that the noise covered their entrance so no one noticed them sneaking in a few minutes late. She'd never seen the room so full of people. Normally the hungry occupants came and went as they pleased within the designated eating times, but now the court was packed full of students and teachers alike.

"Alex! Dix! Over here!"

Alex heard Jordan call out for them and she led D.C. over to where their friends were sitting.

"We were worried you weren't going to make it in time," Bear said as they took their seats between the two boys.

"Us? Late?" Alex asked with wide eyes. "Never."

"Right. I'll remember that next time we have to barge into your dorm to get you up in time for PE," Bear said.

"Once. That only happened once," Alex grumbled. "And I was the one who opened the door and let you in. There was no barging."

Ignoring the stifled sounds of amusement from eavesdropping classmates, her attention moved to the rest of her table. Normally the food court was set up into clusters of randomly shaped and sized tables, but tonight all the furniture was larger, with groups of people seated together. Looking around her table, Alex recognised many faces from her classes last year.

Jordan must have seen her curious expression because he spoke before she could ask. "The first night of every new year we all sit in age-based groups so it's easier to organise getting our new class schedules."

That seemed logical. But unfortunately for Alex, she'd been so overwhelmed by the transition into Akarnae—and Medora—during the previous year that she hadn't had much of a chance to get to know many of her fellow classmates.

"I don't know most of these people," she admitted quietly to Jordan. "Can you give me a brief rundown?"

"No problem." He turned away and called out loudly enough to draw the attention of everyone at their table, "Hey, guys, let's do an icebreaker!"

"Jordan!" Alex hissed.

"What?" he asked innocently. "This way we'll all get to know each other even better."

"Sparker," called one of the guys sitting further down the table. "What gives?"

"You know, an icebreaker," Jordan repeated. "We'll each say something random about ourselves. Something that not many people here know. Fun, right?"

No one else seemed thrilled by the idea, but in true Jordan fashion, he managed to get them all to grudgingly agree.

"I'll start," he said. "My name is Jordan Sparker, and when I was three years old I shoved a pea so far up my nose that it had to be surgically removed. Your turn, Alex."

Turning to eagerly awaiting eyes, Alex's mind suddenly blanked. "I'm Alexandra Jennings—but just 'Alex' is fine—and I, um, like reading?"

She wished she hadn't made it sound like a question. In fact, she wasn't sure why she'd said it, since she didn't read all that much. But it wasn't as if she could have said she was from another world.

D.C. went next, then Bear, followed by Connor and Mel O'Malley, the cousins who Alex had spent some time with in the previous school year. The introductions continued around the table and Alex had a chance to learn about some of her other classmates.

"I'm Savannah Hill, and I'm a virtual reality addict," said a blond girl who Alex remembered from her Delta PE class last year. "The projector in the Rec Room here is way better than the one I have back home, so I'm a little obsessed with it."

"Kelly Gleeson," said the next girl, who had short brown hair and squinty eyes. "My favourite movie is *Beyond the Crescent Moon*."

Next up was a tall, lanky, extremely tanned guy with spiky hair who, when he spoke, sounded like he'd walked straight out of a surfing commercial. "Whazzup! Friends call me 'Blink'. I'm into extremes—extreme sports, extreme food, extreme music—anything extreme. Embrace the rush!"

The introductions continued until the names all blended together and Alex knew she wouldn't be able to remember everyone. Chelsea Jones ... Kimberly Cooke ... Mathew

Parker ... Andrew Nickles ... Tate Golde ... Ruth Voran ... Anna Ford ... Elliott Parvie ... Samuel Hortham ... The names kept coming until there were only two people left.

"I'm Sean McInney," said a bulky guy with long hair. He looked pointedly at Jordan. "I don't like icebreakers."

Alex grinned along with everyone else and turned to the last person who sat directly opposite her, a short girl with mousy brown hair and owlish eyes. She was so tiny that it looked like the slightest breath of wind would snap her in half.

"I'm Phillipa Squeaker," the girl said. "I hate my name, so call me 'Pip' or 'Pipsqueak'. Anything else will result in me shaving off one of your eyebrows while you sleep. You've been warned." Pipsqueak glared threateningly around the table until her scowl transformed into a brilliant smile. "Oh, I forgot to mention that I love rainbow cupcakes and fluffy bunnies."

Alex tried to turn her laughter into a cough but wasn't very successful. Pipsqueak turned to her and Alex tried harder to steel her expression into something more serious, but it was impossible. Just as she managed to get rid of her smile, the small girl winked at her, and Alex couldn't help but laugh again. At least Pipsqueak had a sense of humour. No one else at the table seemed to know how to take the diminutive girl.

"What's the story with you anyway, Alex?" Pipsqueak asked out of the blue. "I mean, you arrive halfway through last year looking like a lost sheep in the middle of a wolf-infested forest, you get potential-tested into some pretty hard-core subjects, you end up in the Med Ward more times than most students do in their entire stay at Akarnae, and then you disappear for the summer without a trace. What's the deal with all that?"

Alex squirmed uncomfortably in her seat, noticing that many of the others around the table were nodding in agreement at what Pipsqueak had said.

"I didn't realise my life was so interesting to you all," Alex said, hoping that if she seemed unconcerned then they would as well. "Would you like a copy of my diary? Perhaps that'll give you some insight into the boring life of yours truly?"

"Yo, sweet!" Blink said with a fist pump into the air. "Count me in!"

"Blink, man, I'm pretty sure she wasn't being serious," Connor said from across the table, with Mel shaking her head beside him.

"Oh," Blink said, deflating. "No fair. You just killed my vibe."

Alex watched the interactions of her classmates and turned back to Pipsqueak who was looking at her, waiting for an answer.

"I have nothing to say that you don't already know," Alex said vaguely. "I transferred here partway through last year, like you said, and I'm not sure why my potential test came back as it did. Believe me when I say I wish the results had been different. My numerous trips to the Med Ward are because of those 'hard-core classes'—as you so appropriately named them. And didn't everyone disappear over the summer when term finished for the year?"

Pipsqueak frowned but the truth of Alex's answers rang clear, despite being somewhat evasive.

"You're just mysterious," the small girl said. "We were in the same classes for a good eight months, but none of us know who you are."

Heads were nodding all around the table and Alex found herself on the defensive. "Is that entirely my fault?" she said to the group as a whole. "Did any of you make an effort to introduce yourselves to me?"

"Whoa, whoa." Blink raised his hands in surrender. "What our Squeaking-Pippa is trying to say is that we want to get to know you better. Anyone who gets sliced and diced by a knife is, like, seriously awesome. We salute you."

Alex was too surprised to react when he actually saluted her. She shifted nervously and repeated, "Sliced and diced?"

"Sure, sure," Blink said. "Despite the bogus food poisoning rumour that went around, everyone knows you were, like, stabbed or something at the end of last year. That's epic."

Alex must have looked panicked because Jordan leaned towards her and whispered in her ear, "It's okay, they don't know what actually happened. But news travels fast and there was a lot of commotion that night with half the teaching staff running off and you coming back all bloodied and everything. Word spread quickly, but no one knows anything solid."

She wasn't sure what to say to all the curious faces staring at her, but thankfully she didn't have to worry about a response because at that moment, lollipops appeared on the table in front of all her classmates. Alex picked up her own, knowing exactly what it was but still looking at it with curiosity.

"Why do we have to get potential-tested again?" she asked, copying her classmates and popping hers into her mouth. Just like the first one she'd tasted, it had a fruity flavour, changing from orange to apple to banana, then mango, passionfruit and pineapple. The taste continued to change as she swirled it around her mouth.

"It's rare, but your potential can change after certain life experiences," Bear answered.

"Does that happen much?" she asked around the lollipop stick.

"Nope, not often," Jordan said. "Bear was bumped up from Delta Chemistry to Epsilon two years ago. Actually, most of the people who are currently in any Epsilon classes weren't there to start with. It's almost unheard of to start out at the academy and be put straight into Epsilon-level anything. Delta, too, sometimes. That's why the harder classes tend to have mostly older students in them."

"Which is why I'm such a freak of nature," Alex mumbled.

Her friends grinned at her but none of them disagreed with her statement.

"Can potentials be downgraded?" Alex asked.

"Sure," Bear said. "I started out as a Beta in Equestrian Skills, but in my second year I was dropped back to Alpha. Horses and I don't mix well."

"Hmm," Alex hummed thoughtfully, mentally crossing her fingers.

She was down to the dregs of her lollipop when she absentmindedly crunched down on the candy to get rid of it faster. She then pulled the stick out of her mouth, wondering what she was supposed to do with it. As if reading her mind, a small plastic bag materialised out of nowhere and she dropped her stick into it. After sealing the bag, she placed it on the table where it blinked out of sight.

Within a few minutes everyone in the court had finished their lollipops and there was a hushed silence as they waited in anticipation to find out their results. Seconds later, the tension was broken as little slips of paper appeared on the tables in front of every student. Alex eagerly picked hers up, scanning her new class timetable.

	MONDAY	TUESDAY	WEDNESDAY	THURSDAY	FRIDAY
06:30—07:30	—Breakfast—	—Breakfast—	—Breakfast—	—Breakfast—	—Breakfast—
08:00—10:00	**Delta PE** *Field/Forest/ Lake*	**Medical Science** *Gen-Sec Lab.3*	**Delta PE** *Field/Forest/ Lake*	**Medical Science** *Gen-Sec Lab.3*	**Delta PE** *Field/Forest/ Lake*
10:00—10:30	—Break—	—Break—	—Break—	—Break—	—Break—
10:30—12:30	**Gamma Archery** *Field 2*	**Core Skills** *Gen-Sec R.5*	**Gamma Archery** *Field 3*	**Core Skills** *Gen-Sec R.5*	**Gamma Chemistry** *Gen-Sec Lab.7*
12:30—13:30	—Lunch—	—Lunch—	—Lunch—	—Lunch—	—Lunch—
13:30—15:30	**Epsilon Equestrian Skills** *Stable Complex*	**Gamma Chemistry** *Gen-Sec Lab.7*	**Epsilon Equestrian Skills** *Stable Complex*	**History** *Gen-Sec R.4*	**Epsilon Equestrian Skills** *Stable Complex*
15:30—16:00	—Break—	—Break—	—Break—	—Break—	—Break—
16:00—18:00	**Epsilon Combat** *Arena*	**SOSAC** *Gen-Sec R.2*	**Epsilon Combat** *Arena*	**Species Distinction** *The Clinic*	**Epsilon Combat** *Arena*
18:00—19:30	—Dinner—	—Dinner—	—Dinner—	—Dinner—	—Dinner—
19:30—22:00	Free Time	Free Time	Free Time	Free Time	Free Time
22:00	CURFEW	CURFEW	CURFEW	CURFEW	CURFEW

She looked up to meet her friends' eyes and sighed in disappointment, sending them a wry smile. "No change in my potential. Next year I want a different lollipop."

It turned out that none of them had any changes either, which was both good and bad; bad because it meant Alex was stuck in Epsilon Combat without her friends again—she only hoped Kaiden and Declan would still be with her—but good because it meant she had their company in all of her other potential-based classes. D.C. was with her in Gamma Archery and Epsilon Equestrian Skills, both D.C. and Jordan were with her in Gamma Chemistry, and both Jordan and Bear were with her in Delta PE. And they would all be together in their age-based classes.

"Whoa, they must be trying to kill you this year," Jordan said as he looked over Alex's shoulder.

Alex squinted at the paper, trying to make sense of his words. But then she noticed where he was pointing and groaned.

"PE, Archery, Equestrian Skills and Combat all in one day? And three times a week! Who did I kill to deserve that?" Alex grumbled. Starting any day with Finn and ending it with Karter was just not nice.

"At least Thursday will be easier," Jordan observed. "Only age-based classes all day. And your Tuesday isn't so bad."

He was right, but that didn't make her Mondays, Wednesdays and Fridays any better. It was going to be a very long year.

"If I can have your attention for a moment," Darrius called out, standing in the middle of the room. "After you've finished dinner, the rest of the night is yours to spend settling in. Feel free to leave here at your leisure, but do remember there's a nine o'clock curfew for first through to third year students, and ten o'clock for fourth years and up."

Alex looked at her timetable again and was excited by the change of curfew that she hadn't noticed before.

"And one final thing," Darrius announced. "Fourth year students, I'll need you to remain behind after dinner to hear about one of your upcoming curriculum options. Thank you."

Apparently that was all he had to say, since menus immediately appeared in front of everyone. Alex eagerly picked hers up and, after a brief glance, she touched the circle beside the lasagne with chips, deciding to treat herself with a glass of bubbly purple dillyberry juice as well.

Within seconds her food appeared and she dug in with relish. She hadn't eaten since Mrs. Gribble's, and after the day's events she was starving.

After she'd swallowed a few mouthfuls, she turned to her friends.

"Why do you think Darri—um—Professor Marselle wants us to stay behind?" Alex asked, hoping no one else at the table had noticed her slip with the headmaster's name.

"I'm presuming, and *hoping*, it's about Hunter's class," Jordan said, cutting into his steak. "We're meant to be able to take Stealth and Subterfuge this year."

"Yeah, I think it's that too," Bear agreed after taking a sip of his drink. "But I guess we'll see."

They finished eating in silence, mostly because there was so much noise in the food court that it was difficult to maintain a conversation. When they were finished their meals, their dirty dishes were whisked away by the TCDs, leaving the table immaculate once more.

Eventually the other students started to leave until only the fourth years lingered. It was then that the headmaster walked over to their table, followed by a lone figure whose face was hidden by a hooded cape.

"As I'm sure some of you have guessed, being in your fourth year means you have the opportunity to apply for Hunter's Stealth and Subterfuge class," Darrius said without preamble. "Since it's an optional study extra, it's held during your free time after dinner for two hours on Tuesdays and Thursdays. There are also mandatory classes held every alternate Saturday morning, along with the occasional whole-weekend assignment. It's not an easy subject by any means, and I recommend you think long and hard before deciding to apply. Hunter, if you will?"

The caped figure raised his hands and pulled back his hood, revealing the darkly mysterious Hunter—or 'Ghost', as Alex knew he was sometimes nicknamed. There was no doubting the man was dangerous, especially considering the cache of weapons strapped to his belt, not to mention those which were likely hidden on the rest of his body beneath the dark cape.

"I don't accept new students lightly," Hunter said quietly, as if knowing they were hanging onto his every word. He glanced around the group with disinterest. "In fact, I'll be surprised if I accept more than a handful of you this year. At best."

Alex's eyes roamed the table and she saw twenty apprehensive and slightly disappointed faces. She wondered briefly why Hunter's class was so highly regarded. All she knew was that she certainly didn't want to be a part of it, not with a name like 'Stealth and Subterfuge'.

"If you want to apply, sign your name on the paper and come along to a trial lesson this Saturday after lunch. Whoever is accepted into the class will join the current students the following Tuesday evening and continue lessons from there. It's my belief that learning alongside those with more experience will encourage you to excel faster."

That just sounded nasty. And it reminded Alex of her Combat class, where everyone else had years of experience and she was a complete novice. Not pleasant.

Jordan nudged Alex in the side and she saw that he'd slid her the paper. She noted that so far everyone had signed it, but she immediately passed it straight on.

"You didn't write your name," said D.C., as if Alex had forgotten.

"I know," said Alex. "I think I have enough to worry about without adding more challenges to my life."

D.C. looked at her with understanding and quickly scribbled her own name before passing the paper on to Bear.

Alex glanced up and was startled to find Hunter's dark eyes on her. The corner of his mouth quirked slightly before he turned his gaze away.

What was that about? she wondered.

When the paper reached him again, Hunter folded it up and pocketed it in his cloak.

"If you don't receive a position in my class, you'll have another chance to try out next year. That said, if you attend Saturday's trial and you are offered a position, it's mandatory for you to accept and you'll be required to participate in classes just like any other subject. All successful candidates will be notified on Sunday evening. If you haven't heard by then, presume that you didn't make it this year."

With those parting words, Hunter turned on his heel and walked away.

"All right, students, that's all," Darrius said. "Enjoy the rest of your evening."

Alex and her classmates rose from their seats.

"Miss Jennings, if I may have a word?" the headmaster called before she could leave with the others.

Alex felt her stomach drop when she realised what she would have to tell him.

D.C. sent her a sympathetic look. "We'll meet you back in our room."

Once the court was clear of people, Darrius remained silent, apparently waiting for Alex to speak first.

"What have you heard?" she asked, her voice resigned.

"King Aurileous contacted me to strongly advise that I speak with you about the events of the weekend," Darrius answered. "Tell me, Alex, what reason could the ruling monarch of Medora possibly have to make such an obscure request?"

Alex shuffled her feet, feeling like a delinquent student.

"I, um, ran into some problems in Tryllin?" Alex said, as if it was a question.

"Did you now? And what might those problems be?"

Alex slumped back down onto one of the chairs, knowing that their conversation would likely not be short. Darrius followed her lead and sat down as well, though much more gracefully.

"To start with, I was accused of being an assassin and locked up in the palace dungeon after I attacked the king and queen during their waltz." Alex winced at how that sounded, so quickly moved on. "Then after I was released, in the middle of Dix's party, Marcus Sparker threatened to kidnap me, I think, but there were too many people around. So that was good. But then today I—um—kind of ran into Aven. Actually, 'ran into' isn't really accurate, since he'd apparently been following me to catch me unawares, but … well…"

She trailed off in a shrug, watching him raise a hand to pinch the bridge of his nose between his fingers as if to alleviate stress.

"Seriously, I'm fine," Alex assured him, hoping it would help.

"Start at the beginning, Alex," Darrius said tightly. "And don't leave anything out."

Five minutes later, Darrius was still pinching his nose. Alex wasn't sure if she should be concerned or not.

"All right, thank you for telling me," he said, finally relaxing his hand and dropping it to drum his fingers on the table. "While Aven's threat is worrying, it's no less than we expected. We'll just have to remain vigilant."

Isn't that what we've already been doing? Alex thought, but she figured it was best to keep her mouth closed.

"I'm not sure how well you'll receive this, but I can't help wondering if perhaps you should attempt to visit Meya soon," he said quietly, as if uncertain of her reaction to his suggestion.

Alex had been looking down at her lap, but his words caused her head to snap up so fast her neck cricked.

"What?" she asked, rubbing at the pain behind her ear. Surely she'd heard wrong. "You can't be serious?"

"Didn't the Library say you would be venturing there at some stage?"

Alex regretted not keeping those words to herself. She'd only told Darrius about it over the holidays because she'd wanted him to tell her how crazy the idea was. No one had seen the Lost City for millennia, let alone been there. She had no idea what would happen if she tried to find the right doorway and step through it.

"Yes, that's what the Library said," Alex admitted reluctantly. "But Darrius, it's a *Library*. It doesn't know the future."

"Who says?" Darrius returned, with a knowing twinkle in his silvery eyes.

Alex opened her mouth but no sounds came out. Was it that much of an impossible jump to believe that the Library was omniscient? *Uh, yeah.* She couldn't begin to follow that line of thinking in her current state of mind.

"Okay, let's say I do decide to hop, skip and jump over into Meya," she said, trying to keep her sarcasm in check. "What then?"

"That's why I suggest you at least consider the idea," Darrius said, "because I don't know the answer. It might be good to get some kind of information about what we're facing. Or, even better, to see if there's anyone there who you can warn about Aven. If his family line is still ruling, they'll need to be made aware of his intentions."

"You do realise that the last humans to set foot in Meya were murdered in cold blood, right?" Alex asked, somewhat heatedly.

"I know, Alex. Truly, I know," Darrius said, holding her irritated gaze and returning it with his own soothing expression. "I don't ask this of you lightly."

Alex blew out a breath and ran a hand across her face. She knew that Darrius was probably more worried about her than she was.

"Why can't you go?" she asked, her tone almost pleading.

"For starters, I'm unsure if I'd be able to access the doorway since I'm not Chosen like you are. But even if I could, until the threat of Aven has passed, I must remain on campus to ensure the safety of the students. The academy wards are at their strongest when the headmaster is in residence. I strongly suspect that if Aven decides to, he'll be able to break through them again. But nevertheless, I'm unwilling to leave and take that chance."

"But you left over the holidays," Alex said, and this time she really was pleading; pleading for him to understand that her reluctance stemmed from fear, and pleading for him to offer to go in her place so she wouldn't have to deal with the challenges the future might bring.

"I only left once, and that was to help relocate your family and assist with the moving of their belongings," Darrius said. "Even then I didn't risk staying away for long, nor were there any students on campus at the time. You know that, Alex."

She tried to think of another argument but nothing came to mind. She knew Darrius would never ask something so dangerous of her without thinking it through. But that didn't mean she was thrilled by the idea. Quite the contrary, considering the potential death-or-dismemberment scenario she could face on such an expedition. Fun times.

"I'll think about it," she agreed finally, not trying to hide her unenthusiastic tone.

"That's all I ask," Darrius said, rising to his feet.

Alex rose with him, bid him goodnight, and headed back to her dorm building, mulling over his words and ignoring what she knew her answer would ultimately have to be. She already had enough to worry about, so as far as she was concerned, her decision about Meya could wait for another day—preferably one in the very distant future.

Five

"Are we all ready for what promises to be a brutal day?" Jordan asked cheerfully at breakfast the next morning.

"Day?" D.C. repeated. "Don't you mean, week? Have you seen our timetables?"

"Year, more like," Alex muttered around her toast, thinking about her cruel schedule.

At least they had all been smart enough to get a good night's sleep in preparation for the unpleasant day ahead. When Alex had returned to her dormitory last night, the four friends had only spent enough time together for Alex to relay her conversation with the headmaster before the boys took off to their own room, leaving the girls to turn in early. Both Jordan and Bear had been bouncing with excitement over the possibility of visiting Meya, but D.C. was a little more guarded, for which Alex was thankful. It made her feel better about her own hesitation.

"Medora to Alex?" Bear said, waving his hand in front of her face.

She blinked, having spaced out for a moment. Then Alex comprehended what he'd said and she chuckled at his phrase. So bizarre.

Her dark-haired friend looked at her strangely. "Are you ready to go? Finn will probably work us near to death today, so we should get down there and stretch before class."

"Yeah, sure," she replied, finishing the dregs of her orange juice.

"I have Combat first up," D.C. said with a grimace as they all stood and walked towards the exit. "But I'll see you in Archery, Alex."

"And we'll see you at lunch, Dix," Jordan said when they parted ways outside.

D.C. waved her agreement and headed off in the direction of the Arena. Alex wasn't sure who had it worse—D.C. for having Karter first thing in the morning, or the rest of them for being stuck with Finn. And then she realised that neither of those alternatives came close to her having Finn up first *and* Karter up last. Her timetable seriously sucked.

"What did you mean about Finn working us hard today?" Alex asked Bear as they walked down to the massive field where their PE class was being held that day. "Doesn't he always?"

He made a face. "It's the first day back after the summer holidays. He usually likes to test us to see if we've just been lazing around for weeks. If we have, he makes sure we regret it pretty fast."

"Oh," Alex said, understanding. She was oddly thankful for the extra Combat lessons she'd been forced to attend over the break, because otherwise she would have been one of the couch potatoes Bear was talking about. And she'd had enough experience with Finn's psychotic teaching style to know that he wouldn't go easy on any slackers in his class, not when he was such a staunch advocate for corporal punishment.

But as it turned out, by the time her last class of the day rolled around, Alex would have repeated their nightmarish PE class over and over again if it meant she could avoid having to face her Combat instructor. And that was because, over the course of the day, the academy's rumour mill had found some juicy gossip.

Gossip that involved Alex.

And Karter.

Together.

Somehow word had leaked out about Alex's training over the holidays, but the rumours spreading around weren't anywhere close to the truth. In fact, they implied a much, *much* raunchier version of what Karter's 'one-on-one' lessons had entailed.

Alex had no idea how the gossip had started, but as the day progressed, it had only worsened. Lunchtime had been awful, filled with gawking eyes, unrestrained laughter, leering sneers and snide remarks. As her first Combat class drew nearer, Alex became more and more certain that she wouldn't live to see another day, not if Karter had heard so much as a whisper of the insinuations spreading around campus like wildfire.

"I hate today," Alex grumbled to D.C. as they left the Stable Complex at the end of their Equestrian Skills class.

"You're going to hate it even more if you don't stop procrastinating," D.C. said. "The only thing worse than going to Karter's class is when you're late going to Karter's class. Which you will be, if you don't get moving."

"But I don't want to go," Alex whined.

"And I don't want to eat a barbecue sauce and peanut butter sandwich for dinner, but I have to since I lost a stupid bet to Jordan," D.C. said. "Sometimes we just have to suck it up and do what we have to do."

"Great words of wisdom, Dix," Alex said, rolling her eyes.

"I'm here to help," D.C. chirped. "Now, get moving."

D.C. actually had to push her to help encourage forward momentum, but once Alex was on her way, she felt a little more confident. After all, it wasn't her fault people were saying such horrible things. She had absolutely no control over what was happening. Karter had to know that.

...Right?

The closer Alex walked to the Arena, the better she felt. Admittedly, she was still anxious, but not so much because of Karter anymore. She was about to actively participate in her first proper Combat class and that was a nerve-wracking concept, especially when she remembered their gruelling exam at the end of her previous year. Nine weeks of training with Karter over the holidays couldn't possibly have brought her up to the same skill level as her classmates, but at least she was better prepared this year.

She entered the Arena with her head held high, determined not to reveal her apprehension. Her classmates were already there, and just like last year, there were only five of them—Brendan, Nick, Sebastian, and—to Alex's relief—Kaiden and Declan. She scanned the area quickly but could see no sign of Karter, and she felt her body relax slightly.

"Hey, Queenie!" Sebastian called, using the nickname she'd been given after tackling the nightmarish obstacle course in their final exam before the summer. "I guess you didn't get enough of us last year, huh?"

"Are you kidding?" Alex asked with fake incredulity as she walked over to where they were all stretching. "As if I could ever get enough blood and gore. I live for this kind of thing. Death before honour, and all that."

They laughed raucously, and Nick actually snorted. Alex hadn't thought her statement was funny enough to warrant such a reaction, but then Declan clued her in.

"I think you mean 'death before dishonour'," he corrected around his chuckles.

Alex thought back over her words and realised how stupid she'd sounded. "Um, isn't that what I said?"

It had been worth a try. But they just laughed even harder.

Despite her embarrassment, their casual camaraderie helped lift a weight off her shoulders. Or it did, until Brendan spoke up.

"So, how was your summer?"

It was an innocent enough question. But the moment the question was out of his mouth, everyone paused and looked at her. She felt her face heat up, knowing they must have heard the rumours. None of them were glaring at her with disgust, so that was something. But they were definitely curious.

"Um," she said. "It was—"

"Jennings!" Karter bellowed, storming into the Arena. He stopped a short distance away and ordered, "Get over here. Now!"

Alex may have actually squeaked with fright. He looked mutinous. His leathery face had taken on a purplish colour, and his icy blue eyes were blazing with fury.

She quickly hurried over to where he stood.

"Sir?" she asked hesitantly, acutely aware of his seething presence.

Without warning, Karter's fist flew towards her face, and it was only because of her developed reflexes that she managed to duck just in time. He came at her again, and she pivoted around on her foot, avoiding contact once more. He then swept his leg out, trying to trip her, but she jumped into the air and, upon landing, she automatically aimed a roundhouse kick at his torso. He deflected her leg with his burly arms, but it was enough to unbalance him, and the move gave Alex the chance to regain her bearings. She didn't have time to wonder why he was attacking her, she just steadied herself, waiting to see what he would do next.

Karter reached a hand over his shoulder and drew a sword from the scabbard strapped to his back. He threw it towards her—with absolutely no regard for occupational health and safety—and unsheathed the blade from his belt, raising it in the air.

"Aw, come on!" Alex cried, hoping Karter didn't intend to continue the fight. "You can't blame me for—"

She didn't get a chance to finish her sentence before he lunged at her.

After spending over two months training with the man, Alex tuned out everything else and fell into a natural rhythm as she deflected his attacks and parried with her own thrusts.

Step left. Deflect. Pivot right. Thrust. Jump back. Duck. Lunge.

Karter was relentless in his attack. Their blades met over and over again and the noise of clashing steel filled the Arena.

They continued fighting for what felt like forever. While Karter had always been hard on her during their training sessions, he'd never focused so intently on destroying her. But he was a man on a mission, and his blows were fuelled by tightly controlled aggression. It took all of Alex's concentration to stay in the fight, and after a while she only had enough energy to respond defensively.

A loud clang sounded when Alex's weapon was finally jerked from her hand, landing on the Arena surface with a mocking thump.

She was breathing heavily but she tried to still her body since Karter's blade was pressed point-first to her windpipe.

"Do you yield?" he demanded.

What do you think? she felt like saying. Instead, she panted out, "I yield."

He lowered his sword and sheathed it at his waist. Alex bent to pick hers up and she handed it to him without making eye contact. Once it was strapped to his back again, he led the way over to her wide-eyed classmates.

"For any of you who might've believed the ridiculous rumours spreading around," Karter said, "that was your proof that they are exactly that: rumours." He stared down each of her classmates and continued in a firm voice, "For the record, Jennings was ordered by the headmaster to undertake remedial Combat lessons with me over the summer holidays. You've just seen for yourselves that she's been training her ass off. If I hear anyone—in this class or out of it—speculate otherwise, look out. I will not be lenient."

Alex gaped at her Combat instructor. Had he fought her just to prove a point? If the awed looks on her classmates' faces were anything to go by, then his tactic had certainly paid off. Alex just wished someone else could have been the guinea pig in his little showdown.

"With that out of the way," Karter began again, his entire demeanour relaxing, "welcome to another year of Epsilon Combat."

Alex felt an irrational urge to laugh. Thankfully, she managed to smother the impulse before Karter could catch her and demand a rematch for her disrespect.

"Labinsky, Gibbs and Baxter, you're all back as first and second year apprentices, so I expect your best performances. James, Stirling and Jennings, since you're not yet apprentices, I expect even more from you to prove yourselves worthy of me keeping you on over the next few years. Understood?"

The six of them nodded dutifully, and Karter continued. "Since we've already wasted enough time, we'll get straight into it. Pair up and find a clear space. The rest of the lesson will be spent revising unarmed fighting techniques."

As Karter walked away from them, Alex felt her heart begin to race—again. Despite the demonstration she'd just been through with her instructor, she was more nervous now. Better the enemy she knew than the one she didn't.

"I call dibs on Alex," Declan said loudly, much to her surprise.

"No way, man," Brendan argued. "I'm the oldest."

"And the ugliest," Nick said with snigger.

Before the conversation could escalate, Kaiden jumped in. It was the first time Alex had heard him speak since seeing him in Tryllin and she struggled not to lose herself in the memory of seeing him—and dancing with him—that night.

"Why don't we let Alex decide?" he suggested.

Oh, awesome. Just what she needed: to pick favourites. That was one way to guarantee getting her butt kicked by them on a regular basis. *Thanks a bunch, Kaiden.*

They were all waiting for her answer, so she said, "Uh, well, fair's fair. Declan was the first to say he wants me."

She groaned inwardly at her wording.

"I mean, he was the first to say he wants to fight me," she quickly corrected. "As an opponent."

She had officially gone beyond digging a hole to the point where she was actually burying herself alive.

Kill me now.

When her classmates had finished laughing—and it took a while—she followed Declan over to the far side of the Arena. Admittedly, she was glad that he was her opponent for the day, since she'd already fought him unarmed twice before. Neither time had worked out wonderfully for Alex, but in her defence, he was built like an armoured vehicle.

"And we meet again," Declan said with a grin, no doubt remembering their previous rounds.

"This time it'll be you who ends up unconscious," Alex threatened, trying—and failing—to sound menacing.

In the end, no one ended up unconscious. Declan came out much less bruised and battered than Alex, but that was hardly surprising. She was pleased that she'd managed to defend against most of his attacks—and she'd even gotten in a few of her own.

"You've improved heaps," Declan said as they walked back over to their classmates. "I didn't have to hold back this time."

"That's what happens when you have ... what did Karter call it? Remedial Combat lessons," Alex said. "You either improve, or you end up six feet under. And I wasn't a huge fan of the latter."

"Well, I'm glad you're still in the land of the living," Declan said. "You sure put on a good show for the rest of us."

Alex sent him a dry look. "My life is complete."

They arrived where their classmates were waiting and stood around for zero-point-two seconds before Karter gave his standard, abrupt dismissal.

Alex followed the boys out of the Arena, overwhelmingly shocked that she'd made it through the day.

"That was awesome!" Sebastian said as they all walked back up the hill.

Alex looked up to find everyone staring at her and nodding in agreement.

"Huh?" she asked, guessing she must have missed something.

"Seriously, Queenie! I can't believe you took on Karter!" Sebastian raved.

Alex frowned. "What are you talking about?"

Sebastian held his hands out in front of him and karate-chopped the air. "You were like, *wham wham*, and he was like, *bam bam*, and then—"

"All right, Seb," Kaiden interrupted, patting him on the shoulder. "Calm down, buddy."

"Sorry, Queenie," Sebastian said. "It was just so awesome!"

"Why?" she asked, confused by his reaction.

"We hardly ever get to see Karter fight," Brendan explained. "We know he can, and he'll often demonstrate things in class, but I can't remember the last time we actually saw him in a full-on proper duel."

Alex snorted. "I'd hardly call what we were doing 'fighting'. I got my butt kicked, in case you didn't notice. What you saw was a picture of my life over the summer holidays."

Sebastian sighed wistfully. "I'm so jealous."

Alex shook her head in bemusement.

"You're wrong, you know," Kaiden said as they reached the food court. "You fought well, regardless of the outcome."

She glanced over to find him looking at her with warm eyes.

"Uh, thanks," she stammered, annoyed that such a simple comment could fluster her. So not cool.

His lips curled up at the corners, almost like he could read her thoughts, and she quickly turned back to the others. "I need to clean up, so I guess I'll see you all later."

"See ya, Queenie," Sebastian said with a final karate-chop.

"You're not eating?" Declan asked before she could move away. "Aren't you hungry?"

"No, I'm fine," Alex lied, but her traitorous stomach chose that moment to grumble loudly. All five of her classmates raised their eyebrows at her, and she added, "I'm just going to eat in the Rec Room tonight."

She really didn't want a repeat of her miserable lunchtime experience. Hiding out seemed like a perfect idea to her, at least until the rumour mill died down a little. She knew how these things worked—if she gave it time, people would move on to the next piece of gossip.

"Snack food isn't very nutritious," Brendan said. "And the Rec Room doesn't provide anything else."

Who did he think he was? Her dad? Yeesh.

"Why don't you eat with us tonight?" Kaiden offered. "It might be a good idea if we all show a united front."

Alex looked at him in confusion, but she noticed some of the others nodding their agreement.

"Um ... Why?" she asked. "Not that I don't want to eat with you guys, it's just ... I'm not sure why you think that's a good idea?"

"Strength in numbers," Nick said. "People think you and Karter, uh, you know ... So, maybe it'll help dissolve the rumours if they see us all together. It's pretty obvious we've just come from Combat. That can only help. If they see we don't have a problem, then they might realise there's no truth to what's being said."

Alex looked at their messy appearances and knew that, if nothing else, the physical evidence would show they'd just come from Karter's class. But she wasn't sure about the rest.

"It can't hurt to try," Brendan said.

"Why do you all want to help me?" Alex blurted out.

"Did you see the mood Karter was in when he entered the Arena?" Nick said. "Next time he might take that out on all of us, not just you. It's for our benefit as much as yours."

He had a point. And she was starving.

"Okay, let's give it a go."

Together the six of them entered the food court and were met with the rowdy noises of students fading instantly into silence.

"Awwwkward," Sebastian muttered from the corner of his mouth as they stood in the entryway with most of the academy staring at them.

Declan leaned closer to Alex and whispered, "This happens every time I walk in here. It's a consequence of being so devastatingly handsome."

She choked back a startled laugh. It was such a Jordan-like comment that she wondered if the two of them had been separated at birth. Either way, his words provided a distraction from the uncomfortable atmosphere.

"Let's grab a table," said Kaiden, gently pressing his hand to the curve of her spine and leading her forward.

As they walked across the room, Alex glanced over and made eye contact with D.C., Jordan and Bear, who immediately moved to join her and the uncharacteristically protective Combat boys. The moment their small group sat down at a table, the whispers started. But Alex found they didn't bother her as much this time around. Maybe it was because fewer people were watching her, no one was outright laughing, and the tone of their quiet comments sounded more curious than malicious.

"I guess you guys were right," Alex told her Combat classmates when they all had food in front of them.

"We're always right, Alex," Brendan said with an arrogant grin. "You should know that by now."

She stuck a chip in her mouth and rolled her eyes at him.

"What I want to know is, who started the rumours, and why?" Jordan said.

He'd been in a bad mood all day, sticking to Alex's side like glue and glaring at anyone who so much as looked at her when he was around. While she'd had the worst first day back imaginable, she was willing to let it go and hope for a better day tomorrow. But Jordan was clearly out for blood.

"I don't know who started them, but I think I know why," Sebastian said.

All eyes turned to him, but it was Nick who explained, "It's because you're a threat now, Alex. They see you as competition. Last year you ... well, you kind of sucked at Combat. And we weren't quiet with our opinions."

"I still suck," she said. "Just less than before."

"No, there's a huge difference," Declan said. "And last year you were terrible, but as far as we knew, you weren't trying to get better. We had no idea about the obstacle courses Karter had you working on."

Alex shuddered at the memories.

"Most of the students here can only ever dream of making it into Epsilon Combat," Brendan jumped in. "They'll never have what it takes, and because of that, they'll always be jealous of us. They thought you were one of them since you, uh..."

"Sucked?" Alex repeated helpfully.

"Yeah," he said with a grin. "But now that you're actually showing your potential, they're lashing out at you. You used to be part of the hive, now you're the queen bee. And not all the worker bees are content to stay in middle management for the rest of their honey-making lives. Since there's nothing they can do about changing their potential, they're acting irrationally. Consider yourself stung."

After a thoughtful moment, Alex said, "That has to be the strangest analogy I've ever heard." She shook her head. "I'm honestly not sure if you're trying to make me feel better or worse."

"Don't worry too much," Kaiden said, stealing a chip from her plate. "It's just the first day back, and people are bored. But they're also easily distracted. It won't take long to blow over; they'll have forgotten all about it soon enough."

Alex nodded and finished her meal in silence, unconsciously sliding her uneaten chips onto Kaiden's plate. She listened to the conversations around her, feeling surreal as she watched her closest friends interact with her Combat classmates. They'd all gone to the academy together for a few years so it made sense that they knew each other. But it was still ... *weird*.

"I'm beat," Alex said, standing up. For the first time all day she noticed that people weren't staring at her. Apparently the academy gossip queens had called it quits and Alex knew she had the Combat boys to thank for that.

"Me too," D.C. said, rising beside her. "It's been a long day."

You have no idea, Alex thought.

Jordan and Bear jumped up from their seats as well, offering to walk the girls back to the dorm.

"Thanks again for tonight," Alex said somewhat awkwardly to her Combat classmates.

"Any time, Queenie," Sebastian said, speaking for all of them.

As soon as they were outside, Jordan said, "'Queenie'?"

"Don't ask," Alex muttered. "Was that as strange for anyone else as it was for me?"

"Definitely," D.C. said. "I'm still trying to get used to sitting with you guys for meals, let alone other students. Not to mention, people who know who I really am."

She said the last part in a whisper, and they all understood she was referring to Kaiden and Declan. The two boys may have grown up in the same social spheres as her at the palace, but Alex knew D.C. still wasn't used to hanging around people who were aware of her true identity.

"It was good of them to do what they did," Bear said. "I think it helped your case, Alex."

"Yeah," she agreed, surprised anew by her classmates' kindness. "I think so, too."

Six

After the frustrations of her first day, Alex expected the week to drag on, but it turned out to be the opposite. Her classes whirled by, in some cases too quickly.

Being back at the academy and seeing the familiar faces of her instructors again was unexpectedly nice. Varin, the odd-looking Viking-like Species Distinction professor, greeted them all boisterously at the start of their first class. The History teacher, Doc, babbled on about places he'd visited over the holidays and things he'd discovered. And Caspar Lennox, the Shadow Walker SOSAC professor, also seemed eager to be back teaching again—even if his mottled-grey skin and blank expression didn't accurately express his joy.

Then there were the other classes and teachers who Alex would have been happy to avoid. Professor Luranda, the Medical Science teacher, was 'kind' enough to greet them with a pop quiz to see how much they'd retained from the previous year. And their Chemistry teacher, Fitzy—or Professor Fitzwilliam Grey—welcomed the class back by experimenting with two unstable chemicals, which resulted in an evacuation of the entire General Sector—or 'Gen-Sec'—building. He had a good heart, Fitzy, but his head wasn't always screwed on right.

Astrid Marmaduke, their Core Skills professor, opened her first class with a long lecture reminding them about the importance of controlling their gifts. She then proceeded to go around the room asking students to demonstrate how far they had come after having presumably—to her reasoning—practised over the summer holidays. When Mel showed off her elemental ability and accidentally set fire to her desk, Connor used his affinity with the weather to try and put it out by making it rain *inside* the classroom. But then he panicked when he couldn't make it stop, so Savannah jumped in to help, freezing the water. This might have worked if the icy result hadn't fallen towards the students' heads like daggers of hail. It was only because Sean raised an invisible shield as a protective canopy above them that no one ended up speared by the frozen shards of water.

Suffice it to say, after that display, Professor Marmaduke had given them theory exercises for the rest of the lesson.

As for PE, Finn was determined to kill them all with his die-hard boot camp to 'whip them all back into shape.' But after Alex's summer of intense Combat training, she found it refreshing to test her increased stamina, most of which had originated from Finn's gruelling classes the previous year. Despite his zapping stick and his harsh demands, Alex had begun to appreciate the value of his class, although she staunchly believed his teaching practices were in strong violation of ethical laws.

In Archery, Alex must have zoned out on her first day, having been too distracted by the circulating gossip. In her second class she learned from Maggie that they would be stepping up their technique over the next few months, which included a course in survival archery with moving targets, rather than simply shooting at the more and more challenging but still stationary boards.

That was sure to be interesting.

By far, Alex was most pleased to be back in her Equestrian Skills class. She hadn't been able to enjoy her first day back because of the rumours and her dreaded meeting with Karter, but her next two classes under Tayla's instruction were much more gratifying. And when Tayla mentioned some of the exercises they would be working towards, Alex felt a thrill of anticipation.

Combat was ... well, it was Combat. Karter's mood was much better when Alex entered the Arena for her second session, which was a relief for her entire class. They continued to practise unarmed combat, with Karter correcting their techniques while pointing out their strengths and weaknesses. Alex apparently had very few strengths and a long list of weaknesses. But she was determined to improve, and the only way she could do that was to continue participating. On Wednesday she was partnered with Sebastian, and on Friday she was against Nick. Both of them crushed her, but she felt a sense of pride at the end of each session when she was able to walk out of the Arena in one piece.

And as for the rumours about her and Karter, it turned out the Combat boys had been right. The whole thing had mostly blown over by the second day of classes, and Alex only heard the rare snide comment as the week continued. Everything had settled back to normal, just as it should have been to begin with.

"Alex?"

"Huh?" she said, pulling herself from her memories of the past week.

"I asked what you'll be doing today while we're at the SAS trial?" Jordan said.

It was lunchtime on Saturday and there was a definite feeling of anticipation in the air. At least for the fourth years, anyway, as they were soon to experience their first taste of Hunter's Stealth and Subterfuge class.

"I think I'm going to visit my parents," Alex said. "They're probably waiting for an update and I don't want them getting antsy about not hearing from me."

Bear nodded. "Sounds like a good idea."

"Say 'hi' from us," D.C. put in kindly.

"Will do," Alex agreed with a smile. "Where are you guys meeting Hunter?"

"Right here," Jordan said. "He'll arrive after everyone else has cleared out."

Alex looked around the quickly emptying food court. "That's my cue to leave."

"Are you sure you don't want to try out with us?" D.C. asked. "It might be fun."

Alex laughed at the thought. "Not by my definition, Dix. But you guys enjoy yourselves."

She stood and hastily left the food court, eager to be far away when Hunter arrived. The last thing she needed was to give the impression that she actually wanted to take part in the class. No sir-ee.

Once outside, Alex walked straight over to the Tower building and headed downstairs into the Library. It was weird; she'd grown so used to coming and going through its doorways over the holidays, but this was the first time she'd been back since school started. The moment she entered the majestic foyer, she felt a sensation similar to a warm embrace, as if the Library was welcoming her back with open arms.

She waved to the surly librarian who grunted in reply, then skipped down the stairs, concentrated on where she wanted to go, willed a door to appear and stepped directly though it—straight into what looked like ancient Egypt.

The Library didn't skimp on details, that was for sure. It had provided pyramids and everything. After seeing their new digs, Alex's parents hadn't cared about being cloistered away in what was loosely defined as a 'building' for the entirety of their stay in Medora. Instead, they'd been thrilled by the idea of gallivanting around amongst one of the Seven Wonders of the Ancient World. Well, *their* world, at least. Medoran history was different. And yet, despite that, the Library had generously accommodated Alex's request for a safe but productive place for her parents to stay. In fact, the ecosystem was so real that the only way Alex knew they were still inside the Library at all was because of its walls. It might look as if the desert's sand dunes continued for all eternity, but upon exploring during her first visit, Alex had walked straight into a transparent barrier—and nearly broken her nose in the process.

Grumbling about needing a warning sign, Alex had very deliberately chosen to ignore the warmly amused voice of the Library echoing in the wind, "*Best watch your step, Alexandra.*"

She had taken those words to heart and now, holding a hand in front of her face to shield against the glare of the artificial sun, Alex opened her mouth to call out to her parents rather than wander aimlessly into another barrier. But she didn't manage to get a single word out before a large gust of wind blasted what felt like every grain of sand in the desert down her throat.

Bending double to hack the coarse grittiness out of her oesophagus, she waited until she could catch her breath before stumbling forward, deciding to head into the nearest pyramid—the only one that was 'real' amid the illusions of others, as she'd painfully discovered on her first visit.

Wiping tears from her eyes after the attack of wind, sand *and* glare, Alex was relieved to find shelter inside the archaeological wonder. Almost immediately she heard excited voices from further in and headed towards them. She found her parents kneeling in a flame-lit chamber at the base of a pillar covered in carved hieroglyphs, talking a mile a minute over each other.

"Rach, honey, can you see—"

"I know, Jack, it's incredible! Just look at—"

"Extraordinary! I can't believe—"

Alex cleared her throat loudly, drawing their startled gazes.

"Alex? What a lovely surprise!" said her mum, Rachel, rising to her feet and brushing sand off her knees. She closed the distance between them and drew Alex in for a hug.

"What are you doing here, sweetheart?" asked her dad, Jack, embracing her after her mother. "Please don't say it's because you have more immortal elves after you for us to worry about. One arch-enemy is enough for any grand adventure, in my humble opinion."

"Aven's not an elf, Dad," Alex said, though she could understand the popular culture comparison—she made it frequently herself. "He's a Meyarin. And can't a girl visit her parents without needing a reason?"

Jack looked at her in a way only a father could. "Once-in-a-lifetime opportunity or not, I still have moments where I wonder if we made the right decision letting you come back here. If Aven's as dangerous as you say..." He trailed off, gathering his thoughts. "You know, if Darrius hadn't told us that the elf can now use the Library to step through to Earth and kidnap you, I'm not sure our decision would have been the same. But if he can get to you no matter where you are, then I guess—"

"—that you might as well be somewhere where you're learning how to not get caught by him," Rachel jumped in to finish. "And you are, sweetheart, aren't you? Learning how to stay safe from him?"

Understanding their concern, Alex tried to reassure them. "I am. And believe me, when my Combat instructor is through with me, Aven won't stand a chance. No one will be capturing me—Meyarin, human, or otherwise."

Noting their still troubled faces, Alex decided it was time for her to divert their attention away from imminent threats to her life and therefore the lives of all Medorans. She took in their dirt-smudged skin and, keeping her tone deliberately light, said, "Now enough about me, I want to hear about what you guys have been up to. It sure looks like you're having fun down here."

That was all it took for her easily distracted, work-loving parents to switch gears, all talk of Aven forgotten. Again Alex was reminded of how they'd seemed to repress what Darrius had told them about Alex's dealings with the Meyarin. But if compartmentalising it all helped calm her parents enough to allow Alex to continue on at Akarnae, then she'd let them repress anything they wanted.

"This place is amazing!" Rachel gushed. "The parallels between Medora and Earth are astounding. Already we've made several new discoveries, and the wonders just keep coming!"

"You should have seen the alluvial deposits we found yesterday," said Jack, practically glowing with pleasure. "I've never seen such nutrient-dense soil before in my life!"

"Who doesn't love a good alluvial deposit?" replied Alex, unintentionally setting her parents off on a longwinded discussion about the importance of fertile soil for ancient crop cultivation.

It was only after listening patiently to their overload of farming information as well as the tangent conversation about the large Canopic vases they'd found a few days ago—including the mummified contents within and just who they might have originally belonged to—that Alex considered her parental duty complete for the day.

With distracted goodbyes and 'be carefuls' from her parents who were clearly eager to get back to their hieroglyphs, Alex willed a return doorway to appear from right inside the pyramid. It opened showing her a view of the Library's foyer, but something unexpected happened as soon as she stepped through the door. With a disorienting swirl of colour, the scenery changed, causing her to land not in the well-lit foyer...

...but in the middle of a forest.

Thoroughly bewildered, Alex turned around once, twice, and then stood there weighing her options. She clearly wasn't in the Library anymore, but she had no idea how that had happened. Never before had she stepped through a doorway and arrived anywhere but where she had chosen.

No, that wasn't right. Her very first foray into the fantasy world had landed her in a forest clearing where she'd met Aven, and then Jordan and Bear. But that didn't explain where she was now—or why she was there.

"Uh, hello?" she called out timidly, wondering what she was supposed to do.

No one answered and she soon realised no one was going to. For whatever reason, the Library had decided to intervene and drop her off somewhere unexpected—and without any instruction whatsoever—and Alex had little option but to simply go with it.

If only she could open a doorway, that would solve all her problems. But when she was in Medora she had to be within the Library in order to will a door into existence. Either that, or she had to have already exited from a doorway that she could then call back into being for the return trip. Neither of those options were available to her at the moment, since technically she hadn't opened the doorway that led to her being lost in the middle of nowhere. That left her with one option.

"Eenie, meenie, miney, moe," she said, closing her eyes and pointing in all directions. When her finger landed, she started off into the forest, stepping cautiously through the thick shrubbery and wishing she'd worn sturdier shoes.

"I hope you have a good reason for sending me here," she murmured, knowing instinctively that if the Library put her there, then it could hear her whingeing.

A branch snapped loudly behind her and the sound reminded Alex that she was in a world where all sorts of monstrous creatures likely prowled through the woods.

Another branch snapped, closer this time, causing her body to tense.

A thick bush rustled only a few feet away from where she stood. The shrubbery was at least twice her height, with a width more than three times that. The rustling increased until the whole bush was moving and Alex's heart began to pound in her chest as she backed away.

When the rustling stopped, Alex released the breath she'd been holding. But it turned into a squeal of fright when something lunged towards her. She scurried backwards until she was pressed up against a tree. But when she caught sight of her 'attacker' she let out a relieved laugh.

"Aren't you cute!" she gushed at the furry little creature that looked like some kind of squirrely possum—fluffy with big eyes and a long curling tail. Hardly the nightmarish monster she'd feared.

Alex knew better than to reach out to touch the animal—knowing her luck, she'd catch some funky disease from it—but she had to admit it was adorable. So much so that she was too busy watching it scavenge for food to notice that the bush was still rustling. A snarl was the only warning she had before a black shadow burst through the shrubbery and caught the squirrely creature in its teeth, snapping its body with a sickening crunch and swallowing it whole.

Alex shrieked and threw herself to the ground just as the animal lunged for her next. It was hideously terrifying; huge and hairy, with unnatural blood-red eyes and dilated black pupils. Talon-like claws ripped into the tree where she'd been standing, and when the animal turned to growl at her, she could see its razor-sharp teeth, each of which was about as long as her hand.

Alex scrambled to her feet when her fight-or-flight instinct activated and bolted blindly into the forest. She had no defence, no weapon, nothing at all. She didn't even have speed to her advantage, since she could hear the creature quickly gaining on her. She wouldn't be able to outrun it. But what else could she do?

At least the dense woodland was working in her favour, helping to slow the beast. She dared not look back; hearing the creature's frustrated growls as it struggled through vines was enough to know that it was still close behind. Too close. She needed to get out of there. She needed to get ... *higher*.

Alex glanced back at the creature as she tore through the forest. While its front legs held lethal talons, its back legs had no claws that she could see. She could only hope that meant it couldn't climb, and with that thought she grabbed onto a thick vine and scurried up the closest tree. But she wasn't high enough when the monster caught up with her, and before she could scramble out of reach, it jumped up and swiped its claws along her back, tearing into her flesh.

Alex cried out in pain and nearly lost her grip, but she managed to hold on and continued to heave herself up. She stopped when she was nearly at the canopy, and shakily rested against the thick tree trunk. Her back was screaming in agony, but she was more concerned about what to do next. The creature was prowling at the base of the tree, snarling and growling at her. She had no way to escape.

And then, out of nowhere, Alex heard voices.

The creature heard them too, and it turned away and looked in the direction of the noise. It jumped into a thick bush until it was concealed entirely from sight, its dark, hairy body camouflaged by the dense foliage.

Just as she was about to call out a warning, three people walked into view. Alex jerked back with shock and shrunk further into the tree, hiding amongst the vines and leaves.

Her reaction may have been dramatic, but it was also justified. Because one of the people was Aven.

Seriously, did she have the worst luck, or what?

"She's nearby. I can sense her," Aven proclaimed.

Alex shuddered at his announcement. Was he talking about her? How did he know she was there?

She peered at the silvery scar on her hand, feeling an unpleasant churning in her stomach at the reminder of when his blood had mixed with hers. Was it possible that...? No, she couldn't bear to consider the thought that he was somehow able to sense her through the scar. It wasn't possible. It couldn't be.

"Are you sure?" Gerald asked. Even from her elevated position, Alex could easily recognise the tattoo-covered man she'd last seen fleeing from the Library with Aven.

"You doubt me, Gerald?" Aven asked dangerously.

"Of—of course not," Gerald stuttered.

"He'd never be so stupid as to doubt you, my prince," said the third member of the group, a woman Alex did not recognise. She was tall and refined, with blond hair and vacant, glassy eyes.

"You're right, Calista," Aven agreed. "He must know how unwise it would be to question my judgement."

Gerald opened his mouth, most likely to apologise again, but Aven quieted him with a look.

"Silence. She's here."

Gerald and the woman—Calista—tensed. They both withdrew blades from belted scabbards and held them at the ready. Alex froze, wondering what they planned to do to her.

"Put your weapons away," Aven said. "This is between me and her."

They did as he commanded, and he stepped closer to the tree in which Alex was perched high above them.

"Come out, come out, wherever you are," Aven goaded as he unsheathed his own weapon.

Alex gripped the tree trunk, her knuckles white. Aven hadn't looked up so there was a possibility that he didn't know where she was exactly. She wasn't going to give away her position, no matter what.

But what happened next was so unexpected that she nearly let go.

In her fear of Aven, she'd forgotten about the dark beast, which soon made its presence known, lunging from the bush and slamming into Aven's torso.

The Meyarin didn't so much as blink. He raised his arm and slashed his blade into the neck of the hairy creature before effortlessly throwing the bulky mass aside with the weapon still imbedded in its flesh. Alex's stomach roiled at the sound of the beast's gurgling whine as it fell limply to the ground.

Aven patted his torn sleeve where the creature had clawed his arm, frantically inspecting his clothes and skin. Alex could see his silver blood dripping from where the monster's talons had swiped into his flesh, but she knew his Meyarin genes would heal the wound soon enough.

"Quickly, Gerald," Aven ordered, snapping his two human companions out of their shock. "We need to leave before Marselle discovers how close we are to his precious school."

It was then that Alex realised Aven hadn't come for her at all. He hadn't been calling for *her* because she wasn't the one he could 'sense'—it was the *creature* he'd been hunting.

Alex let out a stuttered breath of relief but locked her body again when Aven cocked his head to the side, listening with his superior Meyarin hearing. He glanced around with a quizzical expression before shaking his head and turning his attention back to his companions.

While Alex focused on not making any sound that might draw his attention again, Calista reached into her jacket and retrieved a glass vial. She handed it to Gerald who knelt and yanked out Aven's blade, pressing the vial against the slashed neck of the creature. The glass filled with a murky brown liquid as the creature's blood gushed out of the fatal wound.

"That's enough," Aven said.

Gerald pressed a stopper in the top and made to hand the vial to Aven but the Meyarin hissed and backed away. "Remember what I told you, fool!"

Gerald's ink-covered face paled and he hastily shoved the blood-filled container into his clothes.

"Is that all we need, my prince?" Calista asked.

"For the moment." Aven looked down at the lifeless creature. "Such a waste. She had so much potential."

Alex felt the hair on her neck stand on end at his words and she imagined herself in the same place as the animal, with Aven standing over her defeated body.

She shook the thought from her mind and watched silently as he drew out a Bubbler and threw it to the ground. Without another word he led the way through, and as soon as Gerald and Calista stepped in after him, the bubble-gateway vanished.

Alex exhaled deeply the moment they were gone. She couldn't believe Aven had been searching for the very creature that had been chasing her. It was too much of a coincidence.

And Alex didn't believe in coincidences.

"What are you playing at?" she whispered, wanting to know why the Library had sent her there. She, of course, received no answer.

She loosened her grip and considered her next move. There was no way she was going to leave the safety of the tree, but she needed to start moving and find her way back to Akarnae. Aven's words about Darrius gave her hope that she wasn't too far from the academy, so she just had to figure out which direction to go in.

Ignoring the throbbing pain in her back, Alex started climbing higher up the tree. If she was close to Akarnae, then she should be able to get her bearings if she broke through the canopy.

Climbing was hard work. The higher she rose, the more entangled she became in the leaves and branches. But eventually she managed to push through and she balanced precariously on the swaying treetop, gripping for dear life.

Squinting into the distance, she was able to recognise the rising hulk of Mount Paedris, confirming that she was in the Ezera Forest and showing which direction she needed to go to reach the academy.

Shimmying back down, Alex halted her descent when she reached a place where the branches thickly overlapped, making them more stable. She began moving through the trees, crawling more often than walking. It was slow going, but with the advantage of height she didn't fear any more encounters with hairy, snarling beasts. Or Aven, for that matter. She was sure he was long gone, but the last thing she needed was to have another close and personal run-in with him again so soon.

Soon enough Alex's patience waned and her confidence grew, leading her to trust that the branches would hold her weight as she walked, ran, and often jumped from tree to tree. Holding onto the vines for balance and support, Alex felt like a Tarzan wannabe as she moved stealthily through the forest.

Eventually the trees began to thin, bringing her out of the woodland and to the edge of the academy grounds. Just as she was about to climb down to the ground, something caught her eye a few trees away. Her injured back was screaming in agony after all the climbing and jumping and she was desperate to visit Fletcher for some of his miraculous healing salve, but Alex couldn't resist investigating the object glinting in the afternoon light.

She leapt the last few branches until she was able to reach up and grab the object from above her head.

"What is this doing out here?" she whispered to herself, turning the shiny necklace over in her hands.

While the unexplainable resting place of the jewellery was a mystery, what surprised Alex the most, was that it was fashioned from Myrox—a stunning but rare Meyarin steel. The chain was a simple strand of the silver-like material, but it was the pendant that was truly enchanting. It was a miniature depiction of a beautifully crafted archer's bow, with the arrow drawn and ready for release. The detail was incredible, and the glowing Myrox infused the ornament with a lifelike quality.

Alex wondered how such a prized possession could have ended up hidden so high in the trees. It didn't make any sense.

She shrugged to herself and, unsure what else to do, undid the miniscule clasp on the chain and reattached it around her neck. She felt a little uneasy wearing someone else's pendant, but at least this way she wouldn't drop it or lose it in her climb down to the ground.

Branch by branch, Alex slowly lowered herself, wincing as she grappled with the rough bark. Her palms were shredded from all the climbing she'd endured, but that was nothing compared to the throbbing gashes across her back.

When Alex reached the ground she stretched out her cramping arms and legs before setting off through the last of thinning forest. Within a few short steps the academy came into view, and she felt like dropping to her knees in relief. The only reason she didn't was because she wasn't sure if she'd be able to get back up again.

It took her a while to walk around the edge of Lake Fee and hike across the massive field, but eventually Alex made it to the campus and she headed straight for the Medical Ward.

The sight that met her inside Fletcher's domain was not what she'd expected. The Ward was so full of patients that she wondered if she should leave and come back later, but then her back throbbed its disagreement and she grimaced at the pain.

"Alex," Fletcher greeted her, more frazzled than she'd ever seen him. "I take it you're here for the same reason as your classmates?"

She frowned in confusion and looked around the room, noting that the patients were all fourth year students.

"What happened?" she asked, feeling a stab of concern as she searched for the familiar faces of her friends. She relaxed slightly when she couldn't see them anywhere.

"Weren't you with them?"

"No, I was ... elsewhere," she said meaningfully.

Fletcher's eyes lit with understanding. "Oh. I see. Well, some of your classmates pushed themselves too far in their pursuit of a position in Hunter's class. Nothing too serious, mind you, but they certainly weren't being very careful."

Alex looked around the room once more and noticed the various injuries. Cuts and bruises seemed to be the most common ailments, but she also saw a number of bandaged limbs.

"Since you weren't with them, can I assume you'll live until I've herded them all out of here?" Fletcher asked.

Alex swallowed, wondering how long that would take. But she'd already managed on her own while forging through the forest, surely she could wait just a little longer? Her pain spiked again at the thought, but she ignored it and nodded to Fletcher.

The doctor sent her a grateful smile and indicated towards a spare bed in the corner of the room. "I won't be too long," he promised, hurrying off to assist his other patients.

Alex stumbled over to the bed, careful to keep her back to the wall and away from curious eyes. She was wearing a black shirt, which helped conceal the bloodstains, but she was certain the material was ripped from the creature's claws. She sat on the bed with her legs dangling over the edge of the mattress and waited. She couldn't lie down and she couldn't lean on anything—not unless she wanted to stain the white bed sheets or walls with her blood.

She was tired, she was hungry and she was in some serious agony now that she wasn't doing anything to pump her adrenaline and keep her mind off her injury. If only she'd had the foresight to ask Fletcher for some of his pain relief medicine. Then at least she could have been more comfortable while waiting.

It took half an hour for the majority of her classmates to be discharged, but there were still a few left with whom Fletcher was finishing up. She wished they would heal faster.

"Don't tell me you fell out of a tree, too?"

Alex looked up and found herself face to face with Kaiden. She sent him a baffled look. "Why would I have fallen out of a tree?"

Really, considering everything else, it was a miracle she hadn't fallen out of a tree. But how could he have known about that?

"Isn't that what happened to most of your classmates?" he said, leaning against the bed. She turned towards him, attempting to keep her shredded flesh out of sight.

"I'm not sure what happened to them," Alex admitted. "Fletcher said they went a bit crazy in the SAS trial."

Kaiden's eyes flickered briefly over her body, as if examining her for injury. "What about you?"

"What about me?"

"How did you go in the trial?"

She blinked at him. "I didn't do it."

He looked surprised. "Really?"

"Yes, really," Alex huffed. Why was it so hard for people to believe she didn't want any part of Hunter's class?

"How ... unexpected." His lips curled into a secretive smile. "I've never heard of anyone not trying out for **SAS**."

Alex floundered for a response and settled on a lame, "Well, now you have."

He peered intently at her and then chuckled quietly, but she wasn't sure what was so funny. "You're different, Alex, you know that?"

Her tone was wry when she replied, "You have no idea."

He grinned in response and thankfully didn't ask any more questions.

"What are you in here for?" she asked conversationally, shifting her position and barely hiding a wince. "You don't look hurt. Or sick."

"Healthy as a horse," Kaiden confirmed. "So...?"

"I came to report to Fletcher that everyone is accounted for," he said.

"Accounted for?"

"Hunter had all the current **SAS** students out on patrol to keep an eye on the potential initiates," Kaiden explained, waving his hand towards the students still left in the Medical Ward. "We weren't allowed to interfere with the exercise, only to report our observations. He asked me to come and tell Fletcher that everyone is now out of the forest."

"You're in SAS?" Alex was curious despite herself. "What's it like?"

His eyes lit up but all he said was, "It's something you definitely have to experience for yourself."

"Vague, much?" Alex said with a teasing grin. Then she asked, "What was the exercise?"

"I can't tell you that," he said, with an apologetic shake of his head. "Even your classmates weren't told beforehand."

Alex frowned. "How were they supposed to complete the exercise if they didn't know what they had to do?"

"They were given brief instructions that were meant to be interpreted as clues."

Alex looked at him. "Exactly how 'brief' were those instructions?"

Kaiden held his hands up. "Easy, now. Remember, I'm not Hunter. And besides, I had to do the same thing last year. Or something similar, anyway."

"Did you end up in the Med Ward afterwards?"

"Broken collarbone," he admitted, almost proudly. "But it was worth it, since I got a place in the class."

"You're insane," she said. "I honestly don't understand the appeal."

"Don't worry. You'll figure it out soon enough."

That wasn't going to happen, not unless one of her friends made it into the class and regaled her with stories of their stealthy and subterfuge-y adventures. But if they did, then they'd probably be too cool to use words like 'subterfuge-y'.

Alex chuckled at the thought and then grimaced from pain. This time, she failed to hide her reaction.

Kaiden stiffened and Alex thought she caught a flash of concern in his eyes as he looked her over. "Are you hurt?"

"It's nothing," she told him quickly.

"I don't believe you," he said, his gaze probing her face. "I told you why I'm here, what's your reason?"

"Really, it's nothing," she repeated, looking away and hoping he would let it drop. "You should give Fletcher your message and go. It's probably dinner time by now."

"Hey," he said, reaching out to gently grasp her shoulder and turn her back to him.

The movement surprised her and she hissed when her torn flesh spasmed painfully.

Kaiden dropped his hand at her reaction, but then his face hardened with determination and, before she could stop him, he leaned around to look behind her.

She flinched away from him, but the damage was done.

"What *happened?*" he demanded, his tone both concerned and unexpectedly protective.

"It's—"

"If you say it's nothing one more time..." he interrupted, leaving his sentence hanging with the threat.

He wasn't going to let it go, she knew. But before she could decide what to tell him, Fletcher arrived.

"Now that everything is sorted, what can I do for you, Alex?"

She looked from the smiling doctor to the narrow-eyed Kaiden and sighed in defeat. "I was attacked by an animal out in the forest."

There. Done. Just like ripping off a Band-Aid.

Fletcher sent her a look, clearly knowing that she was downplaying the situation. "Where are you hurt?"

She carefully eased herself off the bed and turned around. She hadn't had a chance to look at her injury and Kaiden had barely glanced at the wound, but from both his and Fletcher's sharp inhalations, she could guess it wasn't a pretty sight.

"Alex..." Fletcher breathed. "Why didn't you tell me you were this badly injured when you arrived?"

She turned to face him again but kept her gaze averted and shuffled her feet. "You were busy. I didn't want to interrupt."

He tsked quietly and ordered her to get back on the bed while he went to get medical supplies. When he returned, he instructed her to lie down on her stomach and he lifted the hem of her shirt. The wound was on her lower back so it wasn't too awkward, but she was very aware that Kaiden was still standing by her bed.

Fletcher pressed something wet against the wound and she had to bite her tongue to keep from crying out at the stinging pain. The doctor tried to take her mind off what he was doing by launching into his interrogation.

"What sort of animal did this?"

"I don't know what it was," she said, trying—and failing—to keep her breathing steady as she focused on his question and not the burning of her flesh. "It was big and black and hairy, with creepy red and black eyes, and claws on its front feet. Its teeth were as long as my hands. And its blood was a strange brown colour."

Fletcher's voice was contemplative when he said, "It sounds like a Hyroa. But they're practically extinct. And there certainly shouldn't be any of them left near these parts. What do you think, Kaiden?"

His face troubled, Kaiden responded, "That was my first thought, too, given the description. But like you said, Fletch, they're supposed to be nearly extinct. And definitely not roaming free in the Ezera Forest."

"If that's the case," Fletcher said, turning back to Alex, "how did you manage to get away from it? I've never encountered one, but rumours claim that they're extremely bloodthirsty and move much faster than the average human can run. They're *very* dangerous, Alex."

Gee, you think? she thought, only just managing to keep her sarcasm internal.

"It didn't look like the type of animal that could climb very well, not with different front and back feet," she said. "I decided to use that to my advantage and I climbed up into the trees. But it caught me before I was high enough and swiped me with its claws."

"That must have been intensely painful," Fletcher murmured.

"I've felt worse," Alex said quietly, remembering with vivid clarity the feeling of Aven's ice-like dagger slicing through her back and into her lungs. She shuddered at the memory and turned her head, only to find Kaiden's curious eyes on her. Why was he still here, anyway?

"Nevertheless, this likely caused you no small amount of discomfort," Fletcher pressed. "How much time has passed since you were attacked?"

Alex tried to calculate it in her head. She'd left to visit her parents after lunch and stayed with them for about an hour before she was unceremoniously dumped in the forest. So that meant...

"I think it happened around two-thirty."

There was a weighty silence after the words left her mouth.

"What?" she asked, feeling self-conscious.

"Alex, it's six o'clock," Fletcher said. "You only arrived here about half an hour ago. What were you doing all that time?"

"Making my way back," she answered. Obviously.

Kaiden sent her a probing look. "Back from where?"

Oh. Oops.

"Uh, I was kind of lost in the forest," she said. Until she'd found her bearings, that was definitely true.

"Why were you out there if you weren't applying for SAS?" Kaiden pressed.

"That's an excellent question," Alex said. She then closed her mouth and turned her head to look in the opposite direction, having no intention of answering. The last thing she needed was for Kaiden to learn about the murderous Meyarin hell-bent on using her for his own nefarious purposes. Uh-uh, no way.

She heard him exhale in frustration and she felt a little guilty. But come on. She hardly knew the guy. She didn't owe him an explanation.

"All right, how about this one?" he said, moving around to the other side of the bed so she could see him again. "How do you know the colour of the Hyroa's blood?"

Alex blanched at the new line of interrogation. She absolutely couldn't answer, not without talking about Aven.

Upon seeing her startled reaction, Kaiden leaned in further. He didn't say anything but continued looking at her, waiting for her answer.

"I—I—Uh—" she stuttered.

Fletcher chose that moment to apply some kind of paste to her back, and she couldn't supress the whimper that escaped her lips.

"Perhaps it's best if you leave, Kaiden," the doctor said gently but firmly. "It sounds like Alex has been through quite an ordeal and she could do with some rest."

Alex saw Kaiden hesitate and she braced herself for his response, but he then he relaxed and nodded at Fletcher.

"Thank you for reporting back to me," Fletcher told him. "And for everything else you've done to help as well."

"No problem," Kaiden said, stepping back. He caught Alex's gaze once more, his eyes telling her so much more than any words could express. He was asking her to trust him.

But she couldn't. Too much was at stake. She closed her eyes and turned her head away.

A quiet sigh reached her ears, and then he whispered, "Feel better, Alex."

For some reason, his kind words made her feel worse.

***

"And then what happened?"

It was the next afternoon and Alex was sitting with her friends under her favourite tree by the lake, telling them about the events that had transpired over the past twenty-four hours. Fletcher had made her stay in the Medical Ward overnight and well into the morning, ignoring her protests that 'it was just a scratch'. He'd been worried about infection after seeing the depth of the claw wounds, and because of that he hadn't been willing to seal her injury closed until he was certain his Regenevators had run their full course of healing from the inside out—which had taken all night.

The only visitor she'd been allowed was the headmaster, who had come after Alex had mentioned to Fletcher that there was more to the story, and that Darrius needed to hear it. Both of them had listened intently when she'd detailed what happened to the Hyroa, but neither had known why Aven wanted its blood. Like her, they were relieved that the Meyarin hadn't known she was so close.

Darrius had again reminded her to be on her guard, but he hadn't pressed her further about visiting Meya. He was giving her time to think, just like she'd asked, and she was grateful for his patience.

Fletcher had released Alex before lunch and she'd met up with her friends. They'd stopped by the Medical Ward the previous night, but apparently Alex had been fast asleep. That was hardly surprising, considering how drugged up she'd been on pain meds.

But now the four of them sat and swapped stories. Alex had started first and she was just wrapping up, wanting to hurry it along so she could hear about their SAS trials.

"That was it," she answered Jordan. "Fletcher patched me up, Kaiden asked some probing questions, Darrius reminded me to be careful and then I fell asleep."

"A Hyroa!" Bear whistled. "I can't believe it. Those things are *insane*."

"Do you have a wicked scar?" Jordan asked. "I'll bet you do. Claw marks—that's so cool!"

Alex didn't bother to tell him that it was most definitely *not* cool. Painful? Undeniably. Cool? Absolutely not. Rather than arguing the point, she reminded him about Fletcher's amazing medicines and lifted the hem of her shirt to show that there was no scarring on her back.

Jordan had the nerve to look disappointed—at least until he caught her glare and smiled sheepishly at her.

"Let me see the necklace again," D.C. asked, reaching out to admire the jewellery that was fastened around Alex's neck.

She'd mentioned it to Darrius the night before, but he'd just looked amused and told her to keep it unless asked otherwise. Weird, for sure, but she'd been in too much of a medication-haze to argue.

"All right, enough about me," Alex said finally. "I want to hear what happened with Hunter."

"There's not much to tell," Bear said, snapping a twig between his fingers. "He took us out to the forest and told us we had to prove ourselves worthy of his class. Then he left."

"None of us had any idea what to do," D.C. admitted. "At first we stood there like lost kittens. But then we jumped straight in, coming to our own conclusions about what we were meant to do."

"I figured out that it must have been some kind of scavenger hunt," Jordan said. "The others began to catch on, and everyone kind of branched out and looked for clues. For some reason, most of them ended up climbing trees—and falling out of them. There was a lot of competition to earn Hunter's regard."

"What happened in the end?" Alex asked. "Did you find any clues?"

"All I found was a nest of very unhappy Faendas," Bear grumbled, holding out his swollen hand for Alex to see. She winced in sympathy, remembering her very first Medical Science class where she'd been stung by one of the wasp-like insects whose venom caused instant paralysis.

"I found a stick that was shaped in a 'U'," Jordan said. "I took it to mean 'turn around, you idiot', but even then I didn't find anything." He couldn't keep the disappointment from his tone when he added, "To be honest, we don't know if we were actually *meant* to find any clues. It was a long shot to begin with."

"I guess we'll just have to wait until tonight," D.C. said. "Hunter told us he'll personally visit the people he chooses for his class."

"That's exciting," Alex said brightly, trying to be encouraging.

Bear snorted, while the other two just grinned at her overly enthusiastic response.

"Truly," Alex added. But then she realised just how fake she sounded and laughed with them. "Okay, you know me too well. But I'm still hoping you guys get in, since I know how much it means to you."

"Thanks, Alex," Bear said. "But honestly, it's not looking that great—for us or anyone else. Half our year ended up in the Med Ward, and the rest of us ran out of time and were sent back here more confused than when we started."

"Yeah," Jordan agreed, stabbing the ground with a stick. "I wouldn't be surprised if Hunter didn't take on any new recruits this year."

"Hey, don't count yourselves out just yet," Alex said. "You never know what might happen."

Seven

Late that night a knock sounded on the door to Alex and D.C.'s dorm room.

Knowing D.C. wouldn't knock before entering her own room, Alex presumed the visitor was Jordan or Bear and opened the door without hesitation.

"Good evening, Alex."

Her eyes widened at the sight of Hunter standing there. His dark cape swirled around him, but his hood was drawn back so she could see his face.

"Uh, good evening, sir," she replied awkwardly. She was caught off-guard by his casual use of her name. Not that she minded—she preferred to be called Alex. It was just ... unexpected.

But more unexpected was his presence in her dorm room. What was he...?

Oh! Alex smiled when the realisation hit her.

"You must be here to see Dix," she guessed, excited for her friend, since Hunter's visit meant D.C. must have been accepted into his class. "She's not here right now, she's at the Library. I'm sure you could catch her there, or I can go and find her if you want?"

Alex wasn't sure why she'd offered, especially since she was already dressed for sleep, in her comfiest pyjamas, no less.

Hunter shook his head. "I'm not here to see Miss Cavelle."

Alex thought his response was strange—why else would he be knocking on their door?—but then she realised what he'd said. How did he know who D.C. really was? That was top secret, as far as Alex was aware. But then again, she shouldn't have been surprised, since Hunter was the kind of person who seemed to know everything.

"Jordan and Bear aren't here either," Alex said, wondering if maybe that was why he was at her doorstep. "But their room is just down the hall."

Alex had only a single moment of warning to note Hunter's amused expression, and from it a very strong feeling of dread swept through her.

"I'm not here for your friends, Alex," he said with a smirk. "Congratulations on passing your trial yesterday. You're officially accepted into my Stealth and Subterfuge class."

Um ... What?

Alex wondered if she looked as confused as she felt. "I think there must be some kind of mistake."

Hunter tilted his head, his smirk deepening. "It's not often that I'm wrong."

"Then this is your lucky day," Alex said. "I didn't try out for your class, so there's no way I could've passed whatever your trial was. You have the wrong person."

His dark eyes glittered with humour. "Is that so?"

"Yep," Alex said confidently. "Sorry you wasted your time."

She reached for the door, intent on closing it to end the conversation and not caring how rude the gesture might seem. But Hunter moved to lean against it, blocking her dismissal.

"Tell me, Alex," he said, as relaxed as if he was lounging on a beach somewhere. "Did you or did you not venture into the forest at some point yesterday afternoon?"

Not by choice, Alex thought, but she didn't say that out loud. "Yes, I was there for a few hours. So?"

His lips curled knowingly, and Alex felt her sense of dread rise up again.

"Then you entered the trial zone," he said. "Despite the fact that you didn't sign up for testing, your participation confirmed your entry to my class."

"W—What?" Alex spluttered. "I didn't participate! I didn't even know where the trial was being held!"

"Intentional or not, you actively took part in the exercise, regardless of whether you were aware of it at the time," Hunter said. "And out of all your classmates, you were the only one to succeed."

No, no, no! This was all wrong. Hunter was wrong. This was a prank, right?

Alex backed away from the door and slumped down on the edge of her bed, too overwhelmed to stay on her feet.

"You should feel proud," Hunter continued, still standing in the doorway. "Never before has a student slipped by me as expertly as you did."

Alex rubbed her temples. "I don't understand."

"Should I spell it out for you?" Hunter asked, a hint of mockery in his voice. "It's as I said: you're now a student in my Stealth and Subterfuge class."

She jerked her head from side to side. "No."

"Yes."

"No," she repeated firmly. "I, uh, thank you for your offer, but I'm afraid I have to decline."

There. That should do it. Despite her confusion about whatever trial he was talking about, at least she could decide yay or nay. And for her, it was a definite nay.

"I'm afraid you have little choice in the matter," Hunter said, unconcerned by her growing frustration.

"It's my life," Alex argued.

"Remember the meeting on your first evening back at the academy?" Hunter asked. "Didn't I say that any student who attended Saturday's trial and was granted a position would find themselves mandatorily required to attend classes?"

Alex couldn't recall his exact wording, but she did have a vague memory of him saying something along those lines. But she *hadn't* attended the trial, let alone succeeded in it—whatever 'it' was.

"Yes, but—"

"What's that around your neck, Alex?" Hunter interrupted.

Feeling off-balance from the abrupt change in topic, she looked down at the shimmery Myrox glinting in the light. "It's a necklace. I found it in the..."

Alex groaned as everything fell into place. *No flipping way.*

Hunter actually had the nerve to chuckle at her reaction. "You can keep it as a token prize. No one has ever recovered the target before in all my years of teaching the class, so it only seems fitting considering your exemplary performance. And it may come in handy, especially with the trials you'll be facing in the future."

Alex chose to ignore the implication in his last statement—and the question of how the necklace would 'come in handy'—and she addressed the rest of his words. "You can't do this, Hunter. It was an accident! I wasn't even meant to be out there. Things just ... happened that way."

With an uncaring shrug, he said, "That's not my problem."

"I'll be terrible at your class!" Alex tried, hoping a different angle might work. "I'm not stealthy or subterfuge-y. And I ... um ... I don't like spiders!"

Not her best argument, but she would just have to roll with it.

Hunter arched an eyebrow. "Your point?"

"Not just spiders—all bugs. We don't get along," Alex said. "And I'm sure your class will spend time in the forest and, well, you don't need me squealing every time I feel something crawling up my arm. That would totally ruin the, uh, stealthy atmosphere."

Hunter regarded her for a moment and then pushed off the door, losing his casual appearance.

"Listen to me, Alex," he said with a quiet intensity. It was the first time he'd dissolved his politely official demeanour and she could see he meant business. "Part of my gifting involves perception. It allows me to be aware of the people around me at any given time. Right now I can tell you that there are currently fifteen people on this floor alone. Six of them are asleep, four are catching up on homework, two are gossiping about boys and two more are bouncing around in their room as if drunk on dillyberry juice."

He paused and added, "Coincidentally, those last two happen to be your friends, and the next time you see them, you might want to let them know that their mattresses aren't intended to be used as trampolines."

Alex wished she was with Jordan and Bear right now, not sitting and waiting for Hunter's other shoe to drop. Because she was sure it was about to happen.

"The final person is standing right here: me," Hunter continued. "If you have any basic mathematical skills, you'll have worked out that there's one person missing from my count: you. I can't read you—not at all. Not where you are, not what you're doing. I believe this is because of your own gift and the protection it affords you; an invaluable asset, in my opinion. But that alone isn't enough to warrant your enrolment in my class. I had no idea you were in those trees yesterday afternoon, and not just because my gift didn't sense your presence. Your technique—intentional or not—was nearly flawless."

"But, I—" Alex tried to speak but Hunter continued, not letting her cut in.

"Firstly, you weren't supposed to be out there, so my **SAS** spotters didn't know to look out for you. That was an example of subterfuge at its finest—strategic deceit."

"No, I—"

"Secondly," Hunter pressed, his hard look warning her not to talk over him again, "you avoided all my traps on the forest floor by remaining high above the ground for the entirety of your journey. Again, that was a clever ploy. And thirdly, you moved through the trees like you were born to do so. I only noticed you right at the very end, but it was clear how comfortable you were running and jumping from branch to branch. You claim to lack stealth, but I disagree."

That's just what happens after a few hours of tree-hopping, Alex thought. But she didn't try to interrupt him again.

"Your ingenuity and adaptation sparked my interest," Hunter informed her. "But it was your curiosity that sealed the deal. From my viewpoint, I could clearly see you were injured. And yet, when you noticed the pendant shining in the tree, you didn't turn away, you continued onward to collect it. You exhibited determination, a character trait that's essential in my class. For most new students it's the only requirement for their qualification since, as I mentioned before, no one else has ever found the object of their search."

"Maybe if you made it clear that they actually had to *look* for something," Alex muttered under her breath.

"It's easy to show determination when there's a focus point," Hunter said. "But when the end result is less clear, that's when a person's true character is tested."

Alex sighed, knowing she wasn't going to win against him. He had his reasons—quite a few, apparently—for wanting her in his class, despite her lack of willingness.

"I officially don't like you," she said with exasperation. "And just in case you missed it before, I *definitely* don't want to take part in your class."

"Your opinion has been noted," Hunter said. And with that, he spun around with a whirl of his cape, saying over his shoulder, "I'll see you on Tuesday night, Alex."

She blinked at the spot where he'd been standing and watched as the door closed automatically behind him.

"What just happened?" she wondered out loud, leaning forward to rest her head in her hands.

A moment later the door sprung open again, causing Alex to jump in fright.

"Hey!" D.C. greeted her, walking over to drop her books on her desk. "I just saw Hunter walking down the hall. He nodded at me but didn't say anything, so I guess I didn't make it in. It's probably for the best, anyway. Like you said, things are pretty crazy without having to add an extra class to the workload. And I think—Are you all right?"

D.C. must have finally noticed Alex's strained expression.

"Has something happened? It wasn't Aven again, was it?"

"No, nothing like that," Alex assured her friend. "It's just..."

She had no idea what to say, or where to start. She decided to just blurt it out. "I—"

A loud, rhythmical knock at the door interrupted her words.

D.C. glanced at Alex and said what they both already knew. "That'll be Jordan and Bear. Are you okay for me to let them in?"

"Yeah, sure," Alex said, thankful that she could share her news with them all now to save having to repeat herself later.

"Hail the conquering hero!" Bear cried, barging into the room as soon as D.C. opened the door.

"Thank you, thank you. I love you all, my worthy subjects," Jordan said, bowing pretentiously.

"You got in?" D.C. asked, and when he nodded, she squealed and launched herself at him.

Jordan seemed startled by her reaction, but then he laughed and spun her around. When he put her back on her feet, she turned to look at Bear.

"Not me, I'm afraid," their dark-haired friend said. While he seemed disappointed, it was clear he was ecstatic for Jordan. "Next year, hopefully."

Alex felt queasy. She knew how much the position meant to her friends, and they knew how much she *didn't* want it. She had no idea how they would react. The only good news was, if they decided not to hate her, she would have the comfort of having Jordan in her class.

"I didn't get in either," D.C. told them. "But I'm so happy for you, Jordan. You'll have to tell us all about it. And, oh, the stories you'll have—I bet it's going to be amazing!"

"Yeah, I'm pretty excited," Jordan agreed. "But I wish you guys could've made it, too."

"Next year, maybe," D.C. said, echoing Bear's words.

"Hey, Alex! No congrats for your favourite friend?" Jordan asked, seeing Alex sitting slumped on her bed.

"I'm her favourite," D.C. corrected, elbowing him.

Jordan nudged her back. "You wish."

"Since you guys are arguing about it, I think I should win by default," Bear put in.

Despite her warring thoughts, Alex's lips quirked with amusement. These were her closest friends. Her family, really. If they couldn't accept what she was about to tell them, then no one would.

She stood and walked over to where they clustered near the door. "I'm so happy for you, Jordan. I know how much you wanted this."

"Thanks, Alex," he said, pulling her into a hug. When he let her go, he kept his hands on her shoulders and looked into her eyes. She had difficulty holding his gaze.

"All right, what's going on?" He guided her over to sit on her bed again. "Spill."

She sighed, wishing her friends couldn't read her so well.

Jordan sat next to her, while D.C. and Bear moved to sit on D.C.'s bed facing them.

"I don't know how to say this..."

"It's just us, Alex," Bear said, his voice soft. "We won't bite."

Jordan gave her a roguish wink and added, "Much."

Alex smiled half-heartedly at them, and then she opened her mouth and let the words tumble out. "I got into Hunter's class."

Three pairs of eyes blinked at her.

"What do you mean?" Bear asked, his expression confused.

"I got into Hunter's class. Into SAS," Alex repeated. "He came and told me just before you all arrived."

"But—But how?" D.C. stammered. "You didn't even try out."

"I know!" Alex cried. "It doesn't make any sense! Hunter said that because I was in the forest yesterday on my way back to the academy, to him that meant I was participating in the exercise."

She ran her hands through her hair in agitation and then moved them down to touch the Myrox necklace. "It might've been okay if I hadn't found this. Apparently it was what you were all meant to be searching for. I just happened to have the advantage of height since I was already up in the trees—and not falling out of them, like the others."

Alex stopped talking. She had no idea what her friends were thinking. Did they hate her? Would they turn against her in jealousy? What if they never wanted to see her again?

She sat there fidgeting and waiting for someone to break the silence.

Then Jordan started chuckling.

Alex looked at him in surprise, and turned her disbelieving gaze to Bear and D.C. when they joined in. Soon all three of them were laughing uncontrollably.

"What part of this is funny?" Alex demanded.

"Only you, Alex," Jordan said with clear affection. "This could only happen to you."

"You're not angry?" she asked tentatively.

"Me? I'm stoked," Jordan said. "We're going to have a great time together!"

"I wasn't really asking you, Jordan," Alex said quietly, turning to her other two friends. It was them who had missed out.

But despite her fear, they were both smiling at her.

"Definitely not angry," D.C. promised. "Concerned for you, absolutely. I know how much you didn't want this. But Hunter must have his reasons."

"Apparently he has a few," Alex muttered, but she didn't go into detail. She turned to Bear, more anxious about his reply, since she knew how much he in particular had wanted to be in the class.

"Ghost is a mysterious man," Bear said, still smiling warmly at Alex. "I agree with Dix. He must have his reasons for accepting you, especially since he knew you didn't want any part in his class. You were kind of obvious about it. But I'm sure you're going to learn a lot from him, and I'm just as excited for you as I am for Jordan."

Alex wilted with relief. "I thought you guys were going to flip out on me."

"We wanted it, sure, but we also knew that the chances of getting in were slim to none," Bear said. "Hunter told us that at the meeting. There's no point being disappointed by something we have no control over."

"I guess you're right," Alex acknowledged. Their reactions were much better than she had feared.

They stayed together and chatted comfortably for the next few hours, throwing out ideas for what Hunter might teach in his class. Every new suggestion caused Alex's stomach to flutter with nerves, making her dread the coming Tuesday night initiation even more.

Eventually their conversation began to wind down as the strain of the weekend caught up with them all.

"We should get going," Jordan said, after checking the time on his ComTCD. Curfew meant they had to be back in their dormitory buildings by ten o'clock, but there was no lights-out policy at Akarnae. As long as students were in the building, they were free to do what they wanted. Their exhausting classes provided more than enough motivation for them to be responsible with their own sleeping hours.

Neither Alex nor D.C. bothered to rise after Jordan's announcement as they were already settled for the night, but when the boys reached the door, Alex remembered something.

"Oh, and by the way," she said. "Hunter asked me to tell you two to stop jumping on your beds."

She only had a microsecond to see their startled expressions before the door closed behind them, but it was enough to send her to sleep with a smile on her face.

***

The next two days passed much too quickly in Alex's opinion. Before she knew it, she was eating dinner on Tuesday evening, nervously awaiting what was surely going to be a horrible experience.

"Are you excited yet?" Jordan asked for what felt like the twentieth time in as many minutes.

"Not yet," Alex said. "And the more you ask, the slower the excitement seems to be in coming."

Earlier that day they had both received notes telling them to meet at the forest boundary after dinner for their first two-hour class. They were also given specific clothing requirements that, to Alex's bemusement, included wearing the black cape from her wardrobe that she'd always wondered about. Sitting in the food court dressed head to toe in the dark attire made her feel as out of place as Darth Vader at the beach.

"Aw, come on, Alex," Jordan whined. "It's going to be amazing!"

"You and I have very different definitions of 'amazing'," she told him.

While Jordan was practically bouncing with anticipation, Alex was wishing time would rewind so she could find a way out of the mess she was currently in.

"I'm sure it won't be so bad," D.C. said, trying to sound encouraging. "If nothing else, you're bound to learn heaps from Hunter."

"That's what I'm afraid of," Alex mumbled. The man was too mysterious for his own good.

"It's time," Jordan said, rising to his feet. "Are you ready?"

"Definitely not," Alex answered, but she stood as well. It wasn't like she had a choice. So much for her gift of willpower—what good was it to her now?

Together they left the food court and disappeared into the night. Almost literally, really, given how they blended into the dark with their black clothing.

"If I get stuck in some kind of thorny bush, do you promise to come back and find me at the end of the night?" Alex asked, tripping on her cape for the third time. "This thing is going to kill me."

"It's not that bad." Jordan failed to hide the amusement in his tone. "You just have to learn how to ignore the swishing of the material."

"Ignore the 'swishing'?" she repeated. "That's your advice?"

He chuckled and didn't answer, but Alex found that walking was easier when she didn't focus on the cape as much.

"It's still not very appropriate clothing for the forest," she muttered to herself.

All too soon they reached their destination, where only two other people were already waiting.

"Hey, guys," Pipsqueak said.

"Yo!" greeted Blink. "It's a fine night to discover our inner stealth, am I right?"

"It sure is," Jordan agreed, returning the offered fist-bump.

It was clear that both Pipsqueak and Blink were just as excited as Jordan to have made the cut for Hunter's class. Alex seemed to be the only one with any reservations.

"Did anyone else get in?" she asked.

"Not that I've heard," Pipsqueak answered. "But I didn't know about you, either. I don't remember seeing you at the tryouts."

"It's a long story," Alex murmured, not wanting to explain.

Pipsqueak shrugged. "It's cool you're here. This is going to rock."

Jordan, Blink and Pipsqueak struck up an excited conversation about what they hoped would happen, but as the minutes ticked by, Alex grew more and more anxious. They'd been told to show up by seven-thirty and it was now well after that, but no one had arrived yet, including Hunter. Given the name of the class, Alex wondered if they were about to receive a crash course in what was ahead for them.

"Guys, I think you should keep it down," Alex said quietly, urging the others to settle.

None of them paid her any attention, but Jordan did turn to give her a reassuring smile. He must have just thought she was nervous—which she was. But it was more than that.

A twig snapped and Alex whirled around, peering deeper into the forest. It was too dark for her to see much of anything, but her spidey-senses were on high alert, and she couldn't shake the feeling they were being watched.

She squinted into the shadows until something caught her eye; a stirring of movement accompanied by the sound of a bush rustling.

"Guys, seriously," Alex whispered. "Shut up."

The tone of her voice must have clued them in that she wasn't playing around, and they immediately dropped their conversation.

"What is it?" Jordan asked, stepping closer to her.

"There's something in there," Alex said, pointing into the shadows.

Images of the Hyroa lunging out of the forest caused a shiver to run down her spine.

"What sort of something?" Pipsqueak asked, her voice higher than normal.

Eyes gleaming with the thrill of adventure, Blink said, "Let's check it out."

Alex wasn't a huge fan of the idea, but she was all for strength in numbers, so when the other three began to walk forward she followed along resignedly.

They only had to step a few paces into the forest before they discovered the source of the movement. It was a piece of cloth caught on a tree branch, flapping in the wind.

"Disappointing," Blink said. "But at least we solved the great towel mystery."

Alex didn't think the cloth was a towel, but that was hardly the point. What she was more concerned about was that the flapping noise it made definitely didn't resemble the snapping twig and rustling bush sounds she'd heard. Something didn't add up.

Just as Blink stepped forward to take the cloth from the tree, Alex turned her gaze to the ground, and her eyes widened. "Wait—"

But her warning was too late. Blink had already yanked at the fabric, accidentally activating the trap on which they were all standing. The net-covered ground flew up around them, throwing them all high into the air until they were trapped dangling helplessly in the woven material.

"That was unexpected," Jordan muttered, trying to push Alex's elbow out of his face. There was no room for her to move though, since they were all squished together with their arms and legs tangled in and out of the net. Alex was doubly uncomfortable, since her annoying cape was twisted around someone else and tugging on her throat, nearly choking her.

"Oor—oof—s—nn—m—fce," came Blink's distorted voice.

"What?" Pipsqueak asked. "Ouch!"

"Sorry, but your foot was totally in my face," Blink repeated, his words clear now.

"So you bit me?" Pipsqueak demanded.

"It got you to move, didn't it?" Blink asked. "Mission: success!"

"Quiet, guys," Alex said, preempting their argument. "We need to find a way out of this."

"Anyone have a knife?" Jordan asked.

Alex was too busy trying to keep her cape from strangling her to tell him how ridiculous his question was. As if any of them would be carrying a weapon to class. But then she thought about some of their other subjects and realised it probably wasn't that far-fetched an idea, really.

"Sorry, man," Blink said. "One hundred percent unarmed."

"Same here," Pipsqueak agreed.

"Alex?" Jordan asked.

"I've got nothing," she answered, finally managing to tug some breathing space between her cape and her throat. Now that she wasn't in imminent danger of suffocation, she reached out to touch the netting. "I don't—"

A weight landed in her open hand. She was so startled that she almost dropped the object, and when she realised what it was, she *did* drop it. But she scrambled to grab it before it could fall through the net, despite how shocked—and repulsed—she was.

...Because in her hands was the dagger Aven had used to Claim her, the one that had stabbed her in the back and nearly killed her.

"Uh, actually, I think I might have something that can help," Alex said, her voice wobbling slightly. "Everyone hold on, and I'll try to cut us out."

The ice-coloured blade sawed through the dense netting like it was made of butter. Alex hadn't anticipated such easy results, and she was unprepared when the woven material sliced open around her. She had to drop the dagger to hold onto the net, but she watched as the weapon fell through the air and ... *disappeared*.

Alex was so shocked that she let go of the netting and fell to the ground with a heavy *thump*.

"Ow," she muttered, rolling over and frantically searching the ground for the missing weapon. But she couldn't find it anywhere.

"You okay?" Jordan asked, still dangling in the air above her.

"Yeah," she answered, despite the fact that she felt anything but okay. Where had the dagger come from? And where had it disappeared to? Her last memory of the weapon was when it had been flying through the air towards D.C. just moments before Alex had intercepted the attack. She'd never thought to ask Fletcher or Darrius what they'd done with it after removing it from her flesh. She hadn't *wanted* to ask. Now, though, she wished she had.

"Do you feel like moving anytime today?" Pipsqueak called down, sounding impatient.

Alex was jolted from her thoughts.

"Sorry," she said, getting up and moving to the side.

Pipsqueak, Blink and finally Jordan dropped to the ground, landing much more gracefully than Alex had.

"That was fun," Jordan said. If he hadn't sounded so sarcastic, Alex would have contemplated throwing a rock at him.

"Totally ripping, bro," Blink agreed.

Alex wasn't entirely sure what 'ripping' meant, but she presumed it was a good thing, judging by Blink's glowing expression. Unfortunately, she didn't know the guy well enough to knock some sense into him.

"What now?" Pipsqueak asked, peering into the trees around them.

"Now we begin your training."

Eight

Hunter's words echoed around them, but no matter how hard she looked, Alex couldn't see the teacher anywhere. Not until he stepped out of the forest, appearing before them as if out of thin air.

"Welcome to your first class in Stealth and Subterfuge," he said. "You've just had your introductory test. What did you learn?"

There was a pause as the four of them got over their shock at his sudden manifestation. Then Jordan jumped in.

"Keep an eye out for hidden traps."

"Good," Hunter said. "What else?"

"Don't grab random towels off trees?" Blink suggested.

Before Hunter could respond, Pipsqueak added, "Keep Alex around for when you need a weapon handy."

Jordan and Blink chuckled, but Alex was still too unnerved by what had happened to join in.

"What about you, Alex?" Hunter asked. "Anything to contribute?"

She thought for a moment, not wanting to answer straight away. She'd learned quite a few things during the 'test', but one thing in particular stood out to her.

"Appearances can be deceiving."

"How so?" Hunter prompted.

"The cloth was a diversion, aimed at keeping our attention off the ground. It was a distraction to keep us from noticing the trap."

"And yet, you noticed it," Hunter pointed out. "Even when your classmates didn't."

Just how long had he been watching them? Probably the whole time, Alex realised.

"You'll learn many things in my class," Hunter said, addressing them all, "most of which will come from experience. If you pay attention to what I teach, you'll remain my students for this year and next. It's very rare that I take on apprentices, but if you show a high level of aptitude, I may offer to further your training. At present, I have only one apprentice, and the remainder of your classmates are fifth years."

As he spoke, four people stepped silently out of the forest. They were dressed exactly like Alex—wearing black, black, and more black—and they wore the stupid strangling capes as well. They had their hoods lowered and Alex immediately recognised two of them. She'd already known about Kaiden, but she was pleasantly surprised to see Declan as well.

"Take five minutes to introduce yourselves," Hunter said. "Most of the time you spend together in my class will involve group activities where you need to be able to trust each other. You don't have to become best friends, but you do have to learn to respect one another. Starting now."

He walked over to the tree that held the trap and began lowering the netting down to the ground, leaving his students to converse.

The two classmates Alex hadn't yet met were Skyla Fay, a girl in the year above her, and Tom Barrett, Hunter's first year apprentice. Skyla was tall and willowy, with golden hair framing her classically beautiful face. She barely glanced at Alex and Pipsqueak when they introduced themselves, instead focusing entirely on Blink and Jordan—Jordan more so. When she wasn't looking at either of them, she was staring—rather obviously, in Alex's opinion—at Kaiden. Alex couldn't exactly blame the girl, but still, Skyla clearly had her priorities, and apparently neither Pipsqueak nor Alex rated high on that list.

Tom seemed like a nice enough guy, if quiet. He was also tall, with closely-cropped black hair and skin so dark that he effortlessly blended in with the shadows of the forest.

Once their introductions were complete, silence descended upon them until Blink asked the older students if they'd witnessed them getting caught up in the net. Apparently they had, and mentioned that Hunter had pulled the same initiation trick on them.

Alex was only half listening. She was hyper aware of the eerie forest around her; every little noise intruded on her peace of mind, making her wonder just what might be out there. What if Aven was nearby? Or another snarling beast? She scanned the surrounding trees, anxiously waiting for Hunter to begin the class so that she could be distracted by his lesson.

"I had a feeling I might see you here," a warm voice whispered in her ear, causing goose bumps to rise up on her skin.

Alex whipped around to find Kaiden standing close behind her. The others were deep in conversation about the various ways they could have escaped the trap, and Alex hadn't noticed him approach. Other than in Combat the previous day—where she'd had very little interaction with him—the last time she'd seen him had been in the Medical Ward.

...When she'd turned her back on him.

"Why do you say that?" she asked as she took in his striking features. If anything, he was even more mesmerising under the light of the moon. The way the shadows framed everything from his strong brow to his chiselled jawline—

Chiselled jawline? Alex mentally slapped herself. *Snap out of it, girl. Jeez.*

Kaiden shrugged and his cape rustled with the movement, reclaiming her attention. "Call it intuition."

"Yeah, well, thanks for the heads-up," Alex said pointedly.

"You're obviously here for a reason," he told her, echoing the words of her friends. "Hunter wouldn't have taken you on otherwise."

"That's what everyone keeps telling me," she muttered on a sigh.

"Time's up," Hunter called out at last. "For the rest of this lesson, you'll be paired up and given a task to complete. Phillipa, you're with Tom; Jordan with Kaiden; Blink with Declan; and Alex with Skyla. Grab your partner and come get a piece of paper from me."

This'll be fun, Alex thought sarcastically, noticing the disappointed pout on Skyla's face.

"Tough luck," Kaiden murmured to her as he went over to meet Jordan.

Not sure what to make of Kaiden's comment, Alex stepped forward to take the paper from Hunter, since Skyla didn't seem to be making any effort to move. She opened it and read the words as she walked over to her partner.

Where the little people play,
sing songs, and dance around all day;
only there you'll find a way
to retrieve a figurine of clay.
Follow the mushrooms and you'll be okay,
but do be careful what you say;
for tricky are those pesky Fae,
so take care or there'll be a price to pay.

"Well? What does it say?" Skyla asked.

Alex handed over the paper. "It's a riddle or something."

Skyla scrunched up her face, squinting at the note. "What does it mean?"

"I'm the new student here," Alex reminded her. "You've been in Hunter's class for a year, so your guess is better than mine."

Skyla shrugged and proceeded to buff her fingernails against her cape.

Wonderful.

"You have ninety minutes to follow the instructions you've been given," Hunter called out. "If you're not back in that time, you'll have failed your task."

"What do we do if that happens?" Alex asked.

Hunter looked at her as if the answer was obvious. "You keep going until you're done. Only when you've completed your assignment will you be dismissed."

Alex had to hold back a groan. She was going to be stuck out there all night, she just knew it. Maybe even longer.

"Off you go," Hunter said. "And new students, remember what class this is. You won't have an easy journey."

As much as she wished it wasn't true, Alex presumed that was Hunter-code for, 'I've rigged more traps and you're all going to die'.

Cue: sigh.

"Let's go, Skyla," she said, taking charge and heading deeper into the forest.

"Where are you leading us?" Skyla asked, trailing along behind Alex.

"The clue mentions following mushrooms," Alex said, "so that's where I say we should start. Unless you have any better ideas?"

"Nope," Skyla said, too busy inspecting a tendril of her hair to even watch where she stepped.

"I didn't think so," Alex muttered, too low for the other girl to hear.

Ten minutes later and she wondered if she was developing a nervous tick. While Alex wasn't the quietest person in the world, she might as well have been in comparison to the racket Skyla was making as they walked through the forest.

"You know," Alex couldn't help but say, "I'm pretty sure it's called Stealth and Subterfuge for a reason. Emphasis on stealth. Do you mind picking your feet up when you walk?"

Okay, so that was kind of snarky. But she was anxious to get out of the forest, and so far they hadn't seen any mushrooms, let alone ones that led to places unknown.

"You think you're so special, don't you?" Skyla said.

"Not really," Alex answered, though she figured the question was supposed to be rhetorical.

"Good," Skyla said. "Because let me tell you, you're not. Special, I mean. You're not special at all."

"Thanks for clarifying," Alex said, her tone dry. "I wasn't sure what you were talking about for a moment there. But now I know, I'm not special."

"That's right," Skyla said victoriously. "It's good you can agree. But you should also know that unlike you, I am special. And that's just the way it is."

She's special, all right, Alex thought. During their walk, she had come to the conclusion that Skyla wasn't really the uncaring snob she came across as; she was just shallow, but in a harmless way. While that was better than her being an utter cow, it didn't help their current situation, nor did it explain how Skyla was accepted into Hunter's class to begin with.

"Can I ask you something?" Alex asked, ducking under a low-hanging branch. "Don't take this the wrong way or anything, but how did you get into SAS?"

Hopefully Skyla wouldn't read the obvious message in her words—the 'what *the hell was Hunter thinking?*' implication.

"It's because I'm special, remember?" Skyla said. "I just told you that. Weren't you listening to me?"

"Of course I was," Alex answered quickly, wanting to avoid the impending hissy fit she sensed was coming. "What I meant was, what is it exactly that makes you so, uh, special?"

"Oh," Skyla said. "Well, that's all right, I guess. I hate it when people don't listen when I talk."

Alex didn't say anything, figuring it was best to keep her thoughts to herself.

"Other than my obvious appeal," Skyla continued, and Alex had to fight back a snort of derision, "Hunter recruited me because of my gift. It's very handy in stealthy and subterfuging situations."

Alex knew that 'subterfuge-y' wasn't a word, but at least it made more sense. Skyla's 'subterfuging' sounded like some kind of nasty chemical reaction.

"What's your gift?" Alex asked, holding back all the other comments that wanted to burst from her mouth.

"I can shape-shift," Skyla said.

Alex stopped pushing her way through the leafy woodland and turned to gape at her companion. "Seriously?"

In answer, Skyla's whole body began shimmering and, seconds later, she transformed into an exact replica of Alex.

"Seriously," the Skyla-Alex-copy answered, mimicking Alex's response.

"That's just *freaky*," Alex said, staring wide-eyed at her doppelganger.

Skyla shimmered again and shifted back to her normal self. "I can't hold other forms for too long without getting tired, but it's worth it for the shock value sometimes."

Alex didn't doubt that. She certainly wouldn't get the image out of her mind for a while, that was for sure.

"Shape-shifting would definitely be a huge help with subterfuge," Alex admitted. She didn't bother to mention how sucky Skyla seemed to be with the stealth aspect. "You could literally trick people into thinking you were anyone. That's insane."

"You're insane," Skyla snapped.

Alex jerked in shock and carefully said, "I wasn't insulting you, Skyla. It was a compliment."

"Oh." Skyla twirled a strand of hair around her finger. "I knew that. People compliment me all the time, so I guess I'm just used to it."

Alex mentally shook her head and moved forward again, intent on finding some mushrooms before her partner's 'specialness' began to rub off on her.

Thankfully, they had their first fungi sighting just a few steps later, much to Alex's relief.

After twenty minutes of following the mushrooms, Skyla broke the peaceful silence.

"Are we almost there?"

Alex grumbled under her breath, "I sure hope so."

"What was that?" Skyla demanded.

"I said, 'I think so'," Alex covered. "There are more mushrooms now than there were before. That's probably a good sign."

It was true. At first the fungi had been sporadic at best, dusted around the forest floor so infrequently that Alex had been challenged to find a clear trail. But now that they were further along, the mushrooms practically formed a straight line to follow.

"I'm hungry," Skyla said. "Do you think these mushrooms are edible?"

Why don't you try one and see? Alex thought. But then she realised that if anything happened to Skyla, it would be she who had to carry her out of the forest. So, in a very firm voice, she said, "It's probably not a good idea to eat them. They might be poisonous."

"Yeah, I guess you're right," Skyla said, her disappointment clear. "Oh, look! That's much better than mushrooms!"

Alex turned around to see what the other girl was talking about only to find Skyla walking away from her and heading over to a massive tree. Resting on a branch at eye level was a picnic basket bursting with food.

"Skyla, wait!" Alex said, knowing that the food was clearly a set-up. And an obvious one at that. She had no doubt it would be booby-trapped by Hunter.

"Stop telling me what to do," Skyla hissed, ignoring Alex's warning and stomping towards the branch.

"No, really, you need to listen—"

"Look," Skyla interrupted, "I know you're all, 'blah, blah, let's get this riddle nonsense over with', but I won't take long. And I'll share too, since I'm so nice."

"Skyla!" Alex yelled, trying to get the girl's attention, but she just wasn't willing to listen.

"Seriously, Alex," Skyla said impatiently. "You need to get over your—AHHHH!"

"SKYLA!"

Alex sprinted over to the massive hole in the ground where Skyla had previously been standing. She dropped onto her stomach and wriggled the last few feet, balancing her weight so she wouldn't fall in as well.

"Skyla, can you hear me? Are you hurt?"

"I'm all right," Skyla answered weakly, her voice echoing up the deep hole.

Alex released a breath. "How far down are you? I can't see anything."

"Not too far, I think," Skyla said, her voice shaky. "I didn't fall for long."

"Can you see me?" Alex asked, knowing there was at least some light shining on her and hoping it was enough for the other girl to see.

"Yeah," Skyla answered. "But you're too far away for me to reach."

"Okay, hold on." Alex wriggled away from the hole and stood up. She looked around the area, hoping to find something to help them, and settled on a long, sturdy branch attached to a tree. It took some twisting and pulling—and earned her more than one splinter—but finally Alex was able to yank it free.

She scurried back to the opening of the hole and lowered the branch down into the darkness. "Try to grab hold, Skyla."

After a few moments of silence, Alex wondered what the other girl was waiting for.

"Ready when you are," she added.

"I can't stand," Skyla whimpered. "I think I've sprained my ankle. I can't reach the branch without standing."

Alex had to stifle a groan. She had to get Skyla out of the trap, but how could she do that without a rope?

"Skyla, can you use your gift to lengthen your arm?" Alex asked. "Or just shape-shift it into something long enough to reach me?"

"I don't have supernatural elasticity, Alex," Skyla returned in a pained voice. "I can only shift into other people. And I don't know anyone who has ladder arms."

It had been worth a try, if nothing else.

Standing up again, Alex began pacing around the area, hoping for some kind of inspiration. She'd only taken three steps when she managed to trip on her cape yet again.

"Stupid thing," she muttered, flinging it over her shoulder and continuing onwards. But then she froze as an idea came to mind, and she unclasped the annoying garment and hurried over to the hole, shoving the material down as soon as she was close enough.

"Can you grab my cape?" Alex asked.

"I still can't reach it," Skyla answered, her voice hitching. "Please don't leave me down here."

"I'm not going to leave you," Alex promised. "Are you able to throw your cape up to me? Can you do that? I might be able to tie them together so they're long enough to reach you."

"I think so..." Skyla said, and Alex had to quickly grab the material as Skyla flung it towards her face.

"Good job," Alex encouraged. "Give me a second."

She tied the two capes together, securing them tightly, and threw one end of the cloth back into the hole.

"I've got it!" Skyla cried.

"Make sure you hold on," Alex called down. "And help me if you can."

Now for the hard part, Alex thought, as she strained to lift Skyla out of the hole. It wasn't an easy task given that she was lying on her stomach and could only use the strength in her upper body, but between the two of them, they managed to get Skyla out of the trap. Alex's arms burned from the effort, but she was more concerned about Skyla's ankle. What were they supposed to do if she couldn't walk?

"Can you stand?" Alex asked once they had scrambled a safe distance away from the hole and caught their breath.

"Maybe, if you help," Skyla said in a pained voice.

Alex reached out and gently pulled Skyla to her feet. She was wobbly and couldn't place any pressure on her left foot, but at least she was upright.

"Do you think you can continue? Or do you need me to go and find help?" Alex asked.

"Don't leave me alone out here," Skyla pleaded again, clutching desperately at Alex's shirt. "Please, don't leave me."

"It's all right," Alex soothed. "We'll stay together. But that means we have to finish the task. Hunter was pretty firm about not dismissing us until it's done. Unless—you know him better; do you think he'll be lenient because you're injured? Should we just go back now?"

Skyla shook her head, her face pale. "Tom snapped his wrist in class last year—the bone was poking out and everything. But Hunter just wrapped a bandage around it, gave him a vial of pain reliever, and made him wait until the task was finished before he was allowed to leave with the rest of us. Hunter said it was character building."

Alex felt sick at the thought. "Right. Let's just—let's just hurry up and finish this, then. We'll be back in no time, I'm sure."

Bearing most of Skyla's weight, Alex helped her hobble along the mushroom path deeper into the forest. A few times she noticed more evidence of Hunter's traps—a tripwire that crossed their path; mushrooms of a slightly different shade that led in a different direction; and even a rope snare on the ground that would have trapped their feet and hung them upside-down in the air. Alex wondered what would have happened to them, had they fallen victim to any of those perils.

After what felt like forever, they came to the end of the mushroom trail. It led them into a clearing where the fungi grew in an almost perfect circle. The moonlight streamed through the trees, creating a beautifully eerie atmosphere.

"That's a fairy circle," Skyla said, hopping backwards a few steps and dragging Alex with her. "No way am I stepping in there."

Alex looked at the mushroom ring then back up at Skyla. "Don't tell me you're superstitious?"

"It's not superstition," Skyla said, her voice thick with nerves. "You read the note we were given. Even Hunter knows how dangerous the Fae can be. Uh-uh, no way."

"He didn't say they're dangerous, just that they're tricky," Alex argued, amazed that she wasn't debating the possibility of fairies being real, but whether or not they were a threat.

"He said there could be a price to pay!" Skyla replied, her voice rising. "Everyone knows that if you step into a fairy circle, you might never come back!"

"No, he wrote to be careful what we say, not what we do," Alex reminded the frightened girl. "I'm sure Hunter wouldn't make us do anything that would result in us getting stuck in ... wherever the Fae live."

Skyla folded her arms stubbornly. "I'm still not stepping in there."

Alex sighed and looked at the circle again. It was large, filling most of the clearing. But what caught Alex's eye was the small statue in the centre—apparently the rhyme's 'figurine of clay' that they needed to retrieve. The only way to reach it was by entering the circle.

"All right," Alex said, propping Skyla up against a tree trunk. "You wait here and I'll go get it, okay?"

"No, you can't!" Skyla shrieked. "Then I'll be stuck here all on my own!"

"I'll just be over there," Alex said in her most calming voice. "You'll be able to see me the whole time."

"Not if you disappear—then I'll probably die out here!"

"It's nice to know you're so concerned for my welfare," Alex commented under her breath. Louder, she said, "Listen, the sooner I grab that statue, the sooner we can get out of here. Just relax. We'll both be fine."

Ignoring the desire to hesitate, Alex walked forward and determinedly stepped over the edge of the mushroom ring into the clearing. Once both feet were inside the circle, she released the breath she hadn't realised she was holding. She then turned to look back at Skyla with a reassuring smile.

"See, I'm—"

Alex stopped dead.

...Because Skyla was gone.

Nine

Alex whipped her head around, frantically searching the moonlit clearing. She was in exactly the same place, mushroom circle included. Nothing had changed, and yet, *everything* had changed. Because the clay statue was now missing. And so was Skyla.

"This is like a scene straight out of *The Twilight Zone*," Alex murmured, her body tense with anxiety. "What am I supposed to do now?"

A whisper in the wind answered her: a musical voice, poetic and lilting.

"Enter in, if you dare,
As one who seeks out Meya;
Be strong of mind and pure of heart,
For your journey begins at Raelia."

"Cryptic, much?" Alex whispered, more than a little creeped out.

"*Cryptic is as cryptic does,*" replied the same whimsical voice.

"Are you going to show yourself? Or maybe tell me who you are?" Alex said, squinting into the shadows but seeing no one.

"*I would ask the same of you,*" the voice said, "*but I already know who you are, so there is no need.*"

Alex was muddling over that when a figure appeared directly in front of her, startling her so much that she stumbled backwards.

"Lady Mystique!" Alex cried, trying to regain her balance.

"Hello again, child," the old woman said. "You've come a long way since last we met."

"What are you doing here?" Alex asked, her eyes wide with incredulity. Their last encounter had been at Ye Olde Bookshoppe in Woodhaven—a shop that didn't actually exist, as Alex had since discovered.

"What does it look like I'm doing?" Lady Mystique indicated to the basket she carried. "I'm picking mushrooms. Raelian mushies are the best you'll find anywhere."

Alex gaped at the woman, too surprised for words.

"But I'm more curious about why you are here," the woman said.

"I'm not here intentionally. I just ended up here."

"Did you not step into the circle?" Lady Mystique asked.

"Well, yes—"

"Then you are here intentionally."

Alex didn't bother arguing the point. "I don't suppose you'd mind telling me where 'here' is, exactly?"

"Look around you, what do you see?"

Humouring her, Alex answered, "A forest clearing inside a mushroom circle."

"Look closer."

Alex frowned but did as she was told. As she focused on her surroundings, the moonlight strengthened, illuminating the area. Where the clearing met the trees—just beyond the mushroom ring—Alex could see multiple pathways leading out into the forest. They were all around the edge of the clearing, at least eight different trails, none of which she had noticed before.

"What is this place?" she whispered, feeling a sense of awe.

"This is Raelia," Lady Mystique answered. "In the common tongue, it translates to mean 'The Crossroads'. It's a sacred place. A place of direction, of destiny. Look around and see your choices; which path do you take? Do you go left or right, forward or back? But don't be fooled, for it's much more than a geographical crossroad. Raelia represents opportunity. It yields to the desires of one's heart. It offers temptation, sacrifice, hope and victory. The choice of direction lies with each individual who sets foot within its boundary."

After a pause, Alex admitted, "I'm not sure I understand."

"You will, Alexandra. You will."

"And that I definitely don't understand."

Lady Mystique wheezed out a husky-sounding laugh.

"Why does everything have to be so confusing?" Alex asked, rubbing her forehead.

"Oh, sweet child," the old woman said, patting Alex's shoulder. "When the time comes, you'll have the answers you need."

"I can't wait," Alex said, somewhat sarcastically.

The Lady sent her a wrinkled smile. "It's time for you to return to your friend."

"Hang on a second," Alex said. "When I first arrived here you said something about Meya. Any chance you want to elaborate?"

"Goodbye, Alexandra," Lady Mystique said, with a twinkle in her eye. "It was lovely seeing you again."

"Wait—"

Before she could finish her sentence, the Lady reached out and pressed an object into Alex's hands. Then a gust of wind enveloped her body, the ethereal light dimmed and Alex found herself standing outside the mushroom circle.

"Huh, I guess you were right."

Alex spun around to find Skyla perched against the tree, right where she'd left her.

"Right about what?" Alex asked, trying to make sense of the last few minutes. Peering around, she could no longer see any evidence of the different paths that led out of the clearing. Apparently she wasn't in Raelia anymore, but back in the Ezera Forest.

"You were right about nothing happening," Skyla answered.

"Nothing happened?" Alex repeated, turning to give her full attention to the girl.

Skyla sent her a questioning look. "Nothing. You just picked up the statue and came back."

"Statue?" Alex asked dumbly. She then noticed the weight in her hand and realised Lady Mystique had given her the clay figurine.

"Are you feeling all right?" Skyla asked. "You're looking stranger than normal."

"Yeah, I'm—I'm fine," Alex said, shaking her head to clear it. "Let's just get out of here."

"Wait, I want to try something," Skyla said. "I need to conquer my fear, now I know I'll be okay."

Alex didn't understand. "What are you talking about?"

Before she could say or do anything, Skyla limped three steps forward and entered the circle.

"No!"

"What?" Skyla shrieked, looking around her. "What is it?"

Alex stared at the other girl in surprise. "You can still see me?"

Skyla frowned at her. "Why are you acting so weird? Oh, never mind, just come and help me out of here, will you?"

Alex hesitantly stepped into the circle once again. But this time nothing happened. No wind, no change of scenery, nothing.

So, what was that about? Alex wondered, helping Skyla hobble back through the forest.

"Can I see the statue?" Skyla asked.

"Sure," Alex said absentmindedly, distracted by her thoughts.

She handed the clay figurine over, and the moment they both physically connected with it, colourful light exploded around them and they were whisked through the air, abruptly jerking to a halt a second later.

"Just in time, ladies."

Alex jumped at Hunter's voice, throwing Skyla off balance and causing both of them to fall unceremoniously to the ground.

"Great entrance," Jordan joked, reaching a hand out to Alex while Tom moved to help Skyla.

"Thanks," Alex said, as he pulled her to her feet. "What just happened?"

"Pre-programmed Bubbledoor," he told her. "Once you retrieved whatever object Hunter sent you to find and the both of you held on, it activated. Didn't your note warn you?"

"Uh, no," Alex said, rubbing her bruised behind. "Definitely no warning."

"All right, class," Hunter called out. "Now that you're all back—some in better condition than others—let's see how well you fared."

He asked them to step forward and hand over their strange assortment of objects. Kaiden and Jordan produced a bulky backpack, Tom and Pipsqueak held out a large canvas painting, and Declan and Blink passed over what appeared to be a live animal—something very similar to a squirrel. Alex decided she was better off not knowing how they caught it, let alone how it had activated a Bubbledoor. Some things were best left a mystery.

When Hunter held his hand out to Alex and Skyla, Alex passed him the statue.

Hunter peered at it closely, as did Alex, since she hadn't looked at it properly yet. It was a small figurine of a mushroom. An appropriate choice, considering.

"What's this?" Hunter asked.

Alex felt her brows draw together. "It's the figurine of clay. The one we had to retrieve."

He glanced from the mushroom to Alex, looking at her closely.

"Right," he said, drawing the word out before turning to speak to everyone again. "We're finished for the evening. If you need to see Fletcher, make sure to visit the Med Ward before curfew. We'll meet again on Thursday night."

They started to leave as a group after Hunter's dismissal, at least until he called out, "Alex, a word?"

"I'll wait for you at the edge of the forest," Jordan offered, and she sent him a grateful smile.

Once everyone had left, Hunter asked, "Do you still have the note I gave you?"

"Sure." She reached into her pocket and handed over the instructions.

His eyes flicked over the words and then he looked up at her, gesturing to the mushroom figurine. "Do you want to explain this?"

Feeling confused, Alex said, "What do you mean?"

"And how did you get back here without the picnic basket?"

She blinked stupidly. "Picnic basket?"

Hunter made an impatient sound. "Read the note again, Alex."

She took it from him and did as ordered. The handwriting was the same as earlier ... but the words were different.

Follow the arrows and retrieve the picnic basket.
Beware of traps.
The Bubbledoor will bring you back.

"It didn't say this before," Alex whispered, reading the note again. "And I didn't see any arrows."

"What did it say when you first read it?" Hunter asked.

Alex recited what she could remember of the poem and told Hunter about where it had led her and Skyla. She didn't mention Raelia, though. The story was already odd enough without the supernatural element. And while she knew the people of Medora were no strangers to mysterious happenings, she wasn't quite ready to own up to what she'd experienced with Lady Mystique. Not out loud. Not yet. She'd talk about it later with her friends, but not in the middle of the eerie forest with her intimidatingly perceptive teacher. Instead, she simply told him about the mushroom circle in the clearing and how the statue had brought them back.

"Interesting," Hunter said when she was done. "Are you sure there's nothing else you want to tell me? Like how an unauthorised Bubbledoor transported you back here?"

Alex swallowed and looked away from his piercing eyes. She had no idea, but if she had to guess, her finger would point straight to Lady Mystique.

Silence descended upon them until Hunter finally exhaled, "All right, we'll leave it at that. You can go now."

She nodded and made to escape his intimidating presence, but he called her name again just before she was out of earshot, so she paused and turned back to him in question.

"You did well, tonight," he said. "The traps you avoided after the picnic basket weren't intended for you and Skyla, and I'm impressed you noticed them. I know you don't want to be in this class, but you'll eventually realise you belong here."

Before she could argue otherwise, he turned around with a swirl of his cape and disappeared into the darkness of the forest.
***

"He really didn't give you the note?" Jordan asked later that night in the Rec Room, after Bear and D.C. had been given the rundown of their class.

"Apparently not," Alex said, She grabbed another chocolate bar from the pile, in desperate need of comfort food.

"I can't believe your crazy Lady Mystique has returned," Bear said. "And that, once again, you were the only person to see her."

"I know," Alex agreed. "I have no idea what she was doing there, but I doubt it was mushroom picking. The entire thing was so surreal."

Jordan's night, by comparison, had been much more normal. He and Kaiden had followed the directions on their note telling them to search for a backpack hidden up a tree. Together they had avoided all of Hunter's traps and easily made it back within the ninety-minute window.

"I'm more curious about this Raelia place," D.C. said. "It sounds ... mysterious. Meaningful. Important."

Alex looked over at her friend and noted the expression on her face. "You look worried, Dix. What's up?"

D.C. shook her head. "Nothing. Just thinking."

Alex opened her mouth to ask her more, but Jordan jumped in first.

"So, what happens next?" he asked.

Alex licked melted chocolate from her fingers. "I have no idea. Lady Mystique mentioned something about Meya, but she wouldn't say any more when I asked her to clarify. And then she talked about Raelia being a crossroad and said I'd know what that means when the time comes."

"That doesn't sound good," D.C. said quietly, looking down at her hands.

"Yeah," Bear agreed. "Let's face it, Lady Mystique has a habit of throwing you in the deep end."

Alex groaned. "Can we talk about something else? Something ... normal?"

It turned out that 'normal' took more energy than any of them had left after their full day of classes, so they didn't hang out for much longer before returning to their rooms.

Once they were alone in their dorm, Alex asked D.C. if everything was okay.

"Sure," D.C. said. "I just haven't been sleeping well lately."

Alex understood what her friend was talking about. Being back at the academy and surrounded by people—not to mention the added strain of their exhausting classes—definitely disrupted their sleeping habits. It would probably take them all a few weeks until they were back in a working routine and feeling properly rested again.

"Come on," Alex said, turning out the light. "Time for sleep, then."

***

The next few weeks flew by as Alex got used to her new schedule and ignored the urge to do something more proactive about Aven and Meya. She finally began to settle back into academy life, immersing herself in her subjects—the old and the new. Just like last year, Combat and PE continued to be the most challenging classes for her, but now she could add Stealth and Subterfuge to that list.

It turned out their first SAS class had been an easy introduction, because every class since then had left Alex bloodied and bruised from her attempts at being stealthy in various circumstances. Hunter had also begun teaching them to recognise—and practise—subterfuge in different real life training scenarios, both in and out of his class. By far, Alex's least favourite assignment was when she'd been tasked to break into Professor Marmaduke's sleeping quarters to retrieve a personal item as proof of her intrusion. She had to execute

it so that she was present when the Core
Skills professor discovered the theft, and
Alex then had to find a way to sneak
the item back to the room while convincing
the woman that she must have imagined
the entire thing.

Miraculously, Alex had actually succeeded
in her mission. It helped that her willpower
gift prohibited Marmaduke from reading her
mind. Without it, Alex never would have
pulled off the deceit.

She'd been taking SAS classes for four
weeks now and still didn't want to be an
active participant. But she'd finally come to
accept her position, sometimes even enjoying
what she learned from the surprisingly
patient instructor. Despite his downright scary
demeanour, Alex couldn't help but respect
Hunter—not that she'd ever admit that out
loud.

"What do you think, Miss Jennings?"

"Sorry?" Alex said, snapping back to
the present. She was in her SOSAC class,
with Professor Caspar Lennox staring down
at her from his formidable height.

"I asked for your opinion," the teacher
repeated, his melodious voice washing over
her.

Alex had been so deep in thought that
she had no idea what he'd been talking
about, let alone how she should respond.

"I ... uh..." She cleared her throat, trying to stall. Then she reached up and ran her fingers through her hair. "Um..."

"What's that?" questioned Caspar Lennox, his eyes focused on the hand still tangled in her hair.

Alex lowered her arm and looked at her fingers carefully but couldn't see anything unusual. "What's what?"

Caspar Lennox pointed to her middle finger. "Where did you get that?"

Alex curled her other hand protectively around the ring Bear's brother had given her. "It was a gift."

"A gift?" the teacher asked, his scepticism clear.

"Yes," Alex repeated firmly. "A gift."

"Do you know what it does?"

"I know what it *is*," Alex told him, aware of her classmates' growing interest in their conversation. "But I'm not sure how it does what it ... does."

The Shadow Walker stared at her intently. "See me after class, Miss Jennings."

Alex didn't know what to make of his request, but she was relieved when he moved away to continue the lesson.

The minutes ticked down and when the gong finally sounded, telling them their classes were over for the day, Alex waved her curious friends off and remained behind, waiting for the professor to speak.

"How have you come to possess a Shadow Ring, Miss Jennings?"

"I told you," she said. "It was a gift from a friend."

"And yet, you don't know how to use it?"

"I didn't exactly ask," Alex admitted.

Caspar Lennox held out a mottled-grey hand. "May I see it?"

Alex hesitantly slid the ring off her finger and passed it to him.

The professor peered closely at it while turning it over in his hands, almost like he was looking—or feeling—for something.

"This is a unique piece," he said. "Can I assume you received it from Blake Ronnigan?"

Wondering how he could have known that, Alex nodded in confirmation.

"I've always considered Blake to be a highly perceptive young man. He was wise, I believe, to give this to you," Caspar Lennox murmured, still looking at the ring. "Especially given your ... unique circumstances."

Alex opened her mouth to ask what he meant, but he continued speaking.

"When your need is great, you'll be able to activate the Shadow Essence contained within the stone," he told her, handing back the ring. "But you'll have to immerse yourself fully in the Shadow to do so."

"Ooo-kay," Alex said, drawing the word out. "I don't suppose you could dumb that down a little for me? What you mean by the second part?"

Caspar Lennox smiled slightly at her, his sharp, white teeth standing out against his unnaturally grey skin.

"When the time comes, you'll understand," he promised.

Alex bit back a snarky retort. Why was everyone saying that to her lately?

Before she could question him further, the professor told her not to daydream during his lessons in the future and dismissed her from his classroom.

***

After dinner that night, Administrator Jarvis came looking for Alex to tell her that the headmaster wished to speak with her. She followed him obediently to the Tower building and up to the very top floor to Darrius's office.

"Good luck," Jarvis said as he opened the door for her.

Puzzling over his words, Alex tentatively entered the room. Sometimes when she visited Darrius he would take her to his private study above the clouds that was linked through the Tower into the Library. But this time Alex could see they would be chatting in his official headmaster's office. The huge room held an impressive conference table, but her favourite part was the floor-to-ceiling glass wall that looked straight across the academy campus. Right now the waxing moon streamed light across the grounds, illuminating the beautiful landscape.

Darrius was pacing near the window-wall, and when she closed the door quietly behind her, he barely glanced up at her arrival. She took a seat near the end of the table, knowing he would speak when he was ready.

After a few tense seconds, he let out a frustrated breath and moved to sit next to her.

"Thank you for coming, Alex," he said. "I apologise for the short notice."

"What's up, Darrius?"

He reached for a folder that was resting on the table and passed it to her. She opened it without a word, wondering what was going on. Inside were loose papers, each showing photographs of different people, along with their names and other various details. *Bardie Hicks* ...

Nicholas Reeves ... Lena Morrow ... Travis Flanagan ... Vera Rosta...

Alex wasn't sure what she was looking at until she did a double-take on a familiar face.

"Hey, I know her!" she cried. "Well, sort of."

"Calista Maine," Darrius said. "Was she the woman you saw in the forest with Aven a few weeks ago?"

Alex nodded. "That's definitely her."

Darrius massaged his temples. "I was afraid you would say that."

"I don't understand," Alex said, leafing through more pages. "Why do you have her file? And who are all these other people?"

The headmaster stood and returned to his pacing, a worrying sign that Alex definitely didn't like.

"Darrius?"

He turned to look at her, and his haggard expression filled her with foreboding.

"After you witnessed Aven kill the Hyroa, I began to do some research," he said, reclaiming his seat. "Actually, I started when you first told me about the blood-bonding ritual he tried to use on you. Do you remember when I mentioned the possibility of him having Claimed more than one person over the years of his exile?"

Alex nodded again. Darrius had spoken to her months ago about Aven's charisma and his ability to coerce others into doing his bidding—and how perhaps it wasn't a natural occurrence, but a result of bonding them to him by blood.

"What are you saying?" she asked.

"When you first mentioned seeing a woman named Calista with Aven in the forest, I thought nothing of it," Darrius said. "But after you gave a more detailed description of her, I felt a sense of recognition. It turns out that the woman in that file was once a student here at Akarnae."

Alex wondered why Darrius seemed to think that so significant.

"How many Calistas do you know?" she asked. "It's not exactly a common name, is it? Why didn't you know who I was talking about straight away?"

Darrius looked directly into her eyes when he answered. "Alex, Calista Maine graduated from Akarnae over seventy years ago."

Alex jerked her head back in shock.

"It's true," Darrius said, reading the look on her face. "I studied her case file when I first became headmaster because her gift was so powerful and her disappearance was considered a tragedy."

"Seventy years?" Alex gasped. "That can't be right. She didn't look much older than me!"

"Calista was declared missing by her family when she was twenty-three," Darrius said. "No one has seen or heard from her since then, as far as I'm aware. I think we can now presume that, considering her apparent lack of physical aging, she must have been Claimed by Aven all those years ago."

Alex bit her lip and pointed to the rest of the file. "What about all these other people?"

"They were also students at Akarnae at one time or another," Darrius said, his expression sombre. "Just like Calista, their giftings were powerful; unique, even. And they too have disappeared over the years. I fear they may have met the same fate as hers."

Alex felt the room tip. "What are you implying? That Aven has some kind of gifted ... army? With all of them under his control? He *hates* humans! Why would he use them? And what for?"

"I don't know, Alex," Darrius answered gravely. "But it can't bode well for any of us."

It was then that Alex noticed just how tired he looked. He was not the vibrant man she'd first met. Instead, he was a man burdened with the weight of an uncertain future.

"What do you need me to do?" she whispered.

Darrius captured her eyes with his own silver ones. "You know the answer to that, Alex."

She held his gaze. "You need me to go to Meya."

With an apologetic look and a tone to match, he said, "I know I agreed to give you time, but the circumstances have changed. We need to know what we face, and we need the Meyarins to be aware of what might be coming. Only you can do this."

Understanding the truth of his words, Alex knew her answer.

"I'll do it. I'll go on Saturday."

His relief was apparent in every line of his body. "Thank you, Alex. I know how much you don't want to do this. And I realise how dangerous it may be."

"Don't thank me yet," she warned him. "I have no idea what will happen. I may not even be able to find a way there. And if I do, who knows how receptive the Meyarins will be?"

"I have the utmost faith in you." Darrius smiled warmly at her for the first time since she'd stepped into his office and Alex was relieved to see the cheerful expression back on his face, regardless of why it was there.

"We'll see," she said.

"In the meantime, I don't want you to worry about the rest of this," Darrius told her, indicating the file on the table.

"I'll agree to that if you will," she returned.

"I ... Huh. Well, then," he said, "I guess I'll try if you will."

"Deal," she agreed, holding out her hand to shake on it.

"On that note, it's nearly curfew," he said, after sealing their agreement. "I apologise again for keeping you up."

"No problem," she said. "And despite how much I'd rather not have learned what you told me, I'm glad you trusted me enough to share. At least this way I'll have a heads-up if any zombie-like gifted humans come my way in the future."

Judging by Darrius's grimace, Alex guessed it was too early to be so cavalier about it.

"Sorry," she said sheepishly. "Humour is my best coping mechanism."

That prompted a dry chuckle out of him. "We all have different strategies," he agreed. "You may be pleased to hear that humour is one of the more normal tactics."

Alex gasped dramatically and placed a hand to her chest. "Heaven forbid I do anything *normal*."

Darrius laughed with her, and Alex felt significantly better than she had a few minutes earlier. Whatever was coming in the future, they would all face it together.

That was all she needed to know.

Ten

"Are you sure about this?" D.C. asked.

"Not at all," Alex answered. "But right now, I don't think that matters."

It was Saturday morning and Alex and her friends were standing in the foyer of the Library. Despite her desire for time to slow down, the last few days had passed by annoyingly fast. She'd tried to stall by going to visit her parents again, but they'd been overcome with excitement by some new artefact they'd unearthed. She'd ended up leaving them to their work after a token catch-up that, in Alex's opinion, didn't take up anywhere near enough time. And now here she was, standing with Jordan, D.C. and Bear, and trying to summon the courage to continue onward.

"Where's your sense of adventure?" Jordan asked, nudging her in the ribs. "Just think of how awesome this'll be!"

"I agree with Jordan," Bear said. "This is going to be epic."

D.C. shared a look with Alex, "Any minute now they're going to start grunting and beating their chests, cavemen-style."

"Are we going or what?" Jordan whined, bouncing up and down and acting much younger than his seventeen years.

"We're going," Alex confirmed, leading the way towards the staircase on the far side of the room. She had tried to convince her friends to stay behind, reminding them that she had no idea what they would face and how dangerous it could potentially be. But they would hear nothing of her concerns and adamantly refused to let her go without them. Part of that, Alex knew, was because of their overwhelming desire to see the Lost City, but another part—a larger part, she hoped—was because there was no way they would let her face such an unknown situation alone. Her friends were good like that. Even if they all unanimously agreed to keep any and all details from D.C.'s parents, certain that the monarchs would not be too pleased at the idea of their only child and heir to the throne going off on perilous adventures unknown.

"Do we have a plan?" Bear asked as they started their journey downwards into the Library.

"Nope," Alex said. "You guys know I have no idea what I'm doing. But my best guess is to start in the corridor of doorways and hope for some kind of direction."

"Wicked," Jordan whispered excitedly.

None of her friends had experienced the wonders of the Library quite like Alex had. Sure, they'd heard her stories and witnessed little bits and pieces, but they'd yet to discover first-hand what it meant to be a part of a 'Library adventure'. Judging by the exhilarated looks on their faces, they were giddy with anticipation.

The staircase continued much further down than it was architecturally built to descend, and only when they reached a dead end did Alex will a doorway to appear in the stone wall.

"Ready or not, here I come," she mumbled under her breath, stepping into a labyrinth of corridors filled with doorways that continued out of sight. She knew from previous experience that some of them opened to exotic, even impossible places, while others led to more door-filled hallways.

D.C. moved to stand beside Alex. "Where do we start?"

When Aven had captured the two girls, it had taken him some time to find the doorway to Meya, even with his advanced genes and his direct line of descent from the founder of Akarnae. Alex may not have shared his relation to Eanraka, but she still had something Aven lacked: she was Chosen, and the Library favoured her.

"For the record, I think this is a bad idea," Alex said.

"But it needs to be done," D.C. said. "You said so yourself. We wouldn't be here otherwise."

Alex slumped her shoulders. "I know."

Best just to get it over with, she thought as she stood up straighter, steeling herself with determination.

"Excuse me, Library?" she called out, ignoring the startled and frankly amused looks from her friends. "Can you please show us the way to Meya?"

"Alex, what—"

Bear didn't get a chance to finish his question before a doorway further down the corridor clicked open, revealing a familiar-looking suit of armour.

"Sir Camden!" Alex cried, moving forward to greet the knight.

"Lady Alexandra," he replied with a formal bow. "How doth thee?"

"I'm well, thanks," she said. "But what are you doing here?"

"Did thou not call for an escort?" Sir Camden asked. "Perchance the fair Lady Alexandra and thy loyal retainers be embarking upon a quest for the Lost City? Sir Camden be thy guide!"

Alex stared at the knight, dumbstruck, before she managed to mutter, "This Library sure works in mysterious ways."

"Follow me, Lady Alexandra," the knight offered. "Sir Camden shalt lead the way to thy destination."

The suit of armour did an about-face and began walking down the corridor, stopping to open a door and waiting for them to follow.

"That sounds like an invitation to me," Jordan said, gleefully rubbing his hands together. "I don't know about you guys, but I think today feels like a great day to find a missing city!"

Although D.C. and Bear were just as enthusiastic as Jordan, the three of them unanimously voted for Alex to take the lead behind the knight. *So much for their adventurous courage,* thought Alex. But they needn't have been concerned, because the door led to another hall of doorways. The four of them followed the knight along the new hallway until he opened another door for them, once again leading to more doorways. They continued this routine for some time, until Sir Camden came to a halt in front of another door.

"This be the door thou art seeking," he said to Alex. "If ever again thou needest to traverse this here labyrinth, call upon Sir Camden and I shalt come to thine aid. For the doorway to the Lost City doth not remain in one place, and even one such as thou shalt not find it without a guide."

"Thank you, Sir Camden," Alex said, grateful for his help.

"Thou art welcome, fair lady." The knight bowed to Alex and her friends before he walked to the other side of the hallway and straight through a solid wall.

"Handy little helper, isn't he?" Jordan remarked.

"He sure is," Alex agreed, turning to the door in front of them. There was nothing special about it that marked it from the other doorways, but Alex still felt it was different.

"Do you think this is it?" Bear asked quietly.

"Sir Camden wouldn't have brought us here for no reason," D.C. pointed out.

"There's only one way to know for sure," Jordan said, and reached out his hand.

"Wait, Jordan, I think—" Alex began. But it was too late, he was already grasping the handle and turning it.

Nothing happened.

Jordan jiggled at the handle. "It's locked."

"That was anticlimactic," Bear said.

Jordan dropped his hand and leaned away from the door, before surging forward and ramming his shoulder into it.

"Um, I wouldn't do that if I were you," Alex warned.

"It might just need a little budge," Jordan said, ramming it again. "It's been closed for thousands of years, right?"

"Yeah, but remember, the Library is—"

Before Alex could finish her sentence, some kind of force field slammed into Jordan, throwing him into the air and against a wall across the corridor.

"—alive," she finished weakly.

Jordan groaned and stood to his feet, pressing a hand to his head. "I won't be trying that again."

"It serves you right for being so stupid," D.C. told him. Despite her firm tone, the concern was clear in her eyes as she walked over to inspect the back of his skull. When she was satisfied he wasn't about to die, she placed her hands on her hips. "Do you think Aven would have kidnapped Alex and me if all he had to do was break down a door? Use your brain, Jordan! He needed her to open it for him since she's Chosen—which means it's probably something only Alex can do."

Jordan offered a sheepish smile. "Oops?"

"'Oops' is right," D.C. said. "You're lucky you weren't seriously hurt!"

"Just my ego, huh?" he said, his smile widening.

"That could use more injury from time to time, in my opinion," D.C. replied, fighting her own grin.

Alex decided it was time to jump in. "Should we try this again?"

At their nods, she reached out and grasped the handle, turning it effortlessly. Instead of opening, the door dissolved, leaving the four of them staring at an unexpected sight. It was beautiful, for sure, but that wasn't why Alex was so enthralled.

"I've been here before," she whispered, stepping across the threshold and looking around the familiar forest clearing. It was different in the light of day, but she could clearly make out the mushroom circle that surrounded the area. "This is Raelia."

"Raelia?" Jordan repeated. "The place where you saw Lady Mystique that night?"

"Yeah," Alex said, spinning around. The clearing had been a mystical place with the moonlight streaming through it, but the sunlight brought a new surprise. The trees around them were not of the normal brown wood and green leaf variety; they were silver. Their glittery trunks burrowed deep into the grassy forest floor, and the charcoal-grey leaves shimmered against them creating a beautifully artistic effect. Sporadically dispersed around the area were bushes and vines, their vibrant green contrasting with the rest of the ethereal forest. All in all, it was a fantasy painter's dream landscape.

When Alex turned and noticed the doorway had disappeared, she wasn't worried. She knew she'd be able to call it back into being when the time came. Unlike when she'd been abandoned in the middle of the forest, this time it was Alex who had opened the door and could therefore reopen it for the return trip. But that didn't help with their current predicament.

"Which way do we go?" Bear asked. "There are paths in every direction."

"It's 'The Crossroads'," Alex said. "That's what Raelia means, remember?"

"Choose your path," D.C. whispered, almost too low to hear.

Alex noted the strange tone of her friend's voice. "Dix, are you all right? You're really pale."

D.C. looked at Alex, her eyes haunted. But then she blinked and the emotion disappeared. "I'm fine. Just nervous, I guess."

"Don't worry, Dix," Jordan said. "I'll protect you."

He flexed his arm muscles and wiggled his eyebrows at her. D.C. smiled and tried to swat him away, but he grabbed her around the waist and threw her over his shoulder.

"This is for the caveman comment earlier," he said.

"Jordan! Let me go!" she squealed, laughing madly. "You're molesting the princess!"

"You say molesting, I say assisting," Jordan corrected. "Just sit back, relax, and enjoy the scenic view."

"Of your backside?" D.C. said dryly. "Believe me, it's not all it's cracked up to be."

There was silence in the clearing for a moment before all four of them burst out laughing. Jordan had to set D.C. back on her feet because he was laughing so hard.

"I didn't mean..." D.C. tried to explain, but she couldn't get the words out amid her own laughter. She inhaled deeply and tried again. "I didn't mean for it to come out like that!"

Jordan's eyes were sparkling. "I think we've underestimated you, Princess."

When they all calmed, D.C. said, "We should probably be careful what we say out here. There's no way to know who might be listening."

"Dix is right," Alex agreed. "We need to figure out where we are before we drop our guard too much."

"Why don't you ask the Library which way to go?" Jordan suggested.

"I can try," Alex said. "But we're not in the Library anymore, so I don't know if it'll do any good." Hoping no one else was in hearing range, she raised her voice and called out, "Excuse me, Library, can you please show us which path to take?"

Nothing. No helpful knights, no spotlights, no moving trees, not even a rustle of the wind.

"I guess we're on our own," Jordan said. "I vote we pick a route and see where it—"

THWACK!

"What the—" Alex cried, ducking to avoid being hit by a second arrow that whizzed by so close to her head she felt her hair move from the air it stirred.

"DOWN!" Jordan bellowed, urging the others off their feet.

Alex heard three more whistling noises accompanied by woody thwacks, and realised they weren't being targeted so much as warned. But warned about what, she wasn't sure.

"*Terin mortalis saes fiora en Raelia?*" came an angry female voice.

Alex lowered her protective arm from her head and looked at her friends with wide eyes. When none of them responded to the voice, their attacker repeated the question, sounding even more irate, if that was possible.

"*Terin mortalis saes fiora en Raelia!*"

"How do you feel about fielding this one, Alex?" Jordan whispered.

She sent him a look that told him exactly how she felt. But they needed to know what was going on, so she carefully—and very slowly—rose to her feet, hands raised in surrender.

"I'm sorry, but I can't understand you," Alex called out, feeling like she had a big red target painted on her forehead. What if she was wrong about the earlier shots being warnings?

The silver trees to her left rustled and Alex tensed. But it wasn't an arrow that came out of the forest, it was a young woman.

Or, really, she may not have been 'young', since she was clearly Meyarin, and age was irrelevant for their eternal race.

"I said, what foolish mortals dare trespass upon Raelia?"

The Meyarin was as entrancingly beautiful as any of her kind, with long golden hair, skin the colour of honey and eyes as green as emeralds Those eyes pierced Alex with a burning anger. But she was more concerned about the drawn arrow pointed straight at her heart.

"Uh..." Alex shifted nervously. "Just us. My friends and I. We, um, we come in peace?"

If Alex wasn't so worried about not making any sudden moves, she would have slapped her forehead for such a ridiculous statement.

"You trespass upon sacred grounds," the Meyarin said, her expression livid. "The penalty of which is death."

"Whoa, whoa, wait just a second," Jordan said, jumping to his feet, with Bear and D.C. following. "We didn't come here deliberately. Or, well, not *here*, here, at least. We're looking for Meya. We just got dropped off at Raelia. So not our fault."

"Yeah," agreed Bear, indicating to Alex. "And we wouldn't have known where we were if Alex hadn't been here before."

The Meyarin looked at each of them as they spoke, but her arrow remained fixed on Alex, and now her gaze returned to her as well. "What does your companion speak of?"

"We didn't deliberately come here," Alex repeated. "It wasn't intentional—"

"No," the Meyarin interrupted. "He said you've been here before?"

Alex frowned at Bear, wondering if he'd landed her in even more trouble. But since their being in Raelia was already punishable by death, it wasn't as though she could be executed twice. "I was here about a month ago," she admitted. "At night."

"Impossible." The Meyarin gave a firm shake of her head. "Before today, no mortal has ever set foot in Raelia. You must be mistaken."

"Believe what you want, but I'm telling the truth."

The Meyarin appeared torn by the honesty in Alex's expression, and after a few tense moments, she hesitantly lowered her weapon. "Come with me," she ordered. "We'll see if you speak the truth."

With those words, the Meyarin turned away and headed back into the forest. When Alex stepped over the mushrooms to follow her, nothing changed, and she realised she was actually in Raelia, as opposed to the last time when she'd been transported there from the middle of the Ezera Forest.

"Make haste, mortals," the Meyarin ordered, "or I'll be forced to motivate you."

Alex shuddered at the Finn-inspired thought of the Meyarin running along behind them shooting her arrows. She exchanged anxious glances with her friends, and they all picked up their pace.

After a good ten minutes of silence, Alex couldn't keep quiet any more. "Why are the trees silver?"

The Meyarin's steps faltered, but then she continued striding forward without pausing to turn around.

Alex guessed being human meant she wasn't worthy of an answer, so she was surprised when the Meyarin spoke.

"You're in the Silverwood. That is their nature."

"The Silverwood?" Jordan repeated. "That's so cool! I thought it was only a myth."

"Clearly, that's not the case," came the Meyarin's dry reply. "But it's unlikely you'll ever leave this place to tell anyone otherwise."

That managed to dampen Jordan's excitement.

They continued walking in silence for another five minutes before the silver trees began to change colour. Slowly but surely the bark transformed into a radiant gold, and the leaves turned into a shade of dark honey.

"Are we in the 'Goldenwood' now?" Alex whispered to Jordan, thinking it a valid guess.

Forgetting how good Meyarin hearing was, she was reminded when their guide snorted in response. It was the first non-aggressive sign the Meyarin had exhibited and Alex hoped it was a positive noise, but she couldn't be certain.

"Are all mortals as uninformed as you?" their escort asked.

Alex kept her mouth closed, not sure what to say.

"I think that's a 'no' to the Goldenwood theory," Jordan whispered back.

She looked at him with exasperation. "Yeah, I got that, thanks."

"There's no such thing as a 'Goldenwood'," the Meyarin informed them. "These trees are golden because they form the boundary around the city of Meya."

Alex felt her heart skip with anticipation. She glanced at her friends and saw the starry-eyed looks on their faces. They had grown up hearing bedtime stories of the Lost City. For them, what they were about to experience was comparable to walking into a make-believe world.

With every step through the now golden forest, Alex felt her nervousness increase. Despite the excitement of seeing the Lost

City, she couldn't forget they were about to be in a whole heap of trouble for trespassing upon a sacred site. She had no idea how that would play out. Not to mention, there was also the potentially devastating news regarding Aven that she was supposed to deliver.

They *really* should have come up with a plan first...

The trees ended abruptly at the top of a cliff overlooking a deep valley that stretched across the horizon. The surrounding cliffs were lined with golden trees that glistened in the sun's rays. Around the boundary were thunderous waterfalls spilling into a river that encircled the valley like a moat around a castle. Alex could only just see the distant and jagged cliff face that ended the valley from where they stood, but she didn't stop to wonder just how far the distance was. She was too distracted by her first view of Meya.

"Whoa."

Alex wasn't sure who said it, but it was the only word to describe what they were seeing. Never in her most creative fantasies could she have imagined such a spectacular place. The entire city blazed, like it was lit from within by a silvery luminescence that seemed to flow out of a massive, spiralling building situated in the middle of the valley.

"Their palace really *is* made out of Myrox!" D.C. whispered in awe.

Alex realised that her friend was right. The huge architectural phenomenon in the middle of the city had to be the palace, shining with the light of a thousand suns. Or apparently just shining from the pure Myrox of which it was made. The glow was so strong that it radiated out into the rest of the impressive city, lighting the entire valley, bouncing across the river and up the waterfalls into the forest.

"Incredible," Alex breathed.

"You should feel honoured," the Meyarin said. "Your race hasn't set foot upon the Golden Cliffs for millennia. It's only fitting that you should witness such a sight before you meet your end."

"Could you ease up on the death threats?" Jordan muttered. "If this is meant to be one of our last living moments, you're kind of ruining it."

Faster than Alex could track the movement, the Meyarin had her arrow notched and her bowstring taught with the lethal weapon pointing directly into Jordan's face. If she released it, Jordan would be dead before any of them could blink.

"You'd be wise to watch your words, youngling," the Meyarin hissed. "You'll find that those who I'm taking you to are much less tolerant."

She lowered her weapon, and Alex reached a trembling hand out to squeeze Jordan's shoulder. He didn't seem outwardly rattled, but she knew he must have been shocked by the Meyarin's quick reaction. Neither he nor Bear had ever interacted with Aven, so they hadn't witnessed first-hand the speed and strength the immortal race possessed. Not until now, at least.

"Come along, mortals," the Meyarin said, and she moved closer to the uneven cliff face. "Watch your step, as the remainder of your life will be shortened further if you set a foot out of place."

"We're not climbing down there, are we?" D.C. asked, her voice hitching slightly. "We'll break our necks!"

The Meyarin continued walking until she reached the very edge of the precipice, where she dropped into a crouch. She then balanced on one hand before using it to push herself off the side of the cliff.

"No!" Alex cried, rushing forward in shock. Sure, the Meyarin had threatened their lives, but Alex didn't want to see her dead.

She dropped to her stomach and crawled until she could see out over the edge. Inexplicably, the Meyarin was perched just beneath the cliff top, standing on empty air.

"I have all eternity, but you are aging by the second," the Meyarin said plainly. "Come along, let's not waste any more time than we have to."

Alex gaped at her. "How are you ... levitating?"

The Meyarin exhaled wearily—it was a sign of frustration rather than anger for a change. She stood up on tiptoes and reached up to grasp Alex's wrist, yanking her over the cliff.

Alex heard her friends scream her name as she fell, but instead of plummeting to her death, she landed on a solid surface.

"What is this?" she asked, standing on wobbly legs and staring at the transparent flooring. Despite what her body was telling her, she could see no evidence of any kind of support underneath her. It simply looked like she was floating in the middle of the air.

Alex had to close her eyes when the scenery spun around her. They were very high up, and having what appeared to be nothing under her feet didn't agree with her stomach, regardless of the impossibly stable—but invisible—floor.

"Alex! Are you okay?"

She looked up and saw that all three of her friends were leaning over the cliff and staring at her in astonishment.

"Yeah," she said. "There's some kind of barrier or something."

"It's the Valispath," the Meyarin informed them. "The Eternal Path. It will take us the rest of the way."

"You guys better get down here before you end up coming over head-first like me," Alex warned her friends.

One by one they helped each other down until they were all standing on the transparent Valispath.

"This is so unnatural," Bear said, looking down.

"I recommend that you all take a seat," the Meyarin suggested.

With no other warning, they shot forward through the air. Alex felt the breath leave her when she slammed against the transparent force field surrounding them. She barely managed to choke back a scream as they flew along what she could only describe as an invisible rollercoaster. Every twist and turn moved them lower to the ground and closer to the city, passing over the moat-like river and moving so near to one of the waterfalls that Alex felt the water spray through the apparently not-so-solid force field.

The *Valispath* moved so quickly that within seconds they entered the outskirts of the city, and then they soared in and around, above and even below the silver-glowing buildings. Faces of Meyarins blurred past them, but they sped along too fast to take in any real details other than the fact that they were heading deeper into the city.

"Where are we going?" Alex yelled over the wind. She wondered why—and how—the *Valispath* protected them from falling, when it didn't keep out the other elements.

"Where do you think?" the Meyarin returned. "Are all mortals so unintelligent?"

For the second time, Alex wasn't sure how to answer the generalised—and offensive—question. Instead, she looked ahead to what she guessed was their intended destination.

The Meyarin palace was the jewel of the city. It was truly beautiful, with swirling, slimline towers spiralling high into the heavens. The closer they came, the more easily Alex could see past the overwhelming glow of the Myrox and make out the finer details in the architecture.

"Wow," she breathed when the *Valispath* stopped their forward momentum just near the entrance.

"You can say that again," Jordan agreed, still collapsed against the barrier beside her.

The palace was made out of Myrox, that they already knew, but it wasn't *just* made out of Myrox. Golden vine-like designs wrapped around the silvery Meyarin metal, creating the most breathtaking sight Alex had ever seen. The magnificence was utterly indescribable. It was a palace outside the most imaginative of dreams.

Alex could have stared at the architectural masterpiece for days, but their Meyarin escort cleared her throat, breaking her and her friends' reverential gaze.

"Follow me," the Meyarin said. "And don't speak unless addressed."

Alex and her friends followed their guide up a long set of shining stairs until they reached a massive Myrox and golden-vined archway that led into the palace. Two fearsome guards stood on either side of the entrance, one male and one female. Both had swords and other glinting weapons attached to their dark, Myrox-infused, leather-like armour, along with quivers of feathered arrows and bows strapped to their backs.

Despite their bulk and authoritative stances, they were still beautiful to behold. The dark skinned male was huge, both in height and muscle mass. He had shoulder-length hair and an amused expression on his ruggedly handsome face, while the female had wavy black hair and intense steel-grey eyes.

It's really not fair that an entire race of people can be so attractive, Alex thought.

"*Kyia, frey de gearsa landi?*" the male guard spoke, glancing at Alex and her friends curiously.

"*Hireth en gartha de seafe lae nias,*" their Meyarin guide responded. "*Taern de Raelia.*"

The female guard scowled and raised her sword threateningly. "*Mae keare vars en hersan! Kyia, raesa felin de oarna Raelia!*"

Their Meyarin escort said something in response, and the unknown female guard stepped forward, her steely eyes blazing with anger.

"Stop, Vaera!" their escort ordered firmly in the common tongue, allowing Alex and her friends to understand. "The humans are under my protection until they've been questioned."

"I don't take orders from you yet, Kyia," the female guard—Vaera—spat back.

"But you do take them from me," came another voice.

Alex sucked in a breath at the sight of the Meyarin who appeared at the entrance to the palace. He was ... well, 'wow' didn't quite sum him up. He was not as youthful as the other Meyarins she'd interacted with, but he was just as beautiful, and he stood tall and confident with golden hair and warm, amber-coloured eyes. His demeanour exuded wisdom and kindness, and for some inexplicable reason, his very presence calmed Alex's nerves.

Then she noticed the crown on his head.

"Stand down, Vaera," he ordered.

"Yes, Sire," the female guard said, lowering her sword and ducking her head respectfully.

"Kyia," the crowned Meyarin said to their escort, "it seems I've come outside for a refreshing walk only to discover humans on my doorstep. I trust you have a good reason for bringing mortals into my city?"

"Yes, my king," Kyia said. "I need to speak with you, in private."

Alex was surprised by the lack of deference their escort showed to the ruler of Meya, but he didn't seem to mind. All he did was tilt his head thoughtfully and say, "You and your companions may join me in my receiving room."

The king stepped back inside and Kyia looked at Alex and her friends pointedly before following him.

"At least we know he's not dead," Jordan said. "That's good news."

Jordan was right—that was good news. Aven had tried to murder his father and he'd supposedly succeeded in stabbing him with a dagger, so it was a relief to learn that the leader of Meya was still alive and ruling.

Alex waited for her friends to walk through the entrance and followed after them, but as she moved past the two guards, the male Meyarin stiffened. She turned her head to look at him in question just as he reached out and grabbed her shoulder, spinning her around to face him.

"What are you?" he demanded.

She froze to the spot. "I—um ... What?"

"What are you?" he repeated, shaking her roughly.

Alex winced from his strong grip, but forced herself to respond. "What do you mean? I'm human. Mortal." She only just managed to stop herself from adding a 'duh' at the end of her sentence.

"You smell like one of the Garseth," he said, his dark eyes narrowed and staring into her own.

"I don't know what that means," Alex told him, and his fingers tensed even more.

"Zain, release her!" Kyia ordered, storming back through the entrance.

"*Garseth rai tealon fera de leas,*" the male—Zain—said angrily.

"*Caen de taris en loga,*" Kyia replied, her tone firm.

Zain nodded tersely and released Alex. She automatically reached up to rub her shoulder.

The male Meyarin noticed her movement and his eyes softened slightly. "I apologise, little human. You caught me off-guard."

"Aren't guards supposed to always be on guard?" Alex muttered under her breath.

Zain's lip twitch reminded her yet again about the quality of Meyarin hearing. Oops.

"Come, mortal," Kyia interrupted before Alex could say or do anything else. "The king awaits."

If Alex hadn't been so worried about being pulled back and manhandled again, she would have paused upon stepping into the massive entrance room. Instead, she looked around with wide eyes and tried not to trip over her own feet as she hurried after Kyia.

All Alex could think as she took in the elegant Myrox and gold decor was that

D.C.'s palace in Tryllin had nothing, *nothing*, on the Casa de Meya.

Kyia led the way along an elaborately decorated hallway that seemed to stretch for miles, but thankfully they didn't have to walk too far before she stopped at an intricately sculpted doorway. The door was open and led to a room where Alex's friends were seated in comfortable-looking chairs.

"They wouldn't let us wait for you," D.C. said quietly when Alex sat beside her. "What happened back there?"

"Just a misunderstanding," Alex whispered back. At least, she hoped that was true.

"A word, if you please, Kyia," the Meyarin king said, waving their escort into a side room.

Once Kyia had closed the door between them, Alex's friends turned to her.

"Do you think we should try and sneak out?" Jordan asked.

"What? Why?" Alex asked.

"We were found trespassing upon a sacred site," he reminded her. "You heard what Kyia said. We could be facing a death sentence. That's not my idea of a good time."

"No one said this journey would be easy, Jordan," Alex returned softly. "You know we can't leave yet."

"Why not?" Bear asked, shifting around with agitation.

"For one thing, just because the door is closed doesn't mean they can't hear us," Alex said. "And for another, I'm here for a reason, remember? I have a message to deliver. I have to stay no matter what. But if you want to attempt an escape, I'll try to cover for you."

She wasn't sure how she would do that exactly, but Jordan's gift could potentially shield the three of them and help get them out without discovery.

"No way," D.C. said. "We're staying together."

"But—" Alex started but Jordan interrupted her.

"Dix is right. We're not leaving unless we all go. If you say we stay, then we stay."

Bear nodded his agreement and they fell into an uneasy silence. After what felt like hours, but was only about three minutes, Kyia and the king opened the door and stepped back into the room. Neither of them sat down; Kyia started pacing and the king stared intently at Alex and her friends. When his eyes came to rest on Alex, she felt herself trembling under the weight of his lingering gaze. The tension built and she gripped the sides of her chair, waiting to hear what he had to say.

Finally he broke off his stare and nodded to Kyia, who stopped pacing and moved to stand beside him.

"Welcome to Meya, young mortals," the king said, his voice surprisingly warm. "I'm King Astophe and you've already met Kyia, one of my most trusted warriors."

The king paused and he appeared to be waiting for something, but for what, Alex was unsure. Diplomatic relations weren't exactly her strong point.

"Follow my lead," D.C. whispered, motioning them all to their feet. Once they were standing, D.C. bowed low, prompting the others to do the same

"We thank you for your hospitality, King Astophe," D.C. said regally, rising again. "My name is Princess Delucia Cavelle and these are my friends, Jordan Sparker, Barnold Ronnigan and Alexandra Jennings. We're honoured to visit your majestic city, and we're further privileged that you grace us with your presence."

"You speak well, young princess," King Astophe said. "But the honour and privilege you describe haven't come with permission. Kyia tells me she found you at Raelia—a most sacred site. Even more troubling, she tells me that one of your companions has trespassed upon the clearing before this day." He glanced at Alex and she felt a flutter of apprehension. "Perhaps you would be so kind as to explain yourselves?"

"Certainly, Your Majesty," D.C. agreed, her voice dripping with honey. Alex had no idea what her friend was about to say, but she had a feeling that whatever it was, it would only cause more damage. "We've been sent as a delegation from—"

"Wait, Dix," Alex cut in.

"Alex..." D.C. whispered, her tone begging Alex to not interrupt.

"It's my fault we're here," Alex told her as quietly as she could—not that it would matter given their super-hearing company. "I'm not going to let you guys take the fall."

D.C. looked like she wanted to argue, but then her body relaxed and she nodded.

Alex sent her a small smile and turned to the king, meeting his eyes directly. "I brought them here. I brought us all to Raelia. If anyone should be punished, it's me. But please believe me when I say I had no idea it was a sacred site. And before you chop off my head or hang me or whatever, I have something urgent to tell you. It's about your son—"

The door burst open, causing Alex to jump and spin around. At the entrance to the room stood the male guard, Zain. His nostrils were flared and his furious eyes were targeted on Alex.

"Sire, forgive my intrusion," Zain clipped, not taking his enraged gaze from Alex. "But I have reason to suspect this human is in alliance with the *Garseth*."

"Zain, you said you wouldn't speak of this again," Kyia interrupted, her tone annoyed.

"I said I wouldn't speak of it without just cause," Zain argued, and he hauled someone around the corner and into the room with him. It was another Meyarin, but despite his enchantingly dark features, he was dressed in dirty, ripped clothes and looked like he hadn't showered in some time. He also happened to have his hands and feet chained together with Moxyreel, the impenetrable wire made out of Myrox that could only be damaged by Myrox.

"What's *he* doing here?" Kyia demanded.

"I dragged this traitor up from the dungeons," Zain said. "He's my evidence against *her*."

Zain's finger pointed straight at Alex and she felt her stomach drop. What was going on?

"She's *human*, Zain," Kyia said, exasperated.

"Is she? Do you really believe that, Kyia? Can't you see what I see and smell what I smell?" Zain turned his gaze away from Alex to look at the female Meyarin. "She's different, that much is unmistakable."

At his words and the attention they brought her, Alex had to fight off a bout of nervous laughter.

"She *is* different," Kyia quietly agreed. "But how and why, I'm not sure."

"I can tell you," came the bold voice of the chained Meyarin. His greasy hair fell over his face in waves, and Alex had to suppress a shudder when his cunning eyes bore into her own. "We're very ... *close*, you see. But you've already figured that out, haven't you?"

"I told you!" Zain said. "She's one of the *Garseth*."

"I am not!" Alex said hotly. "I don't even know what a *Garseth* is!"

"Come now, kitten," the prisoner purred. "I've missed you these past years. My life has been so empty without you."

Alex gaped at the Meyarin, and because all eyes were fixed on her, no one noticed his self-satisfied smirk and his strangely warm wink.

"He's lying!" Alex cried. "I've never seen this man—Meyarin—whatever—before in my life."

"What reason does Niyx have to lie?" Zain demanded. "He's already imprisoned for his treachery. Lying would only bring him more suffering, whereas the truth could afford him some comfort to his station."

"That doesn't make sense!" Alex cried. "What if he's lying because he thinks doing so will grant him special favour? It's his word against mine!"

Seeing the unmoved faces around her, Alex took a deep breath and gathered her thoughts. She looked around the room and felt her friends' concern, Zain's alertness, Kyia's uncertainty, the prisoner's—Niyx's—amusement, and finally, the king's calculating gaze. The ruler of Meya raised his eyebrows, expecting an explanation.

"You asked what reason Niyx has to lie, but what about me?" Alex said, keeping her tone as calm as possible. "Why would I want to deceive you?"

Zain laughed without humour. "You expect us to interpret the thoughts of the *Garseth*? Impossible. I wouldn't wish such dark wonderings upon any being, Meyarin or otherwise."

"If you want me to keep up with this discussion, you're going to have to tell me what a *Garseth* is," she said.

"Alex, 'Garseth' is the Meyarin word for 'rebel'," D.C. whispered fearfully. "They think you're one of Aven's Rebels."

Eleven

Alex felt the blood drain from her face. She barely noticed the Meyarins' infuriated reactions to D.C. mentioning their banished prince. If they thought Alex was teaming up with Aven, then she was so dead, no matter what explanation she gave as to why they'd been found at Raelia.

"There's no way you can think I—"

"Your blood is tainted, just like all Garseth," Zain interrupted. "There's no denying it."

Alex shook her head in bewilderment. But then her eyes widened in realisation and she raised her hand, staring at the silvery scar across her palm.

Her fear and confusion dissolved into anger. "Oh, I'm going to *kill* him. I don't care if he's immortal and I can barely keep up in Combat—he's *dead*. Stupid Meyarins ruining my life. Is it too much to ask to just be normal for a change?" She practically yelled the last part of her rant, staring up at the ceiling as if hoping for some kind of divine intervention. When none came, she sighed and lowered her gaze. "I think I can explain. But you need to promise to hear me out."

"We don't need to promise you anything, *Garseth*," Zain said, stepping forward threateningly.

Alex returned the glare he sent her. "Then I guess you don't want to hear about how Aven Dalmarta tried to use an ancient blood-bonding ritual to Claim me so I would open a doorway through the Library and grant him entrance into Meya?"

The silence that came with her exclamation was thick with tension.

Finally, the king spoke. "Zain, please escort Niyx back to his cell and return here immediately."

The guard left quickly, his eyes still wide with surprise.

Silence descended upon them and Alex decided to throw diplomacy out the window by trudging over to slump down into her chair, knowing she would have to wait for Zain to come back before she began her story.

It took barely any time at all for the guard to return, and again he brought someone with him—another male Meyarin, but he clearly wasn't a prisoner. The newcomer was tall and well built, with glossy black hair and warm golden eyes.

"Explain yourself, little human," the king ordered once the door was closed. His gaze was much cooler now than it had been earlier.

"First off, my name isn't 'little human'," she said irritably. "It's Alex."

D.C. winced at her disrespect, but the new Meyarin who had entered with the guard chuckled quietly, and the king seemed to thaw a little with her words.

"Please tell us your story, Alex," King Astophe asked, much more politely.

She took a deep breath and began. "I first met Aven about nine months ago..."

Alex told them about all of her dealings with the disowned prince, including how and why he'd attempted to Claim her, and how her willpower gift allowed her to break through his control. She didn't bother mentioning that she'd been stabbed in the back by the ice-coloured dagger, thinking it was irrelevant, but she did detail her most recent encounters with him, including his newest threats. She also told them about the other gifted humans he appeared to be collecting, and how they seemed to have adopted some of his Meyarin characteristics, like longer lifespans. She ended with how she'd agreed to be a messenger to inform the Meyarins about their Rebel Prince, since she was Chosen by the Library and could therefore open a doorway to their city.

"...And that's why we're here. The Library opened up at Raelia, so, like we said, we weren't deliberately trespassing. It would be great if you decided not to, you know, kill us."

Alex cringed at her lame ending and trailed off into silence.

After a few tense seconds, the Meyarins began speaking to each other in their native language, and she glanced at her friends.

"I'll bet you're regretting not sneaking out now," Jordan whispered.

"Maybe a little," Alex admitted. But she knew she'd done the right thing. The Meyarins now knew about Aven, and that was what mattered most.

When the talking around them ceased, the newest, unknown Meyarin walked over to Alex and knelt in front of her.

"May I please see your hand, Alex?"

Alex wasn't sure if it was because he'd asked so nicely, or because of his mesmerising eyes and kind face, but she didn't hesitate to open her scarred hand for him to inspect. He gently held her palm up to the light and inspected the silver line where Aven's dagger had sliced her skin.

"It healed straight away?" he asked, the curiosity plain on his face.

"Only after..." Alex paused and swallowed. She found it difficult to recount that particular memory as it had been so disturbing at the time and had become even more distressing later when she realised what had happened. "Only after he joined our bloodied hands together."

The image of their combined red and silver blood trickling down her arm was something she would never forget.

The Meyarin nodded in understanding and released her hand. He moved to stand beside Kyia and turned to speak to the king and Zain. "Alex smells like one of the *Garseth* because Aven's blood runs in her veins. I don't believe she's otherwise associated with him."

Alex furrowed her brow. "No, that's not right."

The Meyarin looked at her, surprised. "Are you saying you are one of Aven's Rebels?"

"What? No!" Alex shook her head adamantly. "I'm saying you're wrong about Aven's blood being in my veins. That's just ... not right. Fletcher—Akarnae's doctor—he said I'm all me and there's nothing to worry about."

"You might not be Claimed anymore," the Meyarin told her, "but Aven mixed his blood with yours using an extremely dark ritual. Bonded or not, a trace of his Meyarin heritage lingers within you."

Alex felt the room spin and she was glad she was sitting down or else she might have fainted. Or thrown up. The latter remained a strong possibility.

"This is not my life," she whispered, rubbing her fingers across her face.

D.C. reached out and pressed a reassuring hand against her back.

"Hey, you've got to admit, it's pretty cool," Jordan said. "Not everyone can claim to be part Meyarin."

"Mate, I don't think you're helping," Bear said, seeing Alex's rapidly paling face.

"I still say we need to verify the truth of her words," Zain said to the other Meyarins. "We can all see the mark of the bonding; how can we be sure she's no longer Claimed by the Rebel Prince? What if she's under his control right now and this is all an act? If she truly isn't Garseth, then that will easily become evident. But if she is, then that too will be revealed."

"What's he talking about?" Alex asked her friends, but none of them seemed to know.

"Sire, I wish for your permission to verify her claim," Zain said, speaking directly to the king.

King Astophe looked from Zain to Alex and then to the unnamed Meyarin, who shrugged at the king's unasked question.

"You have my permission," the king said, looking back at the guard. "But Zain, remember that she is human, regardless of all else."

"I won't break her," Zain promised. "I merely seek to uncover the truth."

Alex felt a shiver of foreboding. 'I won't break her.' What was that supposed to mean?

The king nodded his consent and Zain bowed slightly before he turned and led the way from the room.

"Come along, mortals," Kyia said, ushering Alex and her friends out of their seats and motioning for them to follow as she trailed after Zain. The king and the other Meyarin brought up the rear of their procession.

"I don't feel very good about this," Alex whispered to her friends.

"You're not the only one," D.C. said.

The moment they all stepped into the hallway, the floor took off from underneath them. Alex was once again thrown backwards as she felt the power of the Valispath hurtling them through the air. Except this time they were literally moving through the building. They flew through solid walls as if they were open windows; they whisked around Meyarins going about their day; and they rushed higher and higher up one of the spiralling towers until the transparent barrier landed them in a huge, vaulted room.

"I have got to get me one of these," Jordan said as he stood to his feet again, brushing windswept hair from his forehead. Only the Meyarins had been able to keep their footing on the ride, and Alex had no idea how they'd managed not to fall.

"Where are we?" D.C. asked, looking around the massive room. It was empty except for the eight of them, and most of the floor was covered with some kind of padded, gym-style mat.

"This is one of our less commonly used training rooms," Kyia informed them as Zain opened one of the doors nearest to them and disappeared within.

"Training rooms?" Jordan repeated. "Training for what?"

No one answered him, and Zain re-entered the room carrying a sword. With his free hand he immediately unsheathed his own blade from the scabbard at his waist. Held side by side, Alex could clearly see that both swords were made from the shiny Meyarin steel, and one was significantly larger than the other.

Without warning, Zain threw the smaller weapon through the air, straight at Alex. She yelped and instinctively reached out to grab the pommel, grateful for Karter's occasional temper that had prompted him to pull the same dangerous manoeuvre on her in the past.

"Hey, watch it," she said angrily. "Someone could get hurt."

In the blink of an eye, Zain's sword came soaring towards her torso.

Reacting on instinct, Alex spun out of the way, finally cluing in on what he planned to do with her. But they were way too close to her friends for comfort, and if the guard was intent on fighting her, there was no way she would allow anyone else to get hurt in the process.

"Come on, you big oaf," Alex goaded, running away from her friends. She kept running until she was on the firm but spongy mat, far enough away from the others for them to be safe. "If it's a fight you want, it's a fight you'll get."

She hadn't heard Zain chasing after her, so when she turned around and he was directly behind her, she had to suppress a squeak of surprise. Realising she was about to go up against a Meyarin in a sword fight, Alex had to hold back an exclamation of fear.

Oh, I'm so dead, she thought.

Zain's sword came slicing towards her again, and this time she met it with her own blade. The power behind his blow sent her staggering, but she repositioned to hold the sword with two hands, which helped her brace against his supernatural strength. Once she managed to deflect his weapon, she wasn't sure what to do next. She didn't want to attack the Meyarin, but if the alternative was her death, then she only had one viable option.

Defence it is, she decided. She would defend against his attacks, but not provoke him with her own.

The following minutes nearly killed Alex in more ways than one. It turned out that 'defence' was much easier said than done when it came to battling a Meyarin. **Z**ain was stronger, faster and much more experienced than anyone she'd ever fought against—including Karter. Half the time she didn't see his sword flying towards her, and only a natural instinct for survival coupled with some super-keen reflexes kept her limbs attached to her body.

"Is that the best you can do, little *Garseth*?" **Z**ain mocked.

"I told you," Alex panted, avoiding his blade yet again. "I'm not a Rebel!"

"And yet you fight with more fire and finesse than any other mortal I've come across," Zain returned.

"I—What?"

Zain's words caught her off-guard and she only just managed to bring her weapon up in time against his next attack. In her haste to block his move she failed to notice when he swept his leg out and hooked it behind her own, tripping her over, and she slammed onto the ground. Her sword was jarred out of her hand as she lay winded on the not-as-soft-as-she'd-first-thought floor.

Instead of his sword coming down to seal her fate, Zain reached out a hand to pull Alex back to her feet.

"Um, thanks," she said, pressing a hand to her throbbing head. Yeah, the mat was definitely not as spongy as she would have liked.

"You're welcome, little human," Zain said with an amused smirk.

Alex didn't know why he'd stopped trying to kill her, but she wasn't willing to question the matter—not without a sword in her hands. She would even let his 'little human' comment go, so long as he was no longer threatening her life.

Zain reached down to grab the sword she'd dropped and he indicated for her to lead the way back to their companions. She wasn't overly comfortable having him behind her with two blades, so she hurried over to the others as Zain went on to speak with the other Meyarins.

"Are you all right?" D.C. asked, looking pale.

"Yeah," Alex answered, rotating her neck and feeling something pop back into place.

"That. Was. Awesome," Jordan said, staring at her in awe. "Seriously—I've never seen anything like it!"

Alex turned to him. "What are you talking about? That was definitely not awesome."

"From our point of view it was pretty amazing, Alex," Bear said. "We had no idea you could fight like that."

Alex searched for the right words and settled on, "I still have a lot to learn."

"That you do, little human," Zain said, interrupting their conversation. Apparently the Meyarins were done speaking privately. "But you're well on your way."

Alex wasn't sure how to respond to his unexpected compliment, so she ended up saying a quiet, "Uh, thank you."

She had no idea what the big deal was. She'd barely lasted a few minutes in their fight before Zain had won. That wasn't exactly something to brag about.

"As 'enjoyable' as that was, I'm hoping there was a point to that exercise," Alex told the Meyarins. "Did you find out what you needed to know?"

"We were testing whether or not you're under Aven's control," Kyia said, her emerald eyes gazing thoughtfully at Alex.

"And the verdict is?"

"You fight unexpectedly well for one of your kind," Zain answered. "You show great promise, but your strength and skills are your own. You're not under the influence of the Rebel Prince."

Alex had to resist rolling her eyes. She'd told them that, but they hadn't believed her. But despite the inconvenience—and the danger—to her, she understood that they'd had to check. Even if she wasn't thrilled by the way they'd done so.

"Well, that's a relief," Jordan piped up cheerfully. "It would've sucked to have a best friend who was possessed by an evil tyrant. Great anecdote, but definitely not ideal."

"Jordan, seriously. Stop talking," D.C. muttered, shaking her head at him.

"You're such a royal buzz-kill," he huffed. But then his expression brightened and he asked, "What happens next? Can we see more of Meya before we leave?"

While her friends were speaking, Alex was acutely aware of the unknown Meyarin's eyes upon her, almost as if he was searching for something.

"I'd like to try something, if you don't mind?" he said, turning to wait for the king's nod of permission before looking back at Alex questioningly.

"Um, sure," she said, wondering why he'd sought her consent when the king had already agreed.

The Meyarin led her away from the others and back onto the mat. Her heartbeat sped up and her companion chuckled as if he could hear the erratic thumping. Maybe he could, Alex realised. She had no idea just how good Meyarin hearing was.

"Don't worry, Alex," he said, maintaining his earlier informality and putting her at ease. "It's just a little experiment."

"What kind of experiment?" she asked when she noticed him pull a long piece of material from his clothing. While he wasn't wearing head-to-toe armour like Zain, his dark outfit was still like something straight out of a fantasy movie. All that was missing was the cape.

"I spent most of my youth with Aven Dalmarta," he said. "I'm well acquainted with the scent of his blood, and that's why I'm one of the few who can tell it lingers within you, dormant or not. I have no concerns about him holding any control over you—it's clear your mind is too strong for his Claiming to still be active—but I'm curious whether the blood tainting your veins has any other effect. I'd like to test my hypothesis."

"And what *is* your hypothesis?" Alex asked, wondering how much further they would be walking and whether she should ask him to take her back to her friends.

"I'll let you know after I've tested it."

Alex wasn't certain she liked his answer. "Do you have a name?"

He turned to look at her with an amused—and breathtakingly beautiful—smile. "I do."

"And it is?"

"We're far enough away from the others now," he said, avoiding her question. "But just in case..."

He trailed off and knelt to the floor, pressing his fingers in some kind of coded rhythm against the mat. When he stood again, the floor began to tremble and a luminescent Myrox barrier rose up from beneath their feet, encircling them inside an impenetrable dome.

Alex glanced nervously at the sealed force field surrounding them. She couldn't see past the shining barricade, and she knew her friends—and the other Meyarins—wouldn't be able to see inside, either.

"Um, this doesn't make me feel great about what you have planned."

"It's okay, Alex," he said soothingly. "The barrier is for your protection. If it turns out that I'm right, then it'll be best if the others are kept in the dark."

"You know, I really hate it when people are cryptic," she said, irritation momentarily overriding her fear.

The Meyarin laughed. It was a warm, comforting sound that reminded her of sunshine, strangely enough.

"I'm not a huge fan of it myself," he agreed. "My betrothed often gives me just enough information to drive me crazy, while withholding the tiniest detail needed to have everything make sense. She excels in the art of cryptic-ness."

Alex snorted. "Cryptic-ness isn't a real word."

"It could be."

"It's not," Alex said confidently. "And I know what you're doing, by the way."

He tilted his head to the side with a small smile on his face. "What am I doing?"

"You're trying to distract me," she told him.

"Is it working?"

"Yes," she answered, already feeling much calmer.

"Good," he said. "Now turn around so I can blindfold you." *Goodbye, calm.*

Seeing her wariness, he encouraged, "I promise nothing bad will happen."

For some unexplainable reason, Alex trusted the easy-going Meyarin with his warm smiles and kind disposition. She released a heavy breath and turned around, hoping her instincts were right.

"Close your eyes," he instructed, and she felt him place the cloth above her cheekbones and tie it firmly at the back. He then pressed a hand to her shoulder and moved her to face him again.

"What happens now?" she asked, failing to keep the uncertainty out of her voice.

"Now we see just how good those reflexes of yours really are."

Twelve

A rush of air was the only warning she had before her leg was kicked out from underneath her and she tumbled to the ground.

"Hey!" she cried. "What are you—"

Without knowing why, she turned her body to roll out of the way just in time to hear a *thump* behind her—right where she'd been lying a second earlier.

"Take a deep breath, Alex," the Meyarin said. "Let go and *feel* the air around you."

"I don't know what you're—" Before she could finish her sentence she heard a rushing noise and rolled out of the way again, this time using the momentum to lift herself back to her feet. She reached her hands up to untie her blindfold but it wouldn't budge. When she tried to pull it over her head, she realised it was stuck in place.

"Get this thing off me!"

"Calm down and pay attention," the Meyarin said, his voice gentle but firm. "You need to breathe and *listen*."

"I don't understand what you're trying to—"

"Listen, Alex," he interrupted. "Just listen."

The tone of his voice stopped her protests. Whatever he was trying to prove seemed to be important, and he'd been nothing but kind to her. The least she could do was try to do as he asked.

"Okay," she said. "Just give me a moment. I can't hear anything over my convulsing heartbeat."

She took a few deep breaths and tried to focus outwardly. She was blind, that much was true, but she still had her other senses. So when she felt the mat underneath her feet tilt slightly, she knew the Meyarin had decided her reprieve was over.

But this time she was ready.

The movement of the mat told her which direction he was attacking from, and the whisper of air she could inexplicably feel rushing outward from his position told her that he was swinging his arm towards her face. Instead of ducking, she threw her own hand out, meeting and deflecting his blow with her forearm. It wasn't her smartest idea, since she'd forgotten to take into account his Meyarin strength, so all she managed to do was earn herself one mother of a bruise.

From then on, every time she 'felt' the Meyarin come at her, she ducked, jumped, lunged and rolled out of his way.

Sometimes he managed to land a hit, but more often than not her instincts moved her out of his path in time.

Alex wasn't sure how long they were going to keep 'experimenting' when her opponent said, "You're doing great, Alex. Let's try something more challenging and see how you go."

She had no idea what he meant; not until she heard the distinct sound of rasping metal as he unsheathed a weapon.

"You can't be serious!" she cried.

The sharp whistle of steel through the air told her that he was indeed serious.

Her instincts compelled her to duck out of the path of the blade. "You're going to kill me!"

"Just concentrate," he told her. "Open your mind and listen."

"Stop telling me to listen." She jumped back when she felt him lunge towards her. "And let me fight you fairly, with a weapon and no blindfold. You're Meyarin—you'll still win."

"If you have a weapon, you're more than welcome to use it," he said. "And if it makes you feel better, I'm just as blind as you."

"What!" Alex shrieked, dropping to the ground and rolling away from another attack.

Was he honestly fighting her blindfolded as well? Oh, she was so going to end up skewered.

"Can't you feel it, Alex?" he asked, and she sensed his weapon stab towards her again. This time she was too distracted by her fear, and the blade nicked her arm, causing her to hiss as it grazed her flesh.

"I certainly felt that," she said. "Too close, buddy."

His voice was amused when he said, "Buddy? Really?"

"You haven't given me any other name," she said, jumping backwards when his blade swiped at her again. "And what exactly am I supposed to be feeling?"

"Everything," he told her reverently. "Let your instincts guide you."

"What do you think I've been doing?" she huffed. "Building a submarine?"

"You're not letting go completely, Alex," he said. "Listen. Feel. Experience."

Alex stopped moving, ducking only when she felt the blade swing at her again, and tried to centre herself. A few times during their 'experiment' she felt what she thought he was talking about. It was a natural instinct that took over and guided her to move in ways she didn't understand but still made sense. The feeling had so far been sporadic, and the rest of the time she'd just been plain lucky. Now that the Meyarin had a blade, their game had changed, and she was more than ready to even the score. It was time for her to take an offensive position and test the limits of her senses.

When Alex felt him come at her again, she crouched down to avoid the blade and swept her leg out, using his own trick to hook her limb around him and knock him off his feet. It half worked, and she sensed him stumble to his knees, but he recovered quickly and sprang back up, renewing his fight. She twirled around him, dodging another swipe of his blade, and when she sensed she was behind him, she jumped onto his back, wrapping her legs around his torso and reaching down until she held his weaponed arm. But his strength was too much for her and he effortlessly detached her from his body throwing her over his head and onto the ground.

She hit the mat harder than expected and the fall dazed her, taking away all her 'listening' skills. By the time she came back to full awareness, all she knew was that there was a blade flying through the air, straight towards her head.

Alex didn't have time to move out of the way; all she could do was raise her arm to protect her face and hope that the

Meyarin would pull back after he realised he'd hit flesh. But the blinding pain from her wrist being amputated never came. Instead, there was a metallic clang as steel met steel.

Alex's shock almost caused her to drop the weapon that was now in her grasp and blocking the other blade from slashing through her body. Where had it come from?

"You've been holding out on me," the Meyarin said, and Alex could hear the anticipation in his voice. "Now we can *really* experiment."

Alex didn't have the chance to tell him to stop. She felt the strength behind his blade ease for a fraction of a second before he lunged towards her again, prompting her to roll out of the way and jump to her feet, raising her weapon in front of her.

It was then that her entire perception of the world changed.

She still couldn't see anything, but she didn't need to. Everything else was magnified. She could hear, feel, smell and taste the air around her. Her senses drew together a perfect picture that she couldn't have seen with her eyes open. She was suddenly aware, and it made her feel powerful. Invincible. And when the Meyarin sliced his blade towards her, she met his attacks over and over again.

They lunged, they parried, blocked and deflected. They spun, jumped, ducked and twirled. Alex gave as good as she received; never before had she felt so capable with a blade. In the end it was her human weakness that ended their fight, but only when she became so breathless that she could barely draw air into her lungs.

"Enough," the Meyarin said. "I think we've proved my hypothesis correct."

Alex collapsed to the ground and panted heavily, dropping her weapon to the side. A moment later the Meyarin released her blindfold, and she winced at the painfully bright Myrox barrier surrounding them.

Only when her companion sat beside her did she notice that he was also affected by their workout. His breath wasn't anywhere near as ragged as hers, but he was definitely drawing in more air than normal.

"Why are you winded?" she asked, continuing to suck in deep breaths. "You're Meyarin."

"And you just fought like one," he told her with a brilliant smile. "That was incredible, Alex."

"What do you mean?" she asked stupidly. Their fight had seemed like a whirlwind to her, but that was mostly because she'd been blindfolded, right? Her sense of, well, everything had just been distorted ... Right?

"My hypothesis," he said, "do you want to know what it was?"

"Definitely," she answered without hesitation.

"I wanted to test whether the dormant Meyarin blood in your veins—Aven's blood—could be utilised."

Alex felt her slowly calming heartbeat pick up speed again. "What are you saying?"

"Alex, I believe you can choose to access Aven's Meyarin characteristics because of his blood that resides in you," he said. "But whether or not you can only do so under duress is yet to be seen. That's why I blindfolded you—sometimes we rely too heavily on what we see and miss out on opportunities to have faith in what we feel."

"But you couldn't see either," Alex reminded him, her tone thick with accusation at the memory of his risky actions.

"I've participated in many similar exercises before," he assured her. "I wouldn't have let any harm come to you. There was one potentially dangerous situation you faced, but you surprised me when you drew your own blade to save yourself." He glanced around the mat and added, "Your weapon sang beautifully. May I see it?"

Alex raised her eyebrows at his wording, before looking down to where she'd dropped her blade. But there was nothing there.

"I ... Uh ... Um..."

She had no idea how to answer, but fortunately he smiled at her and said, "Don't worry, I'm not going to take it from you. You handled it so well that you've earned the right to keep it hidden, if that's your wish."

He rose to his feet and offered her his hand. Since every muscle in her body ached, she was grateful for the assistance.

"We'd better return to the others," he said, pressing the coded rhythm into the mat again to lower the barrier around them. "I'm sure they'll be curious about what we've been doing."

"What will you tell them?" Alex asked, following as he led the way back to the small group waiting at the other end of the massive training room.

"Just that I wanted to witness your fighting ability for myself, without prying eyes."

"You don't want your, uh, *companions* to know about your hypothesis?" she asked, not quite sure how to label the other

Meyarins, one of whom was the king. "Don't you trust them?"

He turned to look at her as they walked. "It's not *my* companions I don't trust."

Reading the implication in his words, Alex opened her mouth to defend her friends, but he continued talking.

"I know I don't have any input over what you say and do, Alex, but I strongly advise against telling anyone what we just discovered. If Aven learns about the abilities he's inadvertently given you, he'll stop at nothing to get to you."

"He's already pretty desperate to get his hands on me," Alex said. "It's no secret that he wants me dead."

"True as that may be," the Meyarin said, reaching out and bringing her to a halt, "if he learns the full threat you pose to him, he'll be more desperate than ever to keep you from ruining his plans."

"Me? A threat to him?" Alex released an incredulous laugh. "Are you mad?"

"The blood in your veins allows you to use *his* immortal abilities—not general Meyarin characteristics, but Aven's *personal* genetic traits," the Meyarin said, his face solemn enough to instantly erase Alex's disbelief. "Your strength, your speed, your heightened senses; you draw from the essence of Aven's blood when you access those characteristics inherent to the Meyarin race. The connection between you two, even with the bond severed..." He trailed off and shook his head, looking at her with compassionate eyes. "Alex, you're not like his other Claimed victims. You *share* his power. How much of it, only time will tell. But the potential you possess will paint you as a threat, of that there is no doubt."

Alex once again felt like she was going to throw up. "But I'm not—I'm not powerful. I'm nothing like Aven—I'm just me."

"I'm sorry, Alex," he said, his voice gentle. "But it was definitely his power I felt leaking out of you when we fought. That much is true."

"But—But I'm not Claimed anymore!" she said, almost hysterically. Then she gasped. "Wait—does that mean I'm like you now? That I'm immortal? That I'm not *human* anymore?" Heart pounding, she continued blurting out her spiralling fears. "You said I can access the Meyarin characteristics, but that doesn't mean I'm, like, doing it all the time, right? You said the power is dormant in me ... right?"

"Alex, breathe." He sent her a comforting look. "You're definitely not

Claimed, and you're definitely human. You could choose to never tap into Aven's power and live a perfectly normal life. If you do decide to test the limits of the blood in your veins, you'll still remain mortal because you are no longer bound to Aven's life force. But if Aven learns that his power lingers in your veins, he'll either want to kill you more than he already does, or he'll want to find a way to manipulate you to further his own plans. That's why I believe the knowledge of your blood should be kept between as few people as possible. To keep you safe ... or at least, safer."

Alex took a moment to let his words wash over her until she forced herself to be calm again. Only then did she say, "But I trust my friends. I don't keep secrets from them."

"Please, Alex," he said, his expressive eyes begging her to understand. "Don't let them know about your blood. At least not until we know more."

Alex could see nothing but genuine concern in his gaze—concern for her. So, despite how difficult it was, she nodded her agreement. "I won't tell them for now. But I reserve the right to do so in the future."

He released the breath he'd been holding and smiled. "I can accept that compromise."

And with their agreement, the Meyarin resumed walking.

They were almost back to their companions when Alex said, "After all that, are you still not going to tell me your name? You did nearly decapitate me, you know. Surely that earns me something."

The Meyarin chuckled and glanced sideways at her. "It's Roka."

Roka. Cool name.

...And one that Alex had heard before.

She strained her thoughts for some kind of recognition, and finally a hazy memory came back to her.

"*Prince* Roka?" she choked out. "You're Aven's *brother?*"

He laughed at her reaction but didn't have a chance to respond before they reached the others. Her friends must have heard her exclamation, since the three of them were staring at the Meyarin with wide eyes.

"Is everything all right?" the king asked.

Alex couldn't help but stare at Astophe, searching for the similarities between him, Roka and Aven and finding few. Roka had his father's bearing and kingly stature, but his dark hair must have come from his mother, while Aven shared the king's golden locks. As far as Alex could tell, the only thing both Aven and Roka had in common were their eyes, but they didn't inherit those from the king, either. The remarkable colour should have clued Alex in much earlier to Roka's identity, but she'd been a tad overwhelmed by everything else to note the minor resemblance between him and his brother. For all she'd known, golden eyes were the norm in Meya. And there was little else in Roka's appearance—or character—that was mimicked in his evil sibling, at least from Alex's perspective.

"Everything is fine," Roka assured his father, and Alex wondered why they'd been asked the question in the first place. But then D.C. walked over and prodded her arm where the Meyarin's blade had bit into her flesh, causing Alex to wince.

"You're bleeding," D.C. stated. "Why are you bleeding?"

"More interestingly," Jordan said, "why is he bleeding?"

Alex followed his gaze and was surprised to see a few small cuts along Roka's arms that glittered silver. She must have nicked him with her blade, as unfathomable as the idea was. She glanced at him apologetically and wondered what the punishment was for drawing blood from the crown prince of Meya.

Roka's face lit with humour when he saw her expression, probably figuring out where her thoughts were leading her. He tried to reassure her with a smile, but it did little good since the other Meyarins were also staring at the wounds on their prince.

"We're both perfectly fine," Roka repeated. "I merely wanted to experience Alex's fighting skills for myself. And you were right, Zain. She's impressive—for a human, anyway. But she still has a lot to learn."

"How did she injure you?" Kyia asked curiously.

"I was blindfolded."

While the answer was enough of an explanation for Alex's friends, the other Meyarins looked at Roka dubiously. Their super-senses would have allowed them to hear the conversation between him and Alex as they'd walked back across the mat, so the Meyarins would have heard all about Aven's blood in her veins. Curiosity was splashed across their beautiful faces.

"*Trae selve raen de linare*," Roka said quietly, and their expressions cleared as they all nodded.

Alex might not have understood the words he'd said, but she was fairly confident he'd just told them he would explain later. Unfortunately, she couldn't offer the same assurances to her friends.

"What happens now?" Alex asked, wanting to move the conversation along to safer topics.

"Now it's time for you and your friends to go home, Alex," King Astophe said.

"That's it?" Jordan asked, disappointed. "We can't see more of the city?"

"You've seen more of Meya than any other mortal has in millennia," the king said with a trace of amused indulgence. "While your enthusiasm is admirable, you should understand that the last humans to set foot in our city caused a ripple effect unforgotten over the centuries. There are many of our kind who won't take kindly to learning of your presence here. Not all of the *Garseth* were captured with my son's banishment, and those who remain hidden won't hesitate to show their allegiances should a whisper of Aven's return reach their ears. It's for your own safety that I ask you to leave."

Jordan opened his mouth to argue, but Alex interrupted before he could make his opinion known.

"Thank you, King Astophe," she said. "We're aware our arrival was an unanticipated surprise, and we're grateful for the time you've given us. Do you mind if I ask what your plans are regarding Aven?"

The king eyed her speculatively, as if he was deciding what to tell her. "I'll bring the information you shared to the attention of my council, and together we'll make a decision. What happens after that will depend a great deal on Aven's next move."

Alex nodded. It was none of her business, really, and she was surprised that Astophe had answered her. Surprised and pleased. She'd somehow earned the Meyarin ruler's respect, although she wasn't certain how she'd managed such a feat.

"Kyia will return you to Raelia," the king said. "Unless there's somewhere else you can leave from? Somewhere that doesn't involve treading upon our sacred Crossroads?"

Alex winced at the hope in his voice. Clearly Raelia was a very important place for them, but there was nothing she could do about that. "I'm sorry, Your Majesty. We can only return using the door we entered through."

The king sighed in resignation. "So be it."

Alex bowed to him and her friends followed suit. She looked over at Roka, wondering if she should bow to him as well. He must have seen the question on her face and he laughed quietly, shaking his head at her. She chose to interpret that as a 'no', rather than as him thinking her ridiculous. But both options were equally plausible.

"Despite the circumstances of your arrival and the news you've brought, it has been a pleasure to speak once more with those of your race," King Astophe said. "I hope our paths meet again one day."

Alex wasn't sure what to say in response so she smiled and nodded her head.

"I enjoyed fighting with you, little human," Zain told her. "I'll look forward to a repeat performance in the future."

Alex didn't want to be rude to the scary guard by saying "no way in hell", so she kept her mouth shut and once again nodded with a polite smile plastered to her face. The big Meyarin seemed amused by her noncommittal response, if his grin was anything to go by.

"I have a feeling we'll see each other again soon, Alex," Roka said to her. "Until then, stay safe."

The smile she gave Roka was genuine. "You too. And thanks for ... you know ... your experiment. And for explaining things to me. I guess you're not so cryptic after all."

Roka's golden eyes sparkled, the warmth in them so different from his brother's. "Well, I already told you how annoying cryptic-ness can be."

"And I told you that's not a real word," Alex returned.

"Goodbye, Alex," Roka said affectionately, and he followed the king and Zain over to where they had first arrived in the vaulted room. The three Meyarins disappeared from view when the *Valispath* swept them out of sight.

"Follow me, mortals," Kyia said, leading Alex and her friends over to the invisible rollercoaster.

The *Valispath* transported them through the palace and continued until they were outside and speeding across the radiant city. The sun was beginning to set behind the cliffs on the horizon and the fading light illuminated the shining Myrox all around them. Mystical trees glinted high above on the Golden Cliffs in the distance; waterfalls sparkled down into the valley like liquefied rays of light; and the river below glistened as if it contained the essence of a thousand stars. The view took Alex's breath away and she craned her neck to and fro as the *Valispath* moved them towards the top of the cliffs.

She expected the *Valispath* to stop there, but they continued on, speeding through the gold trees as they quickly turned to silver.

"Where are we going?" Alex yelled over the wind.

Kyia turned to look at Alex, one eyebrow quirked. "Raelia, of course. Where else?"

"The *Valispath* can take us straight there? Why didn't we use it the first time?"

"The Eternal Path can take us anywhere we want," Kyia told her. "And you wouldn't have had the chance to enjoy the beauty of Meya properly if you hadn't first witnessed it from the top of the Golden Cliffs."

Alex contemplated that as they continued speeding through the Silverwood and offered a meaningful, "Thank you, Kyia."

The *Meyarin* tilted her head in acknowledgement as the *Valispath* began to slow, soon coming to a smooth stop.

"This is where our journey ends," Kyia said when Alex and her friends were back on their feet.

"Sorry you didn't get to shoot one of us," Jordan said with a smirk.

Kyia mimicked his cocky expression. "There's still time if you want a demonstration?"

"Ah, no," he said, his smirk fading. "I'm good, thanks."

"Let's go before you say something stupid and end up with an arrow through your spleen," D.C. said, dragging Jordan and Bear into the mushroom circle.

Alex smiled at Kyia once more and moved to follow her friends, but she paused when the Meyarin reached out to gently grasp her arm.

"Alex," Kyia said quietly, using her name for the first time. "Be careful. Aven Dalmarta is ... He's the worst of our kind."

Alex blinked at the Meyarin's warning, touched by her concern.

"I will," she promised. "I hope we'll get a chance to meet again, Kyia."

"As do I," Kyia agreed with a slight smile, making her already stunning face even more radiant. With those parting words, she turned and walked away, disappearing into the trees surrounding Raelia.

Alex looked into the woods one last time then stepped over the mushroom boundary and approached her friends.

"Time to see how this return-trip deal works," Alex said. Her intent acted like a command, prompting a doorway to magically appear before them. With D.C., Jordan and Bear all following close behind her, Alex stepped straight through, willing it to open into the painting-and-tapestry-covered foyer of the Library.

"Home sweet home," Bear said once the doorway disappeared again behind them.

"What a day!" D.C.'s eyes were comically wide. "I can't believe we're still alive."

"I won't be for much longer if I don't eat something," Jordan said. "I'm starving."

His stomach rumbled as if to emphasise his words, and Alex realised how hungry she was as well. And tired. Her day had been exhausting, yet it was barely sunset.

"Food, then bed," she said. But she remembered something else and amended, "Food, Darrius, then bed."

Jordan pointed to her bleeding wound where Roka's blade had nicked her arm. "Food, *Fletcher*, Darrius, then bed," he corrected.

"I can barely feel it," Alex argued, but she knew he was right and nodded in agreement.

"Sounds like we have a plan," D.C. concluded, linking her arm through Alex's and leading the way up and out of the Tower.

Thirteen

Alex was jerked violently from her sleep that night when a bloodcurdling scream nearly ruptured her eardrums. She was out of bed and crouching in a defensive position before fully waking, frantically searching the darkened corners of the room for any trace of Aven who she feared had somehow broken into the dorm.

She could see nothing out of place, but the screaming continued as D.C. thrashed around in her bed, clawing at her covers and waving her hands wildly.

"Dix?" Alex called, rushing over to her friend. She reached out to restrain D.C.'s arms to keep them from smacking her in the face. "Wake up, Dix! *Wake up!*"

"*Noooo!*" D.C. wailed. The sound was heart-wrenching and it caused chills to trickle down Alex's spine.

D.C. continued to scream and fight, so Alex roughly shook her. When she finally woke, her demeanour changed almost instantly. One second she was screaming bloody murder, and the next she had her mouth closed and eyes wide open, looking up at Alex in confusion.

"Alex? What are you doing?" D.C. asked groggily, staring at her arms where Alex held them locked in a firm grasp.

"You were having a nightmare," Alex said, releasing her. "You were screaming and everything."

D.C. looked bewildered but then her expression cleared. Just as swiftly her eyes shadowed, and she looked away from Alex, swallowing thickly. "Sorry," she said. "I didn't mean to wake you."

"Hey, you can't help what you dream," Alex said. But then she remembered that sometimes D.C. actually *could* influence what she dreamed. Her friend's gift enabled her to dream *true* dreams—dreams that showed the future. When D.C. had those dreams, she could choose to relive the visions anytime she wanted to gather more information.

"Dix, was that ... Were you dreaming one of your, you know, *dreams*?" Alex asked.

D.C. looked up at Alex with eyes that were calmer than before, but still held a lingering trace of darkness.

"I'm sure it was nothing, Alex." Despite her confident words, she didn't sound certain. "I can barely remember it, so I think it was just a regular nightmare.

Usually I have much more clarity when I have true dreams."

"Do you want to talk about it?" Alex offered.

"N—no," D.C. said quickly. Then she cleared her throat as if to cover her abrupt answer. "I mean, it's late, and I'll probably have forgotten all about it by morning."

"You sure?" Alex asked, not wanting to upset D.C. when she looked so vulnerable. "You know I'm here if you want to talk."

"I'm good, but thanks. And sorry again for waking you."

Alex told her not to worry about it and made her way back to bed. While D.C. seemed to fall straight back to sleep, Alex had trouble relaxing. Try as she might, she couldn't get D.C.'s agonised screams out of her mind. But soon enough the events of her day in Meya and the exhaustion from having to relive every moment—except for the ones she promised Roka not to speak of—during her talk with Darrius caught up to her, and she drifted off into a restless sleep.

That was the first night D.C.'s screams woke Alex, but it wasn't the last.

Every night for the rest of the week Alex was woken by the terrified noises of her thrashing roommate. When confronted, D.C. adamantly refused to speak about her nightmares, continuing to claim they were nothing. And while the night terrors lasted only a few minutes, they were so anxiety-inducing that Alex was rarely able to sleep much afterwards.

Within a few days both girls had dark circles under their eyes, and their lack of proper rest hadn't gone unnoticed by their friends. But more worrying was that their exhaustion was beginning to cause problems in class.

D.C. was the first to reap the consequences when she failed to answer a question correctly in Medical Science. Professor Luranda ended up giving her a detention when her reply was, "Sorry, Professor. I was so bored that I zoned out for a moment there. Can you repeat the question?"

By the time Friday arrived, Alex was definitely feeling the effects of her barely-awake consciousness. Finn had nearly killed her that morning in PE, and she had nearly killed her entire class in Chemistry. Equestrian Skills had also royally sucked because she'd been so out of it during their forest ride that she'd ended up being coat-hangered by a tree. The impact had sent her flying off her horse and onto the ground, resulting in Tayla ordering her to go straight to the Medical Ward where Fletcher had thankfully treated her bruised ribs without comment.

If Alex thought things couldn't get any worse after that, she was soon proven wrong. While Fletcher had been fixing her up with pain meds and a Regenevator to increase the healing speed of her injury, the heavens had opened up, bringing a downpour of rain across the entire academy.

"Perfect," Alex groaned as soon as she stepped outside Gen-Sec and saw the liquid bucketing from the sky. Knowing she was going to end up soaked no matter what, she stepped out into the rain and began to jog over to the Arena for her Combat class. While she ran, her thoughts grumbled about the lack of roofing over the amphitheatre. Sure, she'd had to take the class out in the elements before—rain, hail, snow, shine, *everything*—but she wasn't in the mood to deal with the added inconvenience after the week she'd had.

Such was her luck that when the class actually started, the rain began falling even harder. Fabulous.

She made it halfway through the lesson before finally losing it.

"Fun, hey?" Brendan called over the violent sound of the downpour.

Alex could barely see him through the barrier of water. She could hardly see anything. But since they were supposed to be attacking each other, her lack of vision presented a serious problem.

"So much fun," she returned sarcastically.

The truth was, Alex's tolerance had reached its limit. But she continued to get the stuffing knocked out of her, knowing the class surely had to end soon. She was wet and miserable, and all she wanted was a long, hot shower and a good night's sleep. Was that too much to ask?

Fifteen minutes later, Brendan again yelled to her over the tumultuous noise. "I take it back—this isn't fun anymore!"

Alex grunted in agreement and kicked out at him. They were practising unarmed fighting techniques, so at least they didn't have the added danger of slipping on the muddy ground and impaling themselves on their blades. That was a positive, if nothing else.

"I'll tell you what," Brendan shouted. "Why don't you just let me win and we'll be allowed to finish?"

Ten minutes earlier, Karter had told the different pairs to move out of a practising stance and into an attacking mind frame. As soon as one person managed to overcome the other, the pairs could finish class for the day. It was an uncharacteristic offer from Karter, but his leniency was likely a result of him being unable see his students.

"Me?" Alex yelled back, ducking his fist. "Why do I have to lose? Why can't you let *me* win?"

She heard his faint snort over the cacophony of the rainstorm.

"Why is that funny?" she demanded, swiping her leg out towards where she thought he was. The rain was so blinding that she missed him by about three feet, and she heard him laugh even harder at her failed attempt.

"We both know you're not going to beat me, Alex, and no one would believe us if we acted like you did," he said. "Sure, you're heaps better than you were, but I've been in Epsilon Combat for *years* longer than you. And I'm an apprentice, while you're just a fourth year. You're good, but you're not *that* good."

Normally Alex could handle the banter of the Combat boys, knowing they used taunts to throw off their opponents. But Brendan's mockery just fuelled the fire that sparked from Alex's exhausted state of mind.

She closed her eyes and took a deep breath to still her rising irritation, and her newly determined peace brought a sense of quiet that she'd only experienced once before. Alex suddenly *felt* everything around her. When she opened her eyes, she could see everything so much clearer than before. She watched in amazement as single raindrops fell from the sky in slow motion. She could see the other boys in her Combat class who were spread around the Arena and fighting awkwardly due to their limited vision. It was like switching from a static video to high definition; the added detail was startling. And when she threw her hand out towards Brendan—whom she could now see with phenomenal clarity—he wasn't fast enough to block her blow.

Another punch, an elbow to his stomach, a sideswipe of her foot, and a final roundhouse kick to his torso landed him on his backside with her standing like an avenging angel over his winded body.

"How—How—?" he stuttered, looking up at her in awe as the rain fell onto his mud-splattered face.

"Cat got your tongue, Labinsky?" she said, holding out a hand to help him to his feet.

As if knowing their fight was over, the rain began to ease slightly. Of course.

"How did you move so fast?" he asked when he was standing again.

She brushed a wet lock of hair behind her ear. "What are you talking about?"

"You were like a blur," Brendan said, lowering his voice to a more normal level as the rain continued to lessen. "I barely even saw you move."

"That's because it was raining," Alex said. "The water was so thick I couldn't see you either."

But despite her words, she couldn't ignore the fear that prickled up her spine. At the end of their fight, she definitely had seen him. And she knew how.

"No," he said, shaking his head adamantly. "I mean, yeah, the rain was thick and it made seeing you difficult, but I'm talking about the speed of your attacks. You were insanely fast."

Alex felt her breath catch with his admission but she forced herself to remain calm, even when her memory flashed an image of the cuts and nicks she'd given Roka in their fight a week ago. Had she somehow managed to tap into not only the increased sight, but also the Meyarin attribute of speed during her fight with Brendan? That was definitely a dangerous path to tread. She would have to be very careful in the future.

"I don't know what you're talking about," Alex told him, faking indifference.

"You said it yourself; I'm still not that great a fighter. I think the rain distorted what you think you saw and I just got a few lucky hits in."

Brendan seemed to think about that as they walked to where Karter was waiting. Kaiden and Declan were already standing with him, but Nick and Sebastian had yet to finish their match.

"Yeah, I guess you're right," Brendan accepted before they reached the others. "Maybe you did just get lucky."

Alex tried not to look too relieved.

"Labinsky, Jennings, you're done?" Karter asked gruffly, wiping the rain off his face. It was now only drizzling lightly and Alex had to force herself to not scowl up at the sky.

"Yes, sir," Brendan answered.

"You hurt, Jennings?" Karter asked.

Alex turned to him. "Hurt?"

"Yes, hurt," he repeated. "Injured. Wounded. Damaged in any way."

She looked at him in bewilderment. Sure, she often sustained injuries during Combat class, but rarely did Karter ask her personally if she was okay unless it was obvious she was in a bad state. Otherwise it was just expected that she—and her classmates—would go and see Fletcher if necessary. After class ended.

"No more than usual, sir," she told him honestly. Just like after every Combat class, she was probably covered in bruises, but nothing more serious.

He frowned at her as though she'd said something wrong, then turned to look at Brendan. The apprentice must have been able to read his expression better than Alex, since he quietly mumbled something she couldn't hear.

"Speak up, Labinsky," Karter ordered.

"I said, Alex isn't hurt because she didn't lose the fight."

Karter's eyes flickered in surprise before his face reverted to its natural stoic expression. "Is that so?"

"I just got lucky," Alex said, repeating what she'd told Brendan.

Karter peered intently at her. "Lucky or not, I expect you to keep it up."

He then told Alex, Brendan, Declan and Kaiden that, as per his earlier agreement, they could leave early. Sebastian and Nick would have to continue until one of them won their fight.

As they sloshed their way out of the Arena and up the hill towards the dorm building, the boys conversed with one another while Alex's mind wandered to her comfy bed. Maybe she would get a proper sleep that night for the first time all week.

Just as she was contemplating skipping dinner and going straight to bed, a voice broke through the tired haze of her mind.

"Are you excited about this weekend?"

She looked questioningly at Kaiden as he stepped up beside her. "This weekend?"

"Yeah, you know—our **SAS** getaway?"

Alex stared at him blankly and his lips quirked at her expression.

"Were you paying any attention last night?" he asked. "I mean, I know you got caught in three—or was it four?—of Hunter's traps, but I thought you were just trying to avoid Skyla. I didn't realise you were that out of it."

"I've had a lot on my mind lately," Alex said.

Kaiden's face was sincere but his eyes were laughing at her. "I'm sure you have."

"All right, Mr. I-Know-Something-You-Don't-Know," she said. "What was it that I should've been listening to last night?"

"Well, since you asked so nicely," he said with a wry grin, "tomorrow we have an overnight assessment for **SAS**. We're taking off for the whole weekend, coming back on Sunday night."

Alex groaned. That was the last thing she needed after the week she'd had. But then again, she might actually get a good night's sleep if she was away from D.C.'s screams.

Almost immediately, Alex felt bad for thinking such a thought. It wasn't like her roommate chose to have the nightmares. D.C. was the victim of her own subconscious mind.

"What are you thinking about?" Kaiden asked.

Alex wondered what her expression must have revealed for him to be looking at her with such curiosity, and she quickly relaxed her face. "Nothing. Just wondering what clothes I should pack."

He laughed. "Wow, you're really bad at lying."

She lowered her eyes but didn't try to deny his accusation. Fortunately, he let the matter drop.

"I guess I'll see you in the morning," he said, and she realised they'd already reached the dorm building.

"Yeah, sure," she replied, giving him a tired smile. She headed up the stairs to her room, quietly closing the door when she noticed D.C. curled up in bed.

"Hey," D.C. said softly, rolling over to face her.

"Hey, yourself," Alex returned, crossing the room to sit beside her friend. "Are you okay?"

"Yeah," D.C. said. "Finn let us skip PE because of the rain, so I came back for a nap."

"Really?"

D.C. rubbed her eyes. "Yeah, I was tired."

"No," Alex said, chuckling, "I meant that I was surprised Finn let you out of class. Karter made us keep going."

"You're still back earlier than usual," D.C. said, squinting at the time displayed on her ComTCD resting on her bedside table.

"Yeah, by like, ten minutes," Alex said. "No nanna nap for me, unfortunately."

D.C.'s face crumpled in apology. "Sorry. I know you haven't been sleeping well. And I know that's my fault."

"You can't help it," Alex said with a tired shrug. "And I'll be gone this weekend for SAS anyway, so maybe having the room to yourself will help you move on from whatever is causing the ... episodes."

"Episodes?" D.C. repeated. "You make me sound like a crazy person."

"You know what I mean," Alex said. And then she couldn't resist adding, "And you are a crazy person. Acceptance is the first step to a good, healthy recovery."

D.C.'s lips twitched. "Are you speaking from experience?"

"Me? Crazy?" Alex placed her hand dramatically against her chest.

"You're such a weirdo," D.C. said, shaking her head. "And at this exact moment, you also happen to be a weirdo who is dripping water all over my bed. Go and clean yourself up, would you?"

"Your wish is my command," Alex said with a salute, and she stood up and trudged over to their bathroom for a quick shower before dinner.

***

"This is going to be so awesome!"

"If you say so," Alex mumbled around a yawn the next morning. Once again she'd had little sleep during the night, and she couldn't muster the same amount of enthusiasm as Jordan for their upcoming weekend.

One foot in front of the other, she mentally chanted as she followed her friend down to where their **SAS** class was due to meet at the forest. Even her internal voice sounded weary.

While Jordan continued to babble about what he thought the overnight trip would bring, Alex secretly hoped Hunter would have a change of heart and cancel—or perhaps reschedule to another time.

Unfortunately, he did neither.

"Listen up, everyone," Hunter said when he appeared out of the forest like a wisp of smoke. "This weekend you're going off-campus for some field training. I want you all to grab the bag with your name and inside you'll find everything you need to survive until tomorrow evening." He pointed to a cluster of backpacks under a tree and gestured for everyone to move forward.

When Alex picked up the pack labelled with her name, she had to stifle a grunt—it was much heavier than she'd expected. She watched in bafflement when the much smaller Pipsqueak lifted her own bag with ease, and even the always-whining Skyla didn't complain when she strapped hers to her back. Alex resisted the temptation to see if someone had put rocks in her pack as a joke as she heaved it across her shoulders.

"This assignment is about teamwork," Hunter instructed the group. "You'll need to utilise the skills you've already learned while being innovative enough to adapt to an unknown environment." Hunter pointed to the tree where they'd picked up the bags. Just above head height was an arrow lodged in its bark. "This arrow is specially made to transport you to your destination. Once there, you'll need to follow a set of instructions giving you tasks to complete before the weekend is over. After you've finished, you'll find another arrow which will return you here tomorrow evening. You may arrive earlier or later depending on how well you follow the instructions, but you can be sure of one thing: the only way for you to get back here is by completing the tasks and finishing the assignment."

This is so going to end badly, Alex thought.

"Any questions?" Hunter asked. He may have given them an opening but it was clear he didn't think there was anything left to say.

Alex, however, had many questions—the most prominent of which was whether she could stay behind and let everyone else enjoy the 'fun' field trip without her. But since she already knew the answer, she didn't waste her breath.

Her other concern involved being away from the protective wards of the academy. What if Aven discovered she was gone and decided to come after her? But she figured Hunter had to have spoken with

Darrius about the trip, and the headmaster would never let her leave if he thought she would be in any danger. Besides, she was too tired to start up a conversation that was sure to arouse the curiosity of her classmates. Definitely not worth it.

"You can leave when you're ready," Hunter said when no one responded. "I'll see you all tomorrow evening."

"You're not coming with us?" Alex blurted out. Weren't they going to be supervised?

"Are you afraid of the dark, Alex?"

"What? No—I just—"

"Then I see no need for me to accompany you," Hunter said, cutting her off.

She wondered how he might have responded if she'd lied and claimed she was scared of the dark, but he probably would have just given the same answer.

"Whatever," Alex mumbled, lacking the energy to argue her point. It seemed they would, in fact, be camping unsupervised. Flipping fantastic. An image of the bloodthirsty Hyroa came to Alex's mind and she shuddered, but then she forced herself to remember that they were rare creatures and the likelihood of running into another one was slim to none. Hopefully.

"Right, then," Hunter said when he could see that Alex had let the matter drop. "The sooner you leave, the sooner you'll return. I recommend you make use of the daylight. Night falls quickly where you're going."

Shuddering, Alex dutifully followed her classmates and stepped up to touch the Bubbler-infused arrow. With a whirl of colourful motion she was whisked away from the Ezera Forest only to land shakily in her new environment.

Someone reached out to help steady her and she turned to send them a grateful smile.

"You good?" Kaiden asked.

"Yeah, thanks," she said, and he removed his hand from her arm.

"Come check this out, Alex!" Jordan called.

She glanced towards her friend and gasped at the sight in front of her. "Wow," she whispered, peering out over what seemed to be the entire world.

They'd landed high up in the middle of a cluster of mountains, with three-hundred-and-sixty-degree views all around. Way off in the distance, the land smoothed out until all traces of the woodsy scenery transformed into a never-ending yellow sparseness.

Blink waved a piece of paper around, breaking Alex's wandering gaze. "Do you guys want the good news or the bad news?"

"Good news," Declan said, speaking for everyone.

"According to the Ghost-Master's map here, it looks like we're in the Durungan Ranges," Blink told them.

Alex wasn't sure how that was good news. She didn't know much about the mountain range that spanned the width of Medora, but she guessed it would make for a challenging weekend expedition.

"What's the bad news?" Declan asked.

Blink sent him a lopsided smile. "Bro, we're in the Durungan Ranges. That's, like, so hard-core."

"But you said that was the good news," Alex spoke up, confused. "How is that both good and bad news? And what are we supposed to do here?"

"Well, Alexerina," Blink said, and Alex shot him a warning look at the nickname, "if I'm reading this ultra-military-style map right, it looks like we have to traverse the Ranges. I don't know about you guys, but I'm hungry just thinking about it. Who else agrees that we should break for a snack?"

"Give that to me," Pipsqueak demanded, snatching the paper from him and striding over to the rest of the group.

Alex looked over the smaller girl's shoulder at the basic map Hunter had drawn for them.

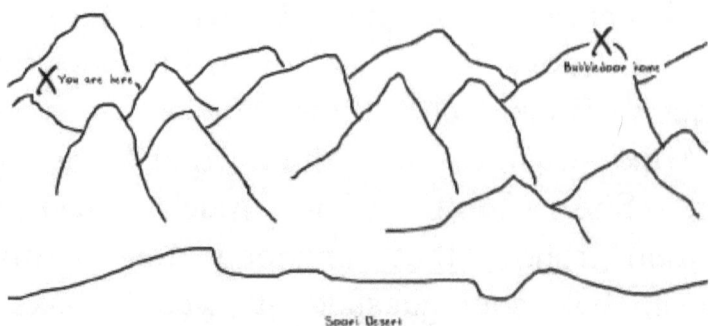

"We can't walk that far by tomorrow night!" Alex exclaimed.

"I'm sure we don't have to walk the entire way," Jordan said, looking at her in a way that silently reminded her of Medora's advanced technology.

"I know that. But still..." Alex trailed off, not sure how to recover from her outburst. Fortunately, everyone else was too busy perusing the map to notice.

"This is obviously Hunter's first instruction for us," Tom said. "I say we take an inventory of what supplies we have in our packs and start walking until we find our next clue."

It was a good suggestion so they sat around in a circle and unloaded their bags to inspect the contents. It turned out that their items were almost identical. Each pack held a waterproof sleeping bag, a bottle of water, an assortment of energy bars and dehydrated foods, an emergency medical kit, a compass, a box of matches and a hunting knife.

Each pack also had one item that was unique to its owner. Kaiden's was a bow with a single arrow; Declan's was a self-inflating raft; Tom's bag contained a banjo-like stringed instrument; Pipsqueak was pleased to discover a fluffy pillow amongst her possessions; Skyla was equally pleased with the hand-held mirror and makeup collection she'd been given; Blink looked overjoyed with the extra food rations in his pack; Jordan pulled a long, sturdy-looking rope out of his bag; and Alex ... well, there was a reason her bag felt so weighty. At the very bottom of her pack, she found a large and extremely heavy book titled, *A Collection of Children's Stories*.

"Seriously?" she said, heaving the tome from her bag to show the others. They sniggered at the look on her face. "Oh, come on! Don't tell me I have to lug this thing over these mountains? Pip, do you want to swap?"

Pipsqueak snorted. "Keep dreaming, Alex. That's what I'll be doing on my lovely, soft pillow later tonight."

"Rub it in, why don't you?" Alex grumbled, staring daggers at the book in her hands. Of all the things for Hunter to give her, why a children's storybook? And a huge one at that?

"We should get moving," said Tom. "I'll take the lead with Kaiden and Declan, since we've been in the class for the longest. And until we figure out what's going on and where we're headed, all of us should keep an eye on our surroundings."

Alex didn't mind deferring to them, but someone else *did* have a problem with it.

"You forgot about me," Skyla said. "I've been in this class for as long as Kaiden and Declan. How could you forget about me?"

Her eyes actually began to fill with tears, and Tom backtracked quickly to avoid the impending waterworks.

"Of course I didn't forget about you, Skyla," he said hurriedly. "In fact, I trust your ability so much that I think you should bring up the rear. They say that the most experienced person should always be at the back to make sure no one falls behind."

Skyla scrunched up her face, thinking hard about his explanation, and then smiled brightly. "You're right. I am the most experienced person—and the most important. I should definitely be at the back. Don't worry, everyone, I'll keep you safe."

"What a nutcase," Jordan mumbled, loud enough for only Alex to hear.

Fortunately, her muffled laughter was covered by the sound of the rest of them rising to their feet.

Tom crosschecked his compass to the map then started leading the group on their journey. After three hours of making their way down the mountain, they rested at the base for a drink and some morning tea. Barely any time passed before they were on their feet again and trekking up the next, much steeper incline. They paused for lunch when Kaiden spotted an arrow sticking out of a tree with a note that read:

Stop here for lunch.

Thanks, Hunter. Very helpful, thought Alex.

It was the middle of the afternoon by the time they reached the top of the mountain. Unlike the lush green scenery on the way up, the peak was bare of trees. It was solid, grey, craggy rock. Glancing over at the other mountains surrounding them, Alex was comforted by the fact that the one they stood on wasn't snow-covered like most of the rest. They evidently weren't as high as most of the Ranges around them, and she was grateful they'd only had to climb the smaller peak.

So far, anyway.

While their journey had been steep, they hadn't had to use Jordan's rope, much to Alex's relief. But that relief was short lived when she saw what lay ahead of them.

Cutting directly through their path across the mountain was a crevasse gouged deep into the rock at least fifty feet wide. It was as if the mountain had been cleaved in two, since the vertical drop fell straight down to the ground way, way below them, where a rapidly churning river flowed at the very bottom.

"Looks like we'll have to backtrack," Pipsqueak said, squinting down at the violent water far beneath them. "Let's just hope we can find a way to cut across the river."

"I think we have different instructions," Declan said, pointing to an arrow that was rooted in a boulder nearby. He retrieved the paper scrawled with Hunter's words and looked grimly at the rest of them.

"What does it say?" Jordan asked.

Declan turned the note around so everyone could read Hunter's instructions.
Cross with caution. It's a long fall.

"No. Way."
Alex wasn't sure if the words were hers or someone else's, but it was likely what they were all thinking.
"Ghost is like, *the man*," Blink said with reverence.
"Shut up, Blink," Pipsqueak said.
"How are we going to do this?" Tom asked the group.
Pipsqueak gaped at him. "You can't seriously be considering crossing here?"
"That's what we've been told to do," Declan pointed out. "So, there must be a way."
"There is," Kaiden spoke up. "But I don't think any of you will like it."

Fourteen

They all looked at Kaiden questioningly as he unstrapped his bow and the single arrow that came with it. Alex hadn't paid close attention to it before, but now she could see that it wasn't like a normal arrow, and the bow was unique as well. Both of them appeared to be made of some kind of heavy, metallic substance. The arrowhead was different too, with little grooves spiking in the opposite direction to prevent it from being pulled out of a target. At the bottom end of the arrow was another surprise: instead of it finishing with the normal feathery decoration, the metal curled into a loop with a hollow centre.

Understanding dawned on Alex and she looked at Kaiden, aghast. "Please tell me you're not thinking what I think you're thinking?"

Despite their predicament, the corner of his mouth quirked in amusement. "That depends on what you think I'm thinking, or not thinking."

"I think you know what I think you're thinking—just like I think you know what I hope you're not thinking."

His smile widened and everyone stared at them.

"I'd like to know what you're both thinking, because I'm sure lost," Jordan said, subtly raising his eyebrows at Alex and flicking a speculative glance between her and Kaiden.

She felt her face heat up under his perceptive gaze, but Kaiden saved her from her discomfort when he jumped in with his explanation.

"I think we have to tie Jordan's rope to my arrow and shoot it into the rock over on the other side of the crevasse," he said. "Then we use it to make our way across."

"Just like that?" Pipsqueak said, throwing her hands on her hips. "Why didn't you say it would be so simple?"

"Hey, it's not his fault we're stuck in this situation," Alex defended. Normally she liked Pipsqueak, but her attitude wasn't helping the situation.

Pipsqueak turned to glare at Alex as if the entire assignment was her fault, but before either of them could say anything more, they were interrupted.

"I don't see why we can't just fly across," Skyla said loftily.

Everyone turned to look at the blond girl who was holding her mirror in front of her face and reapplying her lip gloss.

No one seemed to know how to respond to her peculiar statement, but Jordan tentatively tried to speak up without upsetting her delicate disposition.

"Um, Skyla, how exactly would we fly across?"

She snorted and snapped her makeup case closed. "We'd make wings, obviously."

Alex fought off the irrational urge to laugh. When it appeared that no one else knew what to say, she diplomatically said, "That's a great idea, Skyla. But since Kaiden came up with a solution first, it's only fair that we try his way before giving any other ideas a go. If his arrow doesn't work, then we'll be sure to discuss your plan."

Alex couldn't believe she'd actually just agreed to try Kaiden's suicidal proposal, but compared to making wings, it almost sounded like a sane strategy.

Only almost.

"I guess that's fair," Skyla begrudgingly agreed. "But I still think my idea is better."

Alex chose to let the conversation end there, and she turned to find Kaiden watching her with amusement.

"What?"

He flashed her a humour-filled grin but shook his head. "Nothing."

"How are we going to do this?" Tom asked, indicating to the arrow in Kaiden's hand. "Obviously you shoot it over there and hope it'll hold us, but what's going to keep the rope on this side?"

He had a valid point. But Hunter had already provided the solution.

"We tie it to Hunter's arrow," Alex answered, pointing to the shaft embedded in the boulder where Declan found the note. It was made of the same metallic substance as the weapon Kaiden held—looped end and all—and Alex had no doubt that it was intended for this purpose.

"Let's do this," Declan said, giving Kaiden an encouraging clap on the back.

Jordan handed the rope over to Kaiden who knotted it securely around the loop at the end of the embedded arrow. After tugging against it to make sure it held, he unwound the remainder of the coiled rope and tied the other end to the arrow in his hands.

As a group, they walked to the edge of the crevasse.

"Shoot straight, Kaid," Declan said, as Kaiden strung the bow and pulled it tight.

Pausing for barely a second to aim, Kaiden released the arrow, and it pierced firmly into the rock wall on the other side of the fissure. It was a perfect shot, with the arrow sticking out close to the top of the crevasse—just enough for the rock to not crumble under their weight, but not too far that they wouldn't be able to pull themselves up.

Perfect shot or not, butterflies began to trample around Alex's stomach at the idea of crossing the ravine.

"Who wants to be the test dummy?" Declan asked, cracking his knuckles with anticipation.

No one was eager to raise a hand, and after a few tense moments, Kaiden spoke up. "I made the shot. I'll go first."

Alex reached out and clutched Jordan's arm as Kaiden secured his backpack over his shoulders and stepped up to the rope.

"Here goes nothing," he said, lowering his body over the edge.

Only when Kaiden was sure the rope would hold his weight did he begin to move, using a hand-over-hand approach to swiftly make his way across the ravine. He made it look effortless, but Alex didn't take a proper breath until he reached the other side and drew himself up to safety.

"Are you going to let go of me now?" Jordan asked her with a knowing smirk.

She dug her fingernails in a little deeper for a vindictive moment before she released him, choosing to ignore his amused chuckle.

"Who's next?" Declan asked.

One by one they began to make their way across the crevasse. Blink followed after Kaiden, locking his legs around the rope and pulling himself across backwards. Skyla copied his example, while Jordan adopted Kaiden's faster—if less secure—hand-over-hand approach.

Just as Alex watched Tom pull himself to safety, she heard Pipsqueak's shaky voice.

"I don't have very good upper body strength," the waif-like girl said. "What if I fall?"

"You won't fall," Alex assured her classmate, who appeared to be very close to hyperventilating. "You'll be fine."

"You promise?" Pipsqueak asked, her big blue eyes staring at Alex as if the words alone would keep her safe.

"I promise," Alex said. Really, what else *could* she say? Gone was the snarky girl from earlier, and in her place was a scared teenager needing reassurance—something that Alex could provide.

"Okay," Pipsqueak whispered, and she lowered her body over the edge and quickly wrapped her legs around the rope.

The rest of them shouted encouragement and watched as she pulled herself slowly but surely along. But something happened when she was halfway across and, for whatever reason, she stopped moving forward.

"What's she doing?" Declan asked Alex, the two of them the only ones left to cross.

"I have no idea," she answered, but her stomach tightened at the sight of her classmate dangling motionless so high above the ravine.

"What's the hold-up, Pip?" Declan called.

Pipsqueak didn't answer, but Alex could see that something was wrong when she pulled herself in closer to the rope, almost as if trying to hug it tightly. Even from where Alex was standing, she could see the tremors shaking Pip's body and vibrating along the rope.

"I think she's having a panic attack," Alex whispered fearfully.

Declan groaned. "Worst possible timing."

From the other side of the ravine, their classmates were calling out to the frozen girl too, but she was oblivious to everything around her.

"What are we supposed to do?" Declan asked. "How do we calm her down? If she doesn't move soon, she's going to get tired and..."

Alex didn't need to hear the end of his sentence to know where the 'and...' led.

Tugging firmly on the rope, she said, "How much weight can this hold?"

He looked at it thoughtfully. "Honestly, I'm not sure."

That wasn't the answer Alex wanted, but she'd have to make do with it. "Do me a favour and hold onto it, just in case."

He realised what she intended to do, and nodded, walking to the boulder where Hunter's arrow was lodged into the rock. He gripped the rope and braced himself in preparation for something that *hopefully* wouldn't be necessary.

Alex looked across the ravine to her other classmates and saw they must have noticed Declan's position, as Kaiden and Jordan were now leaning over the edge, supporting the rope on their side. Tom and Blink took up positions behind them to hold onto them if necessary. And Skyla ... well, she did nothing, but that was to be expected.

"Hang on, Pip, I'm coming," Alex called out, deciding then and there that she would never again promise anyone anything in the heat of the moment.

Once her backpack was secured, she wrapped her legs around the rope and dropped over the edge, pulling herself along swiftly.

Don't look down. Just don't look down, she chanted to herself with each swaying pull across the rope.

When Alex approached the halfway mark, she wasn't sure what to do next. Her head was directly behind Pipsqueak's feet, which made having a conversation difficult, but she had to try.

"Pip?"

The other girl didn't answer, so Alex unlocked one of her hands and reached out to touch Pipsqueak's trembling leg.

"*Pip!*" Alex said, much louder this time, and she squeezed her classmate's leg for emphasis. "We need to move!"

Like a whisper in the wind, Pipsqueak's words came to her. "So high. We're *so* high."

"Phillipa Squeaker!" Alex all but screamed. "Snap out of it!"

Pipsqueak continued to babble about the height and Alex realised her words were having no effect whatsoever on her classmate's frozen state.

She had to find a way to calm Pipsqueak. If she were calmer, then she might be able to start moving again.

Alex hadn't spent much time inspecting her emergency medical kit, but she'd heard one of the others scoffing about a fast-acting relaxant. That sounded exactly like what Pip needed. The only problem was that Alex had no idea how to get the kit out of her backpack.

"Just keep holding on, Pip," she said, realising what she had to do. "We'll get you out of here in a minute. I promised, remember?"

Fuelled by her own determined words, Alex made sure her legs were secured as tightly as possible, took a fortifying breath and released her hands until she was dangling upside down in mid-air. She ignored the startled yells from her classmates and focused on retrieving the medicine as fast as possible.

Releasing one strap first and then the other, she craned her neck as she lifted the bag to unzip the main pocket and glanced inside. Being upside-down was disorienting, but she managed to reach a hand in and feel around until she found the medical kit.

A strong gust of wind caught her off-guard and for one terrifying moment she swung uncontrollably. Her legs were almost cramping with the effort of staying attached to the rope. Once she settled again, she wrapped the strap of the backpack around one arm and opened the medical kit, finding the small spray bottle she needed. She clenched it between her teeth and threw everything else into the bag before manoeuvring—quite impressively, in her opinion—the pack onto her back. Muscles screaming, she pulled herself up to grasp the rope again.

After taking a moment to ease her heavy breathing, Alex let go with one hand to retrieve the medicine from her mouth so she could check the instructions. Somehow she had to spray it directly into Pip's face so that the other girl inhaled the contents, and the effect would be instantaneous.

"You so owe me for this, Pip," Alex muttered, placing the medicine between her teeth once more.

She crawled as close to Pipsqueak as possible before she unlocked her legs and let them drop beneath her. It was a precarious position, but the only way she could get to Pip's face was by moving over to her other side.

"Just keep holding on," Alex encouraged around the spray bottle in her mouth.

She awkwardly reached around Pip's body with one arm to grip the rope in the small gap between the other girl's limbs. The new position was almost impossible to hold, and Alex had to hastily swing through the air when she felt her grip slipping.

She released a trembling breath as soon as she was on the other side of Pip and wasted no time in pulling her legs up to lock her body securely around the rope again.

"Time for you to wake up now," Alex gritted out, after taking the medicine from her mouth again.

Pip's protective body-cocoon meant that her head was tilted away from Alex, but it was easy enough to move the bottle into position and spray the fine mist into her face.

Just like the label said, the effect was instantaneous, but Alex hadn't taken into account the full extent of what 'sudden relaxation' actually meant.

"NO!" Alex screamed when Pip's limbs loosened their grip entirely.

Never before had Alex been so grateful for her well-honed reflexes. With barely a split second to react, she let go of the spray bottle and released her other hand from the rope to reach out and catch

Pipsqueak, who had dropped like a dead weight.

"Oh, hey!" Pipsqueak said happily. Her eyes were glazed as she looked up at Alex who was once again dangling upside-down and straining to keep them both from plummeting into the crevasse. Only her steel grip on Pipsqueak's forearms kept the other girl from falling. But the strength required to hold the both of them in the air was taking its toll on Alex and she knew she wouldn't last long if Pip didn't help.

"Pip, you need to snap out of it!" Alex said desperately.

"Are we flying, Alex?" Pipsqueak asked, with a dazed smile on her face. "This is fun. We should've listened to Skyla and made wings. Then we could fly all the time."

"*Pipsqueak!*" Alex shouted. Her body was being stretched painfully from head to toe, with her muscles burning from the strain of dangling for so long.

"Why are you yelling at me?" Pipsqueak asked. "That's not very nice. Oh, look! It's Kaiden. Hi, Kaiden!"

"Pip, what are you—"

Alex didn't get a chance to finish her question before she felt something warm brush up against her side. The rope had been wobbling so much from her and Pipsqueak that she hadn't realised someone else was climbing along it. But when she turned her head and saw Kaiden hanging upside-down directly beside her, she released a shaky breath of relief.

Without saying anything, he reached out and grabbed Pipsqueak's arm just a little further along from where Alex's grip ended, transferring most of her weight into his hands.

"Hey, Pip, how do you feel about a piggyback ride?" he asked the drugged girl.

"Yay!" she cried, and Alex sucked in a painful breath when Pipsqueak bounced around with excitement.

"How are you holding up, Alex?" Kaiden's quiet voice held a tone that she couldn't decipher, and she wished she could turn around again to see his expression.

"I'm ... hanging in there," she answered in a strained voice. He didn't laugh, so she guessed it wasn't the best time to joke about their current predicament.

He'd taken the bulk of Pip's weight from her, but Alex was almost completely drained. She needed to get on solid ground, and soon.

"I'll need you to help me get back upright so we can start moving," Kaiden told her. "We'll both have to reach up and grab the rope with one hand and pull her up together. Do you think you can manage that?"

"I think so," Alex said, knowing she would have to even though she felt like her body was about to tear in two. "Will you be able to carry her? She might be small, but she's heavy."

"I take offence to that," Pipsqueak said moodily. It seemed like her emotions were all over the place because of the relaxant.

"We have a very important mission for you, Pip," Kaiden said. "Do you think you're up to it?"

"You bet I am!" she said, excitement replacing her moodiness.

"In a moment when we're all back up near the rope, I'm going to need you to climb onto me for your piggyback ride. You'll have to hold on *really* tight because we're going to race against Alex and we'll lose if you let go. You don't want to lose, do you?"

"No way," Pipsqueak said, sounding like a small child. "We're so going to win. I promise I'll hold on tight."

"Good girl," Kaiden said, as if he truly was talking to a child. "On three, Alex?"

"One," she said, starting the count.

"Two," Kaiden continued.

"Three," they said together, and they both strained upwards for the rope with their free hands and pulled Pipsqueak up between them. Alex sucked in a terrified breath when Kaiden dropped his legs immediately, dangling by one white-knuckled hand while he helped Pipsqueak wrap her legs around his waist. Once she was secure, Alex released Pip so she could wrap her arms around Kaiden's neck, which left him free to grasp the rope with both hands again.

"Ready?" he called back to Alex.

"Just go!"

With her legs cramped, Alex had to use Kaiden's hand-over-hand method to cross the remaining distance of the ravine. When Tom and Jordan helped pull her up onto solid ground after Pipsqueak and Kaiden, she promptly rolled away from the edge far enough to curl into a ball, waiting for her trembling limbs to relax.

"Alex? Alex! Are you okay?" came Jordan's frantic voice.

"Define 'okay'," she said shakily.

He didn't answer, but she felt someone reach out to take her backpack and she mumbled her thanks.

She heard Tom call out for Declan to come across, and only when she heard the big guy's voice amongst the rest of them did she open her eyes and sit up from her collapsed position. Her body screamed at the move, and she almost bit through her lip to hold back a moan of pain as she began to massage her aching limbs.

Her classmates noticed her movement and began to cluster around her.

"Whoa, that was just ... whoa..." Blink said, apparently beyond a proper sentence.

Alex shook her head at him and continued to stretch out her cramped everything.

"Here, this should help," Jordan said, kneeling beside her with a light green vial of pain relief medicine.

She took it from him gratefully and swallowed it in one go. Her pain disappeared almost immediately and her muscles instantly relaxed. Jordan then pulled her to her feet and wrapped his arms around her. He held her tight against his trembling body, causing Alex to realise just how much she must have worried him.

When he dropped his arms, he moved his hands to her shoulders and looked her sternly in the eyes. "You better not pull a stunt like that ever again."

"I couldn't just leave her, Jordan," she said quietly. "I promised."

He sighed and released her to run his hands through his hair. "I know. But you have no idea what it was like watching you out there. That was just ... I don't even know what to say! I'm supposed to be looking out for you. Dix will *kill* me when she finds out about this. And Bear will find a way to revive me only so he can kill me again. Either way, I'm a dead man. And rightly so."

Alex couldn't bring herself to feel annoyed by his overprotective nature, so she smiled reassuringly and said, "They won't be able to kill you if they don't find out. It can be our little secret."

Jordan huffed out a disbelieving breath, but when she nudged him with her elbow he smiled back at her.

"Eugh. You two are so gag-worthy," Skyla said. "How long have you been together, anyway?"

"Pipe down, Blondie," Pipsqueak said, her expression dazed from the relaxant. "Love is a beautiful thing. I think they're adorable."

Alex looked at Jordan in mortification.

"That's not a very nice face, sweetheart," Jordan said jokingly as he wrapped his arm around her shoulders. He smirked at her when she shot him a disgruntled look and tried to struggle out of his grasp.

"We are not having this conversation," Alex informed everyone. "But, for the record, Jordan is one of my best friends. Emphasis on 'friend'. I can't believe that after what we've just gone through, you're all wondering about something as unimportant as my love life!"

"So you *do* have a love life?" Skyla asked eagerly.

"Unbelievable," Alex muttered, and she turned away from them and stalked over to where someone had placed her backpack. She pulled out her water bottle and took a swig, waiting for the conversation to move on before she joined them again.

"They're just trying to ease the tension."

Alex glowered sullenly at Kaiden when he knelt beside her and reached for his own water.

"I don't see how asking about my relationship status helps," she said. "And it's none of their business, anyway."

"It was only Skyla and Pip who asked," Kaiden pointed out. "The former we know is an airhead, and the latter is currently as high as the clouds. Maybe give them a little leeway, considering."

"I had no idea the spray would do that to her," Alex admitted, her annoyance dissolving as the horror of the memory caught up to her. "She wouldn't do anything. It was like she couldn't hear me. I thought if I got her to calm down, she'd be able to move again. I didn't know what else to do."

"You were incredible," Kaiden said, holding her gaze. "What you did was amazing."

"She *fell* because of what I did," Alex said, remembering the terrifying moment when Pip dropped from the rope. "She could have died."

Kaiden reached out to rest his hand on top of hers. "You caught her."

"I was stupid."

"You were brave."

Looking into his serious eyes, she almost believed him. "We would've fallen if you hadn't come to help," she whispered.

"I don't believe that. You would've found a way to get both of you safely across."

Alex had no response for that, and she lowered her gaze to look at his hand still covering her own. He squeezed lightly and only let go at the sound of someone clearing their throat.

"We—Uh—We should probably get going," said Tom, shuffling his feet and looking uncomfortable.

Alex watched as he hurried off to round up the others, and she turned to look at Kaiden questioningly. "What's up with him?"

Kaiden bit back a smile and rose to his feet, helping her up with him. Despite his amused expression, he didn't answer her question. Instead, he told her something else.

"We found Hunter's next arrow while we were waiting for everyone to cross."

"Fantastic," Alex muttered. "Do we get to throw ourselves off another cliff?"

Kaiden glanced at her. "Don't even joke about that."

"Too early?"

"Definitely. And don't get me started on your 'hanging in there' comment."

She laughed lightly and ignored the playful glare he sent her. "I was quite proud of my wit at the time."

He shook his head at her and she was denied a response when the rest of their classmates came over to collect their backpacks. Pipsqueak was humming quietly to herself and Alex felt a pang of concern.

"How long until she's normal again?"

"Depends," Tom answered. "Usually people sleep it off."

"So, we have to wait until she wakes up tomorrow?" Alex clarified.

At Tom's nod, Jordan dryly said what they were all thinking. "This should be fun."

The sarcasm wasn't lost on any of them. Well, except for Pipsqueak.

"Fun?" she asked, jumping into the conversation. "I love fun. What're we gonna do that's fun? Another race?"

"No, definitely not," Kaiden said quickly.

"That's not very fun at all," Pipsqueak said with a pout.

"We need to move," Declan intervened. "I reckon we only have another hour or so before it's too dark to see."

"Where's the arrow?" Alex asked, looking around for Hunter's sign.

"Over here," Jordan said, leading the way along the edge of the ravine.

When they were all standing around the arrow—but keeping their distance from the edge of the mountain—Tom reached out to grab the paper. His brow furrowed in confusion as he read.

"What does it say?" Declan asked.

Tom held the paper out so they could all lean in and read it.

Time to swim. Don't forget your raft.
And sweet dreams.

"What does that—"

The rest of Alex's sentence was drowned out as the ground rumbled beneath them and an entire portion of it corroded under their feet, dissolving away into nothing...

...And they plummeted down into the ravine far, far below.

Fifteen

Their screams filled the air as they fell faster and faster. Alex knew none of them would survive the fall, even if they managed to avoid hitting the rocks in the river below. They were too high for the impact not to kill them.

She closed her eyes and waited for the inevitable, but when her torso was suddenly yanked upwards, she shrieked and opened them again, and was astonished by what she was seeing.

Her classmates' backpacks had each released a parachute, and those parachutes were easing them safely to the ground.

Alex let out an incredulous laugh, and she heard some of the others joining her.

"Everyone okay?" Declan yelled over the sound of the wind and the churning water below.

Alex couldn't hear everyone's responses clearly, but it looked like they were all fine. Pipsqueak in particular seemed to be having a grand old time.

As they sailed closer to the water below, Alex began to worry about what would come next.

"Declan!" she yelled. She had to call out twice more before he heard her.

"Yeah?" he yelled back.

"The raft! You have to inflate the raft!"

He couldn't hear her over the noise, so she tried to mime it out for him. Her attempt failed miserably, so she spelled out the word R-A-F-T in the air. After a few repeats, his eyes widened with realisation and he looked at the crashing rapids below them.

Since his backpack was acting as a parachute, Alex could see he was struggling to reach around and get the raft out. By his third attempt, she was nervously watching the river come closer and closer. When she was low enough to feel the spray on her face, she heard Declan's victorious exclamation, but that was all she knew before her parachute unattached itself and she fell the remaining distance into the icy mountain river.

Submerged, Alex was tossed and turned as the current dragged her along, unable to draw breath as she was churned through the rapids. Just when she began to fear losing consciousness from oxygen deprivation, something yanked hard on her pack, and she was pulled roughly out of the water and over the side of the inflated raft. After coughing the river out of her lungs and inhaling some much needed air she was able to see that all her waterlogged classmates were already in the vessel, grasping onto the rope-handled sides.

"Can somebody please tell me what this nightmare has to do with Stealth and Subterfuge?" she asked through chattering teeth.

No one could answer her. They all held on for dear life as the raft moved them swiftly along the rapids.

After about half an hour of mind-numbing bumps and repeated body-soaking splashes, the river calmed and they slowed to a more comfortable pace.

"Everyone alive?" Tom asked, uttering the first words any of them had spoken since Alex's outburst upon entering the raft.

Once they'd all acknowledged they were okay—relatively speaking—they decided to make the most of their situation and eat some dinner. The sun was disappearing behind the mountains surrounding them and very soon they would have no light left. That thought alone caused Alex to shiver, and the chill left over from the icy water didn't help her lack of warmth. She was *really* cold.

"Here, Alex," Kaiden said, and when she turned his way, he blew some kind of glittery, gold dust into her face.

She sneezed twice before wrinkling her nose at him. "Why did you...?"

Alex paused mid-question when she felt the most pleasantly warm feeling rush around her body. An instant later, every part of her—including her hair, clothes and backpack—was completely dry.

Her mouth dropped open and Kaiden grinned at her. "My turn."

He handed her a small metal tin filled with glittering dust that she recognised from her medical kit. She looked around and saw that everyone was using the powder in the same way, so she dropped some of it into her hand and, after hesitating only a moment, blew it into Kaiden's face.

He closed his eyes as the warmth enveloped him, and just like Alex, a moment later he was dry.

"What is this stuff?" she asked, her voice full of wonder.

"Quick-Dry," Kaiden answered. "You've never used it before?"

"Never," Alex admitted as she handed the container back to him.

"That's weird," Kaiden said, but he left it at that, much to Alex's relief.

The group ate their meagre dinner of camping rations in silence as they drifted along the river. By the time they'd finished eating there was almost no light left.

"How are we supposed to see the next arrow?" Skyla asked.

"I think we've had all the instructions we're going to get for the day," Declan said. "Hunter's last note had 'sweet dreams' at the end. I'm guessing we're supposed to sleep here."

"As in, here?" Skyla gestured around them. "But we're floating. What if I sleepwalk? I'll end up in the river!"

They all stared at her, until Tom asked what they were all wondering. "Do you sleepwalk often?"

Skyla tilted her head in puzzlement. "Should I?"

Alex had to stifle a laugh at the baffled look on Skyla's face.

"Well, no, hopefully you shouldn't," Tom said, looking around for help from the others.

"Then of course I don't," Skyla said. "Honestly, the questions you people ask!"

"But, you're the one who said—" Tom began, but Alex interrupted his frustrated words.

"I think you'll be fine, Skyla. We won't let you fall into the river, whether you sleepwalk or not."

"But I don't sleepwalk," Skyla said with genuine confusion.

Jordan wasn't the only one who tried to turn his amusement into a half-convincing cough.

"I'm tired," Pipsqueak broke in, changing the course of the conversation.

"Pip's right," Declan said. "I know it's early, but we've all had an insane day. We should get some shut-eye, especially if tomorrow is anything like today."

Alex agreed wholeheartedly. The events of the day had successfully spiked her adrenaline enough to keep her exhaustion at bay, but her week of limited sleep was crashing down on her.

The raft was large enough that they could all comfortably lie down even with its heavily inflated sides. Alex pulled her sleeping bag from her backpack and snuggled inside it, and she had only a few moments of consciousness left to say goodnight before she drifted off to sleep.

**

"Alex, wake up."

Something was nudging her but she wasn't ready to pull herself from her blissful slumber.

"Alex?"

"Maybe if I blow my morning breath in her face she'll wake up?"

"Didn't you see how exhausted she was last night, Blink? Just give her a moment."

"No sweat, bro. Just a suggestion."

Alex wanted to roll over to stop the annoying voices buzzing in her ears so she could go back to sleep. But they continued talking and her consciousness came slamming back when she remembered where she was. Her eyes snapped open and she sat up with a gasp—which turned into a painful moan when she smacked heads with Jordan.

"Oww!" he cried, flinching backwards and holding a hand to his forehead.

"What are you *doing*?" Alex asked, massaging her throbbing skull.

"Trying to wake the dead, apparently," he said. "I have no idea how you slept so well. The rest of us hardly managed a wink."

Looking around, Alex could see that her classmates didn't exactly look well rested. But she felt better than she had in a while, that was for sure.

"Why'd you wake me?" she asked, unzipping her sleeping bag and stretching her limbs.

"The river's ending," he said, pointing to stagnant body of water not too far ahead. "I thought you might want something to eat before we have to tackle whatever's next."

That was thoughtful of him, so she decided not to be annoyed that he'd woken her from the best sleep she'd had all week.

"Thanks, Jordan."

He smiled and handed over her backpack. She wasn't hungry, but she knew she'd need her strength for whatever Hunter had in store for them, so she guzzled down an energy bar and a handful of dehydrated fruit, along with a good portion of water. The bottles they'd been given seemed to have some kind of automatic refill as none of them had run out of water. That was convenient, at least in Alex's opinion.

"What's the plan?" she asked Jordan as she packed away her gear.

He shrugged. "Same as yesterday. Look for the next arrow, follow the instructions, and hopefully make it home later this arvo."

She re-zipped her pack. "I can't wait for this day to be over."

"Aren't you enjoying it at least a little bit?"

Jordan looked so excited that Alex didn't have the heart to bring him down with a reminder of the dangerous situations they'd faced the previous day. "It's been challenging, but we're still alive. So, yay for that," she agreed.

"What are we yaying?" Declan asked, shuffling over to join their conversation.

"Life," Alex said simply.

"A good yay-point, for sure," he agreed with a grin.

"You're chirpy this morning," Alex observed, noting the happy expression on his face.

"Why shouldn't I be?" Declan threw his hands behind his head and leaned back against the raft's side. "The sky is blue, the birds are singing—it's going to be a beautiful day."

Alex looked from him to Jordan and back again, her eyes narrowing with suspicion. "Has someone used the relaxant stuff on you?"

Declan chuckled and shook his head, but then his expression turned solemn and he leaned forward to whisper, "If you get a chance, you might want to speak with Pip about what happened yesterday. She's back to normal now, and I think she's a little embarrassed about it all."

Alex looked over her shoulder at Pipsqueak who was sitting on the opposite side of the raft and staring morosely out at the water.

"Will do," Alex promised.

"All right, guys," Tom said, capturing everyone's attention. "We're not moving much anymore, so I say it's time for us to search around for the arrow on land."

They all agreed, and as a team they leaned over the side of the raft and used their hands to paddle until they reached the riverbank and scrambled out one by one.

Leaving the raft behind but taking the rest of their possessions with them, it took half an hour of aimless wandering in the area before they found the next arrow. In that time, Alex was able to pull Pipsqueak aside to speak with her. It turned out that Pip was ashamed of her relaxant-blurred memories from the previous day, but after a few words of encouragement, Alex managed to cheer her up and she returned to her normal self.

"We have a simple task this time," Tom said, scanning the newest instructions. "It says, 'Continue south until you reach the village.'"

That seemed easy enough, to Alex's relief. But that relief turned into whining grumbles when, six hours and fifteen Hunter-laid traps later, they still hadn't reached the village.

"I'm tired," Skyla complained when they stopped for lunch.

"We're all tired," Pipsqueak grumbled back.

"My feet hurt," Skyla continued to complain.

No one bothered replying that time.

After another two hours the forest began to thin and the greenery started to dry out. The rocky dirt beneath their feet turned into sandy dust, and the air became hotter and dryer.

"I can't believe Hunter would lead us into the Soori Desert," Pipsqueak said, sounding exhausted. "That's so irresponsible of him. The desert is dangerous."

After everything else they'd faced—which, granted, Pip didn't remember as vividly as the rest of them—Alex didn't doubt that the desert was exactly like somewhere Hunter might send them. But it turned out they didn't have to worry about entering the arid wasteland. Because on the outskirts of the forest, just before the woodsy landscape morphed into unending dunes of sand, they found the village.

'Village' was such an inadequate term for the intimidating, fortified walls that surrounded the buildings within. Alex and her classmates scaled a tree in order to get a glimpse into the settlement, but even that view wasn't comforting. The village looked more like some kind of military compound than anything else.

"I have a bad feeling about this," Alex said as they all balanced in the tree.

"I have the same feeling," Kaiden muttered in agreement. "And I think it's about to get worse."

He pointed at something just above her head and Alex realised she'd been so focused on the village that she'd missed the arrow. She reached up and tore off the paper note.

Enter the command outpost at the top of the garrison and retrieve the red envelope.
IT IS IN YOUR BEST INTERESTS TO REMAIN UNSEEN.
When your task is complete, open the envelope for more instructions and the Bubbledoor to take you to your next destination.

"At least there's no riddle," Jordan commented after she read the instructions out loud.

As one, Alex and her classmates all turned to look at him.

"What?" he asked.

"Did you hear the same words as the rest of us?" Pipsqueak asked, her tone almost hysterical. "We have to break into a military outpost—and the command centre, at that! We're so going to prison for this."

"Yo, check out the wicked-looking weapons they're holding," Blink said, pointing to one of the guards walking along the top of the wall carrying some kind of silvery object in his hands.

"Standard-issue military Stabiliser," Kaiden informed the rest of them. "One shot will knock you unconscious for ten minutes; a second shot in that time will kill you."

Alex looked at him questioningly but he avoided her gaze, along with everyone else's. She wondered if advanced weapons knowledge was common in Medora, but for some reason, she doubted that was the case.

"What's our plan of action?" she asked, taking the clearly unwanted attention off him.

"First off, we need to find the outpost Hunter's note refers to," Tom said.

"It's over there," Kaiden replied, pointing to a part of the wall that rose higher than the rest, almost like a tower.

While his answer seemed the logical choice, Alex wasn't sure why he seemed so convinced. Apparently Tom was doubtful as well.

"How do you know?" the apprentice asked.

"I've been here before," Kaiden said.

Alex wasn't the only one gaping at him, but she was the first to get over her shock.

"That sounds like a good enough reason to me," she said, moving the attention off him again. "Now we just have to figure out how to get over there and back without being seen. Any ideas?"

"I don't think we all need to go," Pipsqueak said. "There's no point in everyone getting caught."

"Pip's right," Tom agreed. "The more of us who try to sneak in, the less stealthy we'll be."

"I'll go," Kaiden said. "I already know where to look."

"I'll go with you," Declan said.

"No, I'll go," Jordan said. "My gift will get us in and out without being seen."

When everyone but Alex looked at him in question, he explained how his gift of transcendence could make him and anyone he touched disappear. Their anxious expressions vanished with his words and they were immediately more confident of the mission's success.

"Did anyone think to bring a ComTCD?" Tom asked.

"I did," Skyla said as she pulled her sparkly pink Device from her bag and handed it over.

"That's, um, very pretty," Tom said, holding the glitter-covered piece of tech precariously between his fingers as if fearing the bedazzlement might be contagious. "Anyone else?"

"Here," Pipsqueak said, handing over her plain black ComTCD.

"I'll open a link between us so we can stay in contact," Tom explained, fiddling with both Devices.

"You won't be able to see us while I'm using my gift," Jordan said, securing his and Kaiden's backpacks to the tree.

"I'm not using the holograph function," Tom said. "Just the audio setting so we can hear what's going on around you in case something goes wrong."

"We'll be fine," Jordan said, but he accepted the offered ComTCD and slid it into his pocket.

Kaiden didn't look as confident as Jordan, and Alex was pretty sure she heard him mumble under his breath, "This isn't going to work." But despite his words, he shimmied down the tree, followed closely by Jordan. When they were at the wall, Jordan reached out to grasp Kaiden's shoulder and both of them disappeared from sight.

"Now we wait," Declan said. He sounded as miserable as Alex felt at being left behind. If she could have come up with a valid reason for joining them, she would have. But here she was, stuck sitting safely in a tree and waiting anxiously for their return.

Minutes passed and with them came whispered updates through the ComTCD.

"We're through the gate."

"We've reached the other side of the compound."

"We've found the stairs leading to the command outpost."

"We're on the top of the wall."

"We've just entered the command centre."

"We can see—"

An unknown voice interrupted the update. "General Drock, I sense intruders."

"Search the room!" said another, louder voice. "Seize them immediately!"

"Their thoughts are scattered, General. I can't hear why they're here, but I do sense that they're hiding near the doorway," the first voice said.

"Run!" came Jordan's cry.

"After them!" ordered the authoritative voice.

Alex's heart was thumping in her chest as she imagined the scene playing out in the compound.

"What do we do?" she asked. "We have to help them!"

"If we go in there now, we'll only cause more problems," Tom said. "Give them a few minutes. Between both of their gifts, they should be able to escape."

Alex had no idea what Kaiden's gift was, but unless he could teleport them both out, she didn't see how he'd be able to help their situation.

"Kaiden's been in there before, Alex," Declan said, squeezing her arm in comfort. "He'll have a few tricks up his sleeve, don't worry."

Despite his words, Alex could see Declan was just as concerned as she was.

They waited ten nail-biting minutes before they heard anything, but finally the update came.

"We got away. We're coming back out."

Alex felt like cheering, but she knew it would be stupid to make such a noise. She waited nervously for Kaiden and Jordan to appear, and when they did, she wasn't sure whether to laugh or yell at them. They were panting when they climbed up the tree and it was clear they'd been running for their lives.

"What happened?" Tom asked once they'd caught their breath.

"One of them was gifted," Kaiden said. "A very strong mind reader."

"Did you get the package?" Pipsqueak asked.

The frustrated looks on their faces answered for them.

"You're both safe," Alex said. "That's the main thing. It was a reckless task to begin with, something Hunter never should've asked us to do."

"But that envelope holds the next Bubbledoor," Pipsqueak said miserably. "We need it to get out of here."

"What do you suggest we do, Pip?" Tom sounded irritated. "The entire compound will be on high alert now. And if there's a mind reader in there, they'll all know the moment any of us enter that command centre."

Alex froze and looked up at Jordan. His eyes begged her to stay silent, but she knew what she had to do.

"I can get in there," she whispered. The words stuck in her throat, so she made herself repeat them, loud enough for the others to hear.

"Weren't you listening, Alex?" Tom said. "There's a *mind reader* in there. We won't be able to get within twenty feet of that envelope, not while he's around."

"He won't be able to read me."

Her classmates looked at her as if she was crazy, all except Jordan, who seemed resigned to accept her decision.

"My gift allows me a certain amount of ... um ... choice, when it comes to other people using their gifts on me," she explained vaguely. "The mind reader won't be able to sense me at all, let alone read my thoughts. I'm the only chance we have at getting that envelope."

"Prove it," Pip said.

Alex glanced at her. "What?"

"Prove it," Pip repeated. "Touch my hand."

Giving her a searching look, Alex did as ordered.

Pip's face scrunched in concentration and her grip tightened almost painfully. She was breathing heavily by the time she let go of Alex's hand, staring at her with incredulous eyes.

"Blink, you try," the small girl said.

For the first time since Alex had met him, Blink seemed uncomfortable. But Pipsqueak was determined, and she reached for his hand and joined it with Alex's.

"Do it, Blink. We need to know if she's telling the truth."

Blink looked at Alex in apology and slowly closed his eyes. His body began to vibrate and Alex felt the tremors shake all the way up her arm, but after a few seconds he stilled again.

"You don't look like you're in any pain," he observed, appearing awed.

Alex raised her eyebrows in question. "That's because I'm not."

Pip was still looking at her in amazement. "I should have been able to manipulate your emotions and Blink should have caused your blood to boil, but you didn't feel any of that?"

Alex shrugged, trying not to think of her blood boiling. "I told you..." She felt like a scientific experiment from the looks on her classmates' faces. "Now that your test is over, I'm good to go, right?"

"What's your plan?" Tom asked, the first to shake off his shock. "Regardless of your gift it's not like you'll be able to just waltz in there. And you won't have Jordan to keep you invisible."

"I have an idea," Alex answered, thinking quickly. "But you're going to have to trust me."

Her idea wasn't something she could reveal to any of them, not without compromising one of her best friends.

"We trust you," Declan said, speaking for everyone.

"Skyla, I need you to do my makeup," Alex said, her unexpected statement prompting raised eyebrows from her classmates. "I need to look, um, regal," she continued quickly. "But also like I've been dragged through the desert. Can you do that?"

Ten minutes later Alex was descending the tree while her classmates watched anxiously from above. None of them were happy with the arrangement, especially after she refused to take the ComTCD with her, claiming that if she was discovered then she didn't want the others to end up captured. But really, she just couldn't allow them to hear what she was planning on saying to the soldiers to get into the command centre.

"I'll be back soon," Alex promised, hoping she sounded more confident than she felt.

Skyla had slathered Alex's face with makeup to the point where she looked like a wild mess, and she hoped it was convincing enough to pull off the ruse she was about to attempt. Knowing that the success or failure of their task depended on her, she straightened her clothes and took on a staggering walk, acting dazed. She wobbled all the way over to the gated entrance into the compound, where a commanding voice brought her to a halt.

"Identify yourself!"

When Alex didn't respond, a group of armed soldiers rushed out to meet her. They eyed her suspiciously before one of them stepped forward and repeated the command.

"Thirsty," Alex whispered, making her voice sound raspy. She collapsed to her knees for added effect and was rewarded when the closest soldier called for one of his companions to bring water.

With their Stabiliser weapons pointed at her, Alex guzzled down the liquid as if she were dying of dehydration. When she lowered the bottle, she looked up at the men with an unfocused expression.

"Who are you and what are you doing here?" the closest soldier asked, stepping closer. His black uniform seemed more decorated than the other guards and she presumed that meant he had the higher military ranking.

"I'm Princess Delucia Cavelle," Alex answered, hoping Dix was right about how few people knew what she looked like these days.

The soldier's eyes widened at her exclamation and then narrowed again. "I find it hard to believe the royal princess would be discovered half-dead at the edge of the Soori Desert."

"My travel companions and I were ambushed," Alex said, still kneeling on the ground. "They abducted me and knocked me out. I don't know how long I was unconscious, but when I woke, it took me a while to figure out where I was. I managed to escape but I had no idea where to go. All I could remember was my father once telling me about a military outpost at the base of the Durungan Ranges and I knew if I made it here, I'd be safe."

The soldier's doubtful look remained on his face, but his expression wasn't as harsh anymore. He seemed to be considering her words.

"Come with me," he told her. "The general will be able to verify your story."

Alex pushed herself to her feet with exaggerated exhaustion, swaying for effect. The soldier was considerate enough to hold her elbow until she was steady again, which would have been kind of him had she truly been in need of the support.

He led her past the other soldiers and through the gate into the compound. Instead of having to traverse the entire settlement like Jordan and Kaiden had done, the guard pointed for her to step onto a circle carved into the ground near the gated entrance. Once they were both standing in the circle, he raised his wrist and tapped away at a watch-like screen that was clamped to his arm. Immediately the circle filled with light and Alex felt a rush of wind before she was sucked through the air as if by a vacuum. When the light disappeared, she saw she was no longer outside the gate but standing at the top of the wall, just outside the command outpost.

How convenient.

"Short-range teleportation circle," the soldier told her, seeing the surprised look on her face. "Military-grade. We're still working out the kinks, but it works just fine over small distances."

He motioned for her to enter the tower and it took a moment for her eyes to adjust as she stepped into the building. When they did, she wished she could retreat again.

The atmosphere inside the command centre was thick with tension. There were dozens of armed soldiers stationed around the room, and in the centre stood a man who was clearly in charge. He had close-cropped, salt and pepper hair and wore a black military uniform with weapons strapped everywhere. Alex had to force herself not to take a step back when his piercing eyes turned to stare intently at her. His gaze stayed on her for what felt like forever before it flickered over to her guard.

"Major Tyson, I trust you have a good reason for leaving your post?"

"Yes, General Drock," the soldier said. "This girl came staggering in from the desert and claims to be Princess Delucia Cavelle. She says she was abducted while travelling but managed to escape her captors."

The general's gaze swung back to Alex and, despite her intimidation, she stood up a little straighter, determined to stay in character.

"Does she now?" the general said thoughtfully, turning back to the major. "What of the intruders, Tyson?"

"No sign of them, sir. We have to presume they managed to escape since Signa can't sense them in the compound any longer."

The general swore and Alex narrowed her eyes at him.

"I would prefer that you refrained from using such colourful language in my presence, General Drock," she said, attempting to sound imperious.

The military leader crossed his arms. "Looks like the little princess has quite the tongue on her."

"I'm the heir to the throne of Medora, General," Alex warned, lying through her teeth. "You would do well to treat me with the respect I deserve."

"We'll see about that," Drock said. He turned to one of the soldiers stationed across the room and ordered, "Bring me Signa."

"No need, General, I'm already here," said a man who'd just entered the room. He wasn't dressed like a soldier, but he nevertheless exuded a dangerous aura. And yet, despite her mental warning bells, Alex had difficulty hiding her amused reaction when she realised just how much he looked like the animated villain Jafar from Disney's *Aladdin*. The similarities were uncanny, right down to the large eyes, long face and thin goatee.

"This girl claims to be our royal princess," the general informed the new arrival. "Can you verify?"

Signa turned to look at Alex and tilted his head, his gaze unfocused. After a tense moment, his eyes narrowed and he stepped closer to her. His expression darkened further and he grasped her shoulder firmly.

"Hey!" she exclaimed, trying to shrug off his hand. "Let me go!"

"Signa?" the general pressed. "Is she lying?"

Signa's face remained irritated but he released Alex's shoulder and walked over to the general's side. "I'm unable to hear her thoughts. Any of them."

A few of the soldiers around the room looked astonished, including the general and Major Tyson. Alex rolled her eyes.

"Do you really think my father would allow me to remain untrained in the art of protecting my mind? With all I hear around the palace? Of course not," she said, injecting a hint of scorn into her voice.

"You're too young to have such strengthened resistance," Signa argued.

"I'm a fast learner," Alex rebutted him arrogantly.

The general's gaze was calculating, while Signa looked enraged.

"I don't trust her, General," the mind reader said. "She could be a spy. She's probably in league with the intruders from earlier. I say we torture her for information."

Alex somehow managed to keep her face blank despite her rising fear, but wondered just how much sway Signa had over the general. She had to think quickly before her situation took a turn for the worse.

"There's a simple enough solution," Alex said, following a hunch. "Contact my father. He'll confirm my identity."

"We can't contact the king directly from here," Drock informed her. "We communicate with him through the Warden headquarters unless there's an emergency."

Alex folded her arms. "You don't consider my abduction an emergency?"

"Not if you're lying," he said. "I won't waste the king's time."

"Contact the Wardens, then," Alex said, desperately hoping he wouldn't call her bluff.

"As you wish," the general said, almost mockingly. "But if it turns out you've tried to deceive me, I'll personally see to it that you discover new meanings of the word 'pain'."

Alex raised her chin and tried to appear confident, despite the fact that she was now mentally hyperventilating. "Lead the way, General Drock."

At her words, he spun on his heel and headed over to the far side of the outpost tower and into an adjoining room. Tyson motioned for Alex to follow.

Alex trailed after the general into the smaller office-like room, where her steps faltered. There, sitting in the rubbish bin at the base of a large desk, was a bright red envelope. The good news was that she'd found what she needed without having to actually search for it. The bad news was that she had no idea how to retrieve it, let alone how she would get both it and herself safely out of the compound.

She could have used Jordan's gift right about then, that was for sure.

General Drock moved to the wall of the office and pressed on a touch-screen panel. Immediately a voice echoed out of the Device and asked for identification.

"General Alan Drock, Soori Outpost. Authorisation code one-one-six-four-two-eight. Requesting visual contact."

Within seconds, a projected life-size holograph appeared in front of them. It was a Warden, that much was clear from the uniform, but the person—a woman—had her back to Alex so she couldn't see her face.

"General Drock," the Warden greeted him. There seemed to be something wrong with the audio transference, since the voice was distorted, almost robotic-sounding, while the picture was of good quality. "You're not due to check in until tomorrow evening. Is there a problem?"

"Nothing more than we can handle, Warden," Drock said. "But we've had some intruders in the compound today who we failed to apprehend."

"Intruders?" the Warden asked sharply. "What were they after?"

"We've yet to discover that," the general said. "There's nothing of value here. We didn't get a look at them, but it was probably just some kids looking for a thrill."

"Keep us updated," the Warden said.

"Will do," he agreed. "But that wasn't why I called."

"Go ahead, General."

"After the intruders escaped, a girl stumbled in from the desert. She claims to be Princess Delucia. Can you confirm?"

Alex's heart raced realising that she was about to be discovered, but her feet were frozen to the floor. Maybe they wouldn't torture her if she told them it was all just a joke? Maybe they'd accept her excuse that she was one of those kids 'looking for a thrill'?

For some reason, she doubted that.

The general walked around the room until he was standing next to Alex, and the hologram turned to follow his progress. When the Warden's eyes came to rest on Alex, she wasn't sure who was more shocked. She only just managed to bite her tongue to hold back her gasp of astonishment.

"Good afternoon, Warden Jeera," Alex said, trying to keep her tone calm despite the incredulous look the Warden was giving her. The malfunctioning sound hadn't allowed her to identify Jeera from her voice, but with them both now staring directly at each other, there was no denying their familiarity. "Can you please confirm that I'm the princess so these men won't throw me in a cell and torture me for information?"

Alex added the last part in the hope that Jeera would understand the dangerous situation she would face if the Warden refused to play along.

Jeera's expression continued to show surprise, but she managed to pull herself together enough to speak. "Where have you been, Princess?" she said, to Alex's immense relief. "Your parents have been worried sick."

Alex could see that the men in the room were shocked by the Warden's confirmation of her fake identity.

"My travelling companions and I were ambushed," Alex said, continuing the subterfuge. "I was abducted but managed to escape. Have the others made it back safely?"

The Warden's lips quirked slightly, almost as if she was impressed with Alex's deceit even though she had no idea why it was necessary.

"They arrived just this morning," Jeera said. "But we're all anxious to have you back home at the palace. General Drock?"

He stepped forward. "Yes, Warden?"

"Please provide the princess with the means to return home immediately," Jeera ordered.

She sounded so authoritative that Alex wondered about the chain of command between the Wardens and the military. She would have to remember to ask someone one day—preferably when she wasn't in the middle of the firing line.

"I'll personally lead the princess to our linking Bubbledoor," the general said.

"Thank you, General," Jeera said. "Princess, I'll await you in the receiving room."

The look in Jeera's eyes told Alex that she'd better have a good explanation ready.

Once the Warden disconnected the holograph communication, the room was left silent. After a tense moment, the general cleared his throat.

"I'd like to apologise for my behaviour, Your Highness," General Drock said. "We were on red alert after discovering intruders in our compound, so I was naturally suspicious of your arrival. While that's no excuse, I hope you can forgive my lack of respect."

Alex's demeanour softened at his words. He had every right to be suspicious, especially as she wasn't who she claimed to be. "Consider it forgotten, General. I'd expect no less from a fine, upstanding military commander such as yourself. Your precautions were necessary, but perhaps you might refrain from using so many expletives in the future."

She smiled with her last sentence to tell him she wasn't as offended as she sounded. He chuckled lightly in response, and the gesture transformed his entire face from an unyielding general to an almost friendly father figure.

"Bad habit, I'm afraid, Princess."

"We all have them," she allowed. "But it's something for you to work on, at least when I'm around."

He chuckled again, before straightening up and turning to the others in the room.

"Major Tyson, you'll accompany us to the Bubbledoor," the general said. "Signa, your services are no longer required."

"General, I believe this is a mistake," Signa argued. "I don't like that I can't read her."

"Enough, Signa," Drock said. "You heard Warden Jeera confirm her identity. The matter's closed. You're dismissed."

Signa glared at Alex one last time before he stormed out of the room.

"If you'll follow me, Princess, we'll get you back home at once," the general said, and he began to walk towards the doorway.

Alex had a moment of panic when she realised that she still needed to get her hands on the red envelope. She couldn't leave without it, that much was true. But how could she retrieve it?

An idea came to her, but she wasn't all that confident it would work.

"I'm not feeling so good," she moaned, raising a hand to her head. She staggered a few steps to her right and collapsed onto the edge of the desk before falling off it and landing directly on top of the rubbish bin. A mess of paper fell around her and she managed to get her fingers on the red envelope, hoping all the while that it looked as if she'd just passed out.

"Princess? *Princess!*"

She had barely a second to slide the package under her clothes before Major Tyson knelt down to shake her shoulder.

As soon as she thought it was secure and hidden, she groaned again and opened her eyes.

"What happened?"

"You fainted." Tyson helped her to stand. "You must be exhausted after everything you've been through."

Alex wondered about the odd tone in his voice as he led her out of the room—it almost sounded as if he was amused. But his face was as serious as ever, so perhaps she'd only imagined the flicker of emotion.

"What's the hold-up?" the general asked when they caught up to him in the main room of the command centre.

"I'm just a little tired," Alex said, smiling weakly and not wanting to tell him about her fake dizzy spell. "I needed a moment."

"Don't worry, Princess. You'll be home soon and you can rest then," Drock said, and he motioned for her and Tyson to follow him to the back of the room.

On the wall there was a rectangular section outlined with a white border, roughly as large as Alex's head.

"Just place your hand in the centre of the rectangle and the Bubbledoor will activate," the general told her. "It'll take you straight to the receiving room in the palace."

"Thank you for your assistance, General Drock," Alex said. "I can't tell you how much I appreciate it."

"You're welcome, Princess," the general said, giving her a short bow.

Major Tyson mirrored the gesture, and never in her life had Alex felt like such a fraud. She would have to ask D.C. to tell the king about these two good military men and get them a medal or something.

"I hope we'll meet again in the future," she said genuinely, even if she wasn't in a rush to replay the role of princess anytime soon. With a smile goodbye, she reached for the panel and the Bubbledoor activated, rushing her to her new destination. She had barely landed before she heard Jeera's voice.

"There had better be a very good reason why I just lied to a military general, *Princess Delucia*."

Sixteen

Alex looked guiltily at the Warden whose face showed definite disapproval.

"I can explain," she said quickly.

"I sure hope so," Jeera said. Her dark hair was tied back and her striking blue eyes stared intently at Alex.

Noting the Warden's impatience, Alex quickly summarised the events leading up to her impersonation of the princess, including Hunter's crazy task and how Kaiden and Jordan had nearly been caught. At the mention of the two boys, Jeera's expression flickered with concern until Alex assured her that they'd made it out safely.

"So that's when you decided to go in on your own," Jeera guessed, "because you knew your gift would protect you from the mind reader."

"How do you know—"

"I'm one of the king's Wardens, Alex," Jeera interrupted her. "It's my job to know."

That was interesting news, but Alex let it go and confirmed Jeera's assumption, going on to explain how she'd 'borrowed' D.C.'s royal identity in order to get into the command tent.

"Everything would've turned real nasty if you hadn't stood up for me," Alex finished. "So thank you, Jeera. Really."

The Warden looked at Alex steadily before her expression lightened and she smiled. "You're welcome, Alex."

With the smile still on her face, something about her appearance niggled at the back of Alex's mind. "Have I met you before, Jeera? Other than as a Warden, I mean? You seem ... familiar."

Jeera laughed out loud, which seemed like an odd reaction to Alex.

"No, Alex, we've never met before your impersonation as an assassin."

"Huh," Alex said, but she let it drop. Déjà vu could be a fickle thing.

"I have to ask, did you retrieve the red envelope?"

To answer, Alex pulled the package from her clothes.

"I'm impressed," Jeera said. "That can't have been easy."

"You have no idea," Alex muttered.

"That said, you do realise I can't allow you to keep it, right?"

"What? No, Jeera," Alex begged. "It has our next instructions inside, and the Bubbledoor we need. Plus, it was in General Drock's rubbish bin, anyway. He probably won't even notice it's missing."

Jeera looked at Alex as if judging the truth of her words. Finally, the Warden sighed. "This conversation never happened, understood?"

"What conversation?" Alex said, with a sly grin.

"Exactly," Jeera said, returning the expression. "Now, you need to get out of here before someone sees me talking to you." She handed over a vial that Alex recognised as a Bubbler. "Go back to your friends, finish your SAS expedition, and get back to the academy safely, okay?"

"That's the plan," Alex agreed. Jeera made it sound so easy.

"You might want to have a look at the back of that envelope before you return to your classmates," Jeera advised. "It was good seeing you again, Alex. Do me a favour and tell Hunter that I'll be in touch regarding his teaching methods." With those words, the Warden spun on her heel and left the room.

Curious, Alex flipped over the red envelope and saw there was a small white envelope stuck to its back. Both the envelopes were sealed, and she wondered if General Drock had known they were in his office, let alone in his bin. Had Hunter snuck it in at some stage without the general's knowledge? Either way, the white envelope was clearly intended for Alex, since her full name was scrawled across it in Hunter's handwriting.

Looking around nervously, Alex pulled the envelope off the larger red one, but she didn't get a chance to open it before the sound of chattering voices filled her ears. She shoved the white envelope into her pocket and the red envelope back under her clothes, throwing the Bubbler to the ground.

Resisting the temptation to go straight back to the academy, she directed the portal to open at the base of the tree where the others waited for her return. They didn't notice her straight away and they continued to whisper uneasily to each other while they looked out over the military compound.

Alex smiled mischievously and climbed up the tree as silently as she could. When she was right beside them she asked, "What are we all looking at?"

"Skyla, I swear, if you ask one more stupid question..." Pipsqueak muttered irritably.

"Um, hello, I'm over here," Skyla said, sounding just as annoyed. She turned to Alex and said, "We're all looking for you, and I found you first, so do I get a prize?"

"Alex!" Jordan exclaimed, seeing her perched in the branch beside them.

His startled words caused everyone else to swing around and gape at her, and she began to feel embarrassed by their attention.

"Enough staring," she said. "It's almost dusk. We need to get moving."

"How—How—?" Pipsqueak asked incoherently.

"What our little Squeaker is trying to ask is, how did you get back here?" Blink said. "We haven't seen any sign of you since you entered the gate."

Alex shook her head and said, "You wouldn't believe me if I told you."

"Did you get the envelope?" Tom asked.

She smiled and pulled it from her clothes.

Her classmates whooped excitedly and Alex had to shush them before they were noticed. The last thing she needed was for General Drock to find her outside the compound when she should be safely back in Tryllin.

"Let's get down from this tree and see what we have to do next," Declan said, passing Alex's backpack to her.

When they were all on the ground, they ripped open the envelope. The first thing they withdrew was a set of identification tags, each printed with their individual photo. Kaiden, Jordan and Blink's tags were all given the status of 'Waiter' while Tom's tag labelled him a 'Musician'. Declan, Pipsqueak, Skyla and Alex's were marked as 'Invited Guest'. Their photos were correct, but their names were not. Alex raised her eyebrows when she read that she was supposed to be 'Ally Jones'.

"What do you suppose this is all about?" Jordan asked.

"Oh, hey, I like this task," Skyla said, having found their instructions. She handed the little slip of paper around for them all to read.

You are cordially invited to attend
Sir Oswald Graham's dinner party.
Your identities can be found within this
envelope, along with the roles you will each
adopt for the evening.
Costumes are waiting on the other side of the
Bubbledoor.
Your task is simple:
Retrieve the performer from his accommodation
and escort him back to his home.

"That's it?" Tom said, turning the paper over.

"Maybe there'll be more information with our costumes," Declan said.

"I sure hope so," Pipsqueak grumbled, and she upended the envelope to allow the final item to fall out. It was another one of Hunter's feathered arrows—only a miniature version. At least he was consistent.

"Here goes nothing," Tom said, and he reached out for the pre-programmed Bubbledoor.

One by one they were transported to the top of a tree-covered hill. Their view looked straight down to a small town at the edge of which stood a huge, brightly lit mansion. People dressed in formal party attire were Bubbling into the landscaped garden near the front door, their clothes glittering in the light of the impressive residence.

"We need to hurry," Kaiden said. "If we're supposed to be waiters, we should probably be down there already. And you too, Tom, as the musician."

"You're right," Tom agreed. "We need to find our costumes."

They shuffled around in the rapidly fading light until Skyla called out that she'd found something. Sure enough, there were eight outfits dangling from a tree, attached by labelled arrows to the branch above them. The boys each had a tuxedo, with the waiters' suits completely black and Tom's musician outfit the reverse in white. Declan's guest attire was a dark jacket with a white shirt and silver bowtie.

The girls' outfits were just as dressy, with three formal evening gowns hanging from the tree. Skyla's was pale yellow, Pipsqueak's was bright teal and Alex's was deep midnight blue. All three gowns were absolutely stunning, but...

"Those heels are ridiculous," Alex murmured, pointing to the lethal-looking stilettos on the ground below her dress. "I'm going to break my neck."

"Everyone, find a place and get changed," Tom said, ignoring Alex's comment. "Quickly now, before it's too dark to see."

Only when Alex began to undress did she hear the rustling sound of paper and remember the envelope with her name on it. She pulled it out and opened it, frowning as she read the words.

Alex, this task is more dangerous for you than any of the others.
Stay on your guard.
And don't forget the backpack items.
PS. Ally's mother, Larissa, has many friends.

It seemed that Hunter was back to his cryptic warnings, and Alex had no idea how to interpret his words. But although she wasn't sure what she was supposed to look out for, she would follow his advice and stay vigilant. And as for his comment about the backpack items, there was no way Alex would be able to hide the heavy book under her curve-hugging dress. Hunter's words had to have meant something else.

She finished changing and stumbled back to her classmates, mentally cursing the inappropriate footwear.

Jordan wolf-whistled when she came into view and Alex was glad it was getting too dark for her blush to be easily seen. The attention her arrival brought—from everyone—made her feel beyond uncomfortable.

"So..." she said awkwardly. "Are we going or what?"

"Wait, I have to fix your makeup," Skyla insisted, and Alex saw she was just finishing up with Pipsqueak.

Following orders, Alex sat down on the trunk of a fallen tree while Skyla removed her 'ambushed princess' look and reapplied the cosmetics. Then Skyla twisted Alex's hair up and pinned it softly behind her head, letting a few errant wisps dangle free to frame her face.

While undergoing her makeover, Alex was aware of the others whispering amongst themselves, but she couldn't hear what they were saying. She was relieved when Skyla said she was done, and Alex left her to pack up while she rejoined the others.

"What is it?" Alex asked, noting the hesitant, guilty and determined looks on their faces.

"We think it's a good idea if some of us remain behind, just in case we need a backup plan," Tom said. "Since the waiters are a good cover and I'm the only musician, we've decided that we can probably get away with sending just two guests in. We're thinking Declan and Pipsqueak should go, while you and Skyla remain behind."

"What?" Alex asked loudly. She indicated to herself and Skyla who had just joined them, "Don't we get a say in this?"

"Alex, can I speak with you in private?" Jordan asked.

"Jordan—"

"Alex," he said firmly, motioning for her to follow him.

Once they were out of hearing range, he looked apologetically at her. "It's not you, it's Skyla."

"What do you mean?"

"You know what she's like," Jordan said. "Her head's in the clouds ninety-eight percent of the time. She's harmless but she's also unreliable and we're worried she'll be a liability. We need someone to keep an eye on her, and since you've already had to do so much over the past two days, we figured you should be allowed to sit this one out."

"I don't want to sit it out."

"Please, Alex," Jordan begged. "You can see why we don't want her in there, can't you?"

Alex glanced over to where the others were standing and could just make out their silhouettes in the dark. Skyla was sitting on the tree trunk, polishing her nails in the limited light, while everyone else stood tense and ready. Her voice carried over to them, and Alex cringed when she heard her ask if they would get to dance at the party.

"I do understand," Alex admitted. "But I just wish I didn't have to be the one to babysit her."

"I know," Jordan said softly.

She followed him resignedly over to the others and listened while Tom explained to Skyla that she and Alex would be remaining behind.

"But that's not fair!" Skyla exclaimed loud enough that they had to shush her. "I'm all dressed up and beautiful—I should be allowed to go! Don't you trust me?"

The girl's eyes were filling with tears and Alex realised that it was up to her to intervene. "Skyla, don't you see? You and I have the most important mission tonight. If something goes wrong for these guys, it'll be up to us to complete the task. They're only leaving us behind because they trust us so much."

"Really?" Skyla asked, sniffling quietly.

"Really," Jordan said, playing along.

"I guess that's okay, then," Skyla said, standing taller. "Don't worry, we'll look after you if something goes wrong. We've got your backs."

Alex released a breath and reached for Skyla's sparkly pink ComTCD as Declan handed it over.

"I'll keep you updated on what's happening," he promised.

"Thanks," she said. "Now, you should all get out of here. And Tom, don't forget your banjo-thing."

He looked at her strangely. "My what?"

She pointed to his backpack. "You're the musician, remember. I'm pretty sure you need something to play."

"Right," he said, shuffling over to his pack to retrieve the instrument. "I haven't played in years."

"Hopefully it's just like riding a bike," Alex said.

"What's a bike?"

Alex gave a startled laugh at the absurd comment before she brushed his question off and told them all to leave.

"We'll come get you once we have the performer guy we're meant to find," Jordan said.

"Sure," she replied, trying to act okay about it all when really she was frustrated that she had to stay behind with Skyla. "Take all the time you need."

Alex watched as they made their own path down the hill and crept along under the cover of the now completely dark sky. After a while it was difficult to see them, but she spotted them again once they were closer to the well-lit mansion. One by one they broke away from the group and entered the building.

"We're in," Declan's voice whispered through the ComTCD. "The waiters are heading to the kitchen and Tom's joining the band. Pip and I are going to introduce ourselves to the host."

"Don't forget to use your fake names," Alex reminded.

"Oh, right. Thanks."

It was another twenty minutes before Alex heard anything other than the indecipherable chatter of the various guests and the distorted music from the orchestra.

"Alex, we have a problem," Declan said. "I overheard one of the guests talking about a performer who was in the middle of his juggling act two nights ago when he accidentally dropped a ball into Sir Oswald's wineglass, spilling it all over him. No one has seen the performer since, but they think he's locked somewhere underneath the mansion."

"You've got to be kidding me!" Alex cried. "Do you think he's our guy?"

"Pretty certain, yeah," Declan said. "It makes sense, considering Hunter's instructions to retrieve the performer from his 'accommodation'."

"Do the others know?"

"No, I haven't been able to talk with anyone. But I'll try to get a message to them."

"How will you bring the performer out if he's a prisoner?"

"I'm still working on that," Declan answered. "I'm hoping one of the others might have an idea. I'll update you again in a few—"

His words were interrupted by a loud voice. "What are you doing in here? Who are you talking to?"

"Uh, I was just admiring the view," Declan said.

"Show me your ID," the other voice commanded.

Alex flicked her ComTCD to the visual setting so she could watch what was happening. The holograph rose up out of her Device, showing Declan and another man standing in a small room. The other man looked like some kind of armed security guard.

Declan handed over his identification tag and the guard peered at it before saying, "Dillon Staring? Never heard of you. How did you get on the guest list?"

"I came with my girlfriend. She's a close friend of—"

Whatever Declan had been about to say was interrupted when the door burst open.

"Bro, where've you been? We're all waiting for—Oh."

Alex would have groaned at Blink's horrible timing if she wasn't so worried about sound carrying through Declan's ComTCD.

"Both of you, put your hands up," the man ordered, pulling out a weapon that looked identical to the military Stabilisers she'd seen at the compound.

"What's happening?" Skyla asked loudly.

Alex turned to shush her, but the damage was already done.

"Who said that?" the man demanded, looking around the room. "You there, Dillon, what's that you're holding?"

The man reached out to snatch the Device from Declan's hand and Alex abruptly ended the call, not wanting to give him time to activate the visual setting on his end and see them.

"Skyla, I need you to wait here," Alex said urgently. "You need to be very quiet, understand?"

"Where are you going?"

"I have to go and find out what's happening," Alex told her. "I won't be long—I promise I'll be back soon. But you have to stay here, okay?"

"I will," Skyla agreed. "I won't move until you get back."

Alex swapped her heels for her hiking shoes, lifted her gown, and took off down the hill at a sprint, only slowing once she entered the manicured gardens. Very carefully, she snuck around the various hedges until she was adjacent with the side of the building. Just as she was about to step out of her hiding place and enter the front doors, two burly security guards walked outside and took up positions by the entrance. Alex had to jump behind a peacock statue to avoid being seen.

What now? she wondered, thinking fast.

She dashed from statue to statue, hiding behind large caricature topiaries until she was at the back of the mansion. Moving quickly, she hurried over the lawn and pressed herself against the building, sliding along it until she found a balcony with light streaming through a double-door opening. She could hear the sounds of the party inside; the only problem was that it was two floors above her.

"Good thing I changed my shoes," Alex muttered, as she reached out to grab the vines that decorated the side of the mansion. Her gown made the climb difficult, but after tucking the hem into her underwear—and hoping no one was around to watch the show—she pulled herself up the side of the mansion and over the balustrade onto the balcony. She made sure she was concealed in the shadows before she peered through the doorway.

"Honoured guests," called an impeccably dressed older man from the far side of the grand ballroom. He stood at the top of an elegant staircase that led down from the floor above. "Forgive the interruption, but it seems we have some party crashers amongst us. Your safety is my highest priority, so please assist my security personnel as they scan your ID tags to check for forgeries. Feel free to continue the festivities whilst we ensure all the intruders are accounted for."

Alex watched as the security teams spread out across the room and ran small, glowing devices across the top of everyone's ID tags. Pip was the first of her classmates to be escorted from the room, followed by Jordan, then Kaiden. Tom almost remained unnoticed, but one of the security guards called out for another to scan the musicians.

"Well, this sucks," Alex whispered, as the man on the stairs—Sir Oswald Graham, she presumed—apologised for the inconvenience and told his guests to relax and enjoy the party once more.

Having no idea what to do, Alex scrambled back down to the ground and ran up the hill to Skyla.

"What's going on?" Skyla asked.

Alex told her everything she'd seen, while racking her mind for a solution.

"We need to assume they're all together," Alex said. "Hopefully they'll be locked up in the same area as the performer we're supposed to retrieve."

"Why do we want them locked up?" Skyla asked, confused.

"Because if they're in the same place, it'll be easier for us to get them all out at once," Alex said.

Skyla's voice was surprised when she said, "We're going to rescue them?"

"What else can we do?" Alex said. "Leave them there? No way."

Skyla's silence was enough to show that she agreed, and Alex began to pace while she thought about what to do. Finally she stopped and turned to the other girl.

"I have an idea. But I'm going to need your help." Alex outlined her vague plan, giving as many details as she could before she asked, "Do you think you can do that?"

"You can count on me," Skyla promised.

Alex hoped they weren't going to end up imprisoned with the rest of their classmates. "Okay, then," she said. "Can you grab me Pip's pillow?"

While Skyla was rustling around in the dark for Pipsqueak's pack, Alex dug through the bag closest to her and retrieved the relaxant spray from the medical kit since her own was lost somewhere in the Durungan Ranges. Skyla handed her the pillow and Alex sprayed a liberal amount of the medication onto the fluffy material, being careful not to inhale any of it. She then stuffed the fuming object into her own backpack along with her heels and Skyla's makeup case, securing her bag on her back.

"Ready?" she asked, and at Skyla's nod, the two descended the hill and stealthily made their way to the place where Alex had climbed up to the balcony.

"We're aiming for that room up there," Alex said, pointing to an open window about four floors above them. "Do you see that ledge? That's where we want to go."

"That's high," Skyla said shakily.

"You can do it," Alex encouraged her. "We'll stop halfway, and I'll be with you the entire time."

Skyla wasn't burdened by a backpack like Alex was, but she still had more trouble climbing up the vines. Alex whispered reassurances to her, and when they made it to the second-floor balcony, she and Skyla looked into the ballroom.

"See that guy?" Alex said, pointing to Sir Oswald. "That's him. He's the host."

Skyla's eyes travelled over him, looking more focused than Alex had ever seen. "Got it."

Alex had to trust Skyla knew what she was talking about. After more struggling upwards in the dark, they reached the fourth-floor window.

The room was dark, which was perfect cover for them. Without being able to see anything inside, Alex pulled herself over the ledge, reaching out to help Skyla climb in. The moment both of them were inside, the overhead light flicked on.

"What're you doing in my room?"

Seventeen

Alex held her breath as she stared at the little boy holding a teddy bear and standing in the doorway of what was evidently his bedroom, judging by the toys scattered all about the place.

"Oh, aren't you just adorable?" Skyla cooed, walking towards the child. "Would you look at him, Alex? I just want to wrap him up and take him home."

Alex hissed out a low warning, trying to get Skyla to keep her distance from the wide-eyed boy, but it was no use.

"Hello, there," Skyla said, kneeling a few feet away from him. "My name is Skyla but tonight I'm Samantha. Who are you?"

So much for our fake identities, Alex thought with a mental sigh.

The boy looked uncertainly from Alex to Skyla before he whispered, "I'm not supposed to talk to strangers."

"Are you allowed to talk to friends?" Skyla asked. "Because I'd like to be your friend."

Alex inwardly winced at Skyla's creepy-sounding words, but her intent sounded genuine—and innocent. Regardless, the boy looked confused and Alex was worried he'd make a run for it. She took an anxious step forward, heaving her bag into a better position on her shoulder. Her eyes widened as an absolutely ridiculous idea came to her. Maybe Hunter's cryptic note had been instructive after all.

"Do you like stories?" Alex asked the boy, and the answer was obvious when his eyes lit up.

She knelt to the floor and, holding her breath to avoid the relaxant fumes, opened her pack and reached to the very bottom to dig out the massive book of children's stories.

"Would you like Skyla to read to you?" Alex asked, holding the book out to him.

Seeing the item in her hands, he took a step forward, then another one. When he arrived at Skyla's side, he looked up at her with owlish eyes and said, "I'm Benjamin. We can be friends if you read to me."

"Oh, Benny, you're so cute!" Skyla said in a voice so high-pitched that Alex feared someone would hear. "Let's tuck you in while Aunty Alex brings us the storybook."

Aunty Alex? Wow, Skyla really was a kid person.

Alex zipped up her pack and stood up to find that Skyla had snuggled into Benjamin's bed with him. "Here you go," she said, handing over the heavy book. "Happy reading."

"Look, Benny! There are pictures!" Skyla said. She seemed more excited than Benjamin at the discovery.

"I'll leave you both to it," Alex said. "I'll see you downstairs, right, Skyla?"

"Ten minutes, Alex," Skyla said, tearing her eyes from the book. "I promise I'll be there."

"See you then," Alex said, hoping that would be true.

"Hey, Alex," Skyla called just before Alex reached the door. "You need to swap your shoes. And it'll probably be a good idea to untuck your dress unless you're trying to make a new fashion statement."

Feeling like an idiot, Alex untucked and straightened her gown and swapped back into her heels. She also remembered to grab the compact powder out of Skyla's makeup case, which was essential for their plan to work.

"Thanks, Skyla," Alex said, genuinely appreciative.

She hurried out of the room and down a hallway, finding a staircase and descending to the next floor. When she was there, she snuck into a bathroom to straighten her hair and check her makeup. Once she was satisfied that she didn't look like she'd just climbed up a building, she purposely left the powder brush on the bench and closed the compact, keeping it in her hands. Then she followed the hallway again until she reached the staircase that led down into the ballroom on the second floor.

Alex stood at the top of the stairs and looked out at the scene below, positioned just as Sir Oswald had been when he'd addressed his guests.

I know I need to get his attention, but I wish I'd come up with a better plan than this, Alex thought despairingly. Just like her 'Inebriated Guest' moment at the royal palace, she knew she would likely regret her next move.

Steeling her resolve, she clenched her teeth and slowly moved her foot to the next step down. But instead of resting her heel on the solid stair, she closed her eyes tightly and deliberately overstepped.

The effect was instantaneous.

She fell like a Slinky spring, tumbling painfully down the staircase. The musicians stopped playing and she heard gasps and exclamations all around her. Only when she came to a stop on the hard floor did she open her eyes, finding a swarm of faces all around her.

"Make way, please. Make way," came the familiar voice of Sir Oswald.

Perfect. Just as she'd planned.

"My dear, are you all right?"

"How embarrassing," Alex whimpered, actually managing to fill her eyes with tears. It wasn't all that difficult, considering how painful her landing had been. "Please tell me no one saw that?"

"Of course not, my dear," Sir Oswald lied, kneeling beside her. "Are you injured? Do you need me to call my personal physician?"

"No, please," Alex begged. "I feel humiliated enough as it is."

"There's nothing to be ashamed about," he said, patting her on the hand. "Do you think you can stand?"

When she nodded, he closed his fingers around hers and stood to his feet, pulling her up with a surprising amount of strength for someone his age. The room spun around her and it wasn't hard for her to overdramatise her dizziness. She leaned heavily onto Sir Oswald, apologising profusely when she was finally able to lift her head.

"No need to apologise, my dear," he told her kindly. "Why, it's a pleasure to be able to assist such a beautiful young woman."

Alex almost gagged. He was old enough to be her grandfather. And if he called her 'my dear' one more time...

"What's your name, my dear?"

Alex's eye twitched at the repeated endearment, but she answered him charmingly. "Ally Jones, Sir Oswald. My mother, Larissa, had me listed as her plus one, but she's picked up a stomach bug and thought it best for everyone if she stayed home and I came without her."

Alex held a breath as she waited to see if she was right about Hunter's clue and her 'mother' having lots of friends—hopefully enough friends to secure an invitation to an event such as this.

Her heart raced as she watched Sir Oswald scrunch his face in confusion.

"Larissa Jones?" he said. "I don't believe I know ... Unless..." His eyes lit with comprehension. "Do you perhaps mean Larissa Rolar?"

"Rolar was her maiden name," Alex said, the make-believe story flowing effortlessly from her mouth. "When she married my father she took his surname."

"Not Renwick Jones, surely?" Sir Oswald guffawed. "That slimy old toad! Who would have thought he'd manage to land a catch like your mother? Ha! Well, good on him,

I suppose. There may yet be hope for the rest of us."

Alex couldn't believe he was actually buying her deceit.

"Come, come, dear Ally," Sir Oswald continued. "You must tell me all about how your enchanting mother is faring these days. You clearly inherited her beauty—that much is evident. Too many years have passed since I last saw her..."

Sir Oswald went on to share a memory that included a chicken, a tea set and a thunderstorm, but Alex wasn't paying much attention to his words. She was trying to figure out if she should start laughing or just shake her head in astonishment. She would have to remember to thank Hunter later ... Or not, depending on how the rest of the evening played out.

"—and so, really, I have your mother to thank for setting me up with my darling wife. Oh, how dearly I miss my beloved Bryonie."

Alex had no idea what to say, so she patted him consolingly on the hand that still held her own.

"You're such a lovely girl," he told her. "Kind and caring, just like your mother."

She managed to plaster an embarrassed smile on her face. "That's very sweet of you, Sir Oswald."

"Come along, my dear," he said, taking her arm. "I want you to meet some of my acquaintances. Although, I daresay you will have been introduced to many already, given your mother's commendably active role in society."

"I'd be delighted to," Alex said, but her fear spiked as she tried to figure out how to move her plan along and not get stuck talking with people Larissa's 'daughter' should already know.

"Sir," called a guard, stopping them from going any further. "Please allow me to scan the young woman's ID before you continue."

"That's unnecessary, Quinn. Ally is no intruder," Sir Oswald said.

"All the same, sir, for your guests' piece of mind, I ask you to permit me to check," the guard insisted.

"Be quick about it, then," Sir Oswald said, clearly unimpressed.

"Your identification tag please, Miss," the guard said to Alex, holding out his hand.

"Of course," she said, brushing her hand along her side and frowning in mock-confusion. "I had it pinned to my

dress right here. It was there just before
... when—Oh! I must have left it in the
bathroom. I took it off when I went to
powder my nose."

Alex held out the compact container of
makeup that remained grasped in her hand
as if to verify her words. At least she
hadn't dropped it in her fall down the
stairs.

"Miss, you'll have to come with me,"
the guard said in a no-nonsense tone.

"Come now, Quinn," Sir Oswald said.
"I'm sure this is just a misunderstanding.
Why don't we both escort Ally back to
the bathroom so she can retrieve her ID
and ease your fears."

"Sir, I'd prefer it if you would remain
here with your guests," the guard said.

"Fortunately for me, I don't take orders
from you," Sir Oswald replied firmly.

"Your guest of honour will be arriving
shortly," the guard said.

"And if you cease stalling, then we'll
all be back in time to greet him," Sir
Oswald returned. "Now, lead the way,
Quinn."

Quinn must have realised he wasn't
going to separate Alex from the party's
host, so he abruptly turned and led the
way up the staircase. When they reached
the top and began along the hallway, Alex

had to quickly modify her original plan. Sir Oswald was exactly where she wanted him to be but she hadn't counted on an armed escort. She just had to hope Skyla was in position and not still reading stories to Benjamin.

When Quinn opened the door and stepped into the bathroom, Alex felt some of the tension leave her body at the sight of the pillow resting on the bench beside the powder brush she'd left there. Skyla was ready and waiting, which meant that their plan just might work.

"It's over there," Alex said, pointing to the bench.

Quinn asked Sir Oswald to remain in the doorway and the host grudgingly agreed, ordering the guard to hurry up.

Alex stepped over to the bench. Her armed escort remained a few feet behind her, but she needed him to be closer.

"Oh, look, I left my powder brush here, too," she said. "Silly me."

She giggled as if it was the funniest thing in the world as she reached for the pillow.

"I see the brush, Miss," Quinn said. "But I don't see your ID."

"It's right here," Alex said, gesturing for him to step closer.

He looked at her with narrowed eyes and raised his Stabiliser, edging forward.

Alex's heart thudded in her chest and she prayed that the relaxant would be as fast-acting as it had been with Pip. She stepped towards the guard and deliberately staggered sideways, collapsing onto the ground at his feet.

"Ally?" Sir Oswald called from where he stood at the doorway to the bathroom. He made to move towards her but the guard held up a warning hand, so Sir Oswald remained where he was but in an irritated voice, he ordered, "Quinn, help her."

"Miss?" the guard said cautiously, kneeling down in front of her.

"I guess I'm still a bit dizzy," Alex admitted sheepishly. "These heels aren't helping, either. Would you please help me up?"

Quinn hesitated for a moment before he lowered his Stabiliser and reached for Alex with his free hand. She latched on and yanked him closer, causing him to overbalance and stumble forward. It was the perfect position for her to shove the pillow into his startled face.

"What—"

His eyes glazed over before he could manage a second muffled word, but she kept the pillow pressed against his face for a few more moments to be sure he was mentally out of it.

"Ally, what are you—"

Alex didn't pause to think as she grabbed Quinn's fallen Stabiliser and aimed it at Sir Oswald, pulling the trigger. A blast of light hit him in the chest and he crumpled to the floor where, if Kaiden was right, he would remain unconscious for the next ten minutes.

She stared in shock at what she'd done, but she didn't have the chance to feel guilty because Quinn chose that moment to collapse on top of her. The increased contact with the relaxant had not just sedated him, it seemed to have knocked him unconscious. Alex grunted with the strain of his weight and slid him off her and onto the floor. She then stood and moved over to the doorway to drag Sir Oswald into the bathroom so that he lay beside his guard.

"Skyla? Are you in here?" Alex called.

The door to the toilet opened and a white-faced Skyla stumbled out.

"Do you know how many bathrooms there are on this floor?" she asked hysterically. "Five. Five bathrooms! It's a good thing no one picked up your powder brush, because otherwise I never would have known where to meet you!"

"You did great, Skyla," Alex said. "But we have to hurry before they wake up or someone comes looking for them. We don't have much time."

"All right, all right," Skyla huffed. "You get his clothes."

Alex grimaced as she removed Sir Oswald's jacket, tie, vest, dress shirt, trousers and shoes. She left him in his underclothes, but she still felt uncomfortable at having to undress him at all.

"Here." She handed the clothes to Skyla who transformed so quickly that Alex blinked and said, "Whoa. That was fast."

Standing in front of her was a perfect replica of Sir Oswald, only he was wearing a pale yellow evening gown that was almost bursting at the seams.

"Some people are easier to imitate than others," Skyla said, her voice an exact copy of Sir Oswald's.

"That's disturbing," Alex mumbled and she turned her back so Skyla could change into the man's clothing.

"I'm ready," Skyla said when she was done.

"I'm not sure about Quinn," Alex said, sliding the Stabiliser under Skyla's jacket so that it was hidden from sight, "but we don't have much time before Sir Oswald wakes up, so we have to move."

Neither of them knew where they should go but they figured downwards was the best direction, so they descended a stairway at the opposite end of the hallway, which took them to the ground floor of the mansion.

"What now?" Skyla asked.

"Now you need to ask for assistance."

Alex explained what she had in mind, and once she was sure Skyla understood her plan, she latched onto the arm of 'Sir Oswald' and started fake-giggling. Skyla led them to the entry of the mansion where they caught the attention of the guards standing outside by the doors.

"You, there," Skyla called, and both guards stepped back into the building with alert expressions.

"Sir Oswald?" said the guard on the left. "Is there something you need?"

"This lovely young woman desires to see the juggler perform an act," Skyla told him, her much deeper voice slurring deliberately. "I've had a wee bit too much to drink and I'm afraid I'm a little unsteady on my feet. Will one of you escort us to see my prisoner?"

The guards looked at each other before turning back to their employer.

"Sir, you've ordered that he receive no visitors," the same guard said.

"Well, I'm un-ordering it," Skyla snapped. "Now, take us there at once before my other guests wish to see the juggler as well. We're sneaking away as it is."

"As you wish, Sir Oswald."

The guard stepped away from his companion and led the way down the corridor.

He stopped to open a door, motioning for them to go through first. The door opened to a staircase that took them underground. At the bottom of the stairs they followed a corridor until they reached yet another door, this one guarded by two beefy-looking men.

"Kerway, Stibbins," their escort greeted the other guards. "Sir Oswald and his lady friend want to see a performance from the juggler. Let us through."

The men looked curiously at the trio before the one on the left pressed his ID tag against the touch-screen sensor on the door, unlocking the seal.

"If you'll follow me, Sir Oswald," their escort said, and he led Skyla and Alex into a stone corridor lined with cells, the door sealing shut behind them.

"Ooooh, what a pretty dungeon," Alex squealed girlishly, while secretly wondering what kind of person had a stone prison underneath their home to begin with. "Sir Oswald, this place is simply charming."

"It is?" Skyla sounded as weirded out as Alex felt, but when Alex pinched her, she quickly corrected, "I mean, of course it is. I own the best dungeon in all of Medora. In fact—"

Alex squeezed Skyla's arm and the other girl got the message to stop rambling.

Their guard led them to the very end of the corridor and Alex had to force herself not to react when she saw her classmates gaping at her through a set of bars. Both she and Skyla had to remain in character for their ruse to work, so she barely spared them a glance before she turned to look at the lone man lying on a pallet in the next cell.

"You, juggler," the guard called. "Sir Oswald wishes to see you perform."

The man didn't move from his position. "Sir Oswald can bite my—"

"Are you sure this is necessary, sir?" the guard asked Skyla, interrupting the performer's gruff—and rude—response. "Perhaps your young lady would prefer a stroll in the gardens rather than watching this crass man's pathetic attempts to throw a few balls into the air."

"Pathetic?" the performer repeated, sitting up angrily. He was scruffy looking, which was probably a result of his recent incarceration, and he had a black patch of material covering one eye. "Who're you calling pathetic?"

"I don't want to visit the gardens," Alex said to the guard in a whiney voice. "Those animal hedges give me nightmares. What I want to see is this man juggling."

"You heard my guest," Skyla said. "She wants to see him perform."

The guard looked like he wanted to argue, but when Skyla added a firm, "Now," he relented.

"On your feet, Graver," the guard ordered the man in the cell.

The performer remained in place. "Who's gonna make me?"

The guard wasn't impressed. "You'll do as you're told."

The performer smirked and lay back on his pallet, his hands casually resting beneath his head. "I don't feel like following your orders right now. But thanks for the offer, mate."

The security guard actually growled as he yanked out his ID tag and pressed it to the panel at the entrance to the cell. The lock clicked and he yanked the door open to storm right up to the performer.

"On. Your. *Feet*," he spat, hauling the man up from where he lay.

"Now, that's not a very nice way to treat your houseguest," the juggler mocked.

The guard didn't miss a beat. "I won't ask again," he said in a voice heavy with menace.

Alex had seen enough. They were exactly where they needed to be with the cell now open, so it was time for her to act. She drew the stolen weapon from Skyla's jacket and aimed it at the guard, telling herself that, like the real Sir Oswald, he'd only be unconscious for ten minutes. It wasn't like she was going to kill him—just stun him. He'd be fine.

On that thought, she pulled the trigger. Light flew from the weapon and the guard fell to the ground.

The juggler's visible eye widened and she gave him a comforting smile.

"Hey, I'm Alex," she said. "Hunter sent us to get you out of here."

He appeared both surprised and sceptical. "Us?"

Alex motioned to Skyla and then pointed to her stunned classmates who were staring at her from their cell. "Us," she repeated.

"There's nothing like a good prison break," he said, his stoic features transforming into a beaming smile. "I'm Samson Graver, by the way."

"Nice to meet you," Alex said, aware of how ridiculous their situation was. "As much as I'd like to swap life stories, we really need to get moving."

"Agreed," Samson said, and he pointed to Skyla. "Want me to get rid of him or can you handle it?"

"What's that supposed to mean?" Skyla asked, crossing her arms with a pout. The petulant gesture looked decidedly odd from Sir Oswald's body.

"Uh, she—he's not a problem," Alex told Samson. "He's not who you think he is."

Samson seemed unconvinced. "If you say so."

"We'll explain everything once we're safe," Alex said. She ran her eyes over the performer, noting that he appeared to be standing all right, but she didn't know what might have happened to him in the few days he'd been imprisoned. "Are you hurt or anything? Can you walk?"

He seemed puzzled, but then his expression cleared with understanding and he sent her a reassuring look. "I'm fine, love. They didn't do anything except bore me to death."

"Good to know," Alex said. She reached down and retrieved the security guard's ID tag before leading the way out of the cell and over to her classmates. She could see their mouths moving as they tried to talk to her, but no sound came out of the cell they were in. The moment she touched the ID to the panel the door unlocked, and whatever was keeping the cell soundproofed disappeared. Alex was inundated with so many exclamations that she glanced back up the corridor in concern, hoping the other guards wouldn't hear the disturbance.

"Quiet!" Alex hissed at them as they made their way out of the cell. "We're supposed to be stealthy, remember? Jeez."

Immediately they all shut up.

"Alex, what are you doing here?" Jordan asked, his disbelief obvious. "And why are you with him?"

He pointed at 'Sir Oswald' and Alex motioned for Skyla to join them.

"Hey, guys," Skyla said with a wave. "It's me."

They looked at her blankly, clearly wondering if Alex had managed to drug the host of the party.

"I told you we'd look after you if something went wrong," Skyla continued, oblivious to their confusion. "We totally have your backs."

"Skyla?" Pipsqueak gasped.

"Yeah?" Skyla answered. When Pip didn't say anything further, she added, "I don't have all day, Pipsqueak. What do you want?"

"Uh ... nothing," Pip said, her eyes wide. "Just ... good job."

"We're not out of this yet," Alex told them, and she turned to Samson who was watching their interaction with unveiled curiosity. "Our instructions are to retrieve you and escort you back to your home. If we can get out of the building, can you lead us to your place?"

"That's a little more complicated than it sounds, love," he said. "I'm not exactly a local."

"You don't live in the village?" Kaiden asked.

"No," Samson said, eyeing him warily. "But if we can get to my juggling bag, I have a secret stash of Bubblers that will get us all out of here."

"Where is it?" Alex asked, already knowing she wouldn't like the answer.

"My best guess? Hopefully near the side of the stage upstairs, hidden in the corner behind the fake pot plant. That's where I left it."

Great. Just perfect.

"Here's what we're going to do," Alex said, taking charge. "Skyla and I are the only ones who can be seen walking around upstairs, so we need to get the rest of you outside. There are two guards stationed at the door to the dungeon, and one left at the entrance to the mansion. If we can get you past them, then you'll be outside and you can make a run for it up the hill. Skyla and I will meet you there after we grab Samson's bag."

"But Alex, you said I wouldn't have to do anything else once we found the others," Skyla whined. "I want to be me again. It's tiring holding this man's shape."

Alex looked at her with alarm. "How much longer can you stay as Sir Oswald? He'll be waking up any minute but he'll still need to find some clothes, so we should have just long enough to reach Samson's bag and get out of here. Can you handle that?"

"I don't know," Skyla said. "But I don't want to stay like him anymore. I want to go with the others. I don't like it here."

Alex tried to rein in her frustration. It wasn't Skyla's fault they were stuck in such a dangerous situation, but Alex wished the other girl would be a little more willing to help.

"Fine," she agreed, anxious to get moving. "Skyla, you go with the others. I'll find Samson's bag and meet you all back where we started."

"You're not going on your own," Jordan told her sternly.

"Apparently I am," she replied, with just as much attitude. "None of you can be seen."

"I won't be seen," Jordan said pointedly. "And I'm coming with you, so don't argue."

She frowned at him, but if he was adamant about going with her, then she might as well take advantage of it. "Can you use your gift on me, too? That'll hopefully speed things along."

He nodded, relieved by her easy acceptance.

"Here, take these," Samson said, handing over three juggling balls. "If you need to make a quick escape, throw them as hard as you can at the ground, and run like there's a fire-breathing draekon on your tail."

Wondering what the heck a draekon was but deciding now was not the time to ask, Alex took the balls and handed them to Jordan for safekeeping before she turned back to the performer. "Why didn't you use whatever these are when you were captured?"

"You have the element of surprise," he said. "I was ambushed in the middle of a performance. I didn't have the chance to activate them."

"I heard you spilled wine all over Sir Oswald," Declan said. "Wasn't that enough of a distraction to use whatever is in those juggling balls?"

"Technicalities," Samson said gruffly. "Are we going?"

"We'll head out first and clear the way," Jordan told the others. "Give us a minute to take down the guards before you follow."

When the rest of them nodded, Jordan reached out and grabbed Alex's hand. Almost immediately she felt a tingling sensation and her vision turned slightly blurry as his gift took effect. Only Jordan remained perfectly clear, since he was transcended along with her. But he looked paler than usual, and almost like he was in pain.

"Are you all right?" Alex asked as they hurried towards the door to the dungeons.

"Tired," he said, and Alex knew he didn't just mean physically. "Keeping my gift active the whole time Kaiden and I were in the military compound took it out of me. I tried to get out of the cell earlier, but it's reinforced against gifts, just like our dorms at the academy. The effort drained me even more. But I can keep it up for a while longer."

"Jordan, really, maybe you should go back with the others," Alex tried again.

"I'm not leaving you on your own," he told her. "We're in this together, remember? You're stuck with me, Alex. Deal with it."

She squeezed his hand, knowing she didn't have to say anything for him to understand how relieved she was to have him with her.

"Here," she said, handing him the Stabiliser as they approached the entry to the dungeons. "I've shot enough people today. Can you...?"

"I've got this," Jordan assured her.

"Just one shot, remember?"

Jordan snorted. "As if I'd forget. I don't relish the idea of becoming a murderer."

She nodded in agreement and reached out with the guard's ID, pressing it against the door panel until the lock clicked open.

"It's about time you—Hey, what's going on? Kerway, did you open the door?"

The guards looked at the doorway with confusion as Alex and Jordan snuck through unseen. Jordan quickly raised the weapon and released the quiet burst of energy into Stibbins and then Kerway. They collapsed to the ground, unconscious.

Jordan turned the weapon over in his hands. "Make a note, Alex. I want one of these for my next birthday."

She shook her head at him and waited for their companions to catch up.

When they did, Jordan said, "We'll escort you all to the front door and help with the guard, but then you'll be on your own."

"We'll be fine," Tom said. "Just get us outside."

Eighteen

They hurried up the stairs with the transcended Alex and Jordan taking point. When they reached the front of the mansion, the guard was still there, along with another man in place of the one who had escorted Alex and Skyla to the dungeon. Jordan didn't hesitate in shooting them both, and they fell to the ground with a quiet *thud*. Declan and Blink moved the unconscious men outside and around the corner of the mansion until they were out of sight.

"We'll see you in a bit," Tom said, and he ushered the others out the door.

"Wait," Alex called, taking the Stabiliser from Jordan and asking him to release her from his gift.

"What?" Tom asked her when she was visible again.

She offered him the weapon and said, "Here." At his repulsed grimace, she passed it to Kaiden, who took it from her and held it confidently.

"What if you need it?" he asked.

"There are two of us and seven of you. You need it more," Alex said. "And besides, no one will be able to see us."

"And you have my juggling balls," Samson pointed out, although Alex didn't find that to be much of a reassurance.

"Go," she told them. "We'll see you soon."

She felt proud that she'd managed to refrain from adding a 'hopefully' at the end of her sentence.

"Be careful," Kaiden whispered to her as the others started sneaking away.

"You too," she replied, just as quietly.

"We need to move, Alex," Jordan said.

With that, Kaiden took off after the others and Jordan grabbed Alex's arm, sharing his gift once more.

"I can't wait until we finish this task and get back to the academy," she muttered, leading the way up the main staircase to the party.

"I know," Jordan said, his voice sounding strained. "It's not so much fun anymore. I think I'll sleep for a week once we're back."

Alex could feel him trembling from the effort of maintaining his gift, but she knew it would make things worse if she tried to mother him. And besides, his transcendence was needed to get them in and out of the party unnoticed.

"We'll just grab the bag and bail, yeah?" she said as they neared the dining hall.

"Nice and simple," Jordan said. "Love it."

When they entered the room though, Alex knew it wasn't going to be as easy as they'd hoped. Because standing on the staircase leading down into the hall was Sir Oswald—the real one—with the only difference being his new outfit. Beside him was Quinn, who looked to be extremely dazed from the relaxant Alex had nearly suffocated him with.

"Ladies and gentlemen," Sir Oswald called out, before wincing and pressing a hand to his stomach where Alex had shot him. "I apologise for my absence, but unfortunately I was assaulted and left unconscious in my own home."

Shocked exclamations spread around the guests and Alex dug her fingers into Jordan's hand, pulling him towards the other side of the room where the stage was located.

"Alas, the young woman responsible for my attack is yet to be apprehended, but rest assured that my security team is searching for her as we speak. Due to her actions, I feel that for your own safety I must end the night earlier than planned.

I thank you for your attendance and I look forward to the next time we all meet."

There were murmurs of lingering alarm as well as disappointment, but Sir Oswald's guests followed his instructions and began to leave. Alex and Jordan had to press themselves up against the wall to avoid anyone bumping into them. Just because Jordan's gift could move them through solid objects didn't mean Alex wanted to step through another human being. That was just ... Eww.

The room cleared quickly, but there were about fifteen or so people who remained in place. Alex wondered what they were hanging around for, but she didn't have to wait long before the doors to the room slammed shut and Sir Oswald's previously kind expression morphed into one of hatred.

"I want to know who that girl was, the one posing as Larissa Rolar's daughter," he spat as he stormed down the stairs. "Someone better have answers for me! Who was she and what was she doing in my house?"

"I don't know who she was, Sir Oswald," said a security guard who had just entered the room, "but I might know why she was here. It looks like the performer has escaped, along with the other intruders we detained earlier tonight."

Sir Oswald cursed savagely. "Security? What a load of rubbish. I want you and the rest of your incompetent team gone from my residence immediately, or I'll be locking the lot of you in my dungeon. And don't for a moment think that you'll be compensated for your work tonight. I should be charging you after the mess you've all made."

With gritted teeth, the guard nodded obediently, grabbed the arm of the dazed Quinn and left the room.

When the door was closed behind him, Sir Oswald shouted, "Conference!" and the remaining guests moved to sit at the long, narrow table close to where Jordan and Alex stood like statues.

"Come on," Jordan whispered, barely moving his lips as he tugged on her hand.

But Alex was frozen to the spot because, as the people stepped closer and sat down, she realised she recognised some of them. She couldn't identify anyone by name, but she'd definitely seen them before. As she tried to put the puzzle together, she noticed Sir Oswald speaking through a ComTCD to someone before he abruptly ended the call.

"Are they coming?" a woman asked Sir Oswald, motioning to the Device in his hand.

"Any minute now," the host answered tersely.

Something about his words caused uneasiness to swirl in Alex's stomach.

"Jordan, we need to leave. Right now."

Prompted by her urgency, they edged along the wall until they were beside the fake plant. Just as Alex spotted the juggler's bag, a Bubbledoor opened in the centre of the room, diverting her attention.

Three people stepped out, and Alex barely held back a gasp when she identified them as Calista Maine, the tattooed Gerald and, bizarrely enough, Signa, the mind reader from the military compound.

Only then did Alex figure out why the people seated at the table seemed so familiar.

"Jordan!" she whispered, her already uneasy stomach now churning with dread. "These people—I recognise them from the file Darrius showed me. He thinks they're all Claimed by Aven!"

Jordan gripped her hand tighter in response and she followed his gaze to where Signa was standing—and staring straight at them. Signa might not be able to read her, but he'd sensed Jordan and

Kaiden earlier that day, even in their transcended state.

Their situation had just worsened exponentially.

Sir Oswald was busy informing the new arrivals of the night's events, and he snapped at Signa for not paying attention. The mind reader smirked darkly at the place where Alex and Jordan stood before he slowly turned to the older man.

"Hurry!" Jordan urged.

She reached behind the plant for Samson's bag, handing it to Jordan who slung it over his shoulder. He spun them both around, seemingly intent on running straight through the wall to get them out of there.

They took three steps before their progress was halted. As in, *literally*. It was as if they'd stepped onto a patch of superglue, since neither of them could move their feet so much as an inch. While that was a distinct problem, Alex was more concerned when she felt Jordan's transcendence dissolve around them, bringing her vision into clarity and leaving them visible to everyone else in the room.

"It's impolite to leave a party without saying goodbye," purred a voice that sent shivers of trepidation down her spine.

Alex and Jordan found themselves being physically turned around as if on invisible rotating platforms until they faced the entire group of people. Alex's focus was solely on one person, though. She had no idea where he'd come from, but she was certain he hadn't been there a moment ago.

"I'd say it's good to see you again, Aven, but I'd be lying."

"It's unfortunate you feel that way, Alexandra," he replied. "I, however, am pleasantly surprised by your unexpected appearance. And you've even brought a little friend with you. Would you care to introduce us?"

Alex didn't respond. She looked around the room, trying to figure out who was responsible for their current state of immobility. But with all the potentially gifted—not to mention, potentially Claimed—people in the room, she didn't know where to begin guessing.

"His name is Jordan Sparker," Signa informed Aven. "He's a student at the academy. He has an impressive gift, as we all just witnessed for ourselves. But his thoughts are scattered. He's very difficult to read."

Alex glared at the mind reader who turned his gaze upon her.

"I knew you were lying," Signa said arrogantly. "Those military idiots played right into your hands, didn't they, *Princess*? I was so disappointed that I didn't get to listen to you scream for mercy while they tortured you for information. But it looks like the tables have turned now."

"Silence, Signa," Aven ordered, and the other man quieted immediately.

The Meyarin sauntered slowly across the room, with Calista, Gerald, Signa, Sir Oswald, and another woman following. They stopped directly in front of Alex and Jordan. She felt incredibly vulnerable in her immobilised state, and she wondered why her gift wasn't protecting her. Shouldn't her willpower allow her to decide who could use their powers on her? Why wasn't it working?

Signa sniggered. "It seems that the all-powerful Alexandra Jennings is second-guessing her ability."

Her eyes widened. How could he read her mind now? Something must have changed. She looked around the room and locked eyes with Jordan, specifically where their hands remained linked.

"Are you still trying to keep us transcended?"

A silent nod told her all she needed to know. Someone in the room was interfering with his gift, and because she remained connected to him, somehow her willpower was being nullified as well. She yanked their fingers apart and immediately she felt her feet unstick from the floor, but she remained in position. It was one thing for them to know she was once again mentally protected; she didn't want to reveal her newfound physical freedom just yet.

Signa was staring at her with frustration, evidently unable to read her again. He took a threatening step towards her but Aven speared him with a glance and he retreated hastily. Alex wondered if he'd been following a blood-bonded mental order or if he'd reacted purely out of self-preservation.

"You don't need to know her thoughts to understand her motives, Signa," Aven told the other man. "Her face reads like an open book." He reached out a hand and tenderly stroked her cheek. Feeling violated, Alex shuddered, but somehow managed to remain glued to the spot.

"What are you doing here, Aven?" she asked, trying for nonchalance. "You don't seem like the partying type."

"You're one to talk," spat Sir Oswald. "Who, exactly, are you, Alexandra Jennings?"

Alex sent him a look. "You just answered your own question, genius. I guess you're still recovering from your, ahem, 'power nap', huh?" She managed a taunting smile just to annoy him further.

"Why, you little—"

"Enough, Oswald," Aven said. "Go and see to the others."

Sir Oswald clearly didn't like being ordered around in his own home, but he stormed back to his seat at the table where the other people Claimed by Aven waited.

"You have them all wrapped around your little finger, don't you?" Alex said to Aven. "What did it take to get them on your side? Did you just steal their will from them like you tried with me? Or did you offer them riches and glory in return for their services?"

Aven smiled at her. "What makes you think they didn't come to me of their own volition?"

Alex shook her head in response, knowing he was a first-class deceiver and that there was nothing he could say that she would believe. "Whatever."

"Aren't you curious about your immobility?" he asked. "Perhaps you'll be enlightened if I introduce you to some of my closer associates."

Associates. That was a word Alex had heard Aven use before, and she shuddered at the possibility of it being the term he used for all those he Claimed.

"You already know Gerald Togen," Aven said, gesturing to the tattooed menace crackling his knuckles and sneering at Alex.

"We still have unfinished business, girlie."

Alex wasn't sure whether to snort or cringe, so she kept her face blank and turned her attention back to the much more dangerous Aven.

The Meyarin next indicated to the tall, blond woman who Alex already sort of knew. "This is Calista Maine. You can thank her for your current physical stasis. She has a very useful, very *powerful* gift of telekinesis, which is keeping you fastened securely to the floor."

"So nice to meet you, Calista," Alex said, her voice sugar-coated with sarcasm. "How do you feel about letting us go now?"

The woman just stared at Alex with her scarily empty eyes.

"Oh, Alexandra, how amusing you are," Aven said, without the slightest trace of humour. He turned to the final woman, who had bright ginger hair that fanned around her face like waves of fire. "This is Lena

Morrow. Her gift allows her to neutralise the abilities of others, as I'm sure your friend Jordan can verify. Judging by Signa's displeasure, it seems her gift doesn't work against your own mental fortitude."

"Such a shame," Alex said. "I can't begin to tell you how much I want to be stripped of my will again. We all had a great time that day, didn't we?"

"Yes, I certainly remember the joy I felt when my dagger pierced your flesh," Aven recounted, looking at her thoughtfully. "Speaking of which, I'd like my weapon returned to me."

She was startled by his demand but she answered him anyway—sort of. "Finders, keepers."

He narrowed his eyes. "That dagger was never meant for someone of mortal blood. It won't yield to you."

What a peculiar thing for him to say. "It's a weapon, not a person," Alex said.

"You'd do well to—"

"My prince!" Signa blurted out, with a shocked expression on his face. The mind reader quivered at the look the Meyarin sent him but he continued anyway. "I need a word in private. I believe it's something you'll want to hear."

Aven glared at the man but led him away from the group to the other side of the room. Alex could see Signa whispering urgently, with Aven's expression turning more and more livid by the second. He looked back in their direction with blazing eyes before nodding his head at Signa and striding back over. But instead of speaking with Alex, Aven turned to Jordan.

"Signa tells me you have some colourful thoughts, Jordan Sparker, scattered as they are," Aven said. "I'm curious, did you enjoy your visit to my city? Was Meya everything you expected it to be?"

Alex felt the blood drain from her face as she looked at Jordan. To his credit, he didn't react to the Meyarin's words. But the damage was done.

"How is my family, Alexandra?" Aven asked, turning to her. "Do they miss me?"

"You're disinherited," she reminded him. "I know it's a big word, but FYI, it means they're not your family anymore. Buy yourself a dictionary."

Aven's glorious face darkened and he stepped so close that she almost moved backwards until she remembered that she was meant to be stuck to the spot.

"Do not speak to me that way," he hissed.

She stared straight into his eyes. "I'll do whatever I want, Aven. Because. I. Can."

He growled at her—actually *growled*—before something caught his attention, prompting him to look towards the entrance of the room. He turned back to Alex with a menacing smile that caused her to shiver with apprehension.

"You have brave friends," he said. "Foolish, but brave."

She felt a moment of confusion before the doors burst open and Kaiden and Declan sprinted into the room. Kaiden had the Stabiliser out and immediately started shooting, but after only four shots—leading to four unconscious people—Calista reached out her hand and the weapon soared from his grasp to land in hers. A split second later, both boys flew through the air and landed next to Jordan. The four of them were standing together, frozen in a row.

"Kaiden James and Declan Stirling, my prince," Signa announced. "They also go to the academy. But this one I can't read, nor could I break into his mind earlier today at the Soori Outpost."

Signa pointed at Kaiden, and Aven's face turned pensive.

"I've heard of you, Kaiden James," the Meyarin said. "You're Master Athora's talented protégé, correct? How long have you been studying under him?"

When Kaiden didn't answer, Aven stepped closer to him. "I asked you a question. Answer me."

Kaiden held Aven's stare but his mouth remained closed. In the blink of an eye, the Meyarin threw his arm forward until it made contact with Kaiden's torso, causing him to slam violently backwards and onto the floor, his legs bent at the knees and his feet firmly stuck to the floor.

"Hey!" Declan cried, trying unsuccessfully to break free of his captivity and help his friend.

Aven stood over Kaiden and stared down at him. "I'll ask one more time. How long have you studied under Master Athora? He's managed to evade me for many years and I'd thought him long dead, but I've recently discovered that's not true, is it? So, answer my question, human, or you won't live to hear another."

Kaiden glared rebelliously up at Aven, and Alex felt her heart beat wildly in her chest at his show of defiance.

When it was clear he wasn't going to answer, Aven shrugged carelessly and said, "Pity."

Alex watched in dismay as he unsheathed a long, sharp weapon from his belt and raised it in the air. Even then Kaiden didn't flinch, but everything blurred around Alex and she wondered if she was about to pass out.

When Aven's sword slashed downwards to strike Kaiden, Alex reacted instinctively and jumped forward, throwing her hands out—hands that now held a long, ice-coloured blade. The weapon was slightly different from when she'd last seen it; not a dagger this time, but the length of a short sword. The two blades collided barely a foot away from Kaiden's neck, and Alex had to brace herself to hold up against the Meyarin's strength.

Aven pulled his weapon back quickly, his face startled, before he chuckled darkly. "It seems I've underestimated your gift yet again, Alexandra. I had believed your ability was limited to guard against mental manipulation, but it appears you're protected against physical gift coercion as well. How ... fortunate for you."

He glared over at Calista and the woman looked shamefully to the ground as if it was her fault for not keeping Alex held captive.

"I won't underestimate you a third time," Aven told Alex.

She held his gaze and maintained her defensive position. Only then did he glance down and notice the weapon in her hands.

Aven's eyes widened in surprise. He barked out an incredulous laugh before he held out his hand palm-first and said, "A'enara, come."

Alex couldn't keep the *what-the-hell-are-you-doing- you-weirdo?* expression off her face, and she wondered, not for the first time, if he really was insane. Just what she needed—an immortal, psychotic megalomaniac. Perfect.

"A'enara," Aven repeated, his voice filled with authority. "Come."

Still, nothing happened.

"It's not possible," Aven whispered, looking from the icecoloured blade to Alex's face and back again.

Figuring his confusion was somehow related to the mysterious weapon that kept appearing and disappearing without warning, Alex deliberately tried to ruffle Aven a little more. Remembering a trick he'd pulled once, she ran her fingers down the edge of the blade, willing it to shrink. She tried not to show her amazement when it did so, and instead, she threw the now dagger-sized blade into the air casually and caught it by the handle. Twice more she repeated the gesture, and each time Aven's expression darkened further, his fury growing with her continued flippancy.

"Do you name all your weapons, Aven?" Alex asked. "That's kind of lame, you know. Geeky, even."

"A'enara isn't a name, you foolish girl," Aven spat. "It's an identity. And one whom you're not fit to be in the presence of, let alone wield."

"Yeah, yeah," Alex said, deliberately sounding bored. "Skip the part where you insult me and jump ahead to where you let me and my friends walk out of here. I'll make you a deal—the weapon for our lives."

Aven stared at her for a long moment, then his expression relaxed and he started laughing.

"I truly do find you entertaining," he said. Then his face hardened. "There'll be no deal. I'll take A'enara from you, dispose of your friends and return with you to the academy where you'll escort me to Meya. In return for your obedience, I'll allow you to live."

Alex paled—not at the threat, but at the actual *words*. Or, more specifically, at the audience listening to his words. She could practically feel the questioning stares from Kaiden and Declan at the mention of Meya.

"That's not going to happen," Alex told him, and a trickle of foreboding prompted her to run her fingers along the blade to lengthen it again.

"It is, whether you agree or not," Aven replied. "I don't need you to cooperate for my plan to succeed."

She was ready for him, at least. But she still staggered from the strength of his attack when he launched himself towards her, striking out with his sword. She managed to deflect his weapon, and she could see the surprise in his eyes before his expression turned calculating. Then he lunged forward again, and she forcefully shoved every distraction from her mind as she fought against her impossibly skilled opponent.

He was Meyarin, she was human. Even with his powerful blood rushing through her veins, he had a good thousand or more years of experience on her. He was faster, stronger and much more dangerous than she could ever hope to be. And yet ... hadn't she fought his apparently more skilled brother—wearing a blindfold, no less—and managed to hold her own until her human body had given way to exhaustion? Just maybe she would be able to keep Aven distracted long enough for the others to come up with an escape plan.

Aven attacked Alex at lightning speed, and she somehow managed to maintain a steady defence—thank you, Karter. She tried to let go and sense her surroundings, but she struggled to remember how it had felt when she'd fought with Roka, knowing that her current situation was entirely different. Then, she'd felt only surprise and a little anxiety, not true fear. Now, fear was messing with her attempt to relax and 'listen'. Her defence became more and more difficult with the stress of the moment and the knowledge that if she failed, her friends would die. She refused to let that happen, so she decided to do something stupid.

She closed her eyes.

Alex heard Aven's disbelieving laugh, but she blocked him out and focused on everything else. She focused on the room they were in, on where her feet were positioned on the floor, and on the weapon in her hands.

And then it happened.

Alex felt the shift as her senses expanded and she opened her eyes to see everything was so much clearer than before. She not only saw, but also felt Aven's weapon soar towards her stomach in what seemed like slow motion.

She deflected the blade and thrust out her own sword, aware of the startled gasps in the room as she moved into an attacking stance. Blow after blow she met and returned, and each time she was just as aware of Aven's shock as her own. Her focus wavered when he managed to graze her forearm with his blade, but she continued on, keeping pace with the increasingly astonished Meyarin.

After a particularly jarring strike, Aven pushed her backwards and paused his attack. Alex kept her weapon raised and her eyes narrowed, waiting for his next move. While she was panting for breath, he was barely winded.

"This is an interesting development," Aven bit out. "I'd very much like to know how you're keeping up with me, Alexandra. You fight almost as if you're ... No. You're a weak human, bound by the limits of your flesh. So let me give you a warning. Thus far I've used but a fraction of the skill I possess. If you continue to fight me, you will lose."

"Bold words, Aven," Alex said, trying not to gasp for oxygen. "You look nervous. You're not afraid of a teenage girl, are you?"

Okay, so she was goading him. But she had to hope that her friends were making use of the time she was giving them. She wanted to get out of there alive—she wanted all of them to get out of there alive—so she would continue to play her part until an alternative plan was offered.

"I revoke my earlier offer," Aven said, raising his sword again. "The idea of your death is too appealing. Once you've given me what I need, you'll die just like your friends."

"We'll see," Alex returned, and she launched herself towards him once more.

She quickly discovered that Aven hadn't been bluffing about holding back. Within seconds of their renewed fight, Alex knew she was in trouble. She was exhausted, which wasn't helping her focus, and Aven's increased vigour was startling. The fight was also extremely damaging to her body, which sustained more injuries with each attack.

"Give up, Alexandra," Aven told her after slicing his blade across the side of her thigh. It was a shallow wound, but it was one of many he'd given her in less than five minutes. "You can't fight against a Meyarin and win."

"But I can try," she said through gritted teeth, lunging towards him with her blade.

He deflected her easily, and just as she was about to attack again, the doors burst open. They both turned, and Alex felt her stomach plummet with dread when she saw the rest of her classmates and Samson standing at the entrance to the room.

"Look, dinner and a show," Skyla said excitedly.

Alex would have groaned if she'd had any air left in her lungs.

Without waiting for Aven's order, Calista stretched out her arm and the new arrivals soared through the air and were planted on the ground beside Jordan, Kaiden and Declan.

"More of your friends, Alexandra?" Aven said, his golden eyes glinting with malice.

She didn't respond; she was too busy realising that their situation had worsened yet again—if that was possible. She needed an escape plan, and fast.

Samson made eye contact with her, giving her an idea.

"Thanks for your hospitality, Sir Oswald," Alex called out to the elderly man who was glaring at her from the other side of the room. "Great party. But I think my friends and I have overstayed our welcome."

She shrank her weapon into a dagger, flipped it around so that she held the blade, drew back her arm, and launched it into the air. Her aim was perfect and the pommel end of the weapon slammed into the side of Calista's head. Stunned by the blow, the woman staggered and fell. She wasn't knocked unconscious but she was dazed enough that Alex's companions were instantly freed from her telekinetic hold.

"Jordan!" Alex screamed, ducking as Aven swung his blade furiously in her direction. "Samson's balls!"

That was *definitely* something she never wanted to say again.

"My prince!" Signa cried. But he was too late to warn Aven about whatever thoughts he'd just read, because Jordan had pulled the juggling balls out of his coat and thrown them onto the floor. Dark smoke instantly rose up around them, clogging the air to a near-suffocating point and hiding everything—and everyone—from sight.

"Run!" Samson's grisly voice called out from somewhere in the darkness.

Alex hoped the others were following his order and she spun around in the direction of the exit. But she wasn't quick enough to escape the hand that grabbed her upper arm and yanked her backwards.

"You're not going anywhere," Aven hissed into her ear. "Not until you take me to my city."

She couldn't see him and could barely breathe. The polluted air burned her lungs and she started coughing as she struggled uselessly against his unyielding grip. She fought him in the murky darkness but he wouldn't let her go.

Alex began to feel faint from the lack of oxygen. Just when it seemed her legs would not be able to hold her weight any longer, she heard Aven grunt in surprise and he released his iron-clad grip on her arm. She collapsed to the floor, but just before she blacked out, she felt a pair of warm arms scoop her up and sprint her off towards the door.

Nineteen

"Alex, please, you have to wake up."

A gentle hand stroked the side of her face and she released a pain-filled groan with her return to consciousness. The following inhalation of clean air sent her into a violent coughing fit. She sat up, gasping for oxygen, and tried to clear her lungs of the noxious smoke. All the while, her rescuer ran a comforting hand up and down her back.

"Just take a few deep breaths. In and out. In and out. That's it."

Alex did as she was told until she was able to breathe normally again. She turned her head to see Kaiden kneeling beside her.

"Where are we?" she asked, wincing at the raspy sound of her voice.

"In the gardens at the back of the mansion," he said. "I tried to get us up to our meeting spot on the hill, but Sir Oswald and some of the others nearly caught us when I made a break for it. I thought it best to hide until you woke."

"How long was I out?"

"Less than five minutes," he said. "But you had me worried since your breathing was so ragged. And after your fight..."

Alex looked away to avoid the question in his eyes. She wasn't ready to answer what she was sure he would ask. But he surprised her, and rather than beginning an interrogation session, he stood and offered her his hand. She took hold and he pulled her effortlessly to her feet. He steadied her until she was able to stand unassisted.

"Did the others make it out okay?" she asked as they began to walk back around the mansion, staying hidden behind the hedges and statues.

"Yeah, they're all fine. Samson's chemical cocktail made it almost too easy for everyone to escape," he assured her. "Hopefully they're waiting for us and not planning some kind of suicide rescue mission."

"Unlike what you did," Alex said. "Twice. Care to explain yourself?"

"What's to explain?" Kaiden asked as he ducked under a statue's arm. "The first time you and Jordan took way too long to get back to us that it was obvious something must have gone wrong, so Declan and I decided to investigate. We bypassed stealth and went for the surprise approach. Not that it did us any good. Who were those people?"

Alex figured his comment was rhetorical—or at least that's how she took it—and she pressed for his continued explanation. "And the second time? How did you know Aven had me trapped in the smoke?"

Out of the corner of her eye she saw him shrug. "It wasn't that hard to guess," he said. "Everyone else made it out and said you were right behind us but I couldn't see you anywhere."

"How *did* you find me? I couldn't see anything in that darkness."

Kaiden hesitated, but then said, "I've told you before I have pretty good intuition. Plus, it wasn't hard to hear your struggle with Aven."

"About him..." Alex trailed off awkwardly. She drew a breath and said, "He's not someone you want to go around talking about."

"I'm not stupid, Alex," Kaiden said. "Aven Dalmarta isn't someone I'd choose to have as an adversary. Unlike you, apparently."

"That particular decision was out of my hands," Alex huffed as she pushed a branch away from her face. "He's been after me since the first day I arrived in—"

She stopped speaking, having almost said way too much. She mentally replayed her words and was relieved to note that she hadn't given away anything too incriminating.

But then Kaiden's statement fully registered, and she asked, "How do you know his full name?"

Kaiden didn't answer immediately, but Alex refused to break the silence or change the topic. When they were safely out of the gardens and heading up the hill he explained.

"I've never seen him before, but tonight wasn't the first time I've heard of Aven. I know who he is, where he comes from and why he's no longer a prince of Meya. I also know what it'll mean if he makes it back there. What I don't know is where you fit into the picture, and why Aven believes you can 'escort' him to Meya. Last I heard, the city was impossible to locate."

She bit her cheek and avoided eye contact, even when she felt him waiting for a response.

"I also have no idea how you managed to fight like that," Kaiden pressed. "I've never seen a human move so fast." When she still didn't speak, he added, "Alex, I've gone up against you in class and I've watched you fight others, but you've never shown anything close to the skill you demonstrated tonight. You held your own against a Meyarin. That shouldn't have been possible."

"Guess I'm just full of surprises," Alex said, trying to make a joke of it but failing miserably.

"You saved my life tonight," Kaiden said quietly. "I'm not going to force you to tell me anything, and I'll make sure Declan doesn't either. But you have to know that I'm ... concerned. I was worried when I thought you had Marcus Sparker on your tail, but Aven Dalmarta..."

Kaiden trailed off into a sigh. He stopped walking and reached out for Alex's hand, halting her beside him. Looking straight into her eyes, he said, "Just promise me that if you ever need help, you'll ask."

Alex kept her gaze locked on his. She couldn't escape the emotions pouring out of him. Above everything else, she could see how much he wanted her to trust him.

"I promise," she whispered. And she meant it. But only as a last resort. She would never willingly drag him or anyone else into the mess that had become her life.

He continued looking at her for a moment longer and then nodded, apparently satisfied she was telling the truth. He dropped her hand and she immediately felt a sense of loss at the broken contact, absurd as that was.

"We should keep moving," he said. "I'm sure the others will be worrying about us."

They hurried up the hill in silence, careful with their footing as the light from the mansion faded with every step. Only when they were near the meeting place did Kaiden speak again.

"I'm not sure if you realised in the middle of all that, but your weapon disappeared after it knocked the telekinetic woman to the floor," he said. "It just vanished into the air. What's the deal with that?"

"Honestly, I have no idea," Alex said. "It's happened three times now. It just appears when I need it and disappears again afterwards."

"Aven called it 'A'enara'," Kaiden mused. "I'll see if I can find out anything about it once we're back at the academy, if you want?"

Alex didn't need to think about his offer. "That would actually be really good; I wouldn't even know where to begin looking."

"Consider it done," he said. "I'll let you know if I discover anything."

"Thanks, Kaiden." She sent him a soft smile. "Oh, and thanks for, you know, rescuing me. I don't think I would've made it out of there if you hadn't come back.

But I'm sorry you had to carry me—I'm surprised you didn't break your back."

Kaiden laughed. "You weigh practically nothing, Alex. I've carried much heavier things in Finn's class. I'd choose you any day."

Alex was glad the darkness kept him from seeing her reaction to his statement. 'I'd choose you any day.' Maybe she was taking his words out of context, but so what?

"How did you get me away from Aven, anyway?" she asked, deliberately moving her thoughts along.

"I used this," he said, pulling from his belt the silver Stabiliser he must have stolen back from Calista.

"You shot him?"

"It didn't do much good," Kaiden admitted. "He was barely jolted, when most people would've been out like a light. But it was enough to shock him into releasing you, which gave me the chance I needed to get you out of there."

Alex shook her head in amazement, and she couldn't help chuckling. Her chuckle turned into a laugh, and all the while Kaiden watched her with curious amusement.

"What's so funny?"

"I can't believe you shot him," she said, still grinning. "I wish I'd seen that."

"Maybe one day I'll offer a repeat performance," he said, winking.

Alex sobered at the thought of seeing Aven again in the future. For a moment she regretted her promise to ask for Kaiden's help if needed, but at the same time she couldn't deny the relief she felt at someone else knowing about the threat tainting her life. At least part of it, anyway.

"I can see them! Over there!"

Alex looked further up the hill and saw her classmates running in their direction. The sight of them safe and well almost brought her to tears after everything they'd all been through. When they were within arm's reach, she and Kaiden were drawn into a group hug.

"Are you guys okay?" Pipsqueak asked when they broke apart. "We were so worried when we realised you weren't with us! What happened?"

"Just a minor setback," Kaiden assured them. "We're both fine."

"We'll be even better when we get back to the academy," Alex said in a pointed tone.

Everyone nodded in agreement and looked towards Samson, who rummaged through his bag and pulled out a handful of Bubbler vials.

"We'll have to go through in two groups," he said, "because my Bubblers are cheap knock-offs and they only have enough juice for five people at a time. No one else knows where we're going, so I'll have to come back and bring the second lot of you through as well. Good thing I've got a few of these vials handy."

Good thing indeed, Alex thought suspiciously, beginning to question just how much of Samson's imprisonment and subsequent rescue had been staged by Hunter. In hindsight, parts of it seemed a little too convenient to Alex's mind, like the fact that she had unwittingly crossed paths with Aven yet again—an event that she was certain hadn't occurred by accident, not on Hunter's watch. What, exactly, had her **SAS** teacher been thinking?

Putting aside her questions for now, she watched Samson activate the first Bubbledoor and step through, followed by Blink, Pipsqueak, Skyla and Tom.

While the rest of them waited for him to return, Kaiden guided Declan a short distance away for a whispered conversation, hopefully asking him not to press Alex for details about Aven or Meya. Giving them some privacy, she turned back to Jordan and quickly found herself wrapped in his arms. He hugged her so tightly that she was in danger of suffocating for the second time that night.

"Alex, I was so scared," he whispered in her ear.

She returned his fierce hug, having had first-hand experience—a few times over—of just how terrifying Aven could be.

"I really thought I'd lost you tonight," Jordan continued. "And not just when you weren't behind us coming out of the mansion, although that's definitely something I never want to experience again. But when you fought Aven ... I thought he was going to kill you. His eyes ... I've never seen so much hatred."

Alex frowned in confusion and pulled back to look at Jordan's serious face, trying to read his features in the moonlight. "Wait a minute. Are you saying you were freaked out about *me*, not about Aven?"

At his nod, she gaped at him.

"Are you mad?" she asked. "What about you? You were stuck in the same room the whole time! If anything, you were in way more danger. Aven needs me alive—at least for the moment—but he was more than willing to kill you. Especially after Signa read your thoughts about Meya."

Jordan winced. "Sorry about that. I tried not to think about it, but the more I tried not to think about it, the more I thought about it."

"Like the pink hippo," Alex said, understanding.

Jordan looked bemused. "Huh?"

"You know, the pink hippo," she repeated. Seeing his expression, she added, "When someone says, 'Don't think about a pink hippopotamus', what's the first thing you think of? A pink hippopotamus."

"Riiiight," Jordan said. "I think it's time we got you home."

Alex definitely agreed with him, and Samson chose that moment to Bubble back to them. Without preamble, he smashed another vial and walked through it with Alex, Jordan, Kaiden and Declan following.

They landed in a dimly lit street and the moment they were all steady, Samson started leading them swiftly along the cobblestone pavement.

"Where are the others?" she asked, looking around. "And where are we?"

"Your friends are already waiting at my house," he answered. "And we're on the outskirts of a small town called Dupressa."

"Do we have far to walk?" Jordan asked, wrapping an arm around Alex's waist so she could lean on him for support. She hadn't realised how much she'd been struggling to remain upright until his added assistance made it so much easier for her to keep going.

"Not far," Samson promised. "My house is warded against unauthorised Bubbledoor arrivals. I won the vials we used in a game of Stix and didn't have time to program my access code into them before I was imprisoned. That's why we're stuck walking." The juggler eyed Alex. "Can you last a little longer, love? You sure are a mess."

She frowned and looked down at herself. True enough, she was covered in shallow cuts, and her dress was slashed and bloodied in numerous places where Aven had managed to make contact with his blade. Really, she was lucky she had any material left covering her body, considering the damage. But somehow she was still mostly decent, a fact for which she was grateful.

"I'm fine," she told Samson.

The man raised his eyebrow in disbelief but he didn't call her on the truth of her statement.

They continued walking in silence for another few minutes, and with each step, Alex leaned more and more heavily on Jordan.

"Here we are," Samson said at last, leading them off the street and up to a cottage that was separated from the other houses nearby by a thick row of trees.

As they stepped inside and were greeted by the rest of their classmates, Alex exhaled with relief. But it was short-lived.

"We've found an arrow with our next task," Tom said.

"Another task?" Declan said. "You can't be serious!"

He took the words right out of Alex's mouth. Did Hunter seriously expect more from them? She didn't have anything left to give.

Tom raised his hands. "Don't shoot the messenger."

"Sorry," Declan said, running his fingers agitatedly through his cropped hair. "What does it say?"

"Just that the arrow will transport us to our next destination. We've also been given a bottle of Liquid Light, which doesn't make me feel great about wherever we're going to land."

"Fabulous," Declan muttered.

Alex swayed on her feet, prompting Jordan to tighten his grip around her waist.

"Do you have something we can eat?" Kaiden asked Samson, his eyes taking in Alex's failing energy. "Something to drink, too?"

"I'm fine," Alex repeated, knowing he was only asking for her sake. But she also knew that if she sat down to eat or drink, she probably wouldn't be able to get back up.

"I'm thirsty," Skyla stated. "And hungry."

"We can eat back at the academy," Alex said firmly, and she turned to Samson. "It was nice meeting you. I hope I get to see you perform one day."

"The pleasure was all mine, love," he told her. "Thanks for helping me escape. I owe you one."

Before anyone could argue or ask again for food, Alex sent him a parting smile and stepped out of Jordan's grasp, stumbling over to Tom. She took the vial of Liquid Light from him and reached up to touch the arrow embedded in Samson's wall. Immediately she was whisked away, and when she landed, she couldn't see anything in the pitch-black darkness. She quickly unstoppered the vial in her hands, releasing a brilliant light that illuminated the entire area around her.

All Alex could tell was that she was surrounded by trees, but her attention was diverted when Jordan stepped through, followed by the others.

"Where are we this time?" Pipsqueak asked tiredly.

"It looks like we're back in another forest," Blink said. No one could say his observation skills were lacking.

"I'm cold," Skyla complained. "And hungry. And tired. And—"

"Skyla, you're not going to feel any better whining about it," Tom said.

"But it's true," she said petulantly. "I didn't get to eat anything at the party because Alex and I were too busy rescuing the rest of you from the dungeon. You're welcome, by the way."

"We already thanked you," Pipsqueak muttered. "About a million times."

"It doesn't hurt to show a little appreciation for the risks we took," Skyla huffed.

"We haven't had a chance to thank Alex yet, and she's the one who took most of the risks," Pipsqueak pointed out.

Alex groaned at Pip's words, knowing Skyla wouldn't be impressed.

She was right.

"What's that supposed to mean, Philippa?" Skyla demanded.

"Nothing, Skyla," Alex jumped in. "Pip didn't mean anything. She knows how amazing you were tonight. We couldn't have made it out of there without you. But we're all tired, so maybe instead of talking, we should search for our next set of instructions?"

"Fine," Skyla relented. "Whatever."

Everyone else looked at Alex with gratitude, but she was too drained to so much as offer a smile in return.

"Let's see what we can find," Jordan said. "Alex, stay there and point the light for us, will you?"

"Subtle, Jordan," she said with a snort. But she didn't argue, since she was too relieved he'd given her an excuse not to move. She gratefully slumped down onto a fallen tree and pointed the light around as directed.

"Over here!" Declan called.

They all hustled over to where he stood beside another arrow.

"What is it?" Tom asked.

"It's another map, I think," Declan said. "Alex, turn the light a little."

She did as he asked and Declan held the paper up so they could all see it.

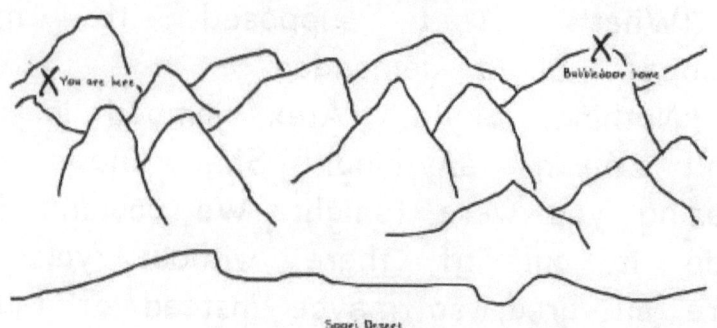

They stared at the map for a few moments before Alex whispered, "Please tell me that means what I think it means?"

"I think it means exactly what you think it means," Jordan said with a grin. "I think we're finished!"

"There's only one way to find out," Tom said with renewed excitement. He pointed at the arrow. "Who wants to try first?"

"Me! Pick me!" Skyla squealed.

No one argued, and she reached out for the arrow, disappearing in a swirl of colour.

"High maintenance, that one," Blink muttered, looking at the place where Skyla had just been standing. "Off the charts."

Again, no one argued, and one by one, the rest of the group travelled through the Bubbledoor until only Declan and Alex remained.

"After you," she offered. "Then I'll come through with the light."

"No way," he said, and he gently took the vial from her hands. "You first."

Alex didn't see the point in arguing, so she stepped up to the arrow. Before she could touch it, Declan called out to her.

"I'm not sure what happened earlier tonight," he told her seriously, "but Kaiden's my best mate, and you saved his life. You saved us all, in fact. I gave him my word that I'd keep my mouth shut about everything that happened, and now I'm giving it to you, too. Your secrets, whatever they are, they're safe with me."

Alex was so tired that she couldn't suppress her overwhelming gratitude, so she reached out and wrapped her arms around Declan's firm torso, grateful to have a friend like him on her side.

"Thanks for coming back for Jordan and me," she said into his chest.

He gave her an affectionate squeeze and replied, "You know me—I love a good fight."

She let him go and smiled up at him, knowing the absolute truth of his words.

"Maybe next time your feet won't be stuck to the ground and you'll be able to jump in and lend a hand," she said light-heartedly. "What's the point in having all those muscles if you can't use them?"

"You were doing just fine on your own," he said. "But next time I'll make sure to bring popcorn for the show."

She swatted him on the arm and he laughed at her pathetic attempt at violence.

"I don't want to have to carry you through, so get going before you collapse," he said, giving her a gentle nudge forward.

She resisted the urge to poke her tongue out at him as she reached for the arrow. Once she landed, she had to blink her eyes until they adjusted to the painfully bright light.

"Here's my favourite patient," came a familiar voice.

Alex glanced around and almost cried with relief when she realised she'd been transported directly to the Medical Ward.

"Look at you, Alex," Fletcher tsked, narrowing his eyes at someone over her shoulder. "Hunter, you have a lot to answer for."

Alex spun around and, sure enough, there stood her teacher, leaning casually against the wall. All around the room her classmates where climbing onto beds, waiting for Fletcher to check the status of their health.

"This is convenient," Declan said, arriving through the Bubbledoor. "But Hunter, teacher or not, we're going to have words about the nightmare you put us through this weekend."

"It's interesting that out of everyone in this room, Alex is the only one who hasn't threatened me," Hunter said with dry amusement.

"I'm too tired to threaten you," Alex said, and then she remembered something.

"But I am supposed to pass on a message from Warden Jeera to let you know that she'll be in contact about your 'teaching methods'."

"I can't wait," Hunter said. Rather than sounding sarcastic, he almost seemed excited by the prospect.

"Did you say Warden Jeera?" Declan asked, and his eyes flickered over to Kaiden who was listening closely as well. "As in, Warden Jeera from the palace in Tryllin?"

"Uh-huh," Alex confirmed around a yawn. "She helped me escape from the military compound after I pretended to be the royal princess. I only wish I'd stayed with her and skipped the fan-flipping-tastic night we've all just experienced."

The only person in the room not gaping at her was Hunter, whose dark eyes glittered with humour.

"What?"

Alex wasn't sure who'd spoken, but she knew the exclamation came from more than one person. She'd forgotten that she hadn't told them how she'd managed to get in and out of the Soori Outpost. *Oops.*

"It's a long story," she mumbled. "And it doesn't matter anyway since we're all here now, safe and sound."

She swayed as she said the words and Fletcher caught her by the elbow.

"You're about to collapse on your feet," he said, guiding her to a bed.

"It's just these horrible shoes," Alex told him, scowling down at her heels as he forced her onto the mattress. She was amazed that she'd made it through the night without breaking an ankle, and she had absolutely no idea how she'd managed to fight Aven while wearing them. "Next time, Hunter, you need to pick more appropriate footwear."

"I'll see what I can do," he said, his voice rumbling with amusement.

"It's not *just* the shoes, Alex," Fletcher said with exasperation. "You look like you've been through a cheese grater."

"It's just a few little cuts, Fletcher. I'll live."

"I'll be the judge of that," the doctor said in his no-nonsense voice.

"Look after the others first," Alex begged. "You know they won't take as long as me. Please, Fletcher, we're all tired. Don't make them wait for me."

Fletcher looked like he wanted to argue, but at her pleading expression, he sighed and relented. "Only if you promise not to move a muscle until I'm done. Agreed?"

"I'm not going anywhere."

He nodded and moved away to begin checking on her classmates while Alex shifted into a more comfortable position and waited for his return. She was almost asleep when she heard the curtains being drawn around her bed and Hunter's voice prompted her to sit up again.

"I have to admit, Alex, I'm amazed by your performance this weekend."

"What are you talking about?" she asked. "You weren't even there for any of it."

Hunter's disbelief was clear. "Do you really think I'd send eight students into the wild without having a way to keep an eye on them? Just because you couldn't see me doesn't mean I wasn't following you."

"You were watching us?" Alex said, incredulous. "Why didn't you help when we needed it?"

"When did you need it?"

She gaped at him. "Are you kidding? Where do I start? Maybe when Pip almost fell off the mountain? Or what about when there was a *mind reader* at the military compound?" She lowered her voice so it wouldn't carry to the others when she hissed out, "A mind reader who just happens to be an 'associate' of a homicidal Meyarin? Kaiden and Jordan were almost captured at the outpost because of him!

And then me—I can't even begin to explain what it was like having to deceive General Drock and Major Tyson. And that's nothing, *nothing*, to how it felt being at Sir Oswald's party when everyone else was imprisoned because your ID tags were counterfeit. Great job with those, by the way."

She broke off, trying to rein in her words, but couldn't resist adding in her still lowered voice, "Am I right in thinking you somehow knew Aven would be there and you sent us along anyway? I'm guessing you didn't tell Darrius—he never would have agreed to that! Did you know Sir Oswald's little party would turn into a Villains 'R' Us sorority group meeting? Because that's what happened. And we barely escaped with our lives. Where were you *then*, Hunter?"

Throughout her rant he continued to look at her calmly, and that annoyed her more than anything else.

"Well?" she demanded.

"First off, if Philippa *had* fallen, don't you think her backpack would have opened her parachute, just like everyone's did when you all fell down into the river?" Hunter asked.

Alex realised he was right. But she hadn't known that at the time.

"What about the rest?" she pressed, unwilling to concede his point.

"Signa's presence was an unanticipated challenge," Hunter admitted. "He was meant to be away from the outpost for the weekend, but his trip was cancelled last-minute. Kaiden and Jordan both have gifts that helped them to evade capture, and the same goes for you. Your creative use of subterfuge tactics made your act all the more believable. If there had been any real problems, I would have stepped in personally, but I also had a man on the inside who would have helped get you out of there if I couldn't. Coincidentally, he was also the same man who helped you get *in* there."

Alex had to think about that before the answer came to her. "Major Tyson?"

"He's a close friend who was willing to assist me in your training exercise," Hunter confirmed. "He admitted to being impressed with your ability to remain calm under pressure. That's high praise from someone of his ranking."

"Why didn't Signa pick up on his thoughts?" she asked, confused. "Or yours, if you were as close as you claim?"

"Upper-level military officers—and Wardens—have to undergo extensive training to protect their minds from intrusion,"

Hunter said. "Signa couldn't read Tyson's thoughts because he wasn't able to break through his mental barriers. As for me, I've undergone similar training to the same effect."

Alex grudgingly accepted his explanation. Not for the first time, she was relieved that her gift allowed her to skip the 'extensive training' and simply reap the benefits of ultra-mind-protection.

"What about Sir Oswald's party?" she asked. "What's your excuse for the way that panned out? And did Darrius know about it beforehand?"

Hunter shook his head. "No, he did not. But leave that conversation to me."

Alex almost wished she could be a fly on the wall for that discussion, since she was certain Darrius wasn't going to be pleased that he'd invested so much effort in keeping Alex safe from Aven only to learn that one of his teachers actively sent her out to meet him, and unprepared at that. In fact, she wondered how the headmaster was able to justify allowing any of his students to go off on dangerous SAS trips away from the academy. But then again, if Hunter was supposedly trailing them wherever they went, it was likely Darrius trusted that the SAS teacher would keep them safe. Either that, or Hunter worked with the 'better to ask forgiveness than seek permission' attitude when it came to his classes. Alex had a feeling the latter was more likely.

"Tonight was the real test of your weekend," Hunter went on to explain. "But remember, I warned you that would be the case."

Alex thought back to the note addressed to her. "You told me it would be dangerous—more so for me than the others. Does that mean I'm right about you knowing that group was meeting tonight?"

"A while ago, Headmaster Marselle asked me to keep an eye on any unusual developments amongst the elite social circles," Hunter said. "When Sir Oswald's dinner party was first announced, I thought it might be a good idea to have an informant on the inside, just in case there was something underhanded going on. As a performer, Samson had the perfect cover. But when he went to audition for the role of entertainer, another mind reader happened to be visiting Sir Oswald at the same time, and Samson's true intentions were discovered."

"Signa?" Alex guessed.

"No. Someone else."

Alex waited for him to offer a name, but he didn't, so she pressed, "How many mind readers are out there?"

"I can count on one hand the number known to me," he answered. "Or, at least those strong enough to be considered dangerous. Your Core Skills professor, for instance, doesn't make the list, since her gift barely allows her to read surface thoughts. Signa Zu, on the other hand ... His gift affords him tremendous leverage into the minds of those incapable of guarding against him—which is most people."

Alex mulled over his words and then said quietly, "Signa couldn't read Kaiden's thoughts. And he had some difficulty with Jordan at first, but he managed in the end."

"Are you asking a question or telling me something, Alex?"

"A bit of both," she admitted. "Why did Signa have trouble reading them?"

"I only have theories," Hunter told her. "You'll have to ask your friends if you want accurate answers."

She nodded in understanding and brought them back to their original topic. "So, Samson was discovered and apprehended, but then what? You decided to send an inexperienced group of teenagers to rescue him? Not your most brilliant plan, Hunter."

"It worked, didn't it?"

"It almost didn't," she argued.

"But it did, and even more perfectly than I could have imagined," he said. "Without your involvement, the night would have remained just a dinner party. But with the mess you lot caused, you managed to confirm the identities of an undercover group of insurgents hiding in plain sight. Or a handful of them, at least. That's quite a success story."

"We almost *died*, Hunter," Alex emphasised.

He looked at her steadily. "Aven wouldn't have killed you."

"He would've killed the others!" she argued.

"No, Alex," Hunter said quietly. "He would have Claimed them."

Alex felt physically ill. "That's a fate worse than death."

"Something we can both agree on," Hunter said solemnly.

"How do you know all this?" Alex whispered. "Did Darrius tell you about everything? About Aven and the gifted people who have disappeared? The people Darrius thinks are Claimed?"

Hunter averted his eyes and appeared to be considering his next words. There was a long moment of silence before he said, "Headmaster Marselle has spoken with me at length, but much of my knowledge comes from elsewhere."

He didn't explain further, and Alex knew she wouldn't learn anything more by pressing him.

"Is there anything else you can tell me?" she asked. "Anything I need to know?"

"I think you already know much more than you should," Hunter said with the barest hint of an approving smile. Then his face turned serious again. "One thing I'll say is that I had a specific reason for sending you, in particular, to Sir Oswald's party. You're right that I thought Aven might be there tonight, and that my allowing you to go in unprepared may seem careless on my part. But listen to me when I say that at no stage were you or your classmates in any real danger, and if you had been, I would have stepped in and pulled you out immediately."

Alex looked at him disbelievingly. "I'm sorry, but did you miss the part where Aven almost beheaded Kaiden? How could you possibly have known a sword would appear in my hands to save him when I still have no idea how that happened? Or what about when I almost suffocated from smoke inhalation? You didn't step in then, did you? Or when—"

Hunter cut her off to ask, "I've told you about part of my gift before, do you remember?"

"Perception," Alex answered, not sure where he was going with this. "You're aware of where people are and what they're doing."

He nodded. "Yes. But I also know what they're about to do."

Alex raised her eyebrows as she digested that. "Are you saying you can see the future?" If that were true, she wondered how similar his gift was to D.C.'s.

"I only see flashes of the outcomes a few seconds before they unfold since the future is dependent upon our choices, but yes, effectively, when I use my gift to concentrate on a specific person, I can see what is about to happen around them. You are, of course, the exception, given your own gifting, but I was able to work around that while you were in the company of others. I could see your future through their eyes."

Alex lingered on his words for a moment before she released an accepting sigh. "So you're saying you knew we'd all make it out of there okay? And that's why you didn't intervene?"

"As I said, I can only perceive events within a short span of time, but I was watching closely, Alex. I knew you would save Kaiden. I knew you'd survive your fight with Aven. I knew you wouldn't suffocate. If I'd seen anything causing a legitimate threat to your lives, I had a plan in motion to get you out. All of you."

"And that plan was?"

"Irrelevant now, since it wasn't necessary," Hunter said.

Alex thought that was a copout response, but Hunter was nothing if not mysterious, so she was willing to let his non-answer slide and simply trust he was telling the truth.

"For the record, a little warning would be nice next time," she said. "Or at least reassurance that you'll be around to help if required."

"My only justification is that you needed to see what you saw and hear what you heard," Hunter said. "And as much as I wish it wasn't the case, you needed to fight Aven like you did so you'd know exactly what you're up against."

Alex frowned at him. "I've gone head-to-head against Aven before. I didn't need a repeat of that to remember how far out of my league I am when it comes to him."

"You haven't fought him physically before tonight," he pointed out.

"I barely 'fought' him at all," Alex argued. "I thought I was holding my own at first, but it turned out he was playing with me."

"Which only shows that you have more to learn," Hunter said. "You'll find a way, Alex. And in the meantime, you'll just have to apply yourself to your training."

"Because I'm such a slacker?" she asked wryly.

Hunter smiled at her fully this time, and the expression softened his whole face, highlighting how handsome he was when he wasn't looking all menacing-assassin-like. But he didn't get the chance to confirm or deny her statement as the curtain was pulled open and Fletcher stepped into the small space.

"Time to get you fixed up," the doctor said.

Hunter took that as his cue to leave her bedside, but when he reached the door, he said, "A slacker never would have made it through my first task, Alex, let alone the rest."

She felt an unexpected rush of warmth from his words—and the tone of approval in them—before she resigned herself to letting Fletcher prod and poke away at her body. He checked her injuries for traces of poison and infection before he healed her cuts and eased her bruises—but not without causing her even more discomfort.

No pain, no gain, apparently.

"If I had my way, you'd be staying here overnight," Fletcher said, handing her a vial of pain reliever.

Alex groaned at the thought, but when the doctor narrowed his eyes, she quickly wiped the grimace off her face and swallowed the contents of the vial.

"Fortunately for you, I don't think there's reason enough for me to keep you under observation when what you really need is a good night's sleep," he said.

"Does that mean I can go?"

He handed her a rehydration toffee, one of the few medicines she recognised, having studied them in her Med Sci class. "Only if you promise to suck on this until it's finished and head straight to your dorm to rest."

"Oooh, I love these," Alex said, eagerly taking the candy-like medicine from him and popping it in her mouth. Within a few swirls of her tongue she began to feel her hunger and thirst disappear.

"Off you go, then," Fletcher said, but when she jumped off the bed and made to leave, he stopped her and removed his lab coat, handing it over.

She looked from the coat back to him with a questioning look.

"It's not curfew yet," he explained. "This might help you avoid some curious glances. And it makes you look like you've come straight from a Chemistry lab rather than been attacked by a pack of wild animals."

"Oh." Alex pulled the coat over her shredded dress. "I guess you're right. Thanks, Fletcher. I'll bring it back tomorrow."

"Just as long as you're dropping it off and not coming as a patient," he said. "No more injuries for a while, okay?"

"I'll try my hardest."

"You always do, Alex," he told her with a disgruntled sigh. "You really need to try harder."

She grinned at him and left the Ward, almost walking straight into Jordan who was waiting outside.

"What are you still doing here?" she asked.

"You didn't think I'd leave without you?"

"Well ... yeah," she admitted. "That was kind of the point of getting Fletcher to let everyone else go. I'm not the only exhausted one."

"But you are the only one who can barely stand without assistance," he said. "And rightly so, considering everything you've been through over the past two days."

"Jordan—"

"We're not arguing about this," he said as he wrapped his arm around her waist to help support her weight again. "I'm going to escort you to your room, with or without your permission."

"Fine," she huffed, grateful for his help but not wanting to say as much out loud. "But you have to promise to go straight to bed afterwards."

"Sure thing, Mum," he said, his voice dripping with false sincerity.

She shook her head in amusement and let him lead—and half carry—her to their dorm building. When they reached her empty room, Jordan helped Alex over to her bed where she sat down and finally kicked off her heels, wiggling her toes with relief. She found a note on her pillow from D.C. saying that she and Bear were in the Rec Room, but there was no way Alex had the energy to meet with them. She would just have to bring them up to speed about everything tomorrow.

"In you go," said Jordan, pulling the covers down so she could slide in under them.

Alex didn't care that she was still fully clothed. Now that she was lying on her comfortable bed, she wasn't going anywhere. But she did at least have the presence of mind to remove Fletcher's coat and drape it over her bedside table.

Lying back with her eyes closed, Alex felt Jordan lean across to tuck her in. When he was done, he bent down and placed a gentle kiss on her forehead.

"Love you, Alex," he whispered.

Her eyes snapped open and Jordan burst out laughing.

"Calm down," he said between guffaws. "I don't mean *love* -love. But you're one of my closest friends—you're my *family*. Of course I care about you." His tone quieted as he admitted, "You really freaked me out tonight. I don't know what I'd do if something happened to you."

She was almost brought to tears by the emotion in his eyes. "Love you too, Jordan. In the same way. And I'm sorry I scared you."

He reached out and squeezed her hand before a mischievous grin spread across his face. "Speaking of the 'L' word ... What's going on with you and Kaiden, huh?"

Jordan wiggled his eyebrows suggestively and Alex couldn't stop the blush she felt spreading across her cheeks.

"I don't know what you're talking about," she mumbled, looking away.

He shook his head in amusement. "If that's how you want to act, I can play along."

She scowled at his knowing expression. "I'm under doctor's orders to get some sleep—something that you're interrupting."

"Fine, be that way," Jordan said, grinning. "I'll see you in the morning. And don't worry, this can be another one of our little secrets."

"I have nothing to hide," she told him, and then with a smirk she added, "unlike you."

"Me?"

She nodded slyly. "I have eyes, you know. I've seen how you look at Dix sometimes. I should be the one asking you what's going on."

His startled expression was all the confirmation she needed.

"I knew it!" she cried, sitting up excitedly. "How long have you liked her?"

"Don't be ridiculous, Alex."

"Aw, come on, Jordan," she begged. "You know I won't tell her anything."

He ran his hands through his hair and dropped down onto the edge of her bed.

"Look, it's not like anything will ever come of it," he said wearily. "She's ... well, you know who she is."

A princess. That was problematic. But still, not impossible.

"You're not exactly a beggar on the street, Jordan," Alex pointed out. "As much as you wish it wasn't the case, you do come from a high-society family. And even if you didn't, Dix is hardly the kind of girl who'd place conditions on her heart. You know that."

He looked at her. "It's complicated, Alex."

"Yeah, well, so is life," she said bluntly.

He rolled his eyes and said, "Don't you have a bedtime schedule to keep?"

"But we haven't finished talking," she said with a Skyla-like pout.

"I'll make you a deal," he said, standing up and re-tucking her blankets. "You tell me about Kaiden, and I'll tell you about Dix. Fair's fair."

She frowned at him. "There's nothing to say about Kaiden."

"Then this conversation's over until there *is* something to say," he said as he headed to the door. "I doubt we'll have to wait long, judging by the starry-eyed expression on your face whenever his name is mentioned. Sweet dreams, Alex."

She remained scowling at the door long after it closed behind him.

"Stupid, arrogant, thinks-he's-always-right best friend," Alex muttered to herself. "He doesn't know what he's talking about."

Yeah. He doesn't know what he's talking about, her thoughts reiterated, as she drifted off to sleep.

Twenty

Something woke Alex in the middle of the night. At first she wondered if D.C. was still having her recurring nightmares, but there was no noise to indicate any distress. In fact, when Alex lifted her head, she could easily see Dix was sleeping peacefully in her bed. So, what had woken Alex from her deep slumber?

When a shadow moved across her field of vision, Alex's heart skipped a beat. She sat up, squinting into the darkness. The shadow moved again and Alex froze.

"Easy, little human. It's just me."

Her eyes widened when she recognised the voice and saw its owner step into the moonlight.

"Zain? What are you doing here?" she asked, gaping at the huge Meyarin. "And how did you get past the bio-sensor on the door?"

"Forgive the intrusion, young mortal, but Prince Roka needs to speak with you urgently," Zain said, only answering part of her question. "He's sent me to escort you to Meya."

Alex stared at the intimidating guard who seemed much too large for her dorm room. "Uh, sure." Then her brain replayed his words and she clarified, "Wait, do you mean right now?"

He chuckled. "Yes, Alex. Right now."

She wasn't thrilled about sacrificing her much-needed sleep—Fletcher would kill her if he found out—but she grudgingly dragged her tired body from her bed.

"Just give me a second to change," she said, grabbing a fresh outfit from her wardrobe and retreating to the bathroom. She quickly peeled off the tattered gown and replaced it with a pair of jeans, T-shirt and a light jacket.

"Okay, I'm good to go," she said, re-entering the room. "Just let me wake Dix."

Alex walked over to her roommate's bed but before she could reach out for D.C., Zain laid a hand on her arm.

"Prince Roka has requested you come alone."

Alex frowned at him. "But—"

"I believe he's already told you why," Zain interrupted pointedly.

"It's Dix," she argued. "She's a princess! Whatever Roka wants to say to me, she can hear. It's practically her job to keep secrets!"

"Even so," Zain said, "I have my orders. Sorry, little human."

"Stop calling me that," she grumbled.

Zain laughed quietly as he used his hand on her arm to guide her to the window.

She looked at him in confusion and pointed to the other side of the room. "Um, the door's that way. We kind of need to use it to get to the Library."

"To the Library, yes," Zain agreed. "But not to Meya. Hold on, little human."

"I told you not to call me—"

Alex clamped her mouth down on a scream when the ground took off from underneath them. Only Zain's firm grasp around her elbow kept her from being propelled back into the transparent barrier of the *Valispath* as it flew them through the wall of her dorm building and up into the night sky.

"No way!" she gasped, as the scenery blurred past them at an alarming speed. When she'd travelled by the Eternal Path in Meya, it hadn't moved anywhere near as fast. They sailed over treetops and rivers, skirted around and above glowing villages and larger towns, and cut straight through the middle of a mountain. And all within seconds.

"This is *insane*," she whispered, taking in their journey with wide eyes.

The *Valispath* seemed to increase in speed until the scenery blurred into unidentifiable shadows. After a minute of what seemed like faster-than-light travel, their transport began to slow, and Alex saw they were soaring through an ethereal—and familiar—forest.

"We've just entered the Silverwood," Zain said.

When the trees turned golden—and their radiance was breathtaking even at night—Alex knew they were almost at the city. The *Valispath* continued to slow to the speed she'd experienced during her first time in Meya—still ridiculously fast, but much less heart-stoppingly terrifying.

When they breached the Golden Cliffs, Alex was again mesmerised by the sight before her.

Meya was a place of dreams during the day, but that was nothing compared to what it was like at night, when moonbeams bounced off the Myrox in diamond-like streams around the entire city. The palace was surrounded by wisps of moving colour that flowed across the valley, to the point where the waterfalls glowed with a pearlescent sheen. Its beauty and majesty were beyond anything Alex could have ever imagined.

"Am I dreaming?" she whispered.

Zain turned his head to smile at her. "No, little human. Behold, the glory that is Meya."

She was too overcome for words, so she nodded dumbly as they flew through the city. Much like the first time, it didn't take long to reach the magnificent palace, but this time the *Valispath* transported them straight through the outer walls and continued until they reached their destination somewhere in the middle of the impressive building.

"I don't understand," she said to Zain when they came to a halt in front of an intricately decorated doorway. "I had no idea the *Valispath* could go beyond Meya—and I guess its surrounding forests, too. But since it clearly can, why doesn't Aven just access it to get back here?"

"The *Valispath* can only be controlled by a Meyarin," Zain answered. "Aven may be one of our race, but the authority of his blood was invalidated with his disinheritance. He lost his rights as a denizen of our city the moment he was stripped of his title and banished. The Eternal Path is one of the many privileges Aven forfeited with his rebellion."

"The Library too, right?" Alex asked. "That's why he needs me?"

Zain nodded.

"What would it take for him to regain those privileges?" Alex asked. "To be able to use the *Valispath* and everything else again?"

"That's never going to happen, Alex."

"But, if it *did?*" she pressed. "What would it take? Hypothetically?"

"For Aven to regain his inheritance, his father and brother would have to be dead," Zain told her bluntly. "If King Astophe and Prince Roka were eliminated, Aven would automatically regain his birthright."

"What about his mother? Couldn't she take the throne?"

"Traditionally, only a king can rule Meya," Zain said. "Queen Niida wouldn't be allowed to hold the position indefinitely so long as she still had a living heir—regardless of his state of banishment. Our laws would defend the right of rulership as belonging to Aven, and we would have no choice but to pledge our allegiance to him or become traitors to the crown."

Alex wasn't sure what her expression must have shown, but Zain squeezed her arm and sent her a comforting smile.

"Don't worry, little human. Like I said, that will never happen." With those confident words, he stepped up to the door.

"One last thing," Alex said. "Could I use the *Valispath*? You know, because I apparently have Meyarin blood in my veins?"

She hated the idea, but if there was the potential perk of using the Eternal Path anytime she wanted, then admittedly that would be pretty awesome.

Zain laughed at the eager look on her face. "I'm afraid not, as it's Aven's blood you possess. His disinheritance technically means your disinheritance."

The Meyarin was clearly amused by her disappointed pout, but he was also intent on keeping them moving. After knocking and waiting for a response too quiet for Alex to hear with her human ears, Zain opened the door and beckoned for her to step through first.

"I was wondering when you two would stop chatting," Roka said, rising from behind his desk and walking over to them.

He was just as intimidatingly beautiful as the first time Alex had seen him—more so, perhaps, since he was wearing some kind of dark outfit with gold trimming that brought out the unique colour of his eyes. He also wore a swirling black and gold cape, which added to his impressive—not to mention, princely—appearance. But the grin on his face was warm and welcoming, and

Alex found herself smiling back at him in response.

"It's good to see you again, Alex," Roka said, reaching out to place his hands on her shoulders. "I hope you've been well?" Before she could answer, he frowned slightly and added, "You're frozen stiff. Zain, please tell me you shielded the *Valispath?*"

Alex hadn't noticed how cold she was until he'd pointed it out. Her body was shivering to fight off the stinging bite of the wind from their journey.

"Forgive me, little human," Zain said, seeing her trembling. "I didn't realise you were uncomfortable."

"Don't worry about it," she said through her chattering teeth. "I was too distracted by the scenery to notice the cold, anyway."

"Be that as it may, we can't have you freezing to death," Roka said, and he unclasped his cape and placed it around her shoulders. It was way too big on her, but warmth immediately began to flow through her body, and she smiled gratefully at him.

"Thank you, Prince Roka."

"I'm not a fan of formalities, Alex," he said. "Just call me Roka."

She furrowed her brow and looked from him to Zain and back again. "But Zain calls you by your title."

"Zain is one of my closest friends," Roka said, "but he also happens to be one of the most respected warriors in Meya's elite guard. Because of that, he often has to maintain a semblance of formality around me, but he doesn't usually call me 'Prince' unless it's for official business, with witnesses present."

"Like when he's picking up a mortal and escorting her to Meya in the dead of the night?" Alex asked dryly.

"A perfect example," Roka said, his lips twitching with humour as he turned to his guard. "For future reference, Zain, you can be at ease around Alex."

"You can also stop calling me 'little human'," she told the guard, for what felt like the hundredth time.

"What would be the fun in that?" Zain asked with a mischievous twinkle in his eyes.

Alex huffed at him but decided to let it go—for the moment, anyway. She followed the two Meyarins over to a set of plush gold couches on the far side of the room and collapsed onto the super-soft material.

"Is this your office, Roka?" she asked, eyeing the opulent furniture complete with a massive wooden desk piled high with all sorts of interesting objects, most of which Alex couldn't begin to identify.

"One of them," he answered, leaving it at that. "Can I offer you something to eat or drink?"

Alex couldn't deny that she was curious about Meyarin cuisine, but it was the middle of the night and she could feel her bed calling her from miles away. She decided not to prolong their discussion for longer than necessary.

"I'm good, thanks," she said. "Why don't we fast forward to where you explain why you needed to speak with me so urgently?"

"I'm truly sorry for disrupting your sleep, Alex," Roka said, and he did look like he meant it, "but I just received news of your encounter with my brother earlier tonight. For so long we've heard nothing of Aven and his dealings—although we do keep tabs on him from time to time—and then to suddenly have you come out of nowhere with your story ... Well, I'm sure you can understand our surprise."

"I definitely can," Alex said. "But I'm still not sure why I'm here?"

Roka looked away and ran a hand through his dark hair before he turned his piercing golden eyes back to her. "Alex, I've spent the majority of this past week trying to convince our ruling council—and my father—not to insist you remain in Meya indefinitely."

"What?" she squeaked.

"You're considered to be our most significant threat right now," Roka said. "With your access to the Library, you're the only one of your kind who can help Aven return to our city. The council members are hesitant to trust the word of a mortal girl whose allegiances they believe could be swayed with the right incentive."

"Aven nearly *killed* me," Alex reminded him. "He also tried to kill my best friend, using me as his puppet! If he'd had his way tonight, he would have killed or Claimed a whole group of people I care about. I would *never* help him, no matter the incentive!"

"Perhaps not willingly," Roka said, "but Aven is a skilled manipulator. And you're young, even for your own kind."

"I'm not an idiot, Roka," Alex said, jutting her chin out. "I know the difference between good and evil."

"Knowing is important," the prince acknowledged. "But there's a great difference between knowing what's right and being able to hold onto it in the face of adversity."

Alex massaged her temples, feeling her earlier exhaustion returning.

"Let me get this straight," she said. "You're telling me that the Meyarin council wants to lock me up? That's a bit extreme, don't you think?"

"I agree," Roka said. "And I've spent many hours arguing on your behalf."

"Why?" she asked. At his questioning look, she clarified, "Why defend me?"

He shrugged his shoulders and sent her a warm smile. "I don't know you very well, Alex, but from what I've seen with my own eyes, I don't believe you would ever willingly betray us."

Alex felt humbled by his kind words and his unexpected offer of trust.

"Thanks, Roka. That means a lot," she said quietly. "But did it do any good? Or should I expect some of your buddies to storm though the door any minute and bind me with Moxyreel?"

Seeing the apprehension in her expression, Roka chuckled. "No, Alex, you're safe here. I'm at a stalemate with the council, but they're willing to stand down for the time being. It helps that my father eventually took your side as well. As King, he holds the most sway with the council. And he seemed to appreciate your ... What was the word, Zain?"

"Spunk," Zain said with a crooked grin. "He definitely used the word 'spunk'."

Roka laughed. "That's right. Apparently he was impressed when you snapped at him and told him to use your actual name instead of, uh ... *other titles*."

"If the king can learn from that, why can't you, Zain?" Alex asked the guard.

"Someone has to keep you in line, little human."

She made a face at him and turned back to Roka. "If I'm not here to be kidnapped, then why *am* I here?"

"I was told you crossed blades with Aven," the prince said. "My informants weren't able to say more than that, so I called you here to make sure you were okay and to find out what happened."

"That's it?" Alex asked, not sure if she was relieved or annoyed. "How is that classified as 'urgent'?"

"I wasn't sure when I'd next have the chance to meet with you, since I didn't want to intrude upon your studies," Roka said. "Education is important."

Alex actually snorted. "So is sleep. And coincidentally, your brother said the exact same thing to me once, just with slightly more condescension."

"As fascinating as that is," Roka said, and she wasn't sure if he was being sarcastic or not, "I'd rather hear about how you ended up fighting him."

Shifting into a more comfortable position, Alex opened her mouth to begin her story, but was interrupted when a knock sounded at the door, followed by Kyia walking into the room.

"Alex, it's good to see you again," said the beautiful Meyarin with a smile so bright it was nearly blinding.

"Hey, Kyia," Alex replied. "Shot anyone lately?"

Roka and Zain both laughed and Kyia's smile widened.

"I'm waiting for your friends to come back so I can get in some target practice."

"I'll remember that for the next time they annoy me," Alex said. "As long as you lend me a bow, too."

"Deal," Kyia agreed, taking a seat and turning to Roka. "Have I missed anything?"

"Your timing is perfect," he said. "Alex is about to tell us what happened tonight with Aven."

Alex looked at Roka, hoping he'd be able to read her hesitant expression.

"It's okay," the prince encouraged her. "Kyia and Zain know everything. You can trust them. Nothing you say will leave this room."

That was good to know, since Alex couldn't help but like both warriors.

"The last time we met I told you how Darrius Marselle thinks Aven has been Claiming gifted humans," she began. "Well, apparently Darrius asked my Stealth and Subterfuge teacher to keep an eye out for anything unusual. Hunter discovered that a man named Sir Oswald Graham was planning a dinner party and he sent in a spy to..."

Alex told the Meyarins every little detail about her evening at Sir Oswald's mansion, and when she was finished, she slumped back on her couch and rubbed her tired eyes.

"How did you feel when you fought Aven?" Roka asked.

"Terrified," Alex admitted.

"No," the prince said, his eyes crinkling with humour. "I meant, how did you feel physically?"

She considered for a moment and answered, "At first I thought I was doing pretty well. I tried to let go and sense my surroundings like you asked me to do when we fought blindfolded, and I eventually managed it, at least for a while. Then Aven told me he was toying with me. I thought he was just being arrogant, you know? But when he came at me again, I wasn't able to put up any kind of fight.

He was too strong and too fast for me to keep up."

"Was he curious about how you were able to defend so well against him to start with?" Roka asked.

"He was surprised, that much was obvious," Alex said. "But I didn't tell him anything."

"Good," Roka said. "We want to avoid Aven learning that his blood empowers you for as long as we can."

"What about the other people he's Claimed?" Alex asked. "Wouldn't they be able to tap into his Meyarin blood?"

"In a sense, yes," the prince said. "But since those humans are entirely under his control, they would only be able to access his Meyarin abilities if he ordered them to do something that required the use of those abilities. You, however, have the choice as to when and how you access the skills inherent to our race. You can use his power without his command, and that makes you ... special."

"Yay, me," Alex muttered, and the three Meyarins laughed at her less than enthusiastic response.

"Is there anything else I need to know?" Roka asked.

Alex shook her head. "I think I've told you everything..." She trailed off as a thought came to her. "Actually, there *is* something else, but I'm not sure if you'll know anything about it. And it's kind of ... strange."

"I'm listening," Roka offered.

She fidgeted slightly and blurted out, "I'm being stalked by a magical blade."

Three sets of eyes blinked at her.

In a dubious voice, Roka repeated, "A ... magical blade?"

Alex was aware of how ridiculous she sounded, but she explained anyway. "There's some kind of weapon that keeps appearing out of nowhere whenever I need it. It's the one Aven used to Claim me, and it's also the one that ended up almost killing me that same day, but I, uh, never told you that part. When it appeared during my fight with Aven tonight, he reacted weirdly and called it A'enara. Does that mean anything to you?"

The Meyarins stiffened.

"A'enara?" Kyia's body was coiled with tension. "Are you sure that's what he called it?"

They seemed to be holding their breath as they waited for her answer. "Positive."

"Roka, *selith raen de A'enara le nada, Aven*," Kyia said to the prince, her tone sounding anxious. "*Torgas fruen halsa de rilona.*"

"Kantaris de Tia Auras frey selia," Roka responded, and he rose from his seat and began pacing the room.

"Does someone want to clue me in?" Alex said. "In case you haven't noticed, I don't speak Meyarin."

"Sorry, Alex," Roka said, sitting down again but clearly on edge. "Can you describe the weapon?"

"Uh, sure," she said, not sure why that was relevant. Surely 'magical blade' was enough of a description. "Size-wise, it changes when you run your finger down the edge of it. I've seen it transform from a dagger into a sword, and it's come to me in both forms. As for the design, it's pretty simple. The pommel is made of some kind of metal—maybe Myrox, but I'm not sure. When it's a dagger, both edges of the blade curve in intervals, like dipping waves, and when it's a sword, the waves stretch out until it's almost straight-edged, but not quite. The only thing that always remains the same is its ice-blue colour. It's ... well, if I didn't have such horrible memories associated with it, I'd admit it's rather beautiful."

During her description, the Meyarins continued to exchange wary glances.

"And it appears out of nowhere when you have need of a weapon?" Zain clarified.

"So far, yeah," Alex said. "The first time I was caught in one of Hunter's traps with my classmates and we needed to cut our way out." She turned to Roka, "The second time was when I fought blindfolded against you here in Meya. And the third time happened with Aven just a few hours ago."

"Can you call it now?" Roka asked.

Alex looked at him in puzzlement. "Um, how?"

"I'm not sure," he admitted. "Can you feel it?"

She tried to keep the 'Are you crazy?' expression off her face when she answered. "Nope. Can't feel a thing."

"Did Aven try to reclaim the weapon?" Kyia asked.

Alex strained her memory. "He said, 'Come, A'enara', as if he expected something to happen, but it didn't do anything. That made him a little ... angry."

"How interesting," Roka said, rubbing his chin thoughtfully.

"Is anyone going to tell me what's going on?" Alex asked.

They looked at each other before Roka answered, "I'm sorry, Alex, but I don't think we should talk about this until we have more information."

"Surprise, surprise," she mumbled. *More secrets.*

"It's for your own protection," Roka assured her. "If you're truly capable of wielding A'enara, then the threat you pose to our city—and the threat Aven will consider you to be to him directly—has just increased tenfold. We can't let anyone else find out about this until we know if our presumptions are correct."

Alex glanced between them, frowning slightly. "I don't understand."

Zain barked out a laugh, diverting her attention to him. "That's because you're about to drop dead on your feet."

She shot him an unimpressed look. "Someone *did* drag me out of bed in the middle of the night."

"And I'm sure that same someone is more than willing to escort you back right now," Roka said with an indulgent smile. "Unless there's anything else you want to discuss?"

"Nope," Alex said. "The only questions I have seem to be ones you can't answer."

"Alex—"

"Don't worry, Roka," she gently but firmly interrupted. "I get it. Really. And I appreciate you looking out for me, even if I don't understand why."

He nodded in acknowledgement and stood, offering her his hand.

"One last thing," Roka said as he led her to the door. "As you're aware, Aven's plans to infiltrate Meya rely on you getting him here through the Library. I was only able to convince the council to let you to remain at Akarnae by assuring them that you wouldn't open a doorway through to Raelia again."

Alex couldn't hide her disappointment. "Are you saying I can't come back?"

Roka curled his arm around her shoulders. "Of course you can. But until we have a better idea of Aven's plans, you'll have to journey here using the *Valispath*."

"But I can't access the *Valispath*. Human, remember?"

The prince grinned. "No, but Zain can."

Alex looked from his brilliant smile to Kyia's sparkling emerald eyes and Zain's highly amused expression before she repeated, for the billionth time that night, "I don't understand."

Roka chuckled at her confusion and said, "I visited your headmaster earlier in the week. Together we negotiated for Zain to take on the role of teaching assistant in your Combat class. He'll be accompanying you back to the academy for the time being and acting as a go-between for communication."

Alex couldn't hide her dismay. "Please tell me you haven't assigned me a bodyguard? Not cool, Roka."

The three Meyarins laughed at her obvious displeasure.

"I have better things to do than babysit a mortal," Zain said. "You'll barely see me."

"Zain's teaching position will allow him some anonymity while he carries out a different mission objective," Roka explained. "His true task is to unveil Aven's plans—or at least attempt as much—and hopefully without gaining my brother's notice."

"Oh," Alex said. "I guess that's okay."

"I'm glad you approve," Zain said, his eyes still laughing at her.

"Sorry if this seems blunt," Alex said, taking in the massive guard's appearance, "but how do you plan on keeping your anonymity when you look like you do? You're kind of like the Incredible Hulk, without the whole pigment issue." Seeing his baffled look, she clarified, "You're not built for blending in, if you know what I mean. And like all Meyarins, you're kind of, um ... physically distracting."

"Aw, does the little human have a crush on me?" Zain teased. "I'm flattered, Alex. Truly."

Alex scrunched her nose at him. "You're probably older than the dinosaurs. I'm not too picky when it comes to age, but I'm confident it'd never work out between us."

Roka laughed openly, and Kyia giggled behind her hand.

"All right, little human," Zain said, clearly amused even if he didn't want to admit it, "it's time to get you back to bed."

With no other warning, he reached down and threw his arms around her waist, hoisting her over his shoulder like a sack of potatoes.

"Let me down, you brute!"

"Say goodnight, little human," he told her.

"'Goodnight, little human'," she parroted.

Roka and Kyia tried—and failed—to hold back more laughter.

"Oh, wait," Alex said as the guard carried her to the doorway. "What about your cape, Roka?"

"Zain can bring it back to me later," the prince said. "It'll keep you warm on your journey to the academy."

Alex watched as Kyia sidled up to Roka's side, wrapping her arms around him as he bent to kiss her forehead lovingly. They waved goodbye to Alex, who tried to return the gesture while Zain manhandled her out of the room. Only when the door was closed behind them did the guard set her down, holding her steady until she regained her footing. He then continued bracing her when the *Valispath* took off underneath them. This time, though, Zain reached out a hand and pressed it against the transparent barrier. Immediately the bitter chill of the wind disappeared.

"Better?" Zain asked, seeing that she was steadier on her feet with the added protection. Not to mention, warmer.

"Much," she agreed, nodding with enthusiasm. "Why didn't you do that last time?"

"Our race is much more durable than yours," he said. "Many millennia have passed since we've interacted with humans. I'd forgotten just how vulnerable you can be."

"That makes sense," Alex conceded.

She watched the scenery as they were transported back through the palace and out into the city. Once again she was transfixed by the view, which was even more stunning now that she wasn't being buffeted by the wind.

All too soon they zipped past Meya and ventured above the Golden Cliffs before the *Valispath* began to speed up again. When they were part way through the Silverwood, Alex turned to look up at Zain.

"So, Roka and Kyia, huh?" she asked. The tender moment she'd witnessed alluded to something much greater than friendship, of that she was certain.

"She is to be his wife," Zain told her. "And one day, our queen."

Alex smiled at the memory of Roka's words about his 'betrothed' from their first meeting. "They're a beautiful couple."

"They are," the guard agreed. "I couldn't ask for two better friends."

"Will you miss them while you're stuck at Akarnae?"

"I'll still see them most days," Zain said, indicating to the *Valispath*. "It's not hard for me to get around."

Handy little rollercoaster, Alex thought as the scenery blurred by at lightning speed.

Soon enough the *Valispath* began to slow down and Alex could see the lights of the academy glinting in the distance, along with the moon reflecting off Lake Fee beneath their feet. The ride came to an abrupt end when the Eternal Path moved them straight through the wall of her dorm building and into her room.

"This is where I leave you, little human," Zain said quietly, not wanting to disturb her sleeping roommate.

"Are you going back to Meya?" she asked, and at his nod she took off Roka's cape and handed it over. "I guess I'll see you tomorrow?"

"You will," he agreed. "It's best if you act like you don't know me, at least not around your classmates. You should also warn your friends to do the same."

"Is that for your anonymity?"

He sent her another crooked smile. "No, Alex. It's so the other humans don't wonder why you're associated with a Meyarin. But I doubt they'll figure out my ancestry considering how much time has passed since one of my kind has been recognised by your race. It's far more likely they'll merely consider me to be intimidatingly large ... and attractive, as you've already pointed out."

"I did not call you attractive," Alex argued hotly. "I said you're distracting. That could've meant anything."

"Goodnight, little human," Zain said with a laugh, ignoring her words. "Get some sleep."

The *Valispath* took off again, taking the Meyarin guard along with it.

Alex shook her head at the spot where Zain had been standing, then stumbled tiredly over to her bed.

As she was drifting off to sleep—again—she realised that not only Karter, but now Zain as well, would be teaching her Combat class the next day. She firmly pushed the thought from her mind, determined to enjoy her last remaining hours of sleep without worrying about what the class might bring.

Twenty-One

"Wake up, sleepyhead."

Alex groaned at the sound of the way too chirpy voice next to her ear.

"Go 'way," she mumbled, burrowing deeper into her blankets.

"Come on, Alex," the voice said. "You'll be late for PE if you don't get up."

"Don't care," she mumbled again.

Her blankets were yanked away and a rush of cool morning air hit her. She sat up with a yelp, reaching blindly for her lost source of warmth.

A quiet snort turned Alex's attention to her roommate who began heartlessly laughing at her predicament.

"Not. Nice. Dix," Alex grumbled, running her fingers through her dishevelled hair.

"But it worked, didn't it?"

Alex didn't waste energy glaring at her friend. Instead, she stood up and grabbed some clean clothes from her wardrobe and headed into the bathroom.

Hot running water was a luxury after two days in the wilderness and Alex used the time in the shower to ease her strained muscles and enjoy a few moments of peace before her day began. When she was dressed, she left the bathroom to find D.C. waiting for her.

"Feeling better?"

"Yeah," Alex said. "Sorry for being such a grump. I didn't get much sleep."

"Are you kidding me?" D.C. said with another laugh. "You slept for almost ten hours straight! You should feel on top of the world right now."

"Actually," Alex said, thinking quickly about what she was and wasn't allowed to share, "my sleep was interrupted in the middle of the night because Roka wanted to speak with me."

D.C. gaped at her. "The Meyarin prince was here?"

"No, Zain was," Alex said. "He came to escort me to Meya. It was so cool, Dix. The Valispath took us the entire way. I've never experienced anything like it."

D.C. was staring at Alex in shock, but then her expression shuttered and she turned her hurt-filled eyes away. "Why didn't you wake me? I would've come with you."

"I'm sorry," Alex said, putting every ounce of sincerity into her apology. "You were dead-asleep and when I went to wake you, Zain told me not to disturb you. I didn't like it, but I also didn't want to argue with him."

D.C. tilted her head thoughtfully, her unhappy expression dissolving into a calculating one. "Prince Roka wanted to speak with you privately, didn't he?"

Alex wasn't sure how to answer, so she nodded, almost shamefully.

"I saw how he looked at the rest of us the other day," D.C. explained. "He doesn't trust us."

"No, Dix, that's not—"

"It's okay, Alex," D.C. interrupted her. "It's not like I don't understand. While he doesn't trust us, it's clear he *does* trust you. I'm not going to ask what he wanted you for, because you're my best friend and I don't want to put you in that position. Keep his secrets, but just know that I'm here if you want to talk, okay?"

Alex threw herself across the room to embrace her friend.

"Thanks, Dix," she said, hugging her tightly. "You're the best."

"It's not like I haven't asked you to keep my share of secrets." D.C. smiled as she pulled away. "It looks as though you're the go-to girl for royal confidences."

"Woohoo," Alex said dryly.

D.C. shook her head in amusement before saying they had less than half an hour left for breakfast.

"Do you mind if we swing by the Med Ward on our way?" asked Alex as she picked up Fletcher's lab coat. "I need to return this to Fletcher."

When they were outside and heading towards the Gen-Sec building, D.C. said, "Jordan told us about your weekend trip. I can't believe Hunter made you do all that!"

"It was pretty intense," Alex said.

Total understatement.

A few steps later D.C. spoke again, quieter this time. "Did you really fight Aven?"

Alex shuddered as the memory washed over her. "Yeah. Or, I tried to, at least. He's ... really good."

"He *is* Meyarin," D.C. reasoned. "Still, I heard you held your own long enough to buy some time and get everyone out of there. I was amazed when Jordan said so. Especially with all the other gifted people on Aven's side."

"We were very lucky," Alex said, honouring her promise to Roka and keeping her new Meyarin abilities secret. "Nothing more."

D.C. appeared doubtful. "If you say so."

They dropped off Fletcher's coat and hurried to the food court to eat a quick breakfast. Jordan and Bear were already waiting for them, finishing the last of their meals.

After Alex had scoffed down her scrambled eggs on toast she turned to Jordan and Bear. "I have some news." They looked at her curiously and she drained her juice before speaking again in a whisper, "Do you guys remember Zain? The massive guard from Meya?"

"He's hard to forget," Bear said, and D.C. and Jordan nodded in agreement.

"Well, he visited me last night and told me he's going to be Karter's teaching assistant for a while," Alex said, deliberately leaving out her trip to Meya.

D.C. eyed her shrewdly, but since Alex's words weren't actually false, she didn't think her roommate would call her on them.

Jordan and Bear were clearly surprised and she quickly finished her explanation.

"He wants us to act like we've never seen him before. It's for our sakes, mostly, since it wouldn't be good for anyone to think we've been in contact with a Meyarin. That said, Zain doesn't actually believe anyone will figure out that he's not human. They'll think he's intimidating—and attractive. His words, not mine."

She scowled a little when she thought about the guard's teasing. *Stupid Meyarin.*

"Why's he coming here?" Jordan asked.

Alex thought about her answer carefully before she responded. "He's going to be keeping an eye on everything, I guess. They heard about what happened with Aven yesterday and they seem to think it's a good idea for me to have a babysitter. Or something like that."

Okay, so she hadn't told the complete truth. But she knew Roka wouldn't be pleased if she gave away Zain's real mission. So she told them what she'd first thought the guard was coming for, and her explanation was believable enough that her friends nodded their acceptance.

"Your very own personal bodyguard," Bear said with a smirk. "You're moving up in the world, Alex."

"I think this is a good thing," Jordan said seriously. "I'll sleep better at night knowing Zain is here to keep an eye on you, just in case Aven turns up again. Meyarin against Meyarin is way better than human against Meyarin, that's for sure."

"I agree," Alex said. "Although it is a little annoying."

"Annoying might just save your life," Bear pointed out.

The gong rang then, telling them to head off to class.

"Remember, you don't know who he is," Alex said to D.C., who had Combat first up.

"Amnesia, got it," the red-head replied before taking off for the Arena, while the rest of them headed to the lake to test their water survival skills in **PE.**

After narrowly avoiding death-by-drowning, the rest of Alex's day passed from Archery—where she had to shoot at moving targets over a hundred feet away—to lunch, and finally to Equestrian Skills where Tayla made them all participate in a game similar to polo, except they had to ride bareback while sitting backwards. It was remarkably unsafe, in Alex's opinion, but Tayla was adamant that it taught them how to feel the horse's movement underneath them. That, and apparently it was a great exercise to help increase their balance and coordination skills.

Alex fell off three times. But that was less than most of her classmates. D.C. landed on her royal behind a total of seven times, and the others hit the ground even more. Needless to say, everyone was relieved when the class ended.

As Alex hobbled from the Stable Complex to the Arena, she wondered how she might get away with skipping her last class. Nothing came to mind, so she stood up a little taller, winced when her backside and shoulder protested from the movement, and entered the colossal structure.

"You're late, Jennings," Karter grunted.

"Sorry, sir," she said, knowing he wouldn't care to hear about how painful the simple act of walking was.

"As I was saying," Karter said, shooting her an irritated look, "my new assistant has more experience than most of you will ever have in your lifetime—combined. When he speaks, you listen. Understood?"

Alex and her classmates nodded their agreement and when Karter was satisfied, he called out, "Zain? Anything to add?"

The Meyarin warrior stepped out from an alcove in the Arena's wall and Alex had to hold back a grin when she heard the indrawn breaths of those around her.

"I think they get the point," Zain said to Karter. "And if they don't, they will."

Alex wasn't the only one who trembled at the look he levelled at them, but she also knew that Zain was really a teddy bear—albeit one who could land her on her back with a sword at her throat without any effort at all.

But still, a teddy bear.

Karter smirked at their reactions and ordered, "Run two laps around the Arena for a warm-up, then grab a wooden staff and find a partner."

They sprinted off as ordered, and when Alex was halfway through her first lap, Kaiden matched her pace and moved closer.

"Do you want to tell me why there's a Meyarin helping to teach our Combat class?" he whispered, after making sure the others were a safe distance away.

Alex schooled her expression into disbelief. "A Meyarin? Really?"

He snorted. "Please, Alex. You can drop the act."

"What are you trying to say, Kaiden?" she asked defensively.

"These days most people don't remember what Meyarins look like, let alone get the chance to see one in real life," Kaiden said, echoing Zain's words from the previous night. "Two in the space of as many days is unheard of. But for some reason, I'm not surprised. And you don't look surprised, either."

Alex didn't say anything, but simply continued to run while stealing glances at him. She wondered how he seemed to know so much, but there was no way she could ask if she wasn't willing to answer in return.

"Just tell me this, is he on Aven's side of whatever's going on?" Kaiden asked, seeing that she was maintaining her stubborn silence.

Alex wasn't going to answer. Really, she wasn't. But after everything he'd been through with her and the secrets he was already keeping, she couldn't not reassure him.

"No," she whispered. "Zain's one of the good guys."

He sighed loudly—how he did that while running, Alex had no idea—and turned to look at her again. "I take it I'm not supposed to know he's not human?"

"That would be preferable," Alex said. "He's aiming for anonymity."

Kaiden laughed at the ludicrous idea, and Alex found herself smiling with him.

"Well, he's *trying* for anonymity," she amended.

"He'll probably succeed," Kaiden admitted. "Very few people would believe that we have a Meyarin on the teaching staff."

His eyes danced with humour as if his words had an added meaning, but they were coming to the end of their second lap and Alex didn't get the chance to ask if there was more to his comment than she understood.

"Hey, Queenie!" Sebastian called over to her, ending their conversation. "Be my partner today?"

"Sure," she agreed, grabbing a staff and following her classmate to a clear space.

The warm-up run had loosened her muscles somewhat, but two hours later Alex was feeling every one of her aches again. Zain had done little more than observe the class and offer advice when needed, but she'd noticed him staring at her on more than one occasion.

Talk about unnerving.

Alex was tempted to skip dinner in favour of another hot shower and an early bedtime, but her stomach complained so she gave in and headed towards the food court to meet her friends. She figured that afterwards she should also pay a visit to Darrius to fill him in on her horror-filled weekend. Unless...

"Hey, Jordan, is there any chance someone's already spoken with Dar—um, Headmaster Marselle about our SAS trip?" Alex asked as they ate. They were sitting at a table with Mel and Connor along with a few other fourth year classmates, so she had to be careful with her words.

Fortunately, Jordan knew exactly what she was asking.

"Hunter made sure the headmaster was informed of ... everything," he told her, the tone of his voice revealing more than his actual answer. "I spoke with him as well, just in case anything was, uh, left out."

Alex smiled at him gratefully. That was one less thing she would have to do, at least. Now, if she could find a way out of her Medical Science assignment that was due the next day...

**

"Recently I had a student come to me and ask an interesting question," said the enigmatic and uncommonly intelligent History teacher, Doc, during class the following week. "This student asked about the historical development of society, specific to our advancement in technology. The question posed was, if society is so advanced, why does Akarnae still teach students using such an archaic curriculum?"

Alex resisted the urge to sit up straighter, knowing that she was the student Doc was speaking of, but not wanting to draw attention to herself. She'd approached the History teacher in his Tower office a few days after the events of the overnight SAS trip—specifically, after having witnessed the military outpost and the high-tech Stabiliser weapons. Too caught up in the adrenaline at the time, she hadn't wondered until later that, if the people of Medora had access to guns, why she and her fellow classmates were running around with bows and arrows and learning old-school Combat techniques. That line of thought, which had kept her awake for hours, had also led her to question why they had an entire class devoted to riding horses when, as D.C. had mentioned during their time strolling along the cobblestone streets of Tryllin, most people walked or used Bubbledoors to travel these days. Out of nowhere, Alex had been burning with questions about why some of the classes at Akarnae were so dated when Medora as a world was advanced in so many ways.

Feeling like an idiot for never having questioned it sooner, Alex had only been able to justify herself with the realisation that ever since her first day at the academy, nothing had made sense to her, so she'd just gone with it in order to retain her sanity. Even the academy's buildings were a juxtaposition of medieval structures alongside futuristic designs. The difference between the Tower and the Gen-Sec building alone was startling, but Alex had simply become used to the idiosyncrasies of Akarnae—and the people inhabiting it.

Or at least, she *had*, until she'd seen the Stabilisers and the military force and realised that her understanding was seriously lacking and she needed to fix that, pronto.

"I didn't answer the student's question at the time since I saw it as an opportunity for a refresher that we can all discuss as a class," Doc went on to say. "So, let's break this down, shall we? Starting with the history of Akarnae—why you're all here at the academy. Who knows the answer?"

Both Mel and Connor raised their hands in perfect sync and Alex hid a smile because, as much as they might disagree with her assessment, sometimes she thought they acted more like twins than cousins. Siblings, at the very least.

Doc nodded at Mel, who cleared her throat and recited, "Akarnae is the only school in all of Medora for people who are gifted. Every five years the headmaster goes on a scouting expedition to search for kids who qualify for enrolment—kids who have or eventually will have a gift. When they're fourteen, the qualifying students leave their normal schools behind and come here to complete the remainder of their education. That's why we're here. Because we were discovered through the scouting process."

"Why come here?" Doc asked. "Aside from it being the only school for those with gifts, of course. But why can't students such as yourselves continue your tutelage with the rest of the populace?"

"We don't *have* to come here," Connor spoke up this time. "But Akarnae is the best place to teach us how to develop our gifts. If we were at a normal school, we'd just be taking normal classes. But at Akarnae, we're in an environment where we can cultivate our abilities and learn how to control them."

"Ah ha!" Doc said, sounding pleased. "Control, Mr. O'Malley. A very important point."

At that, Connor sent a smirk to his cousin, and Alex bit back another smile when Mel responded by pulling a face at him.

"At this point it's worth mentioning that some scholars believe every human being has a potential gift inside of them, but not all of us are able to connect with or access these personalised giftings," continued Doc. "For those of us who can, we have a responsibility to nurture the supernatural abilities within us. That means we must learn to develop them, to *control* them, just as Mr. O'Malley said. Tell me though, have any of you ever wondered why Akarnae—a 'school for the gifted'—only has one class dedicated to actively developing your abilities?"

Alex frowned at the question, mentally adding it to the list of things she should have considered long before now.

"After all," Doc continued when no one answered, "Professor Marmaduke's Core Skills class is the only time you have scheduled to learn control. Would you agree?"

Alex nodded her head along with everyone else, even if in the back of her mind a small voice scoffed at the very idea of the Core Skills class which had, for as long as she'd taken it, taught her next to nothing.

"Does anyone perhaps have another opinion?"

Silent shuffles and fidgeting hands met his question.

"Tell me this, then," Doc said. "Archery, Combat, Equestrian Skills ... These are demanding classes—physically and mentally—which is beneficial for your overall fitness, but they are also hundreds of years after their time. What need have we, in this advanced day and age, to learn the art of duelling with blades? Why send arrows into moving targets? What point is there in straddling an animal intended as a means for transportation when we have access to near instant teleportation? What possible reason could there be for us to teach these classes?"

Hearing her own questions come from his mouth, Alex was hit with a sudden realisation and she spoke without thinking. "It's not about the classes."

Doc raised his eyebrows. "Do continue, Miss Jennings."

Feeling the weight of everyone's eyes on her, Alex tried to rally her thoughts. "It's just—I wonder if perhaps we're looking at this wrong. We're not learning Combat or Archery—I mean, we are, but that's not all we're learning in those classes."

With an encouraging look, Doc said, "Would you care to extrapolate?"

Trying to be as articulate as possible, Alex replied, "Core Skills is dedicated to us learning how to control our gifts, yes?" At Doc's nod, she continued. "Well, what if our other classes, particularly Combat, Archery and Equestrian Skills, are also about control? More than control—they're about discipline. We're not learning how to fight each other or ride a horse or whatever else to use those skills in the world outside Akarnae, but rather, by taking these classes, we're growing our characters. That kind of strenuous training requires strength, patience, endurance, fortitude and a range of other traits that can only improve us as human beings. And..."

"And...?" Doc pressed.

"And," Alex continued, "as you said earlier, sir, people with gifts have a *responsibility* to nurture them, but more than that, I'd like to think we have a responsibility to develop ourselves as human beings as well. That's what these classes offer us. They provide us with the building blocks of discipline and control—both of which, in turn, help us to develop and utilise our giftings."

A smile spread across Doc's face and he raised his hands to applaud her, much to Alex's embarrassment.

"Bravo, Miss Jennings," he said. "You are indeed correct—our curriculum isn't in place on the off-chance that you'll be transported back in time and have to survive a swordfight on horseback followed by an archery tournament. Rather, it is to prepare your character for the future and to assist in the learning of control and discipline in every aspect of your lives—including, perhaps especially, your giftings. Once you graduate and leave these walls, it will be up to you what you do with your abilities. You may enter the workplace in a field where you can use your gifts, knowing that people such as yourselves are highly sought after, or you may decide to put aside your ability and live a normal life. The choice is yours. We can only offer you the chance to *make* that choice, being well-informed based on what we teach you and how we teach it to you.

"All that said," Doc continued, deep in teaching mode now, "there is still some modern day relevance for what we learn here, which is especially helpful should you decide to embark into a future where your gift becomes nothing more than an accessory. Equestrian Skills, for example, teaches you how to respect beings much larger, stronger and arguably smarter than yourselves, and if you ever happen upon a situation where you find another creature of mountable size, you'll have some idea of how to gain control over it. As for Combat and Archery—if after leaving the academy you desire to enter into military service or seek beyond that to become a Warden, your fighting and targeting skills will be required on a daily basis. While more advanced technology is available to those of higher ranks, swords will always be the most accessible means to end a physically aggressive dispute. Or start one, as the case may be. And while bows and arrows aren't common accoutrements for humans outside of the academy's walls, none can argue that, if you can hit a moving target from two hundred feet, you can likely shoot any firearm—or simply throw a stone—with above par accuracy."

Wandering back to the front of the room, Doc finished by saying, "The curriculum at Akarnae may seem dated, but as we have just outlined, its traditions are timeless. It's all a matter of perspective."

With plenty to think about, Alex listened as Doc completed the rest of his class by going over some of the points already raised and expanding on others. She felt better having had some of her questions answered, but there was still one thing she was curious about. Not knowing if it was the kind of enquiry she should make to a class full of students when it might be general knowledge to all Medorans, Alex decided to wait until the end of the day before she sought out the one person who she had a feeling would be able to answer her better than anyone else.

***

"You're a hard guy to track down," Alex said to Kaiden, having finally found him in the stables after asking what felt like every single person on campus for his location.

"Alex," he said, looking at her in question over the back of the horse he was brushing down. "What's up?"

She bit her lip and looked away, wondering if she was making a mistake by coming to him. He already knew more about her than he should, but he didn't know *everything*, and it had to stay that way. However, he *had* told her that she could come to him if she ever needed anything.

"I want to ask you something, but you have to promise not to read into it—and you have to promise not to laugh if you think it's a stupid question," she said, reaching for a curry-comb just to have something to do with her hands while she talked. She began grooming the sleek black coat of the horse she knew was named Eclipse, waiting for Kaiden to agree.

"That depends on what you ask," he said, grinning roguishly. "But I must say, I'm intrigued."

Alex frowned. So far, their conversation wasn't going to plan and it had barely begun. But she decided she might as well jump in and see what happened, so she said, "I want to know about the Soori Outpost."

Kaiden's entire body jerked, and Alex looked at him in surprise.

"What about it?" he asked, his brush strokes becoming visibly tense to the point that Eclipse pinned his ears back in irritation. Kaiden noticed and relaxed his grip, prompting the horse to relax again too.

Confused by his strong reaction, Alex said, "I want to know why it's there. Medora is a supercontinent currently run by a single monarchy, so why is there an active military force if there's no one to go to war against? And do they use other weapons stronger than Stabilisers? Also, I always presumed Wardens were more like glorified guards, but now I'm not so sure. Who has more authority—them or the General?"

Kaiden wasn't tense anymore; that was for sure. But Alex almost wished he was, since he was now looking at her with a scrutinising expression.

She swallowed and focused on moving her curry along the barrel of Eclipse's stomach. "No reading into it, remember?"

"Hey, at least I'm not laughing," Kaiden said. "That's one out of two. Take what you can get."

"I'd rather a judgement-free answer," Alex responded. "With no follow-up questions."

"I'll answer you, but I can't promise there won't be follow up," Kaiden said, moving further along to brush the curve of Eclipse's apple-shaped rump. "Let's start with the Wardens. Don't ever let them hear you calling them 'glorified guards' or it may be the last thing you ever say. And I mean that, Alex."

If his serious expression was anything to go by, he really did mean that.

"Now, in a not-reading-into-this kind of way, am I right to guess that you don't know much about what Akarnae students do after they graduate?"

"Um..." Alex hesitated. "Hypothetically? Let's go with that. From here on out, just act like I know nothing."

Kaiden's lips twitched, drawing Alex's attention to his mouth before she forced her gaze back up to his eyes. Judging by the humour she found in them, she had a feeling she wasn't fooling him at all.

"Well, then," he said, looking down at what he was doing once more. "As you know, there are five years of schooling with an additional two years on top of that should any of the instructors invite you to stay on as an apprentice. Whether you graduate at eighteen or twenty, Akarnae alumni are always sought after for the top positions in any of Medora's workplaces.

It's not so much that we have gifts—though that can definitely be a drawcard depending on your career choice—but it's more that our education here has covered, well, everything."

Alex nodded, having just been over most of that in her History class. "What does that have to do with Wardens?"

"There are two kinds of Wardens, did you know that?" Before she could respond, Kaiden said, "Never mind, don't answer that. I forgot that you *hypothetically* know nothing." He didn't even try to hide his smile at that. "Wardens fall into one of two categories: Swords or Shields. The Shields are intelligence analysts—they come from all different backgrounds and are usually recruited later in life after having the experience of years behind them. They do most of the stuff outside of the public eye, keeping a finger on the pulse of the world and the people in it, so to speak. They are essentially a 'shield' against any threats made by humans and by ... *others* ... who have their own agendas. Wardens like Bear's dad, William Ronnigan, are Shields, and they keep us safe mostly by the use of their collective intellect and intuition."

Alex raised her eyebrows, wondering how Kaiden knew about William. But he continued before she could ask.

"Swords, on the other hand, are the field agents; the Wardens who deal directly with anything the Shields uncover. Swords actively seek out the threats to the kingdom and swiftly neutralise—or eradicate—them."

Alex couldn't help automatically imagining the Medoran equivalent of James Bond. In place of a tux and a gun, her invented figure wore a cape and held a sword. Strangely—or not so strangely, considering—he looked an awful lot like Hunter.

"Other than the obvious, the main difference between the two is that only Akarnae graduates can ever hold positions as Swords—and specifically those who have stayed on as apprentices in Combat or SAS." Kaiden sent her a wry smile as he added, "I'm sure you can figure out how both of those classes are high up on selection criteria for Sword applicants."

Alex returned his expression, understanding completely.

"So you can see how highly trained, combat-ready, stealthy Swords who all have gifts might not take too well to being referred to as 'glorified guards', right?"

Kaiden said. "And while Shields might not mind as much, they both wear the same uniform, so it's better to be safe than sorry since you may never know which one you're talking to."

Alex quickly nodded her agreement. Then she asked, "Warden Jeera—you and Declan seemed to recognise her name when I mentioned her after the SAS trip. Is she a Sword or a Shield?"

Kaiden laughed softly as he grabbed a new, softer brush and moved to stroke it down Eclipse's face while Alex reached for a comb to untangle his mane.

"Jeera's a Sword," Kaiden answered. "One of the best."

"And, um..." Alex wasn't sure why—or if—she wanted to know, but she still pressed. "Do you know her well?"

"You could say that." Kaiden laughed again. At Alex's questioning look, he said, "She's my sister."

"Your *sister*?" Alex wasn't able to mask her surprise. "But—but—"

She thought back over the interactions she'd had with the Warden, from first seeing her while locked in the royal dungeon, to having Jeera follow her and D.C. on their day trip through Tryllin and then finally after the mess with General Drock and Alex's Bubbledoor delivery to the palace. She tried to make sense of the events, but all she could do was tilt her head and stare at Kaiden's face, trying to find some resemblance between them. True, they shared the same dark hair and bright blue eyes, and Jeera's features were just as striking, but ... Nope, there were no buts about it. Now that Alex was looking for it, she couldn't miss it. However, without having been told, she never would have picked it on her own.

"That's really cool," she said, just for something to say—and as a means to not feel like such an idiot for staring at Kaiden longer than was appropriate. "I like your sister. She's helped me out a few times now."

"I know she has," Kaiden responded with an amused gleam in his eyes that told Alex he knew more than he was letting on.

"What—"

"To answer the rest of your questions," he interrupted, "because of everything I just mentioned, Wardens do rank higher than military. They're technically a separate entity but sometimes their assignments overlap, and when that happens, they outrank the General. Their word is law."

"Got it," Alex said, having seen first-hand that Drock had afforded a level of deference to Jeera.

"What were the other things you wanted to know?" Kaiden asked. "Why there's a military and what weapons they have?"

"Said like that, you make me sound like I'm gathering intel against them or something," Alex murmured, untangling the final knot in Eclipse's mane and dropping the comb back in with the other grooming tools.

"I guess I'm just going to have to hope that you won't use this information for evil," Kaiden said with a smirk. "I'm trusting you here, Alex. Don't make me regret it."

Before she could think of a response, he reached for Eclipse's halter and untied the now gleaming horse, leading him into a stall and locking him in for the night.

"Come on, I'll tell you how to overthrow the monarchy on the walk back," Kaiden said, pressing his hand gently to the curve of Alex's spine and guiding her down the aisle past the other stalls of curious-looking equines. She tried to ignore the pleasant warmth she felt through her clothes where his hand was—and failed abysmally at doing so. Only when they were outside again did he drop his hand, allowing her to focus on his words rather than his presence beside her.

"Weapons I can't tell you much about," Kaiden said as they headed up through the grassy fields towards the campus proper. "You have to admit, that's a strange question for you to ask me."

Alex felt him looking at her but she kept her head forward, shrugging slightly. "You seemed to know a lot more about the Stabilisers than anyone else. I figured you were the best person to ask."

"And not your royal best friend?"

Alex shrugged again, having no answer for that.

"Well, as I said," Kaiden picked up, letting Alex's lack of answer slide, "I don't know much, but from what I've ... heard ... Stabilisers are about as lethal as it gets. There's been peace amongst humans in the kingdom for thousands of years so there hasn't been a need to develop anything more than the basics, especially since a sword or arrow can kill just as easily—if not more so."

"No weapons of mass destruction, then?" Kaiden cocked his head at her terminology and she explained, "You know, bombs. Explosive devices that blow large areas up at a time, killing lots of people at once."

"Why would we have something like that?" he asked, looking appalled by the idea. "Who would we want to kill?"

"No, no, it's good you—we—don't," Alex assured him, reaching out to squeeze his arm before quickly dropping her fingers to her side again. "I was just making sure."

Shaking his head, Kaiden said, "The military isn't for going to war against humans, Alex. That hasn't happened for millennia—not since well before Akarnae opened, back when there were places in this world that people wanted enough to fight each other over."

Alex immediately thought of the Library, knowing that battles had been waged over it for hundreds of years until it disappeared. She nodded and asked, "Then why—"

"Medora is populated with more than just humans." Kaiden looked at her in a way that made her realise what he was saying was common knowledge, and yet, he was still humouring her 'act like I know nothing' request. "While we've never gone to war against any of the other races in recent years, that doesn't mean we're not prepared if such an event were to take place. Not that we'd stand much of a chance against them—any of them. Meyarins may be at the top of the food chain, but the others can hold their own. We humans are, by comparison, relatively powerless. But if something ever *did* require a defence on our part, we have an active military in place for that very reason."

Mulling over all the information he'd given her, Alex found that she had no questions remaining. At least, that was the case until—

"There are, of course, the threats posed from beings in other worlds"—Alex literally stumbled at his words—"but as far as I know, we haven't yet encountered anyone who means us harm. So again, it's just a precaution."

Alex forced herself to regulate her breathing and fought the temptation to look at him to gauge his expression. With her eyes focused on the approaching Tower building bathed in gold from the setting sun, she grappled to bring her thoughts together. He couldn't possibly know about her—surely he couldn't. He would have said something, told someone, demanded answers. No, it was purely chance that his final words were so relevant to her personally. When she mustered the courage for a quick glance at his face, she was relieved to find him relaxed and at ease, with no evidence of him knowing more about her than he should.

"Does that answer everything?" he asked as they walked past Gen-Sec and towards the food court. "You don't want to know the blueprints for any secret bases or how to assemble an ITD in under five minutes?"

Alex didn't know what an ITD was, but she figured she was already treading a dangerous line with Kaiden and it was best not to ask any further questions that could show just how naive to the ways of Medora she really was.

"Nothing else. You were perfect," she said. Then realising how that sounded, she fought the heat rising in her cheeks and amended, "I mean, you've been perfect." She wanted to smack herself in the face. "As in, you've answered my questions perfectly. That's what I meant."

Kaiden chuckled warmly. "Well, in that case, I'm glad I could help."

They came to a stop outside the food court, lingering near the entry.

"I'm going to go clean up before dinner," Kaiden said, nodding in the direction of the dorm building.

"Right," Alex said, her hands fidgeting by her sides. "I'll just..." She gestured towards the food court, indicating that she was heading in there. "I'll see you later, Kaiden. And thanks again for ... uh..."

"Being perfect?" His eyes sparked with mischief and she felt her still warm cheeks heat further in reaction to the smile he sent her.

"Don't make me regret coming to you," she grumbled half-heartedly, knowing she deserved his teasing after her accidental gaffe.

"I wouldn't dream of it," he replied, very clearly struggling not to laugh. But then his face turned serious and he stepped closer—almost intimately closer—and lowered his voice to say, "Remember what I told you, Alex. You can always come to me. For anything, anytime. Okay?"

Swallowing around her suddenly emotion-clogged throat, Alex was unable to form a verbal response so she just nodded her agreement.

"Good," he said, reaching forward until his fingers tangled with hers for a fraction of a second before he squeezed gently and let her go. "You go eat, and I'll catch you later."

Fingers tingling, she nodded mutely again. When it looked like he was waiting for her to enter the food court before he left, she spun around and walked through the doors.

As she moved away, it took everything in her not to turn and look back over her shoulder to see if he was still watching.

Twenty-Two

The next two months passed much faster than Alex would have liked. As November drew to a close, her classes became impossibly intense, with the teachers firing assignment after assignment at their students before the term ended for the Kaldoras holidays.

While the theory-based classes were straining her mind to its limits, Alex's practical classes also became more strenuous. PE was close to the top of the list and Finn seemed to take particular pleasure whenever one of them had to be carried off to the Medical Ward.

But PE wasn't the only class that resulted in one or more students having to visit the resident doctor. Alex found herself in the Medical Ward on an almost daily basis—for a variety of reasons—much to Fletcher's displeasure.

The first time was after she became wedged between her saddle and a tree trunk in one of her Equestrian Skills classes. In her defence, an odd-looking reptilian creature had spooked her horse and caught them both by surprise. She was relieved the torn ligament in her knee hadn't led to her falling off to become the reptile's next meal.

Another tree landed her back in Fletcher's domain when she sprained her wrist getting caught in one of Hunter's traps during a SAS fake stake-out one night. It was still, clearly, her favourite class.

Not.

The following week she had to see Fletcher after having a violent allergic reaction to something in her Medical Science class. They were looking at the properties of different animal blood when Alex accidentally brushed her fingers against a murky-brown swab labelled with the scientific name, *Daesmilo Folarctos*. She was rushed to the Medical Ward when she began throwing up within seconds of the sample touching her skin. Fletcher kept Alex in the Ward for twelve hours, all of which she slept away after her energy was sapped from the sudden and debilitating sickness.

Despite her illness, Alex recovered surprisingly quickly, which meant it was straight back to classes for her. And that, of course, led to her next trip to the Medical Ward, when she was knocked unconscious in Combat later that week. She maintained that Zain concussed her on purpose, since he'd deliberately chosen her to help demonstrate a new fighting technique. He'd apparently overestimated her fighting ability. Either that, or he must have expected her to fight like a Meyarin—which was something she was keeping a tight rein on.

On her fifth trip to the Medical Ward, she wasn't alone. Everyone in Fitzy's Gamma Chemistry class was treated after a noxious gas infiltrated their laboratory. That, at least, hadn't been Alex's fault.

Nor was it her fault when all fourth year students were quarantined for forty-eight hours after coming in contact with a sick Foofoo in their Species Distinction class.

That's right. A Foofoo.

As cute as the name was, it didn't come anywhere close to describing the adorable creatures. Alex's heart had melted when she first saw the multi-coloured little balls of fluff. Like every other girl in her class—and some of the boys, too—she hadn't been able to hold back her cooing baby-voice when the Foofoos looked up at them with their big puppy-dog eyes, all but asking to be picked up and cuddled. Which is exactly what Alex and the others had done.

By the time class ended, everyone was sniffling and sneezing—Varin included—and after a quick examination by Fletcher they were sent to his Infectious Diseases isolation room. The illness they'd contracted was the equivalent of a twenty-four hour bug, but the doctor kept them for twice that long to make sure they were no longer contagious.

Despite that particularly miserable experience, Alex couldn't deny that she wanted a Foofoo of her own.

One of the few classes that *didn't* land Alex in the Medical Ward was Core Skills. If anything, though, a trip to visit Fletcher could have only helped improve the subject. For Alex, the class was beyond tedious, since her gift was more like an on-off switch than anything else—with it always turned on. She didn't have to learn control, unlike most of her classmates with their various abilities.

Despite not needing to practise using her gift, Alex *was* experimenting a little to see if her willpower could progress beyond herself. Professor Marmaduke had put the idea in her head at the end of the previous year, and since then Alex had wondered if she could share her gift with others in a similar way to Jordan's transcendence.

So far, Alex hadn't been capable of doing anything different. Then again, she had no way of judging if she actually achieved what she was trying. Which led her full-circle back to believing that Core Skills was a waste of her time, even if she did now understand the bigger picture behind what it was teaching, at least according to Doc's insight into the reasons for the academy's ancient curriculum.

If nothing else, she could say that her Core Skills classes remained predictable, unlike her SOSAC class—or rather, the teacher.

Ever since Alex had returned from her SAS weekend 'adventure', Caspar Lennox had taken an unexpectedly keen interest in her. Whenever she entered his room, his dark eyes found her. If she looked up from taking notes, his gaze was on her. When she left his class, his eyes followed her. The Shadow Walker was already creepy enough without this bizarre, stalkerlike development.

Fortunately, he didn't approach her outside of his classroom. She never saw him anywhere else, but she often had to resist the urge to wait behind after his lessons to confront him about his disturbing stares. Her friends claimed it was all in her head and, while she didn't agree with them, she chose to follow their advice and let it go.

But that was easier said than done.

***

"Miss Jennings, please remain behind after class."

Alex was startled by the unexpected interruption. One minute Caspar Lennox had been speaking about the lords and ladies of Deveraux House, circa two hundred years ago, and the next he was asking her to stay back after his lesson. At her hesitant nod, he continued his discussion as if there had been no change of topic.

'Baffled' didn't come close to describing how Alex felt. She was so intrigued by the Shadow Walker's request that she barely paid attention to the rest of his class. Thankfully, there were only a few minutes left before the gong rang and her friends and classmates filed out the door, leaving her alone with the professor.

Caspar Lennox sat on the edge of his desk and did nothing but stare at her for a full minute. It was unnerving to the point where Alex found herself fidgeting under his gaze.

"Sir?" she asked when she couldn't take the silence any longer. "Have I done something wrong?"

"Not yet," he said, his musical voice floating over to her. "But the future isn't set in stone. I have no way of knowing the choices you'll make."

It was now Alex's turn to stare.

"Never before have I come across a human quite like you," Caspar Lennox murmured pensively.

Alex thought he might have been complimenting her until he added, "I've never known anyone who could find themselves surrounded by so much trouble in such a short amount of time. You truly are a unique individual."

"Uh, thanks?" Really, how was she supposed to respond to that?

The Shadow Walker continued to stare at her. But then Alex realised he wasn't staring at her, so much as *through* her. It was like he was looking for something else, something only he could see.

"The Shadow surrounds you," he said, his bottomless eyes slightly unfocused. "But the Light within you ... I've never seen anything like it. Even the Dayriders pale in comparison."

His words left Alex feeling completely lost. She wasn't sure what question to ask first, so she settled on, "What's a Dayrider?"

Caspar Lennox blinked a few times until his eyes cleared again, and when he spoke, he acted as if she hadn't. "Alexandra, we're all born with Shadow inside us. But, as with anything, it's up to us to decide what we do with that Shadow. We can succumb to its power, or we can overcome it and use it. Our level of control depends upon our ability to resist the Shadow's hold on us. It's a choice we must all make."

He paused, apparently waiting for Alex to respond.

"I'm sorry, sir, but I'm not sure I understand what you're telling me. Or why," Alex admitted. "When you say 'we', do you mean your race? And are you talking about Shadow Essence? Like, with your cape and my ring? That sort of thing?"

Caspar Lennox looked at her steadily and continued, more quietly than before, "Sometimes the Shadow can overwhelm us. The power it offers ... The temptation can be too strong to resist. If we yield to it, it's almost impossible to return to the Light. Unless there's someone willing to help us find our way back."

Alex was well and truly confused, finding herself with more questions than answers. But before she could figure out what to ask the professor, he snapped his head to the side as if he'd heard an unexpected noise in the room.

"Remember my words, Alexandra," he said, rising from his seat with the ever-present cloud of shadows swirling around his feet. "Remember my warning."

When she continued to look at him in bewilderment, he added a firm, "You're dismissed."

She had little choice but to leave, despite the fact that she didn't know why he'd asked her to remain behind in the first place.

"What was that about?" Jordan asked when she met her friends in the food court for dinner a few minutes later.

"I have no idea," Alex said, shaking her head in bemusement.

"Huh," Jordan hummed, but he let the subject drop, probably sensing her confusion.

"Any chance you can help me with my Chem assignment, Bear?" D.C. asked their friend, pulling some broccoli from her stir-fry and wrinkling her nose at the vegetable. "I don't get what Fitzy wants me to do with the Gorgonite. Is it supposed to react in water or in the air? Or just when it's heated up?"

"I finished that assignment a few days ago," Jordan jumped in before Bear could answer. "I can help if you want?"

Alex looked at Bear to find him glancing back at her with an equally knowing—and amused—look on his face. In their eyes, Jordan was so obvious. But, amazingly, D.C. seemed oblivious to his increasing attention of late.

At first, Jordan had kept his intentions subtle. He'd walked D.C. to class, asked her to hang out with him in the Rec Room, and offered to study with her in the Library—as un-Jordan-like as that was. But lately he'd stepped up his game, much to Alex and Bear's entertainment.

"You don't mind?" D.C. asked, looking at him from under her eyelashes.

Alex hid a smile and wondered if perhaps her roommate knew exactly what Jordan was doing. What a conniving little ... princess. Alex almost laughed out loud at the idea of D.C. knowing all about Jordan's infatuation. Because that meant she wasn't discouraging him—which in turn meant she, just possibly, reciprocated his feelings.

Alex could already imagine their cute little strawberry-blond children frolicking around the palace years into the future.

"What are you thinking about, Alex? You have a weird look on your face."

She coughed awkwardly and said, "Uh, I was just thinking about ... cheese."

Cheese? Really?

"You know, mozzarella," she added, seeing their disbelieving expressions. "It tastes so great. All stretchy and ... uh ... flavoursome. Like rubber."

To add emphasis to her nonsensical words, she picked up the slice of pizza in front of her and bit into it, "mmmm-ing" as she chewed.

"Right," D.C. said, looking at her strangely. "Anyway..."

Alex was relieved when they returned to their conversation and the attention left her again. She swallowed her mouthful and glanced up to catch Bear's twinkling eyes. He probably knew exactly what she'd been thinking—most likely because he'd been thinking the same thing. She mock-glared at him, and his grin widened.

"All right, enough Chemistry," Bear said a few minutes later, and Alex nearly choked on her food at his double meaning. "Let's talk about Kaldoras."

"What's to say?" Jordan asked. "I can't wait for Gammy's apple pie."

Alex felt her mouth watering in anticipation. Bear's grandmother made the best food Alex had ever tasted. When she'd stayed with the Ronnigans last Kaldoras, she'd been introduced to Gammy's famous apple pie—and she could honestly say it was too incredible for words.

"I spoke with Mum yesterday and she asked me to confirm you're all coming back to Woodhaven with me," Bear said.

"You know I'm in, mate," Jordan said, shoving a meatball into his mouth and swallowing quickly. "There's no place I'd rather be."

"Me too," Alex agreed, mentally replaying a recent discussion she'd had with her parents about the upcoming holiday.

Alex had been visiting her mother and father at least once a month to check in on them, and thankfully they rarely asked any in-depth questions about what they referred to as her 'elf problem'. It seemed they were content to accept that Akarnae was the best place she could be. Alex, for her part, had decided she was better off not updating them on her latest encounters with Aven, instead opting for the 'what they don't know, won't hurt them' mentality.

During their most recent visit she had asked if they were okay with her spending the holidays with Bear's family again. It turned out that her parents were anticipating being up to their elbows in what they'd discovered to be fossilised bat guano—the Library was scarily well detailed with its depiction of the ancient Freyan ecosystem—so Alex's mother and father had accepted her request to stay with her friends for Kaldoras. She was beyond relieved, given that the alternative was for her to spend the Christmas-equivalent buried alongside them in long-dead animal droppings. *Thanks, but no thanks.*

"Dix? How 'bout you?" Bear asked.

"Yeah, my parents said I can come," D.C. said. "It was easier to convince them since your dad's a Warden"—This also happened to be one of the main reasons Alex's parents were so accepting of her request to leave the safety of the academy—"but I think they're a little nervous, especially with you-know-who running around out there."

Alex snorted into her glass of water and her friends turned to look at her.

"Sorry, your words just surprised me," she said.

"Well, I can't exactly shout his name in the middle of the food court, can I?"

Even though she knew the question was rhetorical, Alex couldn't help but chuckle and say, "Next you'll be calling him He-Who-Must-Not-Be—"

"Good evening, students," interrupted Zain's deep voice as he approached their table. "Alex, do you have a moment?"

She nodded and stood to her feet. The other students had become more used to his intimidating presence, but he was still a sight to behold, especially when he did something as normal as walk through the food court. Plus he was decked out in full warrior gear as per usual, including his sword and various other weapons strapped to his belt, along with his bow and quiver of arrows slung over his shoulder.

Alex mentally shook her head as she followed him out the doors and away from the buildings. She had no idea what he'd been thinking with his intention to remain anonymous. But for whatever reason, no one had yet learned of his origins—as impossible as that was. Were they blind?

"What's up, Zain?" Alex asked when he brought them to a halt near the edge of the forest.

He took in her curious expression and said, "You're such an enthusiastic young mortal. I only wish your eagerness to find answers would overlap into your Combat training."

"Don't start that again, Zain," Alex said in a frustrated voice. "Just hurry up and tell me what you want."

The Meyarin had cornered her a number of times over the previous weeks to find out why she wouldn't attempt to access the power of Aven's blood in her veins. He couldn't understand her aversion to the idea, even when she continued to remind him that her Combat class was made up of decidedly *human* students who would notice if she began to kick their butts to kingdom-come. Their differences of opinion had led to the two of them arguing until they'd agreed to disagree. Or, that was Alex's standpoint. Zain continued to believe she would change her mind if he bugged her enough.

"What's your rush, little human?" he asked, leaning casually against a tree. "If I didn't know any better, I'd say you didn't want to be seen with me."

She was unimpressed with his annoying, but not unexpected, big-brotherly attitude. Over the weeks their relationship had developed to the point where he'd begun to deliberately antagonise her, just like any sibling might do. His jovial and carefree attitude made it easier for her to not fear his daunting power, but at the same time, she'd never had a brother before, and now she knew first-hand just how irritating they could be.

"You might have all the time in the world, but I have to get to SAS in ten minutes," she told him. "Start talking, or I'll start walking."

He laughed at her no-nonsense expression. "You're so much fun to be around when you're all snarky like this. King Astophe was right about your spunk."

"Zain..." she warned.

"All right, all right," he said, rolling his eyes before turning serious. "Roka wanted me to update you."

This wasn't the first time the prince had passed a message along to her via his guard. Alex appreciated the communication more than she could say, since she hardly felt worthy of the royal Meyarin's attention, let alone his continued sharing of information.

"Okay, shoot."

Zain smirked and, in the blink of an eye, he pulled his already strung bow from his back, notched an arrow, and let it fly. A bloodcurdling scream filled Alex's ears and she whipped her head around to see Skyla facing them with her back pressed flush up against a tree—almost two hundred yards away. The girl was frozen in shock, and Alex realised why when she saw that Zain's arrow was embedded into the tree's trunk at the crease where Skyla's neck met her shoulder.

"Zain!" Alex hissed incredulously. "You could have killed her!"

The Meyarin snorted. "Please, Alex. Give me some credit."

Right. He was Meyarin.

But Skyla didn't know that.

Alex hurried over to the terrified girl with Zain ambling slowly behind her.

"You're all right, Skyla," Alex assured her classmate, yanking the arrow from the tree and shoving it into Zain's hands. "You're not hurt or anything. You're fine, see?"

Skyla's frantic eyes jumped from Zain to Alex and back again. "You—You tried to kill me!"

"It was only a warning." The Meyarin waved away her accusation. "I don't tolerate eavesdroppers."

From two hundred yards, Alex doubted a Meyarin would have been able to eavesdrop on their quiet conversation, let alone a human like Skyla. The trembling girl gaped at him but then, to Alex's astonishment, she averted her gaze.

"I was on my way to SAS and I saw Alex talking with someone," Skyla said in a small voice. "I was just curious."

"Curiosity is an admirable trait," Zain said. "But as you've now learned, it's also dangerous. Take more care in the future, Miss Fay."

Skyla nodded her agreement and scurried away from them, heading off to class without a backwards glance.

"I'll be quick," Zain promised Alex, drawing her reeling thoughts back to him and continuing their earlier discussion. "There's nothing new to report from the last update. I'm still trailing Aven, mostly focusing my attention on his gifted humans—the ones we know of, anyway. I haven't discovered any of his plans, and that worries me. I've spoken at length with Hunter and we've been joining forces, hoping that we'll get a lead. So far nothing has turned up. I have to wonder if one of Aven's gifted allies has some kind of disillusioning or protective gift. Every time we get even slightly closer to figuring out what he might be doing, we lose the trail."

Zain began to pace back and forward, his frustration showing through his tense movements.

"What can I do?" she asked.

"Just continue what you're already doing," he answered.

She knew better than to argue with him, since that had never helped her during any of their previous conversations.

"Let me know if that changes," she said. "You know I'll help in any way I can."

"You better get going," Zain said, deflecting her words. "I'll see you in

Combat tomorrow. At least *try* to fight, won't you?"

"*Goodnight, Zain,*" Alex said pointedly, not waiting for his response before taking off for her class.

***

Over the next three days Alex was snowed under with schoolwork. Even their normally leave-study-in-the-classroom History teacher, Doc, had assigned a three-thousand word paper on the relevance of Agnus Cordon's hierarchical government structure and how it compared to the modern day monarchy. Talk about snore-worthy. Alex had literally fallen asleep in the Library while researching the topic.

When Friday night rolled around, she finished the last of her exhausting assignments and decided to reward herself with an early night. She was in the bathroom getting ready for bed when she heard the door to her dorm open and seal shut again. She was about to call out a greeting to D.C. when she heard Jordan's voice in the other room.

"You're overreacting, Dix," he said, sounding exasperated.

"I'm not," D.C. replied. "I really don't think you should go."

"I don't have a choice," came Jordan's muffled reply, his voice quieter than before. "You know that."

"You do have a choice!" D.C. cried. "You're almost eighteen—what are they going to do? Ground you? You don't live with them anymore!"

"Dix, what's really going on?" Jordan asked. "Why are you acting like this?"

There was a loaded pause and Alex stepped closer to the door separating them. She felt bad for eavesdropping, but there was no way she could announce her presence now without it being awkward for everyone.

"I just..." D.C. trailed off before trying again. "I just don't feel very good about this."

In the gentlest voice Alex had ever heard him use, Jordan said, "Hey. Nothing's going to happen to me."

Alex barely made out the words when D.C. whispered, "Promise me you'll come back?"

"I'm only going for the weekend, Dix," Jordan said, his tone still overwhelmingly sweet. "I'll be back Sunday night. Earlier, if I can."

"No." D.C.'s voice was filled with urgency. "I need you to promise. No matter what happens, promise me you'll come back. To us. To *me*."

Alex felt her stomach churn uneasily at her friend's desperate plea. Jordan must have sensed something as well, since it took him a moment to respond, and when he did, his voice was rough with emotion.

"I promise, Dix," he whispered. "I promise I'll come back to you."

D.C. let out a sigh, and there was a rustle of noise where Alex presumed her two friends were embracing after their semi-intense moment. She wondered how long she'd have to wait in the bathroom before she could make a stealthy escape.

"Bear's waiting for me down in the Rec Room," Jordan said. "You coming?"

"Yeah, that sounds good," D.C. agreed. "I probably won't be sleeping for a while yet."

"Still having the nightmares?"

Jordan and Bear had eventually been told about D.C.'s recurring nightmares that had exhausted both girls the week before the SAS weekend. After Alex returned from the trip, D.C. had settled back into her normal sleep routine. Mostly. Once or twice a fortnight she still woke up screaming, but that was about it.

"No," D.C. answered. "Not as often, anyway."

She said something else then, something too quiet to hear, and a moment later Alex heard the door to the dorm room open and close again. Alex waited a few seconds to make sure they didn't come back before she stepped out of her hiding place.

"I thought you might've been here. We don't usually leave the bathroom door closed."

Alex jumped and held her hand up to her fluttering heart.

"Dix! You scared me," she spluttered, seeing her roommate standing next to the window. "I thought—uh—"

"I told Jordan I'd meet up with them in a minute." D.C. looked Alex squarely in the eyes. "Did you hear everything?"

"I'm sorry," Alex apologised, shuffling her feet on the carpet. "I wasn't sure if I should interrupt or not. I didn't mean to listen, but it was kind of hard not to."

D.C. blew a strand of hair out of her eyes. "Don't worry about it, Alex. It's not like you heard anything I wouldn't have told you about, anyway."

"Can I—um, can I ask what that was all about?"

D.C.'s eyes darkened and she turned to look out the window into the night. "Jordan's parents want him to visit Chateau

Shondelle for the weekend. He's leaving first thing in the morning."

Alex felt her throat constrict at the thought of their friend having to spend the next two days with Marcus and Natasha Sparker. "Since when do they want anything to do with him? Whenever they do see him, they don't actually want to see him. What gives them the right to demand his attention?"

"They're his parents, Alex," D.C. said quietly. "You know how much he wants to please them. If they say 'jump' he won't ask 'how high?'—he'll just do it, if only to try to make them proud. He'd do almost anything to earn their love."

"So he's going back to his childhood home for some quality family time? Is that what you're telling me?" Alex asked, more heatedly than she'd intended.

"I don't like this any more than you do," D.C. snapped.

Alex looked into her friend's anguished eyes and could see the truth of her words. "I'm sorry, Dix. I'm just worried."

"I know," D.C. mumbled. "Me too."

"I'd planned on having an early night, but I think I'll come down to the Rec Room with you, if that's okay?" Alex asked, grabbing a hoody to pull on over her pyjamas.

"Yeah, sure," D.C. said, leading the way out the door. "I think that's a good idea. Just the four of us hanging out together. Exactly like it should be."

Alex looked at her friend closely, wondering about the unusual tone of her voice, and then she shook her head and let it go, figuring D.C. was distracted by Jordan's family predicament.

When they reached the Rec Room, Alex walked directly over to Jordan.

"Ah," he said, seeing the look on her face. "I guess I don't need to tell you where I'm going this weekend?"

When she didn't say anything, he placed his hands on her shoulders and sent her a reassuring look.

"I'll be fine, Alex," he said, squeezing his hands gently to emphasise his statement. "I've already promised Dix I'll be back by Sunday night. And I would have to be stupid to break a promise to her. That could mean public execution in the town square, for all I know."

Alex ignored his attempt to joke and looked straight into his eyes, trying to read more than his words. After a moment, she saw how much he believed what he was saying—not the execution part, the coming back part. She would just have to trust that he knew what he was doing.

"Just be careful, yeah?" Alex said, relenting at last.

"You know me," he said with a crooked grin. "'Careful' is practically my middle name."

"Hmm." Alex tilted her head. "I thought your middle name was 'Obnoxious'? Or was it 'Arrogant'? Oh, wait, I know. It's 'Stuck-Up', right? 'Jordan Stuck-Up Sparker'. It has a ring to it, don't you think?"

Bear snorted and D.C. cracked a smile. Jordan's response was to let go of Alex's shoulders and move a few feet away, picking up a cushion from the nearest couch and throwing it at her. She ducked just in time, but it sailed directly into D.C.'s face, prompting what turned into an all out pillow war with Jordan and Bear versus D.C. and Alex. The light-hearted moment was exactly what they needed to turn the tense atmosphere into something much more relaxed, and the rest of the night continued in the same carefree manner, with the four friends enjoying one another's company and laughing into the early hours of the morning.

***

"He's not back yet. He said he'd be back tonight. Where *is* he?"

"Calm down," Bear said, reaching for the pacing Dix and pulling her onto the bed beside him.

It was Sunday night and Alex, Bear and D.C. were in the boys' dorm room, waiting for Jordan to return. They had all managed to keep busy enough over the weekend to keep their fears at bay, but none of them had heard from him since he'd left the previous morning and they were now growing increasingly concerned.

"It's not curfew yet," Bear reminded them. "Don't worry, he'll be here soon."

Despite his comforting words, from her position on Jordan's bed, Alex could see the strain in Bear's features. He was as worried as they were.

As the seconds ticked by, the three friends tried to stay occupied by talking about their upcoming Kaldoras break. But it was hard to remain on the topic for long, especially when every few minutes one of them would glance at the time displayed on their ComTCDs, which only served to increase their anxiety.

At last, the door clicked open. Alex sat bolt upright and felt relief wash over her at the sight of Jordan stepping into the room.

He closed the door behind him, sending them a cocky smile. "I should go away more often if this is the welcoming committee I'll get every time I return."

As if his words broke a spell, the three of them leapt up to greet him.

"Don't even think about it, Jordan Sparker," D.C. said, wrapping her arms around him.

Jordan closed his eyes as he returned her embrace, which gave Alex the chance to look at him properly. His face was paler than usual, but that could easily have been because the temperature outside was turning bitter with the arrival of winter only days away. His rugged-up appearance supported her theory, since he was covered from head to toe—beanie and gloves included.

"Cold back at the Chateau?" Bear asked, noticing as much as Alex.

"Freezing," Jordan said as he released D.C. and grabbed his friend in a one-armed, back-slapping hug. "It's barely been two days, but it feels like I've been gone forever. Yeesh. I need to get a life."

"We've missed you," Alex told him quietly, and Jordan stepped over to her and hugged her last.

"Missed you, too," he whispered in her ear.

Alex's body jerked in reaction to the broken-sounding words that neither D.C. nor

Bear would have heard. She pulled back to look at his face and her breath hitched at the tormented shadows lurking in his eyes. But then he blinked and the emotion was gone, making her question if she'd really seen it in the first place.

Jordan released her and grinned widely as he looked around the room. "What did I miss while I was gone?" he asked, sprawling onto his bed.

Alex was stunned by his one-eighty change of emotion. She sat tentatively beside him and D.C. and Bear resumed their positions on the other bed.

"No way," D.C. said. "You tell us about your weekend first. What happened? What did you parents want?"

Jordan shrugged. "They just wanted to see me."

Alex raised her eyebrows at him—and she wasn't the only one—but it seemed like he was ignoring them in favour of digging through his backpack. Whatever he was looking for eluded him, and he gave up his search and noticed their waiting expressions.

"What?"

"Your parents called you back to their place just to say 'hi'?" Bear asked dubiously.

"Seems like it," Jordan answered. "Weird, huh?"

"Did they say why they wanted to see you?" D.C. pressed. "Or why it was so urgent?"

"Nope." Jordan stood and walked over to his desk. He shuffled some books around before huffing quietly and turning back to them. "I'm starving. Does anyone have any food? I thought I had something in my bag, but I must've left it back home."

Home? Had he just referred to Chateau Shondelle as 'home'? As far as Alex knew, Jordan hated the place where he'd grown up. His home was Akarnae, and his second home was the Ronnigans' house in Woodhaven. Chateau Shondelle was just a cold reminder of a lonely childhood. The only person who had ever actually cared for him had been his brother Luka, but he'd killed himself when Jordan was eleven. All in all, the chateau was hardly a place of happy memories for Jordan.

"Home?" Bear asked, picking up on the word as well.

Jordan froze for a split second before his posture relaxed and he corrected, "My parents' home. Old habits die hard."

Alex was looking at Jordan with concern as he searched for something edible on his desk. When he realised that his search was fruitless, he walked back to his bed and sat down again.

"Sorry to be antisocial, but I'm wiped," he said, covering an almost believable yawn with his hand. "I should try to sleep before my stomach eats my kidneys and keeps me awake all night."

No one seemed to know what to say to that.

"Um, sure," Alex agreed, slowly standing to her feet. "I guess we'll, uh, leave you to it. See you both in the morning."

"'Night," Jordan said, stretching out his legs and cupping his hands behind his head.

Alex looked pointedly at Bear as she and D.C. headed to the door, and her dark-haired friend nodded, understanding her silent request to press Jordan for more information after they were gone.

The moment D.C. and Alex were in their dorm room, they turned to each other.

"Was it just me or—"

"It definitely wasn't just you," D.C. interrupted as she folded onto her bed, holding her head in her hands.

"Hey, are you all right?" Alex asked, sitting beside her friend.

"I'm worried," D.C. admitted after a quiet moment. "I can't help but wonder..."

When D.C. didn't finish, Alex asked, "What is it, Dix?"

The other girl shuddered slightly and raised her head, her expression scarily blank. "Nothing, Alex. I'm sure it's nothing."

Alex was about to protest, but D.C. said she was tired and escaped to their bathroom to get ready for bed. When she came back out, she barely whispered a quick, "Sweet dreams, Alex," before she slid under the covers and rolled over to face the wall.

When Alex settled into bed a few minutes later, she couldn't shake off a sense of foreboding. Jordan was back, safe and sound, so why wasn't she more relieved? Sure, his behaviour seemed a little off, but he'd just spent the weekend with his parents who demanded too much from him and gave nothing in return. That would mess with anyone's head. He just needed time, she figured, and then he would be back to normal.

But as Alex drifted off to sleep, she couldn't get the image of his tortured blue eyes out of her head, and she wasn't the least bit surprised when D.C.'s terror-filled screams woke her up later in the night.

Twenty-Three

"I just wish he'd tell us what happened, you know?" D.C. complained as she and Alex walked away from the Stable Complex, struggling to make a path through the snow that had blanketed the academy grounds during an early season snowstorm the previous weekend. "I don't like that he won't talk to us about it."

Two-and-a-half weeks had passed since Jordan's visit to his parents and he hadn't given them any details about his time away. In fact, Alex had barely seen him outside of classes since his return to the academy, and she was more than a little worried about his continued absence during social hours. She couldn't help wondering if his parents had done or said something to him and, being a typical guy, he'd built up walls to keep everyone else from realising how upset he was.

If Jordan would open up to them rather than avoid them, they could talk about it and try to help him. Or at least remind him that his real family wasn't necessarily related by blood.

"I know, Dix," Alex agreed. "But we can't force him to talk to us."

Unfortunately.

"I wish we could," D.C. said, sounding weary. Her nightmares had returned with a vengeance over the last two weeks, and while they didn't wake both girls every night, her screams interrupted their sleep at least every second day. Both of them had dark circles under their eyes, and D.C. looked constantly ill.

"Maybe you should skip PE and go take a nap?" Alex suggested, worried about her friend.

"You know, I think I might," D.C. agreed, surprising Alex. Normally the red-head wouldn't have given in so easily. She must have been exhausted.

"I'll try to find Bear and see if he'll have a word with Finn for you," Alex offered. Bear's gift sometimes came in handy, that was for sure. While it might not be ethical for him to 'charm' their PE teacher into letting D.C. skip her lesson, his ... influence ... would at least keep her out of trouble for missing the class.

"Thanks, Alex," D.C. said, smiling gratefully.

Alex nodded and took off to find Bear. He and Jordan both had Delta Archery for their final class of the day, so she hurried over to the Archery fields, hoping her friends would be early. Much to her relief, she spotted them quickly and asked for

Bear's help just in time for him to run off and 'speak' with Finn. That left Alex and Jordan standing alone together for the first time in weeks.

"How are you doing?" she asked, trying to subtly examine his appearance. Lately everything about him was just ... drawn.

"I'm good," he said, smiling at her. Despite his words, the usually carefree expression didn't quite reach his eyes, and he failed to keep his gaze locked on her. He looked around as if searching for a distraction. "How 'bout you?"

She made a face at their tense conversation before mimicking his response. "I'm good."

"That's good," he said.

"It'd be better if I believed you," she said bluntly.

He tilted his head and gave another un-Jordan-like smile. "You know me, Alex. Would I lie to you?"

She looked away from him and said quietly, "You mightn't be lying, but I don't think you're telling the complete truth, either."

"Trust me, Alex," Jordan told her. "I've never felt better."

She moved a step closer and lowered her voice. "You can talk to me, Jordan.

I'm good at keeping secrets, if that's what you want. I want to help."

Something changed in his eyes, a glimmer of emotion, but it disappeared before she could identify it.

"That means a lot, Alex," he said. "I'm lucky to have a friend like you. But really, I'm good."

She shuddered at the carefully controlled expression covering his normally animated features. It was like he'd shut out the world. What had his parents done to him?

"Please, Jordan," Alex whispered, not entirely sure what she was begging him for.

"You'd better get to class," he said, reaching out to squeeze her arm in what should have been a comforting gesture. "You don't want to be late for Karter. Or Zain. I'll see you at dinner."

She wanted to stay and convince him to open up to her, but his classmates began to arrive and she knew their time for talking had passed. Not that he'd actually said anything. She wished she could figure out how to bring down his walls. They were only hurting him even more—and his friends in the process. But she wouldn't give up. Maybe he just needed more time. There were only two days left of classes until the Kaldoras break started—hopefully he'd feel more comfortable talking when they were all at Woodhaven.

As Alex hurried over to the Arena, she felt her spirits lift a little, convinced that their holiday together would make everything better. There was nothing like a little quality time to help mend hurting relationships. They would all be back to normal soon enough.

"Ten more seconds, Jennings, and you would have been late to my class for the second time this year," Karter informed her loudly as soon as she entered the Arena.

"I can go back out and come in again if that'll make you feel better?" Alex offered, and then she bit her tongue to keep from saying anything else disrespectful. She'd been so caught up in her thoughts that she'd forgotten to filter them before speaking to her easily enraged instructor. Oops.

Karter's eye twitched at her words. Not a good sign.

"I think it's time for another class demonstration," he said, his voice low and dangerous.

Sometimes my life just sucks, Alex thought miserably when Karter, predictably, picked her for his 'demonstration'. She looked around for Zain, figuring he would be her opponent for the three or so minutes she'd remain conscious—less, perhaps, given the slippery snow-covered Arena floor—but she couldn't see the huge Meyarin anywhere.

"Where's Zain?" she asked, forgetting that she was supposed to be keeping her mouth shut.

"No idea," Karter grunted.

A flicker of worry sparked within Alex, but she didn't have time to think of anything other than her own survival after Karter threw a sword to her and began his attack.

She had a chance of lasting longer than three minutes with Karter, but even so, he was a talented, aggressive opponent. And he was angry. Definitely not a good combination. Plus it didn't help that she was distracted by trying to keep her Meyarin abilities under wraps. It seemed that ever since she'd had a few tastes of what her fighting ability could be like, her body wanted to use the skills it was capable of utilising. So, while Alex was fighting Karter, she was also fighting herself.

No wonder she was so exhausted when he knocked her sword from her hand and toppled her onto the cold, wet snow.

"Again," he barked.

The class couldn't end soon enough, in Alex's opinion. She almost wished Zain was there, since he might have taken pity on her.

Doubtful, Alex thought realistically as she blocked Karter's overhead swing. *Very doubtful.*

***

Zain still hadn't shown up by the time Alex's final Combat class rolled around on Friday afternoon and she was growing concerned. While she hardly counted herself important enough to know the guard's every move, she felt sure he would have told her if he'd planned to disappear for a while. He was her only means of communication to Meya, after all.

His continued absence caused her enough anxiety that she found herself walking up to the headmaster's office after dinner that night to see if he knew anything. While the other students were packing their bags and getting ready for their break the following day, Alex was busy worrying about yet another impossible male in her life.

She was halfway up the Tower staircase when she almost collided with Darrius, who was heading down.

"Alex," he said, surprised. "I was coming to find you."

She blinked at him. "Really?"

"Yes, as a matter of fact," he said. "Let's go up to my office, there's something I'd like to speak with you about."

"Sure," she agreed. "I need to ask you something as well."

She followed him up the stairs and into his official headmaster's office, pausing to take in the beautiful view through the window-wall. The academy looked like a winter wonderland, covered in the thick blanket of snow that still lingered from the previous weekend's storm. It was simply magical.

"Why don't you go first?" Darrius offered, drawing Alex's attention back to him.

She took a seat at the large conference table opposite him before asking, "I was just wondering if you know anything about Zain's disappearance?"

Darrius frowned in confusion. "He's missing?"

"'Missing' might be the wrong word," Alex admitted. "It's just that I haven't seen or heard from him since Monday."

Darrius's features relaxed. "I saw him after lunch today, Alex. Unless something has come up between then and now, let me assure you that he seemed to be perfectly fine."

Alex was surprised. "Why hasn't he been in either of my last two Combat classes?"

Darrius held his hands out as if to show his lack of understanding. "I'm afraid I don't know the answer to that. Perhaps he had somewhere else to be."

His answer didn't sit right with Alex, nor did the Meyarin's lack of communication. He usually updated her every few days with news about Aven. The last time they'd spoken had been on Monday night, when he'd told her about a promising new lead. The anticipation had been rolling off him, which was another reason why she was so concerned about his lack of presence. Surely he would have contacted her by now to update her on his progress?

"Where did you see him, Darrius?" Alex asked.

"Just outside the Arena," he said. "He was speaking with Jordan while waiting for the Delta Combat class to begin."

Alex thought back to lunch and remembered Jordan had left a good twenty minutes before the start of class. That checked out, at least. But it was strange that Zain would have been in the class directly before Alex's and taken off straight afterwards.

"I guess it was a false alarm," she said, though for some reason she didn't believe her own words. "What did you want to speak with me about?"

"Something slightly less pleasant, I'm afraid," Darrius said.

"Let me guess: Aven?"

"Indirectly, yes," Darrius confirmed. "Aside from your off-campus interactions, he's been remarkably quiet in his attempts to return to Meya. He hasn't tried to breach the wards of the academy to get to you, and while he knows about our Lockdown protocol, that hasn't stopped him before. Even with my added security measures, I know that if he wanted to, he could infiltrate Akarnae if that was his wish."

"What are you saying?"

"I'm troubled by his silence," he admitted. "And I'm increasingly concerned because tomorrow I have to deactivate the wards so the students can return to their homes for the holiday. While the Lockdown may not have stopped Aven, it would have given us a little warning. If he decides to come after you tomorrow, we won't know about it until it's too late."

Alex thought about his words and said, "Why don't I leave tonight, then? Would that work?"

"That would be the ideal solution if the wards around Woodhaven were ready to go. But they need another twelve hours before they'll be activated in time for your arrival," Darrius said.

She looked at him with wide eyes. "Wards around Woodhaven? Are you kidding me?"

"Come now, Alex," Darrius chided. "You didn't honestly believe the king and queen of Medora would allow their only child to spend the holidays unprotected, did you?"

"I thought they were happy enough knowing that Bear's dad is a Warden," Alex said, somewhat sheepishly. Now that she thought about it, it did make sense that D.C.'s parents would want extra protection for their daughter. It was ridiculous that none of them had questioned their easy acceptance of the holiday arrangements.

"You should also know that the wards King Aurileous has commissioned play a large role in my approving your stay with the Ronnigans, Alex," Darrius said. "Had he not arranged their construction, I know you likely would've gone with or without my agreement. But at least this way I have more peace of mind about your safety."

"That's ... kind of you," Alex said. "A little overprotective, but kind."

Darrius chuckled.

"These wards," she asked, "are they the same as the ones here? If we have any unexpected visitors, will there be a Lockdown?"

"No, the wards around Woodhaven are significantly different," Darrius said. "The ones here have been constructed and are maintained by the Library. I have very little control over their security protocols, but since they're the most complex wards I've ever encountered, I'm content to keep them working as they are. The ones King Aurileous has commissioned won't be as advanced, but they should nevertheless be quite effective."

He stood and walked over to his desk to pull something out of a drawer. "Do you know what this is?" he asked, handing an item to her.

She squinted at the watch-like, touch-screen device until a memory came to her. "This is a military thing," she said, recalling Major Tyson having something similar strapped to his wrist at the Soori Outpost. "I've seen one before and it activated some kind of short-range teleportation portal when we stood on a circle marking the ground."

Darrius nodded as if he'd anticipated her answer. "ITDs—Instantaneous Transportation Devices," he informed her.

"You and your friends will each be given one of these to wear for the duration of your stay in Woodhaven. They've been adjusted to link with the wards around the entire township—which has in turn been programmed to resemble the carved circle portal. If you find yourselves in any danger, you need only tap three times on the screen and you'll be whisked away to a different location."

"I was under the impression there are some distance-related problems with the transporters?" Alex said, remembering Tyson's words about how they were trying to work out the kinks. "I don't particularly want to be turned into human soup anytime soon, Darrius."

"That's the drawback of the wards," he admitted. At her startled look he quickly clarified, "Not the human soup, Alex, the range. Their lack of long-distance transportation complicates matters. If you have to activate the portal, it'll give you an immediate escape, but you won't be relocated far enough away to avoid capture if Aven remains nearby."

She passed the device back to him. "Then what's the point of this?"

"I'm getting to that," he said. "The plan is that the four of you will carry Bubbler vials on you everywhere you go.

If you need to get away for any reason, you'll activate the short-range teleportation portals, which will distance you from immediate danger and hopefully give you enough time to step through a Bubbledoor without unwanted company. The king has asked that you follow his protocol and Bubble straight to the palace, where he'll keep a constant security detail waiting in the receiving room."

"Why do we need the ITD wrist thingies when we could just Bubble out of Woodhaven at the first sign of trouble?" Alex asked, thinking that would be so much simpler.

"The time it would take to activate a Bubbler and then have you all step through, no matter how swiftly, leads to a certain amount of anxiety," Darrius explained. "And, of course, someone could easily step in after you. The 'wrist thingies' afford an almost instant, simultaneous escape. If nothing else, just humour us, Alex. We're doing this so we can be assured that you're all adequately protected."

"Fine," Alex agreed. Admittedly, she felt a lot more comfortable knowing how secure they would be over the holidays. She would have to remember to thank D.C.'s father the next time she saw him.

"And this brings me back to my original concern," Darrius said. At Alex's blank look he reminded her, "Aven getting to you here before you leave tomorrow."

"Ah," she said, understanding. "Right."

"Initially the plan was to have Woodhaven's wards active and functioning well before your arrival, but the Technos involved in their construction were delayed by—well, you don't need to know the details." He waved a hand in the air, brushing his explanation aside. "What you *do* need to know is that the wards around Woodhaven will activate at precisely eight o'clock tomorrow morning, while the wards here at the academy will *de* activate at seven o'clock. That gives Aven a one-hour window in which he could, potentially, sneak through undetected. It's highly unlikely, but it wouldn't be the first time he's tried something similar."

That was true. Aven had infiltrated the academy when the wards had been down for the students to return after last year's Kaldoras break. That day he'd confirmed his belief that Alex was Chosen by the Library, which resulted in pretty much all the mess she'd been involved in since then. She definitely wasn't keen for a repeat experience.

"So, what's the plan?" she asked.

"To get you, and your friends, out of here the moment the wards at Woodhaven are activated."

She gestured for him to continue, and when he didn't, she questioned, "That's it?"

"I'm afraid so," he answered. "Other than that, you'll need to remain on your guard. I'll be patrolling the boundary of the wards with most of the other teaching staff to make sure students are safe until they leave the academy. You and your friends will remain in the food court after breakfast and wait for me to come and give you the ITDs. Once I'm certain the devices are active, you'll all take a Bubbler to Woodhaven where you can hopefully relax for the next two weeks."

"I like that last part," Alex said. "I'm not sure about the rest."

Darrius smiled at her. "You'll be fine, Alex. Aven will be hard-pressed to sneak past us when the wards are deactivated. The professors and I are not without our own gifts."

He looked at her confidently and for the first time ever Alex realised she had never properly wondered what gifts he and her other teachers possessed. She knew about Marmaduke's low-level mind arts gifting, and she knew parts of Hunter's supernatural awareness, but she had no idea about any of the others. She wanted to ask Darrius straight out what his gift was, but she wasn't sure whether or not that would seem rude—it could be like asking someone what size underwear they wore, for all she knew. She decided her safest bet was to wait and ask her friends later.

"That's all I wanted to speak about tonight," Darrius said, standing again. "You have a big day tomorrow so you should get some rest. Feel free to talk with the others about what we've discussed. I'll reiterate the security protocols tomorrow morning when I hand over the ITDs, but it can't hurt for them to hear the basics in advance."

"No problem," Alex agreed, standing as well. "I'll see you in the morning."

"Just before eight o'clock," Darrius reminded her as he escorted her to the door. "In the food court."

"I think I can remember that," she said with a smile.

"Goodnight, Alex," he returned. "And try not to worry."

Easier said than done, she thought as she descended the staircase.

She hoped the next twelve hours would pass quickly—and without any drama. Then she could relax and enjoy the next two weeks, just like Darrius had said.

***

"Rise and shine!" a chipper voice said, waking Alex the next morning.

"Eugh, what's the time?" she mumbled into her pillow. "Six-thirty," D.C. answered, sounding way too upbeat for that time of day. "We have to meet the boys in half an hour, so get up and get dressed."

"Why're you so happy?" Alex grumbled, sitting up.

D.C. smiled brightly. "Because we're on holidays!"

Alex wasn't sure what had gotten into her friend, but she'd take the overjoyed D.C. over the recently melancholic and exhausted D.C. any day.

"Come on, Alex," her roommate urged. "Get ready so we can go have breakfast. And just think, in ninety minutes we'll be in Woodhaven and we can put the last few weeks behind us!"

Ah. So that was it. D.C. must have presumed, like Alex, that Jordan would be back to normal once they were all away from the academy.

With a hopeful smile of her own, Alex jumped out of bed and dressed in record time. She and D.C. made sure they were packed and ready for the two-week break before they grabbed their bags and headed out the door.

"'Morning!" Bear greeted them when they arrived at the food court. Much like D.C., he also seemed perkier than he had been of late.

"Where's Jordan?" Alex asked, searching for their friend.

"Finishing packing," Bear said. "He'll meet us here when he's done."

"Before eight, right?" Alex had informed her friends about everything Darrius had told her the previous night, but she was slightly nervous about the plan.

"Before eight," Bear promised. "Don't worry, he'll be here."

"How was he this morning?" D.C. asked.

Bear grinned widely, looking happier than Alex had seen for weeks. That was all the answer they needed, but his words confirmed what they'd hoped to be true. "He was Jordan. Finally back to normal."

Alex laughed with relief. Maybe it wouldn't take the entire holiday for him to let down his walls after all.

The three of them ate a quick breakfast and said goodbye to some of their classmates as they came and went from the food court. All the while Alex was acutely aware that it was now after seven o'clock, which meant the wards around the academy were deactivated. But the knots twisting her stomach couldn't completely dissolve her excitement. All she wanted was for Jordan to hurry up and arrive so she could see for herself how back to normal he supposedly was.

The food court had emptied of people by seven-thirty, with everyone leaving early to start their holidays. Alex tapped her fingernails on the table as she anxiously waited for the time to tick by.

"He better get here soon," D.C. muttered, shredding her napkin into pieces.

"Who?" Bear asked. "Jordan or Marselle?"

"Both," Alex answered for her friend, thinking the same thing.

Another ten minutes passed with them all fidgeting restlessly.

"Jordan's really cutting it down to the wire," Alex said, trying to keep her voice light. "What do you think is taking him so—"

She was interrupted by a sudden noise as a hulking figure burst into the food court. She leapt to her feet, fearing imminent attack, but relaxed slightly when she recognised the new arrival.

"Zain!" she cried as the Meyarin approached. "Where have you been?"

"Alex, I need you to listen very carefully," he said, grasping her upper arms and giving her a small, urgent shake.

Alex felt her stomach clench with dread. "What's wrong?"

He stared into her eyes and said, "Aven has the headmaster."

She drew in a sharp breath, and it was only the Meyarin's strong grip that kept her from swaying on her feet.

"He was patrolling with the other teachers when Aven captured him," Zain said. "Never before has Aven had such unrestricted access to Marselle, and now he's going to try to use him to open the doorway into Meya."

"No," Alex whispered, horrified.

"You need to hold it together," Zain said, shaking her slightly again. "I'll use the Eternal Path to warn my people, but I need you to go to the Library with your friends and try to stop Aven before he can force Marselle to open the door."

"What if we're too late?" she asked. "What if they're already through?"

"If you don't see them on your way in, you'll have to assume Aven has managed to Claim Marselle and he's already used him to open the doorway," Zain said. "If that's the case, I want you and your friends to come straight through to Raelia.

We'll need all the backup we can get if we want to capture Aven before he can escape."

"What good can we possibly do?" D.C. asked, stepping up beside Alex and looking at Zain with wide, anxious eyes. "We're not Meyarin. There's no chance we can help fight him."

"If Aven makes it through to Raelia, he won't be alone," Zain said. "He'll have at least some of his gifted accomplices with him. The abilities you possess may help keep the other humans distracted while we capture Aven."

At the concerned looks on their faces, Zain's expression softened. "It might not come to that. We may be able to stop him before he gets through to Raelia, but that depends on you reaching them before they get to the doorway. Go, now, and I'll see you again soon."

"Wait, Zain!" Alex called out as he sprinted away from them. When he paused at the entrance to the food court, she asked, "What happens if we *do* get to Aven in time? If we meet him before he uses Darrius to get through to Meya?"

"Stall him," Zain called back to them. "I'll come along with reinforcements after I reach the palace and warn them."

That was all he said before he disappeared out the door.

Twenty-Four

Alex turned to her friends who looked as shell-shocked as she felt.

"You don't have to come with me," she told them straight up.

"We're not leaving you to face him alone," Bear said firmly.

"Where's Jordan?" D.C. all but screamed. "What's taking him so long?"

"Jeez, calm down. I'm not that late."

The three of them whipped around to see their friend strolling casually through the entrance to the food court with his backpack slung over one shoulder. When he reached them, he dropped it to the ground and grinned at them widely. If Alex hadn't been so freaked out by Zain's news, she would have danced with joy at seeing the familiar, carefree expression on his face.

"Aven has Darrius," she blurted out, causing his grin to evaporate. "We have to stop them before they reach the doorway to Meya."

She didn't wait for him to respond as she sprinted off, knowing her friends would follow.

"Talk to me, Alex. What's going on?" Jordan demanded as they ran along the path.

Alex told him what Zain had said, and finished her quick explanation as they reached the Tower building.

"Are you insane?" Jordan grabbed her arm and spun her to face him. "The entire academy staff is out there making sure Aven doesn't get to you, and you're actively seeking him out?"

"Jordan, it's *Darrius*," she said, yanking her arm back. "If Aven Claims him, he'll be forced to open the doorway through to Meya. And we all know just how bad that would be."

Jordan seemed confused. "What do you mean?"

Alex sent him a frustrated look. "Stop trying to distract me. I know you're protective and you want to look out for me, but I need to get down there."

"Think about this for a second," Bear said, moving to stand beside her. "Are you sure Marselle can open the doorway?"

Alex hesitated. She knew Darrius's access to the Library's secrets was more limited than her own, since she was Chosen while he was only granted the privileges of headmaster. But he'd never said that he *couldn't* get through to Meya. He'd also mentioned that Aven had tried to capture him in the past, but the Library protected its own—except for in the case of their current dilemma, apparently.

"I don't know if he can," Alex admitted. "But Aven seems to think so, and that's good enough for me. We need to find them."

Bear gazed at her steadily for a moment before he nodded. "Lead the way."

Alex didn't need any further permission. She ran into the building and tore down the staircase, sprinting straight past the absent librarian's desk and over to the far side of the foyer. Then she and her friends hurtled down the next set of stairs until they came to a dead end and once more entered the doorway that led to the corridor of doors.

The corridor was tangibly different this time. Instead of a brightly lit hallway, the torches were dimmed. The flames flickered angrily as if the Library itself knew what was happening.

At her summons, Sir Camden stepped through a doorway and into view.

"Lady Alexandra," he said with a bow. "How doth thee?"

"Sir Camden, can you take us to the doorway leading to Meya?" she asked, her voice betraying her sense of urgency.

"Lady Alexandra, perchance I might bring attention to thy companions?" Sir Camden said. "There be an uncanny—"

"Sir Camden," Alex interrupted, "I'm so sorry, but we really must hurry. It's an emergency."

The knight hesitated but then he bowed again. "As the lady doth wish."

Alex and her friends jogged behind the suit of armour as he hastily led them along corridors and through doorways until they stepped in front of the one they needed.

"Thank you, Sir Camden," Alex said gratefully, dismissing the knight.

"Thank me not, Lady Alexandra," he said gravely, "for I fear this here knight hath made a most grievous error in judgement."

"Alex, you said we're in a hurry," Jordan cut in. "You can talk with him later."

His words pulled her gaze away from the contrite-sounding knight just as the suit of armour disappeared stiffly through another doorway. His motions were so rigid that Alex wondered if he'd forgotten to oil his joints recently. But her Tin-Manlike moment passed when a new thought came to her and she recognised the gravity of the situation.

"Aven's not here," she whispered, staring at the closed door while her stomach plummeted with the knowledge of what that meant. He was already through.

"What do we do now?" D.C. asked, just as quietly.

"You said Zain wanted us to go and try to help," Jordan reminded Alex, despite his earlier argument against confronting Aven. "I think we should follow his orders. Maybe if we stop Aven now, they'll be able to imprison him or something, and we'll never have to worry about him again."

"You don't understand," Alex said, with a shake of her head. "Zain wanted us to distract any gifted humans Aven has with him, but the ones we encountered at Sir Oswald's party had incredible powers, remember? My gift can help protect me from some of them, but I can't keep you guys safe. We have no way of knowing what kind of danger we'll be walking into."

Jordan shrugged his shoulders in a casual manner that was at odds with the seriousness of their situation. "What's the worst that could happen?"

While Alex was relieved that he was back to his cheerful self, she didn't appreciate his happy-go-lucky attitude considering the circumstances.

"You could die," she answered bluntly. "Or worse; you could be Claimed."

"You know we're with you, Alex," D.C. said, with both Bear and Jordan nodding their agreement. "But if we're going to do this, we should do it now. Who knows what's happening on the other side of that doorway while we wait?"

Alex nodded and blew out a heavy breath before reaching forward to grasp the handle. She gently pressed it down until, like the last time, the door disappeared in front of them.

"NO, ALEX! *STOP!*"

Alex whipped her head around and gaped at the sight of her headmaster sprinting down the corridor, followed closely by a group of teachers.

"Darrius?" she whispered, her eyes widening with shock.

She moved a step in his direction, only to be stopped when Jordan grabbed her arm and forced her backwards...

...and through the doorway.

She lost her footing when she landed inside the mushroom circle and fell to the ground, Bear and D.C. landing heavily beside her. The doorway disappeared the moment they were through, but not before Alex heard an agonised *"NO!"* come from the corridor behind them.

"Why the hell did you do that, Jordan?" Alex demanded, getting to her feet and glaring at her friend. But he wasn't listening to her. He was staring at the mushroom circle, growing paler by the second.

"You know, I thought I'd conquered my fear," he said shakily, "but I was wrong."

"What are you talking about?" Bear asked heatedly. "And why did you push us in here? That was Darrius yelling to us back there—and he looked fine to me!"

"Jordan?" Alex pressed, looking at the ghostly face of her trembling friend. Her heart started beating erratically, as if she was trying to solve a puzzle that she subconsciously knew she didn't want the answer to. "What fear are you talking about?"

Jordan stared back at her with terrified eyes as he whispered tremulously, "Don't let the Fae take me."

The air left Alex's lungs in a *whoosh* as realisation swept over her and she gasped out, "Skyla?"

Jordan's body shimmered and transformed into Skyla, who looked even more afraid now that she was in her own skin. But Alex didn't have any words to soothe her, since she was too shocked by the other girl's presence.

"If you're here, then where's Jordan?" she spluttered.

The sound of someone applauding caused Alex to spin around, but she couldn't see anyone behind her. She peered into the trees, but there was nobody there. Only when she took a step forward did her world fall apart around her.

"Well done, Alexandra," Aven said, appearing out of thin air. "I expected you to take much longer to figure it out."

"No," Alex whispered, stumbling backwards, away from him. "No."

She continued to retreat, as if distance would change what she was seeing. But no matter how many steps she took, and no matter how many times she blinked, the image remained the same. Three people stood in front of her: Aven on the left, and Calista Maine on the right. And between them was Jordan, staring blankly out at the space in front of him.

"Jordan?" came D.C.'s whimper.

Alex flicked her gaze to the side just in time to see D.C., Bear and Skyla lifted up and suspended in mid-air thanks to Calista's telekinetic ability. Skyla looked confused and scared, but Bear and D.C ... There were no words to describe their ravaged expressions.

"Hello, Princess," Aven said, looking up at D.C. "You didn't see this one coming, did you?"

"You—!"

"Now, now," he admonished. "A princess must always remain polite. Tell me, dear, sweet Delucia. When did you realise your dreams were failing you?"

D.C. paled and her gaze swept over to Jordan, then Alex, before she looked back at Aven. "I don't know what you're talking about."

"Is that so?" Aven asked with a smirk. "Are you saying you haven't been waking from recurring nightmares for the last few months? Nightmares where you see the boy you so deeply care for surrounded by nothing but shadows?"

Alex wanted to step in and help D.C., but she wasn't sure what to say. Especially because her roommate's nightmares had been recurring. But how had Aven known that?

"I have to ask, Princess," he said, "was it frustrating when, no matter how hard you tried, you could never discover any details in your dreams? Almost as if you were being ... blocked?"

"How?" D.C. whispered.

"One of my associates is gifted in the art of neutralising the abilities of others,"

Aven informed her. "It's a very useful skill."

Alex remembered the woman he was talking about from Sir Oswald's dinner party—Lena Morrow. Once again she was grateful that her own gift kept her safe from manipulation, but she wished she'd had the foresight to consider the scope of Lena's ability on others.

Hindsight truly sucked.

"I have Lena to thank for keeping you in the dark," Aven continued, "since darkness was all that your dreams contained. It was fitting, really. I particularly loved how you lost so much sleep fretting over your, ahem, *friend*."

D.C. looked horrified. The idea that someone had been tampering with her gift must have terrified her, especially when it had been occurring so frequently.

"You'll regret this, Aven," D.C. seethed.

"I doubt that, Princess," Aven said mockingly. Then he turned to Calista and ordered, "Keep them quiet."

Immediately Calista focused her gift to snap their mouths closed. Alex could hear her friends trying to talk, but the only noises they managed were trapped in their throats.

"You have my gratitude, Alexandra, for helping me return to my homeland," Aven said. "I couldn't have done it without you."

She couldn't speak. Not because Calista's gift worked on her. It didn't. Her mind simply couldn't come to terms with what was happening.

"Actually, that's not entirely correct," Aven mused, deliberately drawing out his words. "I needed you to get me through the doorway, that much is true. Did you really think Marselle could have helped me? I would have found a way to Claim him long ago if that were the case, regardless of how protected the Library keeps him. No, Alexandra, he doesn't have the access you do, which is why he won't be opening another doorway to save you. It's also why only you could assist me in the end. But you proved to be much more tenacious than I'd ever expected of a human."

"What can I say?" she managed to croak out. "It's a gift."

"The literal implication isn't lost on me," Aven said, his demeanour souring before he brightened again. "But no matter. I only had to find your weakness. It was really too easy; all I had to do was capture someone dear to you."

Alex's eyes flickered over to Jordan who stood silently between Aven and Calista.

"I don't mean Jordan," Aven said, seeing where her gaze rested. "I'm speaking of your beloved headmaster. And my deceit was twofold, since you had the added concern that he would grant me access where you resisted. It was perfect, really."

"Roka will stop you," Alex told him confidently. "Zain has probably already warned him that you're here. They'll be arriving any moment."

Aven laughed deeply. "Zain? That poor excuse for an elite guard is half-dead right where I left him with my arrow sticking out of his shoulder blade. No, Zain won't be warning anyone."

Alex felt her stomach clench with fear for her friend but she refused to believe Aven. "You're lying. An arrow to the shoulder would never kill a Meyarin—least of all Zain. It would take way more than that."

"I love that you still have such naive optimism," Aven said with dark amusement. "I almost feel guilty about bursting that little bubble of yours."

She fisted her hands to hide their trembling. "Then don't."

"Denial isn't a healthy state of mind, so I'll tell you a secret," he said. "There's a creature, Alexandra, whose blood is so repulsive to Meyarins that it can incapacitate us at the briefest of physical contact. Among my kind, it's called the Sarnaph. Your race titles it *Daesmilo Folarctos*, but it's more commonly known as a Hyroa. Have you heard of it?"

Pictures flooded Alex's mind. She saw the day so many months ago when she'd witnessed Aven slay the terrifying, violent beast. She saw the Meyarin urgently checking his clothes and backing away when Gerald tried to hand him the vial of blood. She heard Fletcher comment on how the species was considered nearly extinct. And lastly, she heard the name *Daesmilo Folarctos* reverberate around her thoughts as she remembered the severe 'allergic reaction' she'd had after touching the murky-brown swab of what she now realised was Hyroa blood.

Aven had no way of knowing that there was Meyarin blood in her veins that apparently reacted just as negatively to the Hyroa blood as his own would. That was one secret she would do well to keep from him.

"Whatever you're about to say, I won't believe you," Alex told him boldly. "I don't care about incapacitating blood or whatever, because I saw Zain only a few minutes ago. You wouldn't have had time to attack him and then follow us through the Library."

Aven smirked at her. "Are you sure it was Zain you saw?"

"Of course it was..." Alex closed her eyes when she realised just how well Aven had played them. "Skyla."

"Yes, Skyla," Aven confirmed. "Your friend has an impressive gift. If she wasn't so simpleminded, I might have considered adding her to my collection."

Alex quaked at his words, but he continued before she could say anything.

"Even without Claiming her, it wasn't difficult to convince her to assist us, but she was a painfully slow student. We had to meet with her a number of times so she could learn her script, so to speak. Such a foolish child. But we managed to make her believe she was important enough for your Stealth and Subterfuge teacher to consider taking her on as an apprentice next year. She was under the impression that today's events were a test to see how well she could remain in character as both Jordan and Zain."

"Why are you telling me all this?" Alex asked, her heart racing at the rapidly darkening tone of Aven's words.

"I thought you might appreciate the truth before you could no longer hear it from the source," he said offhandedly. "The girl performed admirably, but she wasted too much of my time learning her role. And I ... Well, my patience with her has reached its limit. Calista?"

It happened in a split second. Alex didn't notice the command in Aven's words. All she heard was a whimper and a *crack*, followed by the sound of Skyla's lifeless body dropping to the ground.

"No!" Alex gasped, seeing Skyla's face pressed into the snow, her neck bent at an unnatural angle and her empty eyes staring out into nothing.

All it had taken was one word from Aven and Calista had broken Skyla's neck without lifting so much as a finger.

Alex glanced fearfully up at D.C. and Bear who were still trapped by Calista's power. Tears were streaming down D.C.'s face as she stared at the girl on the icy ground, and Bear looked more haggard than Alex had ever seen him.

"Don't you want to know how I managed to pull all this off?" Aven asked. "Even I, as brilliant as I am, couldn't have fooled you without help. Aren't you curious about Jordan's role in all this?"

No, Alex begged him in her mind, already knowing that whatever he was going to say would bring him great joy and her great pain.

Please.

Don't.

But Aven couldn't hear her thoughts, and he continued, almost gleefully, "Aren't you curious about how long your friend has been in my service?"

Alex felt her entire body stiffen with dread.

No.

"I don't believe you," she said. But she couldn't help dragging her eyes back to Jordan's scarily blank face.

"Dear, sweet child," Aven purred. "Didn't we already decide that denial is unhealthy?"

"You're a liar, Aven," she returned heatedly. "I know you. All you do is lie."

His golden eyes flashed. "Watch your tone, Alexandra."

She stared at him defiantly. "Make me."

Alex watched Aven bury his rage beneath a relaxed smirk. "Jordan, tell Alexandra to be quiet."

Jordan's empty eyes stared straight through her as he opened his mouth and said, "Alexandra, be quiet."

Alex felt her breath stutter at the sound of her friend's dismissive monotone. "Jordan?" she whispered.

Jordan lowered his gaze again, his expression showing no emotion. Alex watched him for a moment before she turned her face up to capture Aven's triumphant look.

"What have you done to him?" she demanded.

Please, please, let him only be drugged.

Aven tilted his head to the side as he stared at her, and then a smile broke out on his face. It quickly turned into a laugh. It took a full minute for him to calm down enough to gasp out, "Do you truly not know? How can you be so blind?"

She didn't respond. She didn't want confirmation of what she feared was true.

"Jordan, show Alexandra your hand so she can see my mark for herself."

At his words, Alex had the answer to what she'd refused to believe. When Jordan raised his hand, the glowing scar across his palm was all the evidence she needed.

No.

"Release him, Aven." Alex's voice was unrecognisable to her own ears. It was as cold and hard as steel. "Let him go and I'll allow you to leave this place. You can do whatever you want in Meya and I won't stop you. I won't tell anyone you're here. Just let Jordan go."

Aven laughed again. "What makes you think I'm keeping him here?"

That made Alex pause. "What are you talking about?"

"Jordan," Aven said, his voice authoritative, "tell Alexandra how you came to be in my service. Give her every detail, using your own words and emotions."

Jordan blinked and his blank face cleared of its empty expression. "Alex," he whispered brokenly, stepping forward to reach out to her.

"Stop," Aven commanded. "You'll only speak to her. Nothing more."

At his order, Jordan froze to the spot, and his anguished face begged her to understand. It was the most expressive he'd been since his return from Chateau Shondelle three weeks earlier.

Wait a second.

Chateau Shondelle.

Jordan's unusual behaviour.

No.

"Jordan?" Alex breathed, hoping desperately that she was connecting the dots incorrectly.

"I couldn't say anything," he told her, his voice pleading with her to understand.

"I was ordered to act like normal. There was nothing I could do."

"Tell her everything, Jordan," Aven said, his voice firm. "From the beginning."

Jordan swallowed thickly and whispered, "I had to, Alex."

No.

"Aven says my brother is alive. He's going to help me find Luka."

No. Wrong. All wrong.

"Alex, you have to believe me," Jordan begged. "It was the only way."

"Tell her the complete truth," Aven commanded again. "Tell her how you came to be in my service."

With emotion-filled eyes, Jordan said, "I went back to the chateau for the weekend because my parents asked me to. I didn't want to go, especially since I knew you, Dix and Bear were so worried. But they said they had something important to tell me."

He hesitated for a second before he continued. "When I arrived at the chateau, Aven was there. He and my father are ... close. I swear, I had no idea. I tried to escape, but Lena was there too, neutralising my gift so Calista could hold me captive. It was horrible. I was trapped."

His eyes shadowed at the memory until they brightened again. "But then my father promised me that everything would be okay as long as I listened to Aven. Then they'd let me go. So, I listened. And what I heard—Alex, I don't know what to say."

Alex didn't know what to say either. All she knew was that with every word of his, she felt as if her heart was being ripped out of her chest. Judging by D.C.'s muffled sobs and Bear's choked expletives, she wasn't the only one falling apart.

"Aven told me that Luka faked his own death," Jordan continued. "I didn't believe him at first. But then he showed me some surveillance footage dated a month ago—a *month* ago!—where Luka broke into a Techno lab in Mardenia. He's alive, Alex. Can you believe it?"

No.

"My parents told me they've been trying to find him for years," Jordan said. "Apparently they've known all along that his suicide wasn't real, but they didn't want to tell me because they knew how upset I'd be. I was so angry with them, but they said that no matter how hard they looked and how close they'd come, they've never managed to find him. I would've been devastated if I'd known he was out there and I couldn't contact him. They did the right thing."

No. Wrong. Stop.

"But then Aven made me an offer," Jordan continued. "He said he'd help me find Luka if I did something for him first. I had to help him get to Meya. All I had to do was use my gift to hide him and Calista so we could all slip through the doorway when you opened it. It was almost too easy to orchestrate everything, especially after I suggested we use Skyla's ability to help us. She took on Zain's appearance to get you going, and then she made herself look like me to make sure you opened the door and came through. It was perfect."

Alex struggled to draw breath into her lungs.

"I'm sorry, Alex," he continued. "I know how important you thought it was to keep him away. But Kyia and Zain and Prince Roka, they all lied to us. It wasn't Aven who murdered those humans and tried to steal the throne—it was Roka. He framed Aven, making it look like he was innocent, while Aven took the fall and the banishment for his brother's actions. Aven's the victim here, Alex."

Try convincing Skyla of that, she thought.

There was no way the Jordan they knew and loved would fall for such a fictitious story. And he would *never* refer to Aven as a 'victim', not after everything the Meyarin had done.

Alex turned to look at Aven with hate-filled eyes. "That's not Jordan talking. My friend would never believe the words coming out of his mouth."

"Finish your recount, Jordan," Aven ordered, ignoring Alex.

When she turned back to Jordan, she found him looking at her with eyes full of hurt.

"It *is* me, Alex," he whispered. "I'm still me. Aven Claimed me for my own protection. It'll help him keep me safe while he saves Meya from its evil rulers. And after that, we're going to search for Luka together. A brother for a brother, that was our agreement."

Alex couldn't accept his words.

"Your agreement?" she repeated, despite her better judgement.

"Jordan," Aven interrupted. "Answer truthfully. Did I offer to Claim you?"

Jordan hesitated, but then he whispered a quiet, "No."

Alex's blood turned to ice.

"Did I Claim you against your will?" Aven pressed.

Jordan's answer was even quieter this time. "No."

She felt like an invisible hand was squeezing her windpipe.

Aven grinned victoriously and asked his final question. "Then tell us, Jordan, how did you come to be in my service?"

Jordan's vibrant blue eyes stared straight at Alex when he said, "I asked Aven to Claim me. It was my idea. And I don't regret it."

NO!

Alex felt as if the ground had been pulled out from underneath her. "No! *NO!*" she screamed out loud, adding to the horrified sounds coming from D.C. and Bear. She couldn't keep the tears from welling in her eyes as she begged, "Tell me it's not true. Please, Jordan. *Tell me it's not true!*"

"It's for the best, Alex," he said, his voice anguished. "You'll see."

She had to hold back a sob at his brainwashed words. Where was her cocky, overprotective best friend? Where was the Jordan she knew—the one who would never have surrendered to Aven, let alone *asked* for a life of controlled servitude?

"Jordan," Alex whimpered, unable to say more.

"Alex," he whispered. "I'm sorry."

His apology broke her. Tears poured down her face, dripping down her cheeks and landing on the snow-covered ground, melting the ice as her blood remained frozen in her veins.

Her grief nearly brought her to her knees, but she knew that she had to keep it together and protect her friends until help arrived. Darrius might not be able to step through the Library into Meya, but she had to hope he'd find another way to summon reinforcements.

"As touching as this is, it's time for us to leave. I have a rebellion to lead."

Alex snapped her head up at Aven's words and croaked out, "Over my dead body."

He smirked at her. "That's one thing we agree upon."

She wiped a shaky hand across her eyes, preparing herself for what she knew would be her final battle with the Meyarin. He no longer needed her, so he would have no problem killing her.

Just like Skyla.

Alex swallowed back fresh tears as the shock of such a pointless murder hit her anew.

Focus, she told herself. *Grieve later. Focus now.*

"Ready when you are, Aven."

"You misunderstand me, Alexandra," he said, his eyes glittering. "I'm not going to fight you."

She frowned in bewilderment. Didn't he want her dead?

"You seem confused," Aven observed. "I have to admit, I do enjoy toying with you."

At the look she shot him, he sighed mockingly.

"I can see you're not in the mood for games, so we'll end this quickly," Aven said. Then he called, "Jordan?"

Her friend turned to look at Aven, and Alex wished she could run away and hide in the forest for the rest of her life just to avoid the pain she was currently feeling. But she would never leave D.C. and Bear, not when their lives could end like Skyla's had at one word from Aven. Or two words, as the case may be, since they were the exact words he spoke to Jordan with his next command.

"Kill her."

No.

Twenty-Five

Jordan stepped forward at Aven's order. Alex had been too focused on his face earlier to notice the cape he wore that concealed a sword belted to his waist. But she could see it clearly now, since Jordan had pulled it free.

"Don't do this, Jordan," Alex begged, stepping backwards as he continued to stalk towards her. "I won't fight you."

Her words meant nothing to him. His eyes were unfocused and his body obediently followed Aven's orders. Alex knew exactly what that felt like—having no control, but being able to witness everything that was happening. More tears leaked out of her eyes at the thought of her friend trapped in his own mind while his body prepared to fight her, maybe even kill her.

"Do it now, Jordan," Aven ordered louder. "I don't have all day."

"No, Jordan," Alex said. "Don't listen to him. Fight him!"

But her words were useless. Jordan's eyes narrowed as he raised his sword a fraction and lunged towards her.

"No!" she cried, jumping out of the way. "Don't!"

He came at her again, swiping his blade at her torso, and again she jumped away.

"I won't fight you!" she repeated. "I won't!"

"Then you'll die quickly," Jordan said, his voice devoid of emotion as he swung his weapon towards her neck.

It might have been his words, or the strength she could see behind his attack, but something within Alex shifted and a fierce resolve came over her. If she could make it out of Raelia alive, then she might be able to find a way to help him. Anything was possible; she was living proof of that. So, rather than avoiding his attack, Alex needed to disable him—hopefully without causing too much damage in the process.

"A'enara!" she yelled instinctively, and the glowing weapon appeared in her hand before she'd even finished calling its name. The ice-coloured blade—which was again the length of a sword—intercepted Jordan's blow, with blue sparks flying furiously between them.

Alex barely heard Aven's enraged growl as she focused on defending against Jordan's next strike.

Her friend was rated Delta in Combat. That was only one level down from Alex, and he'd been taking the class for years.

He was more than capable with his blade. But he now also had Aven's Claim on him, supplementing his strength, speed and skill. It also didn't help that, while half of Alex's mind was concentrating on staying alive, the other half was trying to come up with a plan to get Jordan out of there in one piece. So far, both halves were at a loss for ideas.

"Stop playing around, Jordan," Aven ordered. "Finish her."

Alex frowned at the Meyarin's words. But then she jerked in surprise when Jordan disappeared, using his gift to make himself—and his weapon—invisible. Only a deep-rooted survival instinct caused Alex to raise A'enara in time to intercept Jordan's sword when she sensed his attempt to slice her in two.

Definitely not good.

"That's more like it," Aven called out smugly.

Concentrate, Alex told herself. *Concentrate or you'll die. Concentrate or Bear and D.C. will die, too. Concentrate or you won't be able to help Jordan.*

Remembering her blindfolded fight with Roka, Alex closed her eyes and let go of everything else to focus on the power within her. It was waiting for her, just under the surface, welcoming her acceptance like a warm embrace.

She opened her eyes again when she felt the air move around her and she raised her weapon, blocking Jordan's invisible attack. Again he lunged at her, and again she defended. She jumped when she felt his leg swing out to trip her, and she kicked out towards where she thought his torso was while he was undefended. Her foot landed hard and she heard him stumble backwards with an "ooof" sound.

When he came at her again, she was ready for him. But rather than letting him continue to attack her, she made the first move, beginning a quick series of swipes and lunges for him to defend against. The problem was that she didn't want to hurt him, which severely restricted her ability to incapacitate him. Unlike when she'd fought Roka, Jordan was *human*. It was difficult to injure or kill a Meyarin, but humans were much more vulnerable.

That was why having the upper hand in the fight didn't turn out so well for Alex. The moment her blade skimmed lightly across where she thought Jordan's forearm was and he hissed in pain, Alex hesitated. Her sword stilled in the air when Jordan became visible again, clutching at his bleeding arm.

"You wounded me," he panted, exhausted from the fight as well as having to maintain his transcended state. "For that you will die."

"Listen to yourself!" Alex cried. "That's not you speaking, it's Aven! Resist him!"

"Enough!" Aven roared, striding over to where they stood. His infuriated glare could have set the snow on fire. "How are you are able to fight an invisible opponent?"

She stilled at his question, recalling Roka's warnings to not let Aven discover the truth of her blood status. "I've been practising," she said evasively.

"Answer me!"

"I did," Alex replied, remaining as deliberately vague as possible.

He took a menacing step forward but then froze, tilting his head as if listening to something only he could hear.

"No," he breathed, his eyes quickly looking around the clearing until they fell on his companion. "Calista, stay here and keep them occupied for as long as you can. Then come and find us."

The woman nodded and turned her focus back to D.C. and Bear who remained suspended in the air.

"You," Aven said to Alex, capturing her in his burning gaze. "You're coming with us."

"I'm not going *anywhere* with you," Alex argued, raising her blade defiantly.

Aven didn't so much as blink as he said, "Jordan."

Alex dreaded the thought of continuing the fight with her best friend. But this time Aven's order had a different meaning, and she discovered his intent a moment too late when Jordan reached out to grasp the Meyarin's shoulder and they both disappeared.

She wasn't quick enough to tap into her new senses again before both her hands were yanked behind her back and her sword was forced from her grip. A'enara disappeared immediately and she hissed at the pain of her arms being tugged almost out of their sockets. Before she could so much as cry out, the pommel of Jordan's sword smashed into her temple.

She was unconscious before she hit the snow-covered ground.

**

A stinging pain forced Alex back to half-consciousness, and a second sharp slap to her face woke her completely.

Ouch.

She opened her eyes and winced at the throbbing pulse beating through her skull. Aven stood directly above where she lay in the icy snow, looking down at her with flared nostrils.

"The reason you're still alive is because I need an answer. If you tell me quickly, I'll be merciful and end your life just as fast. If you delay, I'll take great delight in prolonging your pain."

"At least one of us will be happy," Alex slurred. "That's something."

Clearly her damaged head was affecting her judgement. *Note to self: don't antagonise the murderous psychopath.*

Aven snarled at her.

Oops. Too late.

"Answer me!" he demanded loudly, causing Alex to wince in discomfort.

"It might have escaped your notice, but I can barely remember my own name after that sucker punch, let alone what I'm supposed to be answering," Alex said. "And where are we, anyway?"

They weren't in Raelia anymore, that much she could tell. But judging by the colour of the forest surrounding them they were still somewhere in the Silverwood.

"How did you fight Jordan when you couldn't see him?" Aven repeated his question, barely reining in his temper.

"You didn't tell me where we are," Alex singsonged. "Quid pro quo?"

Before she could draw a startled breath, Jordan was kneeling beside her in the snow with the point of his sword resting against her windpipe. "Answer him!" he growled.

Alex couldn't utter a single word, she was too consumed by the fiery blue eyes staring at her out from her friend's face. She reached out her hand without thinking and stroked his cheek, whispering, "Oh, Jordan."

His gaze flickered with what she thought was genuine emotion at her touch, but as he pressed his blade into her skin reality washed over her. This wasn't her best friend. This was Aven's puppet. And he was willing to kill her for his master.

"Answer him now or I'll slit your throat," Jordan threatened.

Alex stared from his eyes to her hand on his cheek and back again. On her third glance, something other than his hardened expression caught her attention. Maybe it was because she was dazed from the bump on her head, but the swirling darkness in her Shadow Ring seemed more beautiful than usual.

A whispered memory came back to her.

"When your need is great, you'll be able to activate the Shadow Essence contained within the stone ... But you'll have to immerse yourself fully in the Shadow to do so."

Then another memory came to her.

"Alexandra, we're all born with Shadow inside us. But, as with anything, it's up to us to decide what we do with that Shadow. We can succumb to its power, or we can overcome it and use it. Our level of control depends upon our ability to resist the Shadow's hold on us. It's a choice we must all make."

A choice. That's what Caspar Lennox had told her. So, she would choose.

"Help me up, will you?" she asked Jordan. "I won't answer while this wet snow soaks through my clothes. It's icky."

Jordan looked to Aven, seeking permission. At the Meyarin's terse nod, Jordan kept his blade steady against her neck with one hand while he used the other to yank her to her feet.

The Silverwood blurred in Alex's vision while she wobbled on her unsteady legs and fought the urge to vomit. *Okay, that wasn't my smartest idea.*

When she could see clearly again, she sought Jordan's eyes. "You're my best friend," she told him quietly. "Remember that I love you. Bear, Dix ... we all love you. Don't forget."

His eyes flickered again but his grip on her remained strong.

"Don't give up," she whispered thickly. "We'll find a way to save you."

"Time's up, Alexandra," Aven cut in. "Answer the question, or I'll have to motivate you." He dropped his voice and added, "And I can guarantee you won't like how I choose to do that."

Alex looked at Jordan one last time before she turned to Aven. "You still haven't figured it out, have you?" she said. "I'm surprised. It's so obvious."

His blistering glare spoke more than his words ever could.

Throwing caution to the wind, she smiled darkly at him and said, "Allow me to show you, then."

If I can fight like a Meyarin, maybe I can run like one too, Alex reasoned. It was worth a shot, anyway. She took a deep breath to centre herself, elbowed Jordan in the stomach, forced his sword away, and sprinted off into the forest.

The scenery whizzed by at an alarming speed, and her throbbing skull rebelled painfully against the rapid movement. She could hear Aven screaming at her, and her heightened senses picked up that he was following close behind—too close. But she only needed a head start, and that was what she'd achieved.

Using the same principle Roka had taught her, Alex concentrated on her surroundings. She felt the air as she ran, she smelled the wood of the trees and the fresh snow at her feet. She heard her footfalls and those of Aven catching up to her. She saw everything in crystal-clear detail. And when she held out her ring hand and narrowed her gaze, she saw even more. In, around, and through her very flesh swirled light and dark, both battling for dominance. It was beautiful. Entrancing. But Alex couldn't pay it the attention it deserved—she had to focus.

"We're all born with Shadow inside us ... We can succumb to its power, or we can overcome it and use it ... It's a choice we must all make..."

Alex knew the choice she had to make, and what she had to do to make it. Caspar Lennox had told her, months earlier.

"...Immerse yourself fully in the Shadow..."

Alex closed her eyes as she ran at an impossible speed. She didn't need to see where she was going—she could feel everything around her. Trusting her heightened senses, she acted on instinct, scrunching her hand into a fist and focusing inward at the Shadow swirling within her body, encouraging it to move down her arm and towards the ring.

The spine-tingling sensation was unlike anything she'd felt before. The effort to maintain her concentration caused her head to throb more painfully, and she nearly lost both her grip on the Shadow and her ability to keep running when her attention wavered. But then she thought of her friends—D.C. and Bear, who she needed to make it back to, and Jordan, who she had to leave behind for now—and that gave her the strength to hold on.

When she felt like the weight of the world was in her fingers—or really, just the one finger—she acted instinctively again and threw her fist forward, away from her body. Her eyes opened in time to see a thick cloud of dark, swirling Shadow fly from her hand and engulf the wintry landscape in front of her.

One step, two steps, three steps, and she launched herself into what she presumed—and hoped—was a Shadow-fuelled portal. Although she had no idea what she was doing, her intuition told her to channel her thoughts towards her destination—just like with a Bubbledoor—so she did exactly that, coercing the Shadow towards a single place: Raelia.

The darkness surrounded her, pulling at her clothes and slamming her body into invisible walls as it fought for her submission. Alex remembered Caspar Lennox's words, how he'd said that Shadow was powerful. Dangerous, even. He'd warned her about the need to resist. Not fight; just resist.

So, that's what Alex did.

Instead of fighting her way through the darkness, Alex recalled the rest of Caspar Lennox's words.

"The Shadow surrounds you. But the Light within you ... I've never seen anything like it."

Light. That was what Alex needed to focus on. Not the darkness, but the light.

She thought about the faces of her friends. Bear. Dix. Jordan. She remembered the day they'd first entered Raelia together, how they'd joked and laughed even in the most worrying of situations.

Then she thought about the other special people in her life. She pictured her parents and their enthusiastic zest for adventure. She remembered Kaiden dancing with her at the palace in Tryllin, just as she remembered Declan hugging her and promising to keep her secrets. She thought about Roka's trust in her, Kyia's approving smiles, and Zain's annoying 'little human' jabs. She recalled Darrius's kindness, Karter's grudging respect, Hunter's faith in her and Fletcher's unending concern for her well-being.

They were her light. And they were what kept Alex from yielding to the Shadow, which was trying desperately to overwhelm her. Rather than submit, she fortified her mental defences and screamed out a single, commanding word: "RAELIA!"

This time the Shadow listened to her, surrendering to her control.

The disorienting force abated instantly and Alex fell to her knees as the ground became steady under her once more. She opened her eyes and they widened in surprise. The Shadow Ring had done exactly as she'd ordered, delivering her directly to Raelia, but it wasn't the Raelia she'd been expecting. Instead of the snowy landscape, she was in a moonlit clearing.

Moonlight.

As in, nighttime.

What...?

Not only was it nighttime, but there was also no trace of snow. The landscape looked exactly like it had the very first night Alex had stumbled upon the clearing months ago.

"Enter in, if you dare,
As one who's been to Meya;
Be strong of mind and pure of heart,
For your journey began at Raelia."

Alex jumped to her feet, swayed on the spot and pressed a hand to her throbbing head. She knew who the singing voice belonged to, even if she couldn't see the owner.

"Lady Mystique?"

"Hello again, Alexandra," the old woman said, appearing in the middle of the circle.

"How—how did I get here?"

"You activated the Shadow Essence in your ring," Lady Mystique said. "A dangerous undertaking, especially for one so full of Light. But you managed to gain control over the Shadow, and now you'll be able to do so with much less resistance in the future. Two Walks remain in your ring. Use them wisely."

Alex shuddered at the idea of ever having to use the ring again. "What I meant was, where's the real Raelia?"

"You'll be back there in a moment, child," the old woman assured her. "But I wished to speak with you, to give you a warning, before you're reunited with your friends."

Alex wasn't sure she could handle any more bad news. "What is it?"

"It won't take long for Aven Dalmarta's power to rise again, despite Meya's best efforts to resist," Lady Mystique said gravely. "There are too many Garseth hiding out in the city, ready and willing to serve him. King Astophe and Prince Roka will need all the help you can give them."

"Me? What can I do?" Alex asked. "My part in all of this is over. I was supposed to keep Aven from getting through the doorway, and look how well that turned out."

Alex was barely holding her emotions together. It was as if shock had finally settled on her and she was completely numb. She couldn't think about anything, least of all what Aven was going to do next.

"Alexandra, listen to me," Lady Mystique said. "Your role has barely begun. You have much left to do, more than you can possibly imagine. You must—"

"No," Alex interrupted with a firm shake of her head. "I *must* nothing. In the last hour I've given Aven free access to Meya, I've watched a classmate die and I've been attacked by my best friend—who I've now lost to my worst enemy. I'm sorry, but I can't have this conversation right now."

The old woman's face softened and she reached out to take Alex's hand in her own. At her touch the throbbing pain in Alex's head disappeared, along with all the other aches from her fight with Jordan.

"I know you don't want to hear it," Lady Mystique said softly, "but it's important that you listen to me. You must train, Alexandra. You must train with the Meyarins."

Alex stared at her. "What?"

"You must build your stamina," Lady Mystique continued. "You must learn how to call upon the Meyarin blood in your veins at a single thought, without hesitation. It won't take Aven long to realise how you managed to escape him and why you fight so well. He's cunning, dangerously so, and when the time comes, you must be ready to face him—and win. You can only learn so much with a human instructor, regardless of how capable your Karter is. You need to learn how to use your Meyarin abilities *from* a Meyarin."

"That's not—I can't—" Alex took a deep breath and tried again. "I don't *want* to fight Aven."

"I know, child, I know," Lady Mystique said, squeezing Alex's hand. "But when the time comes, you may be the only one who can."

Alex struggled to control her emotions, overwhelmed by the weight of responsibility she felt resting on her shoulders.

"There's something else you need to know," the old woman said, her tone gentle but firm. "They are words written of old. To what they refer, no one is certain. But I believe you must be made aware of them."

She released Alex's hand and pulled a faded piece of parchment from her coat.

It was withered and crumpled and looked as if it had survived more years than should have been possible.

"Open it," Lady Mystique urged.

Alex hesitantly did so, finding a beautiful script in an unknown language, with a translation directly underneath.

When Day and Night combine and fight
Against one Enemy
Then Dark and Light shall meet mid-strike
And set the Captives free.

She read it a few times before turning her eyes back to the old woman. "Am I supposed to know what this means?"

Lady Mystique just looked steadily at her. "You will when the time comes."

Alex didn't have the strength to fight for more information. She tried to hand the paper back, but the old woman said, "Keep it."

"What happens now?" Alex asked, looking around the clearing.

"Now you go back to your friends. They'll need you in the coming times, just as much as you'll need them."

Alex felt her throat close painfully, but she forced out a whispered, "What's going to happen to Jordan?"

Lady Mystique stared at her for a long moment before she answered, "That will depend on you, Alexandra."

With her declaration still echoing in Alex's ears, the old woman disappeared, as did the darkened clearing. Alex's head spun at the abrupt change in landscape and she closed her eyes. When she reopened them, it was daylight again, and she was standing in the middle of the snow-covered Raelia.

And she wasn't alone.

Twenty-Six

The clearing was full of people—beautiful Meyarins, mostly—and all of them were looking at her with startled expressions. But her attention was solely on her two friends sprinting her way.

"Alex," D.C. sobbed, slamming into Alex and wrapping her arms around her. "We thought—We thought—"

D.C. couldn't finish her sentence, but she didn't have to. Her fierce embrace said enough, as did Bear's tormented face when he reached them and circled his arms around the both of them.

"Jordan?" Bear whispered against Alex's hair.

Alex knew what he was asking. She wished she could tell him what he wanted to hear, but she couldn't. She shook her head and held her friends close as her own tears began to trickle down her face.

Alex felt Bear shudder in anguish and she absorbed D.C.'s sobs as they racked through her entire frame. The three friends held tight to each other while they grieved for their friend, remaining like that until someone cleared their throat nearby, breaking them apart.

Alex wiped her eyes as she stepped back and turned towards the source of the sound. "Zain?" she croaked, unsure whether or not he was real.

The Meyarin's face was alarmingly pale and he held himself as if he was in pain. But he still smiled at her and said, "It's good to see you, little human. You scared us all for a while there."

Alex released a broken breath and launched herself at him, hugging him fiercely. He grunted but wrapped his arms around her in return.

"Aven said you were dead," she whispered into his solid chest. "He said the Hyroa blood would kill you."

"It almost did," Zain told her, his voice weak. "If your headmaster hadn't found me while he and the other teachers were out protecting the academy, then I fear I would have soon passed on from this world."

Alex pulled away so she could study his face. "How long ... How long were you out there?"

"Aven caught me by surprise on Monday night," Zain said. "Right after I finished speaking with you. I told you I'd found a lead, but it turned out to be a trap. Aven and Jor—Aven and his Claimed accomplices managed to overpower me."

Alex inhaled sharply at his near slip. She appreciated him changing his sentence at the last second, even if she knew what he'd been about to say.

"I found Zain near the perimeter of the wards," another voice said, and Alex spun around to find Darrius standing directly behind her. "He was barely conscious, but he managed to say two words: 'Jordan. Claimed.'"

Alex swallowed heavily and looked at the ground. So much for avoiding the painful truth.

"Fletcher immediately sought to stabilise Zain while I and some of your other teachers took off in search of you and your friends," Darrius continued. "But I knew we were too late for Jordan. I'm so sorry, Alex."

She clenched her teeth to hold back another round of tears, but she was able to choke out, "It's not your fault, Darrius."

"Nevertheless, I didn't listen when you came to me with your concerns about Zain," the headmaster continued, shaking his head regretfully. "I should have looked into the matter further. I didn't think for a moment that one of my own students might have been in on Aven's plans, let alone two of them."

"Skyla didn't know what she was doing," Alex said quietly, barely able to say the other girl's name. The memory flashed across her mind and Alex's breath caught at the image of Skyla's lifeless eyes gazing out from her unnaturally still body.

"I know, Alex," Darrius assured her. "Your friends have already told me what happened here."

Alex looked around the clearing, noticing again how many people were lingering inside the mushroom circle. As well as the numerous Meyarins, Alex was surprised to see Hunter, Fletcher and Caspar Lennox talking quietly to each other. Fletcher was peering over at Alex as if trying to assess her for injuries, and when she attempted a shaky smile for his benefit, he relaxed, if only slightly. All the while, the other two teachers remained deep in conversation.

Alex might have questioned Darrius about their presence had she not been distracted by the absence of someone else.

"Where's Calista Maine?"

"She got away," Bear said, as he and D.C. stepped closer. They each took one of her hands, as if they needed the contact as much as she did.

"When everyone arrived, Calista managed to force them back with her gift long enough to disappear into the forest," D.C.

said, her voice thick from crying. "I presume she's with Aven now, wherever he is."

"Speaking of Aven, how *did* you get away?" Zain asked. "And why did you appear back here through a cloud of Shadow?"

"I believe I can answer the second part of your question," came the smooth, melodious voice of Caspar Lennox as he approached. "I see you figured out how to use the ring, Alex?"

She nodded and let him explain to the others. It didn't take him long, and then it was Alex's turn to fill in the rest of the story. That part was much harder. Fortunately, Bear and D.C. had already informed them of what happened in the clearing, which meant Alex could focus on what she'd experienced after regaining consciousness and how she'd escaped Aven. Even so, the pain of Jordan's Claiming pierced her heart like a dagger.

As if he'd read her mind, Caspar Lennox caught her eyes and whispered, "Sometimes the Shadow can overwhelm us, just as it did your friend,"

His words took Alex back three weeks, when he'd said the same thing to her. She had been confused at the time, but now she wondered if his true meaning hadn't been about the Shadow but something else entirely.

Alex gasped as the realisation flooded through her. She yanked her hands free of her friends' and moved directly in front of Caspar Lennox.

"You knew, didn't you?" she accused the Shadow Walker. "You knew what would happen to Jordan, and you didn't try to help him. That stupid Shadow metaphor you gave me—you knew all along that Aven was going to Claim him and you did nothing to stop it from happening!"

She ended on a sob and had to bite her tongue to keep from breaking down in front of the Shadow Walker. And everyone else.

"I didn't do *nothing*," Caspar Lennox told her while the others watched with baited breath. "I prepared you for what was coming. I warned you about the strength of temptation. And, if you can remember our conversation, I also told you that it's almost impossible for someone to return to the Light once they've yielded to the Shadow's temptation."

Alex choked back another sob and attempted to control her emotions.

"Alexandra," Caspar Lennox said, gently but firmly, "do you remember how I concluded my words to you?"

She couldn't speak, so she just shook her head.

"I said it's almost impossible for someone to return, *unless there's someone willing to help them.*" His melodious voice softened further and he said, "Your friend is not without hope, Alexandra, not so long as you are a child of the Light. But to help him, you must be willing to fight for him. It won't be an easy task."

"But he's *Claimed,*" Alex whimpered.

Caspar Lennox stretched out a mottled-grey hand and rested it on her shoulder. "As were you, once."

"Jordan—" Saying his name hurt, and she winced before trying again. "Jordan's gift won't help him like mine helped me. I don't know any other way for him to escape Aven. It's a miracle that I managed it, and that was solely because of my willpower gift."

"Then perhaps you need to follow the etiquette of a five-year-old," the Shadow Walker said, somewhat mockingly, "and learn how to share."

"I don't—" Alex stopped talking when she realised what he was saying. "Do you think it's possible?" she whispered. "Do you really think I can learn how to extend my gift to include others?"

"I wouldn't have suggested it if I didn't believe it to be possible," he told her.

"I don't know where to begin," she said. "I've been trying, but I have no idea what I'm doing or how to strengthen it."

"To build any muscle, you must exercise it," he said. "Practice makes perfect."

"But how am I supposed to know if it's working?"

Caspar Lennox stared at her with a calculating expression before he nodded once as if to himself. He flicked a glance towards the others in their group and then turned back to her, stretching his hands out. The cloud of Shadow that was constantly at his feet rose at his command and surrounded the two of them, wrapping around them like a cloak.

Alex began to panic as they were enveloped by the swirling darkness. "What—"

"Be calm," Caspar Lennox said. "I wish to speak to you without the others hearing. The Shadow will give us privacy from the eyes and ears of those around us—Meyarin included."

She shuffled nervously and waited for him to continue.

"I know of someone who may be willing to assist in the strengthening of your gift," the Shadow Walker said. "I'll speak with him over the holidays and see if I can convince him to help. He rarely accepts new students these days, so it may come to nothing. But he owes me a favour. I'll let you know the outcome when classes resume in the New Year."

"Thank you, sir," she said, her voice wobbling slightly.

His mottled face filled with compassion. "Take heart, Alexandra. All is not yet lost."

The Shadow dropped from around them until Alex could see the clearing and everyone in it once again. Everyone except Caspar Lennox, who had apparently said all he needed to say before disappearing.

Alex blinked at the spot where he'd been standing. "How did he...?"

"He's a Shadow Walker," Bear said, seeing her puzzled expression. "They move through the Shadows. It's what they do."

... *Right.*

"Can we ask what that was all about?" Darrius said.

"Um, I'm not sure I'm supposed to say," Alex said. Caspar Lennox must have had a reason for concealing his message, and she didn't want to reveal anything without his permission.

The headmaster eyed her thoughtfully before nodding his head in acceptance. "There's something else you should know,

Alex. After you stepped through to Raelia, Sir Camden appeared and spoke with me. His words made little sense at first, but then I learned that somehow he'd felt the presence of Aven while he was concealed by Jordan's transcended state."

Again, the mention of her friend's name pierced her.

"Just as the knight was about to warn you, something stopped him from speaking," Darrius said. "That same thing forced him to leave you and move through another doorway. It's my belief that Calista Maine must have been using her gift on him."

They'd been played the whole time. No wonder Sir Camden had looked like his joints were rusting over—he'd been as stiff as a board because of Calista's telekinetic hold on him.

"It's not your fault," D.C. whispered, sensing Alex's anguish. "You had no way of knowing. None of us did."

"What about Skyla?" Alex asked, just as quietly. "She's dead. There's no changing that now."

"What happened to Skyla is..." Bear's voice choked with emotion but he took a deep breath and pushed through it. "What Aven did to her is unforgiveable. That's not on us, so don't take on that guilt,

Alex. If you do, Aven wins one more victory today. Don't give him that."

Alex knew he was right and she forced back a fresh wave of tears. Enough crying. The Jordan she knew wouldn't want her to drown in her sorrows. He'd want her to stand up and fight. Fight for what was right. Fight to make things better.

"Alex? I'm sorry to interrupt, but can I have a word?"

She turned and found Roka and Kyia standing a few paces away.

"I'll be back in a moment," she told her friends.

When she reached the Meyarins, Kyia surprised Alex by pulling her into a comforting hug.

"I'm sorry about your friend," she said softly.

No more crying, Alex reminded herself. She managed to breathe out a quiet, "Thank you."

Kyia nodded and offered her a compassionate smile before she walked away to speak with a group of Meyarin guards.

"Walk with me, Alex," Roka said, offering her his arm.

She latched onto it like a lifeline and waited for him to speak. When he did, his words surprised her.

"Are you okay?"

She blew out a breath of air. "Physically, sure. Emotionally, not so much."

Roka squeezed her hand gently. "If there's anything I can do to help, you need only ask. The same goes for if you want to reach out to Kyia or Zain. We're all here for you, Alex."

She looked up at him in disbelief. "Are you for real? Aren't you going to lock me up or something?" Seeing the question in his eyes, she clarified, "You've managed to keep Aven away from Meya for over a thousand years, and now, thanks to me, he can come and go as he pleases. Everything that happened today is *my* fault, Roka. Aren't there consequences for something like that?"

They reached the other side of the clearing and Roka stopped, turning Alex to face him.

"None of us blame you, Alex," he said. "What you did was justified considering the deceit surrounding Aven's plan. He's a master of manipulation. There was no possible way for you to realise the truth."

"I should have known," Alex argued. "I should have figured it out."

"How?"

"I don't know!" she cried. "I should have felt something was wrong!"

Roka's face softened at her tortured expression. "You had no way of knowing, Alex. We all thought it was impossible. If anything, the fault lies with us."

She frowned at that. "What are you talking about?"

"We were overconfident in our ability to keep him out," Roka said. "It was my idea to send Zain out for information, but we did that in secret as our council didn't believe it was necessary. We had so much faith in our own race that we forgot the power some humans possess. Skyla Fay's gift ... Never would we have imagined such a deceptive ability. Nor would we have thought to link it with the gift of your friend Jordan. But Aven has spent so much time amongst your kind that using humans' gifts is second nature to him. And because of that, he managed to slip by us."

Roka paused, deep in thought. "If your headmaster hadn't found Zain, then I fear all hope would have been lost. He would have died, Aven would have killed you and your friends and then arrived unnoticed in Meya, intent on destroying us. But Zain's warning came in time for us to ruin Aven's plan. We know he's here now, and although we're not sure where he's hiding, he's lost the element of surprise."

"How *did* Zain warn you?" Alex asked. "Darrius said he was nearly dead and could barely talk."

"Your doctor is extremely skilled." Roka's gaze moved to the other side of the clearing, where Fletcher stood hovering around Zain. "He was able to stabilise the effects of the Sarnaph blood—the Hyroa blood—long enough for Zain to find the strength to call up the *Valispath*. Fletcher was distressed by Zain's refusal to remain in bed, but he consented so long as he was able to continue his treatment and assist with any injuries you and your friends might have sustained. Darrius and Hunter travelled on the Eternal Path with them, as did the Shadow Walker."

"I thought the location of Meya was supposed to be a secret to humans?" Alex asked.

Roka shrugged. "Zain was too weak to fight them off, and his urgency to warn us of Aven's arrival was too great for him to wait any longer."

"But doesn't it worry you?"

"Your companions won't be able to come back without using the *Valispath* or one of your Library doorways," Roka reminded her. "And besides, the time may soon be coming when humans are once again aware of our existence."

"What about Caspar Lennox?" Alex asked. "He disappeared from here without using the Library or the Eternal Path. All he needed was his special shadow magic, or whatever it's called."

"Shadow Walkers are an unpredictable race," Roka said. "Even my people don't fully understand the scope of their abilities. It's quite possible that they've always been aware of the location of Meya and have just had no interest in our city. We're not enemies, nor are we allies. We've had no need to interact before now—before you, really. And it was clearly you who Caspar Lennox came here for today."

Alex wasn't sure what to think about that.

"I have to ask, Alex," Roka said, his voice strangely hesitant, "I heard you giving your account to the others, but is there anything else you can tell me about Aven's plans? His whereabouts?"

Alex had omitted to tell the others about her time with Lady Mystique, but the old woman had told her something that Roka probably needed to hear.

"Um, there is something I didn't mention," Alex said, and she went on to tell Roka about when she'd first seen Lady Mystique at Raelia during her SAS class. Then she told him about how the Lady had been waiting when the Shadow Ring transported her to the moonlit clearing.

"She said it wouldn't take long for Aven to become powerful again," Alex warned. "Apparently there are still many willing Rebels hiding out in the city."

Roka's face was grave. "Did she say anything else?"

Alex tucked a strand of hair behind her ear and quietly admitted, "She said I need to learn how to use my Meyarin abilities and that I should begin training with one of your race so that when the time comes, I'll be ready to fight Aven. She seems to think I might be the only one who actually can fight him. And she gave me this too, but I don't know what it means."

She handed the crumpled piece of parchment to Roka and he skimmed the words twice before his golden eyes captured hers, his expression unreadable.

"I've heard this prophecy before," he said, returning the parchment to her. "The translation is disturbingly accurate."

"It's a Meyarin prophecy?" Alex asked with surprise, not sure why Lady Mystique would have had it in her possession.

Roka shook his head. "No. I heard it from a Tia Auran in her native tongue. Many, many years ago."

"What's a Tia—"

"I'll have to look into this, Alex," Roka interrupted, sounding distracted. He blinked and his eyes cleared as he focused on her again. "As to the training your Lady Mystique recommended, I have to say I agree with her."

Alex met his concerned gaze and whispered, "Roka, I don't want to fight Aven again."

She'd said the same thing to Lady Mystique, and just as the old woman's had done, Roka's eyes filled with compassion.

"I'll help you, Alex," he promised. "I'll personally make sure you're ready, in case that time comes. But I also hope your Lady Mystique is mistaken. And I give you my word that I'll do everything in my power to ensure she is."

Alex blinked back more tears. She couldn't keep eye contact with him without breaking down again, so she averted her gaze.

"Do you know why this place is called Raelia?" Roka asked her.

Alex kept her eyes on the snowy ground and shook her head.

"This is the place where my father stood millennia ago and declared Aven's sentence of banishment. My brother had already disappeared after trying to murder us, but my father chose to make known the consequences of his betrayal, if only so the *Garseth*—Aven's Rebels—would know the fate that awaited them. My father called this place 'Raelia' as a reminder to us all."

He reached out for her and tilted her head up until she was forced to look into his eyes. "Life is full of crossroads, Alex. Full of choices. There are many paths we can take. It's up to us to decide which ones lead in the right direction."

Despite her resolve, she couldn't stop the fresh tears that slid down her cheeks. "I don't know what to do, Roka."

"Yes, you do," he told her gently. He placed a hand against his heart and said, "Your answer is here." Then he pointed towards the other side of the clearing. "And your answer is there."

She turned and saw her friends clinging to each other as they mourned the fate of their friend.

"Go to them, Alex," Roka said. "Everything else can wait. They need you now."

When Alex nodded, he pulled her into a warm embrace, wrapping his arms around her and holding her close. A long moment passed before he released her, promising to be in touch soon so she could begin her training.

As she began to walk away, Roka said, "Remember, your friend isn't lost to you yet. Don't grieve as if he is."

Alex knew he was right. And she knew that if she was going to save Jordan, she needed to be strong enough to fight for him, as Caspar Lennox had said. Maybe to fight *against* him again. And when the time came, she would make sure she was ready.

With determined strides, Alex walked across the clearing to rejoin her friends. "It's time for us to leave."

"Alex, I'm not sure—" Darrius started to say, but she cut him off.

"We're going, Darrius," she said. "We're on holidays and we're going to Woodhaven as planned."

D.C. and Bear looked at her with surprise, as though they'd thought their situation had changed now that Jordan was no longer with them. But Alex was going to make sure everything remained as normal as possible until their friend returned to them.

Darrius eyed her appraisingly, observing her unwavering expression. He pulled three military ITDs out of his pocket along with three Bubblers. "Take these with you. The wards are activated now," he said.

Alex and her friends took the objects, although she knew they would have no need of them now that Aven had what he wanted.

"We'll see you in two weeks," she told Darrius. "But if you hear anything before then..."

"I'll contact you immediately," Darrius promised. "Just as I expect you to do the same."

She nodded and asked, "Are you all coming back with us?"

"We're waiting to speak with Prince Roka; he'll return us to the academy afterwards," Darrius said. "Hunter has some information about Aven's Claimed humans and we need to work out a strategy to ensure they remain out of Meya. Aven doesn't have access to the *Valispath*, but he's now able to use the Library's doorways to bring others here. We mustn't allow that to happen."

"Let me know if I can do anything," Alex offered, secretly hoping they wouldn't.

"That's very kind, Alex, but you've already done more than we have the right to ask," Darrius said. "Go to Woodhaven, and try not to worry about the rest until you have to."

That was easier said than done. But she would try to follow his advice.

"Wait, little human," Zain called out as she and her friends were walking away. "I'll activate the *Valispath* and escort you to your destination."

"Zain, I'm not sure that's the best idea..." Fletcher tried to advise him, but the warrior waved away his concern.

"I'm fine," he said dismissively. "Never better."

His words might have been more believable if he hadn't slurred them while tripping over his own feet.

"It's okay, Zain," Alex told him. "We'll go back through the Library. You look like death warmed up, so you should probably follow Fletcher's instructions until the Hyroa blood is out of your system."

"I could still beat you in a fight," Zain grumbled.

Alex cracked her first real smile since she'd arrived at the clearing. "I reckon I could take you."

"By the sounds of your talk with Roka, we might soon have the chance to discover whether that's true or not," he said, an excited glint in his eyes.

Meyarin hearing really didn't allow for any secrets, Alex realised with a pang of annoyance.

"I guess we'll have to wait and see," she said. "But I don't want to win by default and be stuck listening to you whinge about me taking advantage of your weakened state. So pay attention to the good doctor's orders and get better quickly, yeah?"

He mumbled something under his breath but nodded in agreement.

Alex smiled softly again as she turned to lead her friends into the middle of Raelia. A door opened almost immediately by her will, and the three of them halted in front of it.

"What're we going to do now?" D.C. whispered, her voice wobbling with emotion.

"We're going to continue on with our lives as much as possible," Alex said. "That means we go to Woodhaven, and while we're there, we'll come up with a plan."

"A plan?" D.C. repeated.

"A plan to get Jordan back."

Saying his name hurt, but Alex's resolve was strengthening by the minute. As Roka had said, she wouldn't grieve for her friend because he wasn't yet lost to them.

"We're going to fight for him," she continued. "He needs us to fight for him. And we're going to find a way to bring him back to us."

Bear's face still reflected his sorrow, but now it showed a trace of hope as well. "Do you really think we'll be able to?"

"I'm certain of it," she said, her confidence leaving no room for doubt.

D.C. looked at her, tears still glittering in her eyes. "What makes you so sure?"

"He promised, Dix," Alex told her gently. "Remember that night in our room? You made him promise to come back, and he promised he would. He promised that no matter what happened, he'd find a way back to us—back to you. The Jordan Sparker I know would never break a promise. Not to you, Dix. Not to the girl he loves. Not to the girl who loves him back."

At her words, D.C. broke into heaving sobs. Neither she nor Jordan had acknowledged the depth of their feelings to each other, but they would have the opportunity one day.

Alex would make sure of it.

On that thought, she ushered Bear and D.C. through the doorway and turned to glance back at Raelia one last time.

A crossroad. That was where she was. Multiple paths lay before her, but she knew which one she had to take.

Alex closed her eyes and took a deep breath, thinking about the challenges she would have to face. But it would be worth the struggle.

It had to be.

Decision made, Alex opened her eyes and stepped through the doorway after her friends, her mind focused on a single thought.

Hold on, Jordan. We're coming.

Alex's journey continues in the
next instalment of next instalment of

THE MODERN CHRONICLES
BOOK THREE
DRAEKORA

ACKNOWLEDGEMENTS

In the first book of this series my acknowledgements were nearly as long as the story itself. So this time, I wish to say a huge bulk 'thank you' to everyone I mentioned all over again—God, my parents, my brother and the rest of my wonderful family and friends. Your continued support, encouragement and love gives me the strength I need to wander through this beautiful thing called life, and I'm forever grateful to you all.

To add just a handful of additional mentions, thank you also to everyone at Pantera Press for yet again doing everything in your power to continue making my dreams come to light. Special thanks go to Ali, who is not just my publisher but also my freebie therapist. I can't thank you enough for listening to my irrelevant musings on an embarrassingly frequent basis (I still haven't tried that sideways toaster grilled-cheese, but it's on the top of my list). Also, massive hugs go to my incredible publicist—'My Susan'—for opening so many doorways of opportunities for me this year. Extra gratitude for the fact that no matter where I go, you always make sure I end up with a hot chocolate in my hands. That alone is a testimony to just how awesome you are.

Copious amounts of thanks also go to my editor, Glenda Downing; the fabulous editorial team at Pantera Press (especially my masterful copyeditor James Read and my amazing proofreader, Lucy Bell); as well as the wondrous cover-making talent at XOU Creative. This story wouldn't be what it is without you all contributing your own special kinds of magic.

I'm also hugely grateful to all of my fabulous early readers, with special mentions to Dana Summer, for your overwhelming and unquenchable enthusiasm; Emily Davison, for your emotional investment in the story and its characters; and Frannie Panglossa, for fangirling with me over Twitter for hours on end.

And last but most definitely not least, I want to thank you, my readers. Every time you contact me via my website or social media to gush about Alex and her friends, it warms my heart to see how much you love them and the journey they're on. I can't promise it will be an easy ride, but I can assure you we'll travel with them together, following wherever their paths may lead. Thank you for sticking by them, thank you for sticking by me. I can't wait to see which doors we'll step through next!

Lynette Noni grew up on a farm in outback Australia until she moved to the beautiful Sunshine Coast and swapped her mud-stained boots for sand-splashed flip-flops. She has always been an avid reader and most of her childhood was spent lost in daydreams of far-off places and magical worlds. She was devastated when her Hogwarts letter didn't arrive, but she consoled herself by looking inside every wardrobe she could find, and she's still determined to find her way to Narnia one day. While waiting for that to happen, she creates her own fantasy worlds and enjoys spending time with the characters she meets along the way.

Raelia is the second of five books in Lynette's YA fantasy series, *The Medoran Chronicles*.

Lynette loves to chat with her readers—connect with her online:

www.LynetteNoni.com
Facebook.com/Lynette.Noni
Twitter.com/LynetteNoni
Instagram.com/LynetteNoni

www.ingramcontent.com/pod-product-compliance
Lightning Source LLC
Chambersburg PA
CBHW032029120726
47901CB00001BA/10